THE STONE OF INNVERICUM

BOOK 1

The NaraRose Series

Kate Rosevear

ISBN-13: 9798582327264

DEDICATION

To my family for their constant support and love,
to Tash for her patience,
thank you.

CONTENTS

ACKNOWLEDGMENTS

There are many people to thank for helping me finally finish this story.

Firstly to my parents, for keeping the initial copy locked away in their safe at home and reading several versions along the way. My mother's wonderful proof reading skills and encouragement, that helped to kick started the final version. And, for actually taking me on all those magical holidays to the Isles of Scilly as a child, where it all began.

To Cornerstones Literary Consultants for concise and thorough editing reports and ruthless advise.

To Christopher Little's Literary Agency for the inital wonderful encouragement and delightful belief.

To the amazing and talented Darren Bourne at Aspire Defence, who's incredible artistry brought Halgelen alive on the front cover in shattered glass format and creating the bleak Moorlands as his backdrop. He also changed my pencil sketches to the detailed map of NaraRose.

To my publishing team for all of their help and amazing service.

To my long term and solid friend, Tash. I will always cherish those hilarious Monday evenings spent awash with tea and chocolate trying to edit an unfathomable amount of words. Rereading and rereading until our eyes hurt. Thank you…..

To my wonderful friends The Barron's. For their introductions and enthusiastic encouragements.

To many other wonderful friends, and especially Jules, for all of their support, jokes and at times just not talking about the book, as it was taking so long to complete.

To my immediate family. Francis my husband and three amazing children, George, Alice and Jess for their constant love, support and encouragement, even when I stubbornly won't have any self belief.

And, lastly to you, Simon – here it is. A promise I had to keep. My friend, my brother.

PROLOGUE

Eight Generations Before Daniel...

Ostric, the God of Darkness, stood before Turgred, Earth Guardian of the Pixies, materialising from a contorted monochrome fog into a Tribeling, not that dissimilar to himself. Turgred clasped his dagger so tightly that the whites of his knuckles made his fist appear frozen around the handle. He knew such a weapon would do nothing to harm the mighty God, but somehow it made him feel safer. He glanced uneasily at the three Tribelings beside him, Eadric, Creoda and Penda. Ostric's presence had ceased their stormy fighting. A battle born, in Turgred's mind of futile origin, for one Tribe was never capable of supremacy over the other. Ostric's appearance had showed the gravity of their mistake.

"You have made me proud." Ostric's deep words shook the ground and drilled, like the relentless hammer of a craftsmen's tool. "Such anger and hatred, it makes me strong." Ostric stretched his newly formed arms to the sky. Turgred lowered his gaze, unable to bear the radiating heat, or the disconcerting way Ostric's eyes changed colour. Only Creoda, leader of the Arramond Imps, seemed to welcome his presence, and tantalisingly flicked her red hair.

"I have a gift for you all," He scattered a path of black powder into the air. Turgred was careful to avoid every particle as it drifted like snow, the slightest touch deadly. "You will be first to receive,"

Ostric declared, pointing at the tall, lean Elf. "Eadric, first Water Lord of Caradoc. Enter the black bog." Turgred followed the line of Ostric's outstretched hand, with ash dripping from his arm, disappearing into gloppy, bubbling pools. The Elf hesitated, as if rooted to the very fabric of the earth.

"Well," Ostric said, "I won't ask twice." Eadric placed his bow and arrow on the ground and shed his cloak. He glanced at his few surviving foes, with not a flicker of emotion. Then, carefully and slowly he stepped into the bog. Turgred shuddered violently as an unnaturally long howl left Eadric's mouth and wrapped itself around them all like snakes. The leather of Eadric's boot caught alight, and flames hungrily ate at his leg.

"Now retrieve your gift," Ostric commanded. With red swollen eyes and sweat coursing, Eadric shakily obeyed; the alternative Turgred knew for him would be death. His hand reaching into the bog to find. Turgred looked away. Finally the raw moan subsided. The Water Lord stood swaying like a young sapling, battered but still alive. Turgred could tell something had changed in the Elf; despite the obvious pain, there was a new, ruthless hunger that shown in his eyes.

"That, Elf," Ostric broke Turgred's thoughts, "has turned your water into an Element. Take, your gift, *The Stone of Innvericum*, to Caradoc, put it in the water's source. Learn how to use it well. But, to those of you who don't, be warned they will burn as you just have." The rank stench of Eadric's singed flesh, made Turgred wonder how many Elves would die trying. Ostric's gifts were never without pain.

Next, Creoda was the given the power of fire, her namesake, Fire-Maker, made real. Her joy was clear for all to see and Turgred was certain this would make her Tribe, the Imps, unstoppable warriors of uncontrollable might.

Then Penda of the Sprites took the power of air, but suffered bitterly as Ostric froze her body to near death. Turgred had known he would be the last. For he had been the reluctant warrior, only drawn into battle when no other route was possible. He grew more and more anxious, as his fate drew near.

"Turgred," Ostric finally addressed him. He stood alone, with only the relentless Moorland breeze for company. Ostric floated across the ground towards him, his limbs merging between swirling trails of ash. "My only disappointment," he sneered, "...weak in your resolve to battle, hesitant to kill. So... it's taken me time to decide what to give you." Ostric leant in closer and touched the grass in front of Turgred's feet. The green blades shrivelled to dust, revealing cracked, dry soil beneath. "Your land," Ostric's desolate gaze bore into Turgred's resolve, "has suffered the same fate as this. Now, take it," he held the barren clump of earth aloft. "Place it on your chest." Turgred was unable to move.

Suddenly, a white searing light blocked Ostric from view. Turgred stumbled, glimpsing Istria, the Goddess of Light. Her silvery hair fell like a flowing river, magnetically alluring between the black ash. Turgred felt unnervingly drawn to her, like a moth, hopelessly smitten by the warmth of a lamp.

"You're brave, Istria," Ostric snarled, "appearing before me like this."

"That as it may be, Ostric, but you cannot have it all your own way." Istria raised her white staff and pointed at Eadric, Creoda and Penda in turn. "Take heed, leaders, you must learn to use your new powers wisely." A ball of tumbling black ash hurtled through the air. Turgred dived and rolled. Istria flicked her staff, engulfing the ash in a barrier of light. "Don't Ostric!" she shouted. "Turgred," Istria called, "don't touch the earth, enough damage has been done. Take these and go." Turgred saw something glint, flying through the air. Stretched to his limit, he caught a simple, stubby cup, with curved handles. Around his extended wrist appeared a twisted amulet of bronze. "Use them well..." A clatter of thunder knocked him sideways, losing Istria's words. A warm pulse rippled across his chest, softening Ostric's commanding roars. His vision faltered into a mess of black and white lines. He scrambled to his feet and ran, blindly desperate to reach the gate of Poldaric.

PART I

1

FIRING AN ARROW

Nestled in his hand was a torn fragment of his brother's trousers. Daniel scanned the tiny bedroom, moving his gaze over the familiar wooden bed and square patchwork quilt. Isaac hadn't slept. Daniel moved to his desk. The wooden chair lay at an angle on the floor. Isaac's model boat was broken, its mast and sail bent, and hull crumbled in two. The room's little round window swung ajar. The metal handle, pulled away from the frame, hanging limply. Daniel crammed the cloth into his pocket.

"Where?" Daniel looked at his friend, Seb.

"By the harbour wall, on the south side of Trevarian."

"How many?"

"I don't know..." Daniel noticed his fingers drumming against his leg. Seb only did that when he was nervous.

"Why were you out?" It's mid *Dark Exchange*..."

"Because I was." Seb pushed the wooden door open. It creaked loudly. "We must go."

"Are you sure it was Isaac?" Daniel pointed through the window, "It could have been anyone, and he's just gone somewhere?"

"It's him. I know… as you said it's *Dark Exchange* and he's not here is he?" Daniel shuddered, still in disbelief that someone had managed to take his brother from right under their noses, including his all-powerful father.

Daniel quietly closed Isaac's bedroom door and hurried across the cold flagstones, into the simple kitchen. He snatched a carcass leg from the wooden table and headed down the west corridor. He gnawed the chewy meat, and silently pushed open his parent's door. His father, in bed, wheezed, the eiderdown rose and fell rhythmically. Daniel gazed around room questioning if his parents asleep state affected the strength of their protection spell. Unsure, he moved on, and beckoned Seb to follow.

Once they reached the narrow entrance porch, Daniel ran his hand tenderly along the cobbled wall, not wanting to light the candle. He found the door key, and the tall, thin cupboard that held all the important stuff. He ignored the hazy image of a skull on its front panel.

"We're going to need these," he said to Seb, and filled his holdall with arrows. "And," he said, "take this." He gave Seb a spare *Element* pouch.

"But it's your mother's," Seb held it like it was a piece of stale fish.

Daniel frowned, "I'll take it when we're outside."

When he was satisfied he'd got all he needed, he ducked under the low slate mantle. His head span like a whirlpool, as the cold *Shadow* air hit. He looked around. It was still pretty dark, so no one should see him leave.

"Which way?" he whispered. Seb's eyes darted from side to side.

"There… past the Dorian dwellings."

"Where most of The Council live!"

"Look,' Seb snapped, "you're the Grand Master's Elfling… and it's Isaac we're rescuing." Daniel was about to ask him what the hell was going on, but Seb shot off. Daniel tore after him. At full pelt they fled through the cobbled streets, passing oak doors emblazoned with family crests, that Daniel knew well. He was thankful there were no lights on, anyone normal, he thought would be asleep. Seb slipped from the usual route into a narrow alleyway. Suddenly engulfed by unforgiving stonewalls, Daniel could feel The Council's magic. Seb slowed to a jog, the passageways darkened, and every corner felt like a circle. After, what seemed like a *Shadow* of running, the familiar harbour wall came into view. Daniel ran up the granite steps to the coastland path, skirted hurriedly eastwards and onto the Great Lake.

The mighty bridge swung into view; its overpowering granite archways strode across the water. Daniel hated every stone, a permanent reminder, that his Trevarak Elves were joined to their Eastlings rivals. He was beginning to tire, his legs ached, and heart hammered, but he dared not stop, Isaac was too young to be out alone. Daniel jumped over the weathered boulders, feet plunging into the finer sand, where he stopped to allow his breath to settle.

"Look," Seb pointed to the bridge. Daniel fixed his gaze. Six Elves, huddled. Daniel suddenly regretted not waking his father. In the middle, was the unmistakable shape of his brother. "Stop!" he hollered, but the hungry lake ate his cry. He scanned the nearby cottages nestled in the dunes. Surely someone was awake?

"What are they doing?" Daniel grabbed the viewing spell from Seb. "They're...," he began to shake, "pouring water on his skin!"

"We should have woken your father." Seb said. "He needs to see this, they have to be punished this time."

"It's too late, Isaac won't survive if we don't do something now. Those Eastlings won't stop." The raw flesh on his brother's cheek was as clear through the spell, as if Isaac stood just a step away. Daniel's anger began to boil.

"I'll go to the eastern steps," Seb said, "try to cross the bridge." Daniel ignored him, as he reeled through all the spells he knew; something that would get to the bridge, scare them. Daniel recognised, Thaen. That Elf had always hated his family. Their eyes locked. Thaen began to pull Isaac to the edge of the bridge. His younger brother was no match; but Daniel could see he was putting up a fight. Beads of sweat travelled down Daniel's forehead. If Isaac fell into the water...

"Leave him alone," Daniel shouted. A scream rippled in reply, a gurgling squeak, which travelled into Daniel's soul and lodged itself tightly. Slowly and carefully, Daniel pulled his bow off his shoulder and took an arrow from its holdall. He would prove to his father that he was capable of handling Thaen and his thugs. With trembling hands, Daniel positioned the string between his thumb and forefinger. It slipped and quivered before notching securely. He flexed his firing arm, the bow tautened. Waves created long pale fingers across the sand. He drew in a controlled breath and chose his mark. With a last check of the wind direction, he released the arrow. Momentarily, the arrow hovered, before disappearing between the murky line of water and sky.

Time stood still, as a mirage of shapes and shadows danced in patterns. A black silhouette sliced his vision in two. Daniel immediately knew and sank to his knees, dropping his bow heavily to the sand. Like a rabbit bolting from its hole, the Eastling Elves scattered across the bridge.

Daniel slowly removed his tunic. He walked purposely towards the edge. His foot plunged knee deep into the cold lake. He allowed the familiar surge of energy to run up his leg.

"Daniel, what r you... h... wah... doing?" Seb was running across the beach frantically waving his arms. "You'll burn! You'll die! You can't save him now... we need your father. Get out..." But Seb's words slipped past him like a waterfall, splashing into his subconscious. He had to save his brother.

2

WATER PRISION

Daniel's eyes stung as he looked through the gloopy mire. Beneath him, a foreboding endless expanse of murky black. The lake seemed heavier, thicker even, compared to the water he'd experienced in Algor. The secret practises under the watchful eye of his mother. He took a few more strokes fully submerged to get away from the shoreline. He resurfaced, filling his lungs to bursting before diving again.

He opened his eyes, trying to master water vision, his mother's favourite lecture. Tiny golden flashes, with flickering tails appeared, rising from the cold depths, darting like shoals of fish, and filling the space with a rich yellow. More and more came, until they formed a glowing wall. Daniel froze, treading water, suspended like a puppet on strings. Entranced by its moving patterns. The light became brighter, blinding even. He turned away and kicked with all his strength, breaking the lake's surface. He had made it halfway to the bridge. Scanning the foamy peaks, something caught his eye by a strut arch. In and out of view, buffeted by white spray. Daniel plunged back under and swam on.

Drawing closer, Daniel began to bob like an empty bottle, pulled by a magnetic force towards the bridge. Kicking and flaying his arms, he fell into a swirling current, tumbling and struggling for air. The weight of the water pressed him onwards. He hit the stone. Grazing his face, he groped along the rough edge, until he could pull his head and shoulders out of the water. To his side was a body, covered by soaked undistinguishable garments, face hidden. Patches of red puffy skin glared through torn holes. A wave of putrid salty pile rose in his throat. How could this happen to his brother? His mind raced, he had to get him out of the lake, there still might be time. With all his strength he pushed. Single-mindedly he found an unmelodic rhythm.

The waves tugged at his every move. Drums beat in his head, warning him to stop. Reeds curled around his ankles making him stop and have to untangle. His lungs throbbed with the effort. He had never been in water for so long and prayed to the Water Lord, it would end soon. His strength failing. His only motivation to save his brother.

Daniel finally hit stiller water, his feet touching the lake floor. A strange gurgling, almost like giggling followed him as he climbed out. Shaking his head, he knocked the water out of both ears and began to drag the body, soaked and exhausted up the shoreline. He knelt beside the limp form and flipped it over. An arrow with a long, coloured shaft, bounced up. He squinted and wiped his face. Hot water spluttered from his mouth; as he recognised its markings. The sand around him darkened and between every shudder, he began to sense a wall of coloured cloaks. His strength ebbed into the sand. With shaking hands, he carefully dragged the body onto a drier ridge. The cloaks parted as he approached. No one was offering help. He took a deep breath and raised his gaze. Elves, young and old, had gathered, filing the shoreline for as far as he could see, standing like jailers.

"Why isn't he dead?" he could hear them whisper. "How come he isn't burnt?"

"Is it his arrow?"

"Perhaps he's Ostric's messenger?" Each whisper gathered momentum and spread through the jittery crowd.

"Daniel..." Seb burst into the open, almost falling as he did. He shuffled awkwardly. "That's... that's impossible... you're alive... Thaen!" Seb stood with his arm outstretched, pointing. For the first time, Daniel could see that it wasn't his brother, but an Elfling to the

Eastling leading family – now dead at his feet. His actions began to fall like a mass of metal chains, choking and consuming. Thaen was hardly recognisable, his skin covered in weeping scars, his eyes burnt red and flared open. Most of his hair had gone, leaving charred holes in his skull. Daniel stared at the green and blue markings of the arrow. It was his arrow! The air escaped from his lungs.

"Daniel Elf Trevarak." Trembling, he raised his gaze. His father, no longer the contented snorer tucked under an eiderdown, but Caradoc's Grand Master, angry and powerful. The gathered Elves moved to let their leader through. Seb sank to one knee, with his head bent. His father's bitter scowl increased as he strode by him. "I'm convening The Council of Caradoc," he thundered to the audience. "Let this message be heard by all those who need to be present."

Noah knelt beside Thaen; his fingers encircled the arrowhead and Daniel saw his fist whiten as he began to mouth a silent spell. Carefully he folded Thaen's arms, and brushed aside the remaining strands of hair, before closing his charred eyelids. After what seemed to Daniel like a life sentence of solitary confinement, Noah sent a single water droplet skywards, and began to chant a prayer. The gathered Elves joined in, their united voices rippled across the lake. Daniel felt a shiver take root within the pit of his stomach – he knew his father would never forgive him. The Grand Master rose to his feet, as if he carried the weight of a lake on his shoulders, and met his gaze. Daniel trembled.

"You will follow me to the Great Hall of our forefathers and be tried by the Trevarak Council, for the crime of taking another Elf's life and the crime of entering our sacred lake." He turned and walked away.

"Father… wait, I can explain." Daniel grabbed his belongings, throwing on his tunic. He shouldered his bow and ran between the Elves. They scattered, like flies from a carcass.

"Daniel, you'll only make it worse," Seb called.

"How?" Daniel stopped and turned to face him. "How can this be any worse? This wasn't meant to happen, this was their fault not ours."

"Then… why? Why… shot? And why… not tell me?" Seb was

shaking. "Tell you what…" Seb threw his hands in the air. "What? How stupid can you be?" Are you hiding something else? No one… ever… our age… has entered the waters without burning!" Seb was shaking. The surrounding crowd murmured their agreement.

"This is the reason I never said anything," Daniel bellowed, but swayed like the sail on a boat, at the hatred in his friend's gaze. "Just go…" Daniel said more quietly, "you can't help me now. Stay out of this, or you'll be convicted too." Daniel watched the realisation dawn in his eyes. Seb looked frantically around as the crowd's mood changed their next victim in this hideous crime. He bolted like a hare. A wall of water ran up Daniels legs, reached his chest, and engulfed him completely. Imprisoning him in a pulsating tube of swirling dips and troughs. The full extent of his troubles made clear. He'd seen a cage like this before, but then he'd been on the other side. It had surrounded an Elf who was later sentenced and sacrificed to *The Water Lord*. Daniel reached out to touch the spinning waves; a drop stung his finger leaving a red blister. Darkness magic used to control prisoners. He felt sick. The tunnel began to move, hovering and rippling over the ground. He had no choice, go where it dictated, or be burned.

3

THE COUNCIL OF CARADOC

D aniel's water prison stopped pulsating, froze in mid-air before sloshing into the ground, with images of Thaen's face burned and raw face glaring in every puddle.

Disorientated and alone, he stood on a patch of barren shoreline, by a flat granite slab. It took a moment to work out where he was, then he saw the majestic grey steps. Why was he at the main entrance, only the Elf Council were allowed that privilege. Several Elves had followed his prison, they stood along the formal plinth and ornamental pathways. He was here because it gave plenty of room for everyone to come, watch and wait.

He gazed up at the powerful Great Hall. Trevarak's majestic landmark, matching the Unity Bridge in stature. He had only ever been allowed inside twice. The last time had been to celebrate his father inauguration as Grand Master, where everyone came. Even other Tribelings from other lands.

A member of The Council appeared and beckoned for him to follow. The wave of his hand was a simple movement, but it said more to Daniel than if it had been an angry shout. He wished he could run; but there was nowhere to go, they were too powerful; and would eventually find him. He wondered where his mother and Karn were. He thought of Isaac - *had his little brother escaped? Did they even know he was here?* He scanned the crowd but couldn't see them. Surely they knew, his father did? He slowly began to climb. A fountain of colour reflected off the stained-glass window. He turned. The crowd has started to chat a single monotonous low hum. He didn't understand, he just wanted them to stop. The door creaked loudly. Two enormous thick panels of oak decorated in line drawings of their ancestry. He crossed the threshold, looking up at the solid granite door frame, feeling the cold air wrap itself cruelly around him. The doors shut behind, quickly and loudly. The final clunk trapped in his fears.

The elaborately vaulted ceiling soared in a multitude of wooden arches, interspersed by a rich blue wood, that flickered with thousands of flickering lights. It reminded Daniel of Caradoc's enchanting *Dark Exchange* sky. Everywhere he looked hung giant carved panels, depicting Elves performing spells, images of Algor and scenes of glorious battles. They all emanated a soft blue glow. Daniel could sense the magic, as if it was in the air he breathed.

He stood just inside the doorframe; the Elf who had summons him had disappeared. He tried to run over in his mind how to explain what had happened, to justify his actions. Would they understand he was only trying to rescue his brother. That he hadn't used magic to touch the Water. He hadn't meant for Thaen to die. He hadn't started it. He looked into the gloomy corners of the hall – *where was everyone?* He thought of his water prison. If his father had created the prison, why had he used darkness magic to hold him there?

Then someone appeared. Then another and another. Dressed in formal cloaks, each representing a tribe, resplendent in their family colour, depicting honour and history. They came from all sides of the room, floating like ghost, into a horse shoe around the hall. The hairs rose across Daniel's neck.

"Daniel Elf Trevarak." He faced the speaker - Lucas, his father's deputy. A family friend and Seb's father... surely that was good? His gaze moved to a grey patch that appeared before him etched into the dark wooden floor, noticeable yet not bright.

"Stand in the marked square," Lucas commanded.

Daniel could smell burning sage and felt himself being pushed forwards. He struggled but was powerless against the invisible force that propelled him. With little effort from himself he reached it quickly. When both feet were inside, a ring of water rose to his waist. He watched as seats then appeared and The Council began to settle, adjusting cloaks and removing water pouches to place them on the floor beside. Some Elves removed their hoods, but others didn't. He recognised most. They supported his father and trusted his family. Surely another good sign? He looked about for his father but couldn't see him. Then images started to appear. Distorted figures of Thaen's burnt body flashed across the surrounding water. Daniel clenched his fists to try and stop himslef from trembling.

"Daniel Trevarak, you are here before us charged with two serious crimes, the like of which we haven't seen in Caradoc for many *Turns*. What do you say?" Lucas had risen from his chair to speak. Daniel felt his breath quicken and throat restrict.

"I was trying to save my brother," he blurted. "The Eastlings had dragged Isaac from our dwelling to the bridge over the Great Lake. They were torturing him with our Power Element, I could see his burns through a viewing spell." Daniel heard an echo of the word *spell* rush around the room, accompanied by the same giggling he'd heard from the lake. He instantly stopped speaking.

"Surely Isaac wasn't pulled from his room?" Thansim asked, a female Council member, renowned for her knowledge of Istria. "Under the nose of our Grand Master?" Her spectacles rested on the end of her nose.

"No... no... I mean, yes. He was... and none of us heard him being taken."

"I think that is almost impossible..." she laughed. "Your father, not to mention your mother, are two of the most skilled Elves within Caradoc - it would take a whole heap of magic to achieve deception against them."

"Kind Thansim, I'm sure Noah will be touched by your words, but we need to hear the facts," Lucas replied. "So how did you find out?" Lucas asked. "Why were you the only one to know? Lucas placed one hand back on the arm of his chair.

"I wasn't the first to know, I was woken and told." Another Council member removed his hood; it was Clements, his father's spell master. "Then by whom? Who woke you and how did they manage that, when everyone else slept?" Daniel didn't want to say, he knew he would get Seb into trouble. "Time is not on your side Elfling, it is very important you tell us truthfully. We have various spells, as you know, to make you otherwise, and none of them are pleasant."

Daniel took a deep breath, he had no choice. "Sebastian Trevarak woke me, he came in through Isaac's window, which was already broken. Then crept into my room." There were gasps around the room. Lucas sat back down with a jolt.

"Is he allowed through your house protection spell, has he been given entry?" Clements had walked a few paces towards him.

"Uh, yes..." Daniel hesitated. "He has... everyone knows that." Rumblings mixed with a ripple of exchanged looks went around the horseshoe.

"But why not wake your father? This was a serious matter." Lucas's face had turned an ashen colour. "He would have dealt with the situation properly and you wouldn't be standing here!"

Daniel felt swamped by a wave of prickling heat. "I was trying to handle it alone. I wanted to prove... I mean, I had a hunch it was Thaen and his followers and I wanted..." Daniel trailed off unable to find the words.

"Well..." Clements cleared his throat, "you've certainly proved something this *Turn*, but perhaps not what you wanted." Daniel swallowed hard.

"Did any of you see what happened?" Lucas's voice was flat and toneless, "The Eastling Elves on the bridge?" Lucas sought confirmation from the rest of The Council.

"None of us," Camundra replied. His blue cloak seemed to be the brightest of them all. Adorned with gems that sparkled. He was third in line to rule Caradoc.

"I find that so hard to believe," Clements said. "Twelve, all asleep, unaware. Or perhaps some of us are not being honest."

"How can that be?" Daniel blurted out, feeling the panic rise. "It was just there on that bridge." He pointed at one of the tall glass windows. "I know it was early, but surely one of you." An Elf, who hadn't spoken and sat on the far left-hand side, removed his hood. His cloak plain and old. His father... Daniel instinctively lunged towards him.

"Don't," Noah shouted. Daniel pulled back. "Father, I know this is..." his throat tightened. "But, I was only trying to save Isaac - he was burnt and limp. Why were they doing that? Why am I here and not them? I know I should have woken you..."

The door to the Great Hall suddenly swung open and in strode a willowy Elf. Daniel instantly recognised him. It was Tonurang, the leader of the Eastling Elves, his father's rival. Daniel had rarely seen him in the Trevarak settlement and had never known an Eastling Elf to enter the Great Hall without specific permission. A cold wind whipped through the room as the oak doors closed.

"Greetings..." his voiced deep and pronounced, "Council of Caradoc or should I say Trevarak. I am sure you understand why I am here. I have come to make sure justice is done. This is a most terrible crime..." his words ricocheted off the walls, "it cannot and must not be taken lightly. Punishment must be appropriate." Daniel glanced back at his father but was unable to read his expression. Tonurang proceeded forwards, as if he knew exactly where he was going, beckoning to his four henchmen to follow.

"Please do continue, don't let my presence stop the proceedings, I am so keen to understand where you have got to." Tonurang's footsteps were unusually loud. He circled the horseshoe. No one said a word. Tonurang then took a droplet from his pouch and flicked his hand; a chair appeared, taller, grander than the others. "I see you are not being as hospitable as usual." The Council shuffled awkwardly aside to let him in. His four guards stood like stone status shrouded in long grey cloaks and thick hoods, flanking his chair. Their bow and arrows not visible, but Daniel knew they were somewhere.

"But why fire an arrow Daniel?" Lucas asked.

"I hadn't a choice," Daniel struggled to find his words, "I couldn't reach Isaac in time. When they saw me... Thaen was holding him over the edge, threatening to drop him into our *Water*." Thansim got up from her chair.

"There are always choices, Daniel," she said in a voice that sounded different to how she spoke before. "Why not use a spell?" A lump rose in Daniel's throat. She paused, "Why not send a warning signal, if you chose an arrow? The Eastling Elves are our neighbours." And she smiled at Tonurang. "I didn't mean for the arrow to hit anyone. I aimed above their heads, I was just trying to scare them into letting my brother go…"

"There," Tonurang said loudly, "I didn't mean for an arrow to hit anyone…" in a mocking voice. "Opps sorry what a mistake," he laughs. "How ridiculous is that…?" Tonurang points "he… is clearly a threat to our society, with such dangerous and impetuous reactions. Could we all go around shooting our arrows at anyone we liked…?" he gestured extravagantly and sprang up from his chair. This was met by mumblings of agreement.

"There was provocation," Lucas interjected.

"And Daniel doesn't usually get into trouble," Clement said.

"Rubbish," Tonurang replied, "he's often been in trouble, only three *Turns* ago he had to be dragged off my Elfling, who were battered and bruised."

"That's not true," Daniel shouted.

"Not to mention," Tonurang ignored him, "his secret adventures onto the Moorlands of NaraRose. I saw him return just recently from such a trip. " He let the words linger. "For all we know he could be in league with the Imps." The Council shuffled within their positions and began to hold private discussions.

"Silence," Noah shouted and slammed his foot on the wooden floor.

"Is this true, Daniel," Lucas asked, "have you been onto the Moorlands of NaraRose?"

"Yes, and your Elfing came with me." Something inside Daniel erupted. Daniel had never felt so angry. He glared at his father expressionless face. What was wrong with him? He saw Tonurang smirk, then he realised what he'd done. His shoulders sank. "It's true," Daniel quietly whispered, "but it's not like that."

"I don't think everyone heard you," Tonurang said.

"I have been on the Moorlands, but only to explore; find out what it was like. I've NEVER met an Imp," Daniel implored. "I SWEAR my actions haven't brought harm to anyone."

"No harm?" Tonurang shouted. "But it's against Elf rules… rules in place for all our safety. Why should you be the one to flaunt them? You've entered our sacred waters, crossed our borders and killed an Elf." Discord filled the Great Hall, as if the Elves had turned into an angry swarm of flies. Daniel had no answer, *what had he done*? He didn't want to die.

"And by the look of you," Tonurang wouldn't stop, "you've been in our sacred waters before. Are you something special?" He spat his words. "How are you, without years of training, able to remain unharmed?" Daniel stood shaking. "And you, Noah Trevarak, our Grand Master." The whole Council turned, "Hiding something from your own council? Your eldest Elfling can somehow touch our Power Element without using magic! Is he even an Elf?" Daniel's father didn't move. His gaze, fixed and strong. Lucas called several times for calm.

Daniel sank to his knees, his strength suddenly gone. Voices bounced off the walls and filled his head. Snippets of information hit him like arrows. He put his hands over his ears and squeezed his head. His heartbeat slowed.

"The only punishment," Tonurang declared, "for such a blatant disregard of all that Caradoc holds dear, is the same as the crime that he's just committed and that's death! You all have no alternative."

"No," Daniel screamed inwardly. "No, you can't mean that… Father!" he whispered. He looked up to see Noah standing, staring at the glistening flecks in the ceiling, the creatures Daniel had heard so much about but had rarely seen - The *Glows*.

It took a while before everyone settled. Once there was silence Noah rose to his feet. "I think you have all said enough, especially you, Tonurang Eastling," his voice laced with venom. "I don't think we as a Council are able to **decide**. There is much more at play here and I for one, will make it my duty to find out what else is going on. So, the only option left open it to seek advice from Istria and now it is her time to speak."

4

THE SUN FESTIVAL

Eleanor paused, drew in a long slow breath, and gathered her strength. Then, stepped from her doorway. It was the *Turn* she'd been waiting for – *The Sun Festival*.

Despite the early *Shadow*, wild singing had already begun; mixing harmoniously with drumbeats, laughter, and chattering. Eleanor paused, scrunching her fists into a ball, and drew in the intoxicating cocktail of sweet chestnuts, dried cinnamon and pine. The trees ahead were a jumbled mixture of assorted leaves. Through the twisted network of branches and shadows, she could just make out a long line of tents and marquees. Each one dotted with fires and coloured flags. Adjusting her sack, she straightened her hair and set off.

A long-bearded Sprite peered over a burning pit, with sweat dripping from his brow. Irregular piles of terracotta bowls stacked in rickety piles on wooden trestle tables. He must have brought the goods to sell but made no effort to strike up an *exchange*. The Sprite's eyes flashed bright green - a warning. Eleanor hurried on.

Behind the next series of tents, each stall holder wore thick fur coats, they must have come from the North, where it was always cold. Having to travel through *Dark Exchange* to arrive at the beginning of *Light,* in order to set up such a display. Each table groaned with goods, arranged by colour, in intricate designs. Rich, red patterned pottery, glared against shiny green trinkets, and stood out against a multitude of dull wooden figures. Eleanor went on, browsing from one side of the pathway to the other, lost in the variety. Everything from clothes to furs, pots to necklaces, tools to food. Then she remembered the errand she had to do for her mother. She knew the treat of being out alone, would come with a price. Standing on tip toes, eventually she spied somewhere tucked from the main path that might help.

As Eleanor drew closer, she realised the stall was part of an elaborate tent. An intricate network of cupboards, tables and boxes, piled high with racks of wools, cottons, hemp and hessian in differing colours and patterns. Fabrics even hung from canopies, on long poles flanking the white turrets. No one seemed to be about, except an elderly couple, white-haired and deep in concentration over a selection of red wools. Eleanor carefully ran her hand over the creamy folds of a smooth hemp, that sat invitingly on the edge of a table; perhaps her mother would make a shawl from it?

With a slight breeze an aged Sprite appeared. Slightly hunched, with thick black frizzy hair interspersed by faint yellow streaks. Eleanor almost giggled, she'd never seen a hair style like it. A pointy, long, angular face stared through the thick hair, like an old snarly fox, except the Sprite's nose was rounder and not black or shiny. There was no brown fur either, but a thick dark cloak from head to toe. A strange colour for a Sprite, Eleanor thought, who owned such colourful fabrics.

"Can I help you, Spriteling with black hair?" She clipped the ends of her words. Eleanor groaned, why wouldn't Sprites just give up on her hair colour, so what if it was different.

"I'm looking for material for my family to make into clothes." Eleanor noticed the Sprite wasn't even listening and followed her gaze to see what she was so intently staring at. But there was nothing there except the rest of the materials, the older couple had moved away and no one else had taken their place.

"Puh," she barked and met her gaze. Her eyes startlingly emerald and fiercely piercing. "My cloth is of the highest quality and took time to weave, what could you possibly have that I might be interested in to make an *exchange*?"

Eleanor stammered. "Ropes," she said. "I've made them. There's no one else here. So... take a look." The old Sprite began to laugh and started to turn away.

"I have all the ropes I need in this tent. Now go away." Eleanor couldn't believe how rude she was. Just because she was young! Scrabbling around in her satchel, she pulled out one of her ropes. She'd show her. "Look, they're strong." The old Sprite lifted her hand, as if to shoo her away. "Everyone comments on how good my ropes are." Eleanor heard her chuckle, as she turned around. Spontaneously the rope began to glow and wriggled in Eleanor's hand, emanating a pale, yellow. Eleanor glanced at the Sprite, and then at the rope. Their eyes locked. Quickly, Eleanor began to shove it back into her bag, angry with the Wind Master, *who had let her down again*! She had prayed to her that this wouldn't happen again... and especially in front of this old crow!

"I've changed my mind," Eleanor fumed, "I don't want any of your cloth - forget it."

"It glowed!" the Sprite rasped, "At your touch."

"No," Eleanor replied, "you're mistaken. It didn't." The old Sprite walked slowly around the side of the table,

"It also moved in your hand. I saw it clearly."

"You couldn't have," Eleanor said, "you're wrong. That's just rubbish." But the ends of Eleanor's fingers tingled at her lie. Unexpectedly the old Sprite lunged, clasping long, slender fingers around her shoulder and started to chant musical words. Eleanor felt like a fish snared at the end of a hook. A gusty, playful breeze danced around them, as if commanded by the music. Quickly it filled with dust and began to swirl in circles. Unable to move, Eleanor watched a cloudy mass approach, growing thicker. Faster and faster it went. In an instant, it filled her eyes, mouth and lifted her off the ground. Around and around, she tumbled, powerless.

Several moments later, Eleanor plummeted, as if she'd been miles up in the sky; and landed dishevelled and bemused, on a thick white fur rug, amongst a pile of dust. As it settled, Eleanor reached for her dagger.

Haphazardly placed objects and trinkets crammed every corner of her surroundings. A tree bed grew across part of the floor; and its branches covered most of the ceiling. A multitude of leaves rustled as breezy gusts seeped in through the canvas walls. Tucked away to one side was a stone hearth, accompanied by an enormous wooden chair, big enough for at least three of her sisters to sit in. It rocked by itself.

"Apologises for the abrupt arrival. But you gave me no choice." The old crow appeared, with her arms raised. The dark cloak had gone, replaced by a startling yellow gown. A long line of dust floated from her outstretched hand. "Don't move, this shouldn't hurt," she said. The grey moving shadow shot across the room and burst into Eleanor's face. "This will mean you might listen. You young Spriteling's these *Turns* are all the same. Keen to jabber on, not to listen." Eleanor sat paralysed on the rug. "My name is Morwena," she said, "au Leona du Gwent. I am one of the Sprite Elite." Eleanor fought against her hold. "There are only three of us and together we have a greater ability to use our *Power Element – Wind*, than any other Sprite alive." Eleanor knew that, and also knew what they were capable of. She really didn't want to be stuck in a tent with one. "We've been waiting… waiting for several generations to find '*The new Wind Whisperer*'."

The hold on Eleanor broke. "Why are you doing this?" she shouted. "That spell - I couldn't move!" Eleanor rose to her feet. "And where am I?" Morwena turned and shuffled away, muttering something about not listening. Her dress dragging across the floor. Eleanor spotted an opening in the tent, and bolted, scrambling over padded chairs, cooking pots and a cauldron. Running straight into a chest. Holding back tears, she furiously rubbed her leg. "You… you… that spell… me in here,' Eleanor gasped, looking at the hole in her tights where blood had already appeared. "After I showed you my rope, didn't you… why, why did you do that?" Morwena's eyes changed from green to a steely black, which gave her the look of a wild *Darkness* Creature Eleanor had seen in books.

"I didn't only see it move," Morwena's step quickened, "I saw it glow in your hands. Has it done that before?"

"Yes."

"When?"

"Whilst I was making them," Eleanor edged around the trunk.

"Are you one of the Paraquinn Sprites?"

"Yes, why?"

"I knew your Grandsprite."

To steady herself, Eleanor reached for the canvas roll. "You can't have," she challenged.

"Huh," the old Sprite's gaze went to rest on a book that lay alone on a short-legged bench. The old book lay lifelessly, startlingly dull against the jewel-embellished furniture it sat on. "Do you know why the rope does that?" Morwena asked.

"No," Eleanor whispered, "I've not shown anyone before."

"Good... they probably wouldn't understand." Morwena opened the large, aged brown cover, and ran her finger down its spine, as if she was stroking a young Spriteling's face. "I will teach you, give you answers - like I taught your Grandsprite."

"Teach me! Teach me what? And... that's not true, I would have known if you were in Grandsprite's life, and she never mentioned you." Eleanor knocked over a saucepan as she lost her footing. "And I knew everything about her," Eleanor voice was trill, "and... she died in the Great Fire! So don't speak her name." Morwena's lips moved then returned to an arched frown, as if she was going to say something, but thought better of it. The fire crackled and spat angrily. "If you want to learn," Morwena announced, her voice rose as if to silence any more interruptions, "meet me, in four *Turns* from now, on the Moorlands of NaraRose. You haven't been through your Passing, so there is much to learn."

"Uh? Why would I do that?"

"I know you are looking for answers. And I am the only one who can give them to you. So you must find *Obakeech,* our sacred valley. If you make it, you will be rewarded with what you seek." Eleanor shivered as she stared at the white pages of the book flickering madly from side to side. "Now..." Morwena's voice was distant, "you've been with me for too long. Go... take what materials you want and leave." A long pale finger extended through the misty grey cloud that had already begun to obscure the tent from view. The finger almost touched Eleanor's nose. A sharp tug pulled on her satchel. A rope began to wriggle its way through the flap. The dust grew thicker and Eleanor once more felt herself being lifted off the ground,a s the tope slipped from her bag. When the dust had cleared, Eleanor was back in front of the material stall. But this time there were several Sprites about. They all turned to look at her. Her hand lay on the cream hemp. Looming menacingly over her, was a completely different stall holder, thick set with his hands on his hips.

5

THE SILVER BOWL

Eleanor steadied herself, trying to make sense of what had just happened. The stall holder cleared his throat, with a crackle and a line of spit fell from his lips. Eleanor slowly took her hand from the hemp and slowly dusted off her dress, stalling.

"What are you doing?" He slammed his fist over her bag. His bulging fingers covered most of the front pocket.

"I'm... er choosing materials..." Eleanor stumbled backwards. "As the old Sprite... Mo... Morwena told me to. She said take what I needed."

"Who?" his mouth curled downwards. "There's no one else on this stall... I'm the owner, and there certainly not anyone else in my tent." His chin protruded from his face, his breath smelt of stale junipers, "And I did NOT tell you to take my cloth."

"But that's im... impossible," Eleanor stuttered. "I've just been pulled into that tent and... and... locked by a spell. Morwena du Gwent; or something like that, told me she'd known my Grandsprite, and to take what I wanted."

Another Sprite came closer, "So," she hissed as if her mouth was unable to open wide enough to speak clearly. She was much taller than Eleanor, with a thin pinched face, "you're saying you know one of the Sprite Elite and that she was here in that tent." A few other Sprites began to laugh around them. "Don't you think some of us would know that? Especially him. Don't you think we would sense her?"

"It's true," Eleanor said. "She's here."

"Don't lie," the stall holder shouted. "This is my stall and mine alone - now give me back those materials unless you have something impressive to exchange, or I'll call a member of the Council." Eleanor opened her bag, trying to control her shaking hand. Underneath a series of different materials, she had no idea how they got there, she managed to grasp some ropes.

"There," she said and threw him four. "They should be good enough." She scooped up the cream hemp for her mother. She wasn't going to wait around for his answer. He began to grunt and examined one as if it was a precious piece of gold.

"Morwena was here," Eleanor said to them all, "... I'm not lying. There is something wrong with your awareness spells, if none of you sensed her." She began to run. The stall holder's angry words didn't quieten until she had jostled her way back into the main thoroughfare.

Standing amongst the crowd, Eleanor felt as if she'd stepped into another world, not of excitement remained. A Spriteling's cries made her jump, Sprite's that brushed against her, a potential threat. She nearly took her knife out on an old Sprite who walked into her. Had she really just met one of the Sprite Elite? Flown in the air? And even worse... would her parents hear about what she'd done at the stall? She moved over to a jewellery display and tried to absorb herself in the selection of silver rings. Her eyes flickered over the patterns, but her mind wouldn't rest. She had to go back - she had to check... *make sure she hadn't gone mad.*

This time, Eleanor took a different path, skirting behind the main stalls, deep amongst tall, concealing pines. Feeling safer blanketed by the silvery half light and away from the festival. Drawing nearer, the back of the white tent appeared into view. Eleanor checked no one was about and pushed her satchel into a thick leafy bush. *She'd collect that later.* Then slowly crept nearer. The coarse voice of the stall holder calling out the merits of his wares, boomed through the air.

His back of his head, full of thick matted hair, glared against the white of the tent. She checked again no one could see her. With shaking hands, Eleanor stepped over the main guy ropes, untied several linking catches and wriggled into a gap between the linings.

A completely different interior, confronted her. She sank to her knees and rubbed her eyes. Eleanor slowly rose, sinking into the tent wall. Surely she'd hadn't made it all up? She took another look, sullen and confused. A shiver travelled down her back, as the interior began to change. The whole tent shifted and blurred, as it imploded. Two images flickered in a mirage, before Morwena appeared kneeling, hunched over the same book. Eleanor instantly melted into the lining. Morwena flicked steadily through the tattered pages, before settling on a page, tenderly running her palm down its facing. Her other hand rose into the air. A delicate silver bowl appeared. Eleanor could see intricate carved images rippling over the metal, but none of them she recognised. Without looking, Morwena put her hand into the bowl, and drew out a line of dust. Eleanor leaned in, hardly daring to breathe. The dust span into a circle, wider and wider so that it grew and encased the old Sprite's body. A moving column, mirroring the one that had transported her into the tent. Suddenly it dispersed, spraying wildly. Eleanor shrank to the ground, breathing rapidly. When she dared to look again, the dust had gone and Morwena was gently rocking back and forth in the chair by the fire.

"This had better be good, Morwena," came an angry voice. Eleanor jumped grabbing hold of the main guy rope to stop herself from falling. A hunchbacked stocky sprite stood rubbing her hands in front of the fire. Eleanor couldn't see where she'd come from.

"Oh, stop being so grumpy, Moranta," Morwena snapped. "Have patience… you won't be disappointed." Morwena rose stiffly from her rocking chair and shuffled towards her companion.

"But, I haven't been summoned like that," said Moranta, "for a very long time and dust travel is not my preferred way of getting around these days. I'm far too old and far too…" She was interrupted mid-sentence by a sprinkling of silvery sparkles falling from the canvas eaves. They swirled around in a spiral and formed into the shape of a body. Eleanor clasped her hand to her mouth. As the shape became clearer… she recognised the figure. He was one of the most talented and, in some circles, feared Sprite within Vearmoor.

Blaydoc, head of The Council. Eleanor panicked - had he come to punish her for taking the material without a proper Exchange? He reappeared only a few feet from where she crouched. If she stuck out her arm, she could probably pull on his long grey plait.

"What is the meaning of this, Morwena?" Blaydoc demanded. "I've never been dust summoned without my specific permission. I was in the middle of a council meeting. Chairing the damn thing... How am I to explain? I just disappeared. They fear us enough as it is... damn you." Eleanor's throat dried. *He must be, she realised, the last member of the Sprite Elite – she was looking at all three of them.* Morwena gave a curt bow and held up Eleanor's rope! Moranta and Blaydoc stopped talking and shuffled over to Morwena's outstretched arms, where the rope lay. Blaydoc picked it up.

"Beautifully made, intricate detail, not seen anything like this for a long time. The colour is perfect and its strength apparent. So... who made it?"

"A young Sprite..." Morwena replied.

"Oh no..." Blaydoc raised his arms, "don't tell me you think you might have found *The Wind Whisperer...* again," he exclaimed, "from just one rope!"

"But it moved and glowed in her hands... she had no idea what she was doing. It came naturally," Morwena snapped. "But you've failed once before," Blaydoc had raised his tone, "don't you remember, the consequences were not pretty? Surely you wouldn't want that to happen again?"

Eleanor's hands went cold. She pulled away and sank to the ground. Surely Morwena wasn't talking about her Grandsprite? The forest fires, that terrible *Turn* when her Anna had died, danced before her eyes. In a daze, she tried to stand up. Suddenly a blast of wind came from nowhere. It knocked her squarely off her feet and send her flying into the air, collapsing crumbled into a canvas wall.

"What is going on back there?" Eleanor could hear the stamp of heavy boots, as she tried to clear her thoughts. "It's you? What are you doing here again?" The angry stall holder's voice boomed. Eleanor groaned and rolled over onto her side, a pain rolling down her back.

"I'm not..." she gasped for breath, and scrambled to her feet, only just managing to dodge his giant flaying hand. With the speed of a hare, she got up and ran up the side of the tent, skirting agilely around the back, leaping ropes as if she was a cricket. Falling into the bush she'd grabbed her things, ignoring the abusive threats. She wasn't going to give him a chance to catch up. Without stopping she fled deep into the woods.

6

OBAKEECH

leanor slowed, finally surrounded by the smooth bark of long branches, bowing to the ground. The distinctive silvery trees denoted her Paraquinn district. They wrap themselves comfortably like a best friend's hug. She fell to a fast walk. A neighbour waved. Eleanor tried to smile back, but it felt more like a grimace, she hoped he wouldn't notice. The long path of worn down bark-chippings passed her friend's carved cedar door. If Johanna was in, she would know what to do. But no washing hung from branches, or music floated from open windows. Eleanor quickly hurried on.

Lifting the heavy iron handle, she fell against the familiar oak door. It couldn't open quickly enough. The *Turn* she'd waited patiently for so long, had become a disaster. Wearily, she climbed the wooden staircase, comforted by the solid enclosing trunk, and away from prying eyes. Her hand slid along the worn, carved handrail, created by her father. She hoped that her family wouldn't be at home either. She needed time to think. Try to make sense of everything that had happened. Surely Morwena was mistaken. One of the Sprite Elite couldn't possibly think she might be *The Wind Whisperer – A Sprite who, according to legend, would unite them all against* The Darkness - it almost made her laugh.

One hundred and seventy-seven, one hundred and seventy-eight.

She threw her satchel over the nearest hook, untied her boots, and ran across the room to the pile of giant cushions. Her family platform had never looked so reassuring. She hit and shoved a few pillows, to get the perfect position, then collapsed into the middle, resting her head to gaze over the lattice sidewall, at the network of lanterns, tracing their lines between the trees. She drifted off into a world of thought.

Chattering, loud and cheerful filled the room. Eleanor groaned.

"Look!" Amber squealed, "E's back. What did you find?" Eleanor pointed to her satchel on the hook. She had no idea what materials were in there, except the cream one. Amber ran over, before Eleanor got a chance to stop her. She rummaged uncaringly before quickly pulling them out and throwing the contents over the floor.

"Your bag is bigger than it looks. There's loads. How did you manage it?" Before Eleanor could reply, everyone spoke at once, admiring the cloth, and deciding which one to have. Eleanor felt sick. What if they found out she'd practically stolen them?

"These are great, sis, I'm impressed. Did you do this all alone?" Eleanor glared at Amber. Her mother gently tapped Amber on the arm and came over and gave Eleanor a hug.

"Ignore her, she's only miffed as she didn't do so well on her first outing alone!" Amber started to rant her protest. "You seem tired," she said as she held Eleanor to arm's length. Eleanor savoured her lavender scent. "You, alright, darling? Did everything go to plan? You were so excited earlier."

"I'm fine." Eleanor looked to the floor.

"Nothing happened at the festival, did it?' Her mother tilted her head to one side. "There, Elerday." Eleanor's favourite sister stood just behind her mother. "I said she shouldn't have gone out alone. Look at her... she's pale – something's happened. Look, see… was someone unkind to you?"

"Mother." Elerday came over. "Don't fuss, she's fine, right, E?" Eleanor nodded. "It's been a big *Turn* for us all. Leave her alone."

Their father came into the room. He was drying his hands on a towel and gave Eleanor a wink. He looked like he'd appeared from his workshop and hadn't gone to the festival at all.

"E's done well," he said, "so...," he said loudly and waited for everyone to listen, "she'll be allowed to go to the Paraquinn music festival this *Late Shadow*." There were gasps from her sisters, followed by a host of protest, that they had never been allowed to go when they were her age. Eleanor smiled at her father, she couldn't believe it, what had come over him. He normally stuck to his rules. Maybe this *Turn* would get better after all.

"So..." he said in a loud voice, "you ALL need to be ready in one *Shadow!* I'm not waiting a moment longer, so go, hurry, get ready, as I've got the tickets and you can't go without me!" He started to laugh as they scurried off in various directions. The jumble of shrieks trailing behind like ribbons.

"Thanks," Eleanor bit her thumbnail.

"Hurry, E, you'll be late." He took her thumb from her mouth and squeezed it gently. "Are you sure everything's ok? I overheard your mother fussing. You do look pale."

"Er... no... nothing," she paused to decide, "... it's ok." He raised his eyebrows. "Honestly, Papa, I think I'm more tired than I thought. It's been a big *Turn* - everything's fine. "I'll go and change." She hurried away; wandering if she'd made the right decision by not saying anything.

Running along the connecting branch, Eleanor steadied herself on the rope ladder, down the three steps and flung open her bedroom door. Her sister, Elerday was just above. She could already hear her shuffling around. Eleanor collapsed onto the bed, sinking into her favourite fur. With her face buried, the glow of her rope, and Morwena's black eyes, were still imprinted images. She wearily sat up. *What was she going to wear?* She walked over to her wardrobe, and pulled open the heavy slated door. Her eyes scanned the rail of tunic dresses, all hand me downs from her sisters. Nothing she could call her own and good enough to wear tonight. She sighed, it was rubbish being the youngest sometimes. A strange fizzing sound filled her ears. She shook her head. It didn't go away. She looked around her room, holding onto the door for support. It was coming from behind her chair in the corner. It went away, so Eleanor went to light the candle on her bedside table. Her chair still had the same bundle of clothes from *Early Shadow*. She reached over to the pillar candles on her trunk and struck a match - it was too dark in her room. It instantly went out. She tried three times; the last match's extinguished smoke spiralled up into the air and floated towards the corner. Eleanor's stomach tighten as she followed the dusty grey line. The noise grew louder as the smoke approached the chair. Eleanor reached for her pillow. The smoke floated behind the chair as if it had a mind of its own. The fizzing, started to bubble and pop, forming the shape of a head! Eleanor pulled her pillow over her mouth and stifled a scream. The head grew and pushed her chair scrapping along the floor. With a clammy palm, Eleanor grasped for her water tumbler, anything to throw.

"Don't," croaked a voice through the smoke as a body joined the head, with a slightly crooked back and hunched features. Eleanor lowered the tumbler.

"It's you," Eleanor stammered. "How did you break our protection spell?" A misty outline of Morwena hovered in the corner of her bedroom. Fading and changing shape. Eleanor could still see the murky corner walls behind.

"Silence, Spriteling, I have little time to explain and I can't hold this spell for long enough to apologise as well. Now listen. We must meet next *Turn* at the *Sixth Shadow.*"

"Are you really here?"

"Is that important?" Morwena exasperated tone was sharp. "No, of course I'm not actually here. This is my dust image. Don't you know anything?"

"Uh..." Eleanor shuffled uncomfortably. The smoke sighed, "next *Turn,*" she repeated. "Follow the falling sun out of Vearmoor and onto the Moorlands of NaraRose. Walk south-eastwards towards Caradoc." A gust of wind buffeted the image.

"Where? Wait!' Eleanor blustered. "Why the urgency?"

"Find a solitary yellow gorse bush covered in bees within a valley." The swaying ghostly image billowed in and out. "You'll know when you find it - it's *Moorland Obakeech.*"

"I don't know where that is..."

"Oh, for the sake of the *Wind Lord*. Use some initiative. Ask for help if you have to! Otherwise just, follow the sun and don't be late. It's not hard..." The image evaporated. Eleanor groaned, staring in frustration at the trail of dust as it pipped and popped, through the gaps in her wooden floor. The rumpus from her sisters filled her room once more.

"Why me?" Eleanor yelled, thumping her bed as she landed on her back, submerged by her duvet. "*The next Turn*," she groaned, "*that's ridiculous. I'm not going....*"

"Eleanor, are you alright?" her father called, "could I hear someone?"

"No, Papa, of course not. I'm talking to myself about what to wear. I'll be there in a moment!"

"Well, hurry up. It's time to go." She looked down at her dress - she hadn't even changed! She hurriedly brushed her hair, removing all the twine from the day and tied it loosely into a knot at the back of her head. She pulled the nearest dress from her wardrobe and quickly swopped it for what she was wearing. The folds spilling into place, not nearly quickly enough. Trying to make some effort, she put on her late Grandsprite's gems and stared into the mirror. The gems sat perfectly at the nape of her cheek bones. Her face was still pale, but hopefully no one would notice. She pinched her cheeks and rubbed beeswax into her lips. Grabbing her shoulder fur, she flew to her bedroom door.

7

THE BLUE CROSS

Noah raised his arms. The heavy silence filled the room, smouldering with discord. Daniel looked up at the ceiling; *The Glows* bounced erratically. *How had his father managed to communicate with them?*

His stomach churned, bubbling furiously. *The Glows* burned brightly, casting a white over the blue and threatened to dominate the room. The Elves of The Council held up their arms, palms open. Daniel prayed to the *Water Lord*, Istria and anyone who was listening. He would make amends, never be so hasty again, never go into the scared waters, never use his bow, no matter how much he loved it. Anything, just anything they would spare him.

The Glows began to calm. This didn't ease Daniel's nerves. Their light receded, drawing into each burning fleck, as if the life had been sucked out of the hall. Their decision made. The Council lowered their arms and sat back into their chairs. Even Tonurang was silent, a hand resting under his chin as he stared blankly. They all knew and he didn't… Daniel lent on his bow, nestling it tightly under his arm, trying to draw strength from the smooth wood. Words flowed from his father he didn't understand. The water around him disappeared. He blinked as the last few drops splashed his face. He forced an image of his body burning at the centre of a sacrifice pyre away.

"Council members," Noah paced like a studious professor, "and our guest, Tonurang Elf Pengarin Eastling, *The Glows* have answered my call. As a Council, if we cannot come to an agreement, they will have the overriding say." Every member nodded their head. Daniel's whole insides twisted at the flint expression on his father's face. No one was listening to his prays. Istria, *The Water Lord* or his father hadn't...

"Do you find Daniel Elf Trevarak," Noah paused, "guilty or not guilty of the unlawful death of another Elf and violation of our power element?" Daniel noticed his voice displayed anger, not pity. Daniel's chest tightened. He closed his eyes, this time he saw his mother's face weeping as she threw his ashes across a lake. Only a few *Shadows* ago his sole thought had been of breakfast. How could he now be standing where he was, having killed someone? "*Wake up, wake up*," he wanted to run, or open his eyes to a new realisation it had just been a bad dream. Tonurang rose from his chair, and began to pull his cloak on, carefully fastening each buckle.

"Our guest can answer first."

"Guilty, there is only one right answer."

Daniel's cheeks went hot.

"Lucas?" Noah turned away from Tonurang.

"Not guilty, I believe he was provoked," Lucas replied. Daniel's eyes filled with water – was there hope? Might The Trevarak Elves rally to his family?

"Eliwane?"

"Guilty. I have my concerns, Noah," she said. Daniel's shoulders sank, she was a Trevarak. His knees wobbled as if his body's weight had suddenly become too much. The remaining ten Elves gave their verdict.

"It is even," Noah declared. "So, while I am still the overall Leader of Caradoc," Daniel saw his father look at Tonurang. "I will sentence in accordance with *The Glows'* recommendations. Again each Elf raised their arms skywards. This time Daniel was finding it hard to focus. He swayed like a fragile sapling. Blue lines of light pulsed from their outstretched hands. Casting a pale mangled pattern, of earlier *Light Exchange*. Daniel covered his face and fought to stop the tears from brimming over. Through the cracks between his fingers he saw a deep blue cross appear, melting across the beams of wood, until it hung directly above him. The ceiling went black. His sentence was sealed into Caradoc history.

"Daniel Elf Trevarak, you've been found guilty by The Council of two serious crimes to the Caradoc way of life." The cold words cut through his skin. "The Elves of NaraRose aren't a Tribe who let the taking of another's life go unpunished and we are not a Council who allow our sacred power element to be violated in such a way." Thick aromas of burning sage filled the room. "But Istria had spoken. Therefore…" his father cleared his throat, "your sentence is not death, but banishment. Banishment from your homeland, in accordance with our Goddess' recommendation. You'll be sent onto the Moorlands of NaraRose, unable to return into Caradoc."

The dark blue cross brightened and *The Glows* reappeared. Daniel fixed his gaze on a small door at the back of the room and allowed its wood panel to form the word 'banishment'. Out alone onto The Moors, *where no one lives*? He'd never survive. He choked and spluttered. It took time before he realised his father had finished speaking and it was Tonurang's voice he could hear.

"Death should have been his punishment," Tonurang shouted, "however I'm satisfied with this ruling, as it has come from Our Lady. He'll never be a threat to my Elves again. I will wait by the Raven exit," Tonurang paused, "make sure it is executed quickly. If not Noah Trevarak, my Elves will take over."

Daniel rocked unsteadily; as if a strong wind had filled the hall. Tonurang walked pompously around the circle. The footsteps of his guards, hit Daniel like batons. *Don't fall, Don't fall,* he ground his fingernails into his palms. The Eastling Elves disappeared quickly through the oak doors sucking the air from the room as the doors slammed shut. Daniel shuddered, but refused to fall.

8

THE RAVEN EXIT

"Listen, Daniel." His shoulders moved. "Can you hear me?" The words lapped over him. "There's little time, my Elfling." Daniel savoured the warmth. "Lucas and The Council will escort you to the Raven exit. Once you've crossed the border, a spell will be cast that prevents you from re-entering. Be strong. You have to go through with this, it's the only way." Daniel pressed his head into his father's chest.

"Why did you not wake me? Why? I wish, I wish..." his father muttered. "I could have prevented this. Isaac would be safe and Thaen would be on trial not you."

"I know, I know," Daniel sobbed. "I just wanted... to," but he lost his words. He lay still, breathing slowly in and out. "...can't you stop this, you're the Grand Master?"

"Even I can't. But *The Glows* have spared you for a reason. You must be able to survive. And your ability to swim in our Power Element is a miracle; how could you keep it from me?" Daniel saw deep lines of anguish in his father's face. "Why didn't you trust me? Does your mother know?" Daniel couldn't reply. Noah took his face in his hands. "You must trust me, when I say that something is wrong here." His father's voice filled with the same anger that Daniel had heard earlier. "It may be better you're out of the way. Istria always has her reasons."

"But... how can this be for the best," Daniel spluttered. "The Moors are haunted with *Darkness* creatures and no one survives?"

"We have to go, my old friend," Lucas interrupted. "We don't want to give the Eastling Elves any excuse to take over the proceedings." He laid a hand on Noah's shoulder.

"Just a little more time."

"Listen Daniel," his father pulled him closer. "Remember two things. Firstly, the power elements of *Water* and *Earth* are aligned and can make a good partnership. Secondly, try to find a Sprite Elder called Morwena; tell her you're my Elfling. She will help you, I know she will. Use your bow and that instinct of yours, it will serve you well." His father's embrace went stiff. "I can't come with you. I have to stay here."

"But father, I can't go alone."

"Lucas will be there. Remember, Daniel," his father's eye's glistened, "you are my Elfling, a member of the ruling family of Caradoc. *The Glows* and Istria have saved your life for a reason, be strong, fight and survive."

Daniel was helped up by Lucas. He stumbled across the hall. Daniel could feel his father's gaze heavily on his back. "I am with you," Lucas said. But he faded in and out of sight, as the great doors flung open, flooding the hall with the clear blue light of Caradoc. Daniel raised his arm and covered his eyes. Two more Council members appeared, and manoeuvred him to the granite steps. They stood like tall stone pillars. Lucas began to speak, reading from a scroll, broadcasting his verdict. Murmurs ran through the crowd, gasps, loud and raw. The whole of the Trevarak Elves had gathered. Elders, joined by their Elfling's united in families, huddled together. He searched the crowd for his mother, Karn and Isaac... Isaac, his father had said, he could have saved Isaac, *so didn't he?* His body swayed, until a guard tightened his grip.

Daniel tried to ask the Elf about Isaac, as he was pulled down the steps. The pathway broadened, and eight Council members appeared forming a impassible cage, several he recognised who had been family friends. None of them showed him any care. He frantically searched, in the throng for his family. A few of the crowds' whispers seeped into his conscious. Cutting like a sharp knife... *Good riddance, I say... He must possess Darkness magic; how else would he be alive? How could the Trevarak's do this to us? Why does he not burn?* Through a fleeting gap Daniel saw the Raven exit, sitting aloof and proud at the end of a broad valley, flanking the treacherous Grey Lake. The two stone boulders weren't impressive, but the valley they sat at the bottom of, was a fortress of stone. Several times before, he'd run past the gates without a second glance. It was where his friends played Scoop and Rat. Its soft sand made the game harder. His entourage reached the Mid lake. Tall reeds surrounded the edges. They became engulfed in a reed archway, which sheltered them from the falling water of the jagged rocky cliffs. Funnelling the crowd to follow behind. The roar from White Falls on their eastern side deafened all words. The walk was slow and haphazard. One wrong footing and the reeds would give way into the lake. Eventually the Raven Stones appeared clearly, as they climbed down a steep pathway onto the plateau. The carved handles sat at their midst, shining a bright silver. Sitting like guards at the base of a sheer wall of flat rock. Daniel could hardly believe that they were the only things that stood between him and The Moors; and would trap him out of his homeland forever.

A voice rang out. He recognised it instantly - his mother. The crowd jostled, Daniel could see the top of her head pushing her way through. Finally, he could smell her rosemary.

"Let me through, Eliwane, that is my Elfling," Anta snapped.

"Anta, you don't have much time, Tonurang is on the war path."

"I don't care, let him try." Daniel saw his mother's eyes flash in defiance. She pushed the guards aside. He couldn't move as her voice soothed him. She refilled his quiver with arrows and stole a water pouch under his tunic. "Daniel, you are important, *The Glows* have spoken for you." She wrapped an oilskin around his shoulders and put bread into every pocket. "But why, why not ask for help?" She stifled a sob. "How could you fire an arrow?"

"I didn't mean for it to hit him." Daniel sobbed. "You have to believe me."

"I do... I do."

"You need to leave," one of the guards said gruffly.

"Don't speak to me like that, Tiawain," Anta snapped back. "My Elfling is about to be banished. Find it in your heart to give me another moment." Daniel could see the fury in his mother's expression, mirroring that of his father's earlier. "When you're on The Moorlands, Daniel," she said in a hurried whisper, "call on me... I will come... I promise." And she dropped something into his pocket.

"But how is that possible?' Daniel mumbled.

"Just do it... promise me." He nodded, as she stroked her hand slowly down his face. "Remember, Daniel, remember... I'll always love you. Just stay alive." Her arms moved away.

"Wait, you can't go," Daniel begged. "Isaac, Isaac, I don't know what happened to him."

"Neither do we." Daniel felt as if his stomach had been punched.

"No... tell me. Where did he go?"

"I don't know. Daniel, but I will find him, you have my word," his mother whispered. "Our family will be reunited."

"Your time is up," Tiawain demanded. Anta was roughly pulled away. Daniel watched as her hands were bound, as if she too, now a prisoner. One by one his respected family were being stripped of their status, all because of what he had done. Determined hands pushed him forwards. He found himself alone, like a bull in an arena. The guards retreated to form an arch behind him. Only Lucas remained.

"Stand back a little," Lucas's voice sounded shaky, as he drew from his pouch a line of water droplets, using a silver funnel. He dropped one at a time onto each boulder. In the corner of his eye Daniel spotted Tonurang, standing on a ledge, surrounded by the same bodyguards. Daniel bit his lip and looked away. The Raven stones started to move, scraping along the ground like nails across a board. They heaved and moaned, painfully slowly. Eventually, a black void was exposed, letting in dank air.

"Daniel, it's time." Lucas spoke softly. "Remember what your father said about *Earth* and *Water*. And I promise to stand by him... whatever happens."

"It wasn't Seb's fault," Daniel said quietly. "He was not to blame."

Lucas smile was laced with pain. "I'm afraid, Daniel, it's too late for that."

The water slammed against the shoreline, the same beating swish and slosh that had been present all his life. He took his first step; with Lucas's firm grip digging into his shoulder.

"Use your wit, Daniel," he said urgently, "you can survive, you are much stronger than you realise." He pressed his own Element pouch into Daniel's chest. "Now go. May the Water Lord be with you."

The crowd began to hum. The same low deathly note. Bidding him good riddance. Daniel fell between the stones, trying to see into the dark. He could hear Lucas begin to chant his *Banishment Spell*. He dared not look back. He couldn't have the last image of his homeland, of his own tribe's mistrust, imprinted upon his memory. The chant grew to a crescendo as if Lucas was performing for the crowd. Daniel crept into the gloom above him revealing a funnel shaped path. Daniel forced himself to go on. Soon he had to duck as the tunnel narrowed, and crouch on all fours, crawling along in the dirt to follow it upwards. Mud covered his hands and dirt flicked into his eyes. He pushed his way through a mass of dangling roots.

A scrapping sound scratched at the tunnel. Daniel turned to see The Raven stones were closing. His heartbeat rose, as he hadn't made it out yet! With a resounding thud they closed, much more quickly than when they'd opened. He was in complete darkness. The air quickly thickened and filled his lungs with gloopy dust. Daniel picked up his pace, frantically scraping at the earth, until his head hit into something. He couldn't go any further. Wildly he scratched and pushed with his shoulders. Soil fell into his hair and down his neck into his clothes. Several stones tumbled by. He wildly hit the ceiling, willing it to give way. Eventually a thin shaft of light appeared. Thrusting his hand through, he could feel prickly grasses. Grasping hold, he scratched at the hole, pulling handfuls of earth away, until it was wide enough to heave himself through.

Every nerve in his body was alive. He leapt to his feet. Standing tall on The Moorlands. He covered his eyes against the glaring light. He'd heard of Elves being blinded. The hole quickly refilled with soil and grass, as if he'd never been through, sliding into place commanded by Lucas's powerful spell. He felt a trembling start in his stomach, that rippled through his body in waves of panic. Caradoc's entrances invisible to him? He thought at least he would be able to see them still. *Was he no longer an Elf?* A bitter wind wrapped its cruel claws tightly around his shoulders and settled into his heart. Was this what it was like to no longer be part of a Tribe?

9

BLANK SPACE

"I've sent the others on," Eleanor's father said. He was dressed in his best navy waistcoat, white shirt with deep green tartan trousers. "They will meet us at the Great Oak. I thought you and I could walk there together," he gave her a smile. Once through the front door, Eleanor linked her arm through his. They ambled on in a peaceful silence.

"Papa," Eleanor eventually said, "did Grandsprite ever mention a Sprite called Morwena?" Her father stopped, unhooked his arm. "Why do you ask?" His face had a funny sort of half smile, that Eleanor couldn't work out if it was concern or disinterest.

"I... I don't know," she stammered. "Uh, someone said to me, a friend, that Anna had known her..." Eleanor turned away. "I mean, imagine one of our family knowing a Sprite Elite."

"Be careful... tell your friend," he cleared his throat, "I mean around Morwena... that is, if she, or you, have ever come across her." "She's incredibly powerful, and... somewhat unpredictable." He linked her arm again. "She and your Grandsprite were once good friends," he said, "but their friendship didn't end well."

Eleanor was about to shout *seriously Grandsprite knew her...* but found that she couldn't get her words out. Her head had started to ache, and a sickness flushed over her. She watched her father pick up a long stick transfixed by its beauty, as an unusually prickly heat stabbed through her arms and legs. He was talking, as he examined the wood. Then as suddenly as it all came, the pain stopped. Eleanor let out a huge sigh, "Papa," she said shaking herself, "I can't believe you're actually saying that Grandsprite knew her." Francis looked up, "Oh but she did, for a long time, I'm sure I told you this when you were young. Grandsprite never spoke of her again after they parted ways." Eleanor grimaced, she wished she'd listened more. "She's," Francis continued as he went back to look at his stick. "The type of Sprite who is only with you... for as long as you're useful." He started to look around the forest floor, searching. "But I believe her heart is in..." Eleanor's hearing became muffled. She placed her hand on the smooth silver trunk, to steady herself. The heat and sickness came back with intensity. Her father's voice sounded like he was speaking into a bottle. Eleanor felt her feet were on fire. She doubled over, and vomited. "Eleanor... what's wrong?" But she couldn't feel the grip of his hand. She glanced at her feet, panic rippling. They had merged into the ground. She tried to cry out, but no sound materialised. She went to rub away the sick from her mouth but couldn't.

"Father...," she whispered, her voice, weak and distant. Eleanor knew his arms were around her but wasn't sure if she'd fallen or floated into them. Mist covered her vision. Pain numbed her senses. *Where had her father gone?* Then abruptly and cruelly, her world went black.

*

Eleanor opened her eyes and peered blearily at the furrowed, weathered face. Slowly, she traced the deep crinkles that weaved across the skin, meeting at green eyes, tinged with hues of greyish red – her father. She tried to sit up, but couldn't, consumed once more by the same dense cloud of nightmare that had taken her before. This time, images of tormenting, matted trees and wild grey shadows seeped into all of her senses. Her body was weak and helplessly buffeted along, seemingly going nowhere. On and on, she drifted. Voices of various tones bellowing commands. One, louder than the rest, urged her to be strong, fight. She was important. A hand, from nowhere pale and young, took hold of hers, and held on with a fierce grip.

She saw her father's green eyes once more, piercing through a gap in the dense forest, reflecting hope and willing her to follow. It took every fibre of determination to pull herself nearer.

"Drink, Eleanor, you must drink." Eleanor felt the dry edges of her lips crack as cool water filled her parched mouth. The hand that poured was not her father's; too young, pale and glossy. Eleanor tried to remember whose it was, but the effort was too much, the mire returned, bowling her over like a northerly wind. This time hazy images of flying creatures lifted her above Vearmoor. She saw a Sprite dressed in black with long floating hair, her arms swirling around her body. Beside her was a Tribeling, surrounded by fire. Eleanor called out to warn them both, but the fire turned, and headed in her direction. Eleanor began to run away, the thrill voice rippling through the flames, like the peal of gentle bells. Eleanor opened her eyes.

"Eleanor, Eleanor, can you hear me?" Her father's voice was like the call of a greenfinch, startled and desperate. The images disappeared along with the fire.

"Thank the *Wind Master*, you're alive!" The sweet honeyed wood sap from her father's workshop, exuded from strong arms that engulfed her.

"Where am I?" she whispered shakily.

"Home... you're home darling, and back with us." Eleanor closed her eyes, trying to take it all in. Was that her Passing? Had she made it? Would she become an adult Sprite? Tears flowed, as she sank into her feathered pillow.

"We thought we'd lost you," her mother, Rachel, said. Eleanor looked into her gentle, caring face. "You were stone cold," she continued, "and wouldn't stop shaking - I just kept praying we couldn't lose you when all of my others had survived. That wouldn't be fair. Our precious youngest - we've been so worried. We tried everything," her mother tilted her head, "but nothing worked, nothing...until..." She hesitated, her usually soft features creased into a frown.

"Not now, Rachel," her father interrupted. He placed his hand on her mother's shoulder. "Our E needs to rest," he said firmly.

Eleanor studied the worried lines across her mother's face, feeling the weight of their silence. Suddenly she remembered... flashes... images. *The pale hand holding hers... willing her to fight.* She tore her gaze past her mother's mop of curly brown hair, into the corner, where she had last seen the old Sprite. Could she have been in her Passing?

*

Eleanor had slept for several *Turns*. She woke, as Elerday clattered into her room, carrying a wooden tray. Eleanor heaved into a seating position, trying to ignore the tiredness, as the tray landed heavily on her lap.

"There... lazy bones." Elerday went to sit on the end of her bed. A fine selection of red berries, rosemary flavoured bread, and a steaming cup of mint tea. She was being spoilt. "You've been sleeping forever," Elerday said.

"I should try and get out of this room, shouldn't I?" Eleanor dipped her bread into her tea.

"Good," Elerday shot her a look. "We'll go as soon as you've eaten and dressed, it's about time you used those legs of yours."

Eleanor sighed, "Do you think mother will let me?"

"Of course – why wouldn't she? You're not planning to go far are you?"

Eleanor smiled, "Nuh...." Her sister's face took on an inquisitive frown. "It's just... well...," Eleanor continued, thinking of a way to get some time to herself, she had missed her meeting with Morwena and she had to talk to her. "You've all been so good, mother, you, father.... And done so much, maybe you would like your own time, instead of nursing me?"

"Oh... never satisfied!" Elerday replied. "If it was me I'd be revelling in all the attention."

"Yuh..." Eleanor paused. "It's just..." Eleanor's words stuck in her throat, "I... er... need to do something... by myself."

"Really? That's a bit odd after all you've been through."

"No, really I do." Eleanor hated lying. Elerday stood up and went to open the window shutter, put fresh water into her bedside jug and slowly began to hang up the laundry. Eleanor ate her breakfast, waiting.

"Eleanor," Elerday said in a serious tone. She came back to sit on the bed, "what could you possibly need to do alone?"

"Oh, it's nothing," Eleanor felt trapped, "really nothing." She reached out and held her sister's hand. "I just wanted to get you all something. A thank you." Her sister raised her eyebrows.

"Well, there's no need to go alone. I can come too, we'll go together, and I won't say a thing to the others."

"But then it won't be a surprise for you," Eleanor replied.

"I insist... and you'd better tell me what you're hiding, on the way. Remember it's me, not Amber, who's listening." Elerday opened her bedroom door and closed it quietly behind her without a backward glance.

Eleanor got out of bed and reached for the handle of her wardrobe. She would have to come up with a better excuse than that, if she was going to ever have any time alone. She began to take off her white tunic but struggled to get it over her head. She stared at the face in the mirror and the mass of tangled black hair. She held a strand up and wondered if it had gone even darker? That was all she needed, something else to make her even more different. Roughly she brushed out the knots and half-heartedly plaited one side. It was beyond her to do much more, then headed out of her room.

"Where is everyone?" she said as she entered the sitting room. Elerday had a heavy looking bag on her back, her web tied to her shoulder and a dagger. "You look like you're going on an expedition."

"No... no, I'm just being prepared. Anyway, Father's working, and the rest went on the great berry pick, so it's just you and me." Eleanor wished she'd known that... she could have taken more advantage of it. "We don't have to walk," Elerday said, "we could use dust travel, now you've, you know... gone through your Passing."

"No... never... I'm not trying that again."

"It won't be the same as last time, you've done the hard bit." Eleanor could tell Elerday's mind was set. She was testing her for lying to her earlier.

"Ok," Eleanor said quietly, "just once." She began to whisper the Transformation spell. A sharp shiver zigzagged cruelly.

"I can't do this," Eleanor gave up. "Look I've tried, can't we just walk now?'

"What? You're not scared, are you?" Elerday taunted.

"That's not fair. It just hurts," Eleanor protested, "really hurts."

"I could always ask Holly to take you! Call her back from the berry pick. She's with Dairren - I'm sure she wouldn't mind."

"No, you wouldn't." Eleanor looked at her sister who had transformed and was hovering in a moving silhouette above the floor, as if it was the most normal thing in the world.

"Ok, ok."

"And," Elerday continued to taunt, "I'll tell mother that it hurts. You know how much she'll fuss."

"That's mean." Eleanor stared at her sister's floating outline, allowing the hammering from her father's workshop to wash over her. She said the spell again, her fist firmly clenched and teeth clamped together, braced against the pain. It began in a wave that rose from her feet as if she'd stood too close to a roaring fire. Eleanor tried to think of something else – music, her favourite Tanna nuts - but nothing worked, her mind blurred and body shook. A bolt of heat burst into her chest.

"Stop, E, don't, you're shaking," Elerday shouted, "This isn't right!" Eleanor opened her eyes. She looked at the ground, but it wasn't under her feet. She stretched out her hand to the ceiling and touched its smooth oiled surface, *but where was her hand, in fact where was her arm?*

"Uh?" Elerday whispered. "I can't see you!" Eleanor looked at her sister's ghostly image and then at the blank space where her body should be.

"This isn't normal, is it?" she said quietly.

"Uh... no wah! You've totally disappeared; even your outline has gone. Wow!" Elerday rose slowly to Eleanor's level. "Think how difficult you'll be to spot," Elerday said and gave a mischievous smirk, "and all the things you could get up to! I've never seen this before. Not even the Sprite Elite can disappear! Or can they? Oh who cares, you can!"

"Don't tell anyone, will you?" Eleanor began to say the reverse spell. She fell onto the wooden floor, her body reformed. "I need to think about everything that's happened over the last few *Turns.*"

Elerday gently landed beside her. "Sure. E, but you can't keep this secret for long."

10

THE TENTH SHADOW

Light seeped into Eleanor's room. She stretched lazily, listening to the competing songs of the Finch and Larna birds, before covering her ears and snuggling back into her pillow; wondering if she could just grab another *Shadow's* rest. Her door creaked ajar and Elerday poked her head around.

"You awake?" she whispered.

"I am now..." Eleanor rolled onto her side, as Elerday crept in. "It's about time. I've been fending a torrent of questions from Mother, late into *Dark Exchange*. She was really mad with me."

"With you, why?" Eleanor rubbed her eyes.

"Probably because you were asleep and weren't there to argue with. She found out about your transformation... or more like complete disappearance." Eleanor pointed to the end of her bed. Elerday jumped in. "But how? Who told her?"

"I have no idea... but you know how things are seen and Sprites find things out around here. I'm not surprised! Anyway, are you going to tell me or not?" Elerday buried herself under a silvery fur. "I've been thinking about what you said *how you needed time to think about all that had happened*. I think I deserve the truth, especially after taking the heat for you."

Eleanor let out a sigh, lit a candle on her bedside table and waited for the soft glow to brighten her room. Her words came out slowly at first, because she found it difficult to explain, without sounding crazy. Eventually she gathered momentum, retelling the entire story of her encounter. Including the bit that Morwena thought she might be *The Wind Whisperer* and summoning the other two Sprite Elite to tell them! She ended by saying how she had been convinced Morwena had helped her to survive her *Passing*.

After a long pause, where time tenderly hovered between reality and a dream, Elerday replied in a slow mumble. "So it's one of the Sprite Elite we have to thank for saving your life." Her bright green eyes deep in thought. Eleanor cocked her head to one side.

"I promise I'm not lying. You know that, don't you?"

Elerday bit her lip. "I know you're not lying, you couldn't possibly be making this up! Halfway through your Passing, when all you were doing was spasmodic twitching..." Elerday demonstrated, but it didn't make Eleanor laugh. The was an awkward silence, before she said, "Anyway, we thought we'd lost you; then something changed. So I suppose it could make sense, but, how she did it, I don't know."

"It was Morwena, I know," Eleanor replied. "I hardly believe it myself. Why would she help me?" Eleanor gulped down some cold water. "I can still see her dark eyes coaxing me."

"You don't think I could be *The Wind Whisperer*, do you?" Her stomach tightened.

"Hmm..." Elerday frowned, "you can't be, I'm sure, as that would be too wild. But look, you are a bit strange and we've all tried not to make you feel, well, different."

"You're not making sense," Eleanor felt her face flush.

"Don't you remember all the impressive things you did when you were younger?" Eleanor thought for a moment.

"No?" She hadn't done anything exceptional. "Like what?"

"Oh, for the sake of the Wind Lord! You hovered as a baby Spriteling. You didn't crawl like we did. You talked to all sorts of insects and birds and even performed a few spells that Ma and Pa couldn't do."

"But I don't remember."

"Well, we haven't talked about it for ages," Elerday said, getting up from the bed.

"Why not?"

"Everyone was worried."

"Worried about what?" Eleanor asked.

"That what happened to Grandsprite might happen to you, so we protected you from preying eyes, kept you close and I suppose, pretended nothing was different. You should be talking to Pa or Ma about this, not me." Eleanor shivered despite being under the bed covers.

"I suppose you're now going to tell me that Morwena thought Grandsprite was *The Wind Whisperer* too?" Eleanor saw Elerday's mouth open to reply – then shut. Eleanor rolled over and stared at the ceiling. She couldn't believe it. How had everyone kept this from her? Was she that blind to notice?

"Oh, this came." Elerday took something from her pocket and held it into the air.

"What is it?"

"A letter, silly. Dropped into our box at the bottom of the trunk... very old fashioned, two *Turns* ago." Eleanor scrambled to open the envelope. It had the seal of a green oak leaf and golden sparkles flew out as she lifted the flap. "That's odd," Elerday leaned in closer. "What does it say?"

"Give me a moment." Eleanor's eyes flowed across the words. Her heart beat faster. "Has anyone else read this?"

"No wah. I took it out of the box before Holly saw. You can thank me now if you like! Why?"

"It's from Morwena. It says - come this *Turn*, at the *Eighth Shadow*, to Obakeech, on The Moorlands of NaraRose, find the solitary yellow gorse. Look there's a sketch." Eleanor showed her the paper.

"The image moves," Elerday said in shock. "Have you ever seen a drawing do that?"

Eleanor shook her head. "Time is running out," she read on. "The winds are turning. If you want answers, you must come now."

"That's it! That's all it says..." And slumped into her pillow.

"Perhaps I should go," Eleanor said out aloud. Elerday swung her legs out from under the covers and jumped from the bed; her eyes wide and glazed. "Are you crazy, you can't? You have no idea what that Sprite is capable of, and... outside of Vearmoor! That's mad." Her face was red and her nose stuck out. "Also, how does she know you're recovered, is she somehow spying on you... us?"

"That's creepy, I admit," Eleanor replied, "but you lot have been hiding things from me. I hadn't even realised about Grandsprite. So maybe Morwena might tell me the truth and help me understand. Then I can put a close to all this mess. And... **so what** if she knows what I'm doing, she hasn't hurt me."

"That's ridiculous. And you can't be angry with any of us, we've only be trying to protect you! Anyway, it's only been a few *Turns* that these things have happened, hasn't it?"

There was a long drawn out pause. "No wah... there's been other things."

"What?" Elerday's face was contorted in anger.

"I will tell you on the way. Come with me," Eleanor said calmly. "Come to meet Morwena and then I won't make any mistakes. Together we'll be safer. And it won't take long. No one will find out we're gone. Just explain to Mother we're out for a long walk - help me recover. We're going to meet Johanna or something - she'll cover for us." Eleanor held her breath.

"We must be home by the beginning of *Dark Exchange*," Elerday said.

"Agreed," Eleanor nodded, hardly able to control her nerves.

11

THREAD-LIKE RIBBONS

Daniel stared at the foreboding sky, wondering how his father could have thought banishment was the best option; surely death would have been quicker. This was going to be slow, painful, lonely and a drawn out form of torture. He wanted to hit something. And what happens if his *Element* ran out? Which it would. There was no way of replacing it. He wouldn't be able to perform spells or defend himself. **And...** how was he going to find food or shelter in this barren landscape.

Buckling his oilskin tightly across his chest, he stamped the ground, clinging to the water pouch his mother had given him, the rosemary scent still lingered. He must be careful with every drop - he'd promised her.

It was colder than expected, Caradoc wasn't like this, the wind didn't pierce your skin there. He knew he couldn't stay where he was for long; too exposed. Listlessly, he gathered the arrows that had fallen when he'd scrambled from the tunnel. He was putting off the inevitable. He had to decide where to go. The Moors no longer held any beauty, stripped from the wonderment he had felt, during those forbidden adventures with Seb. Seb, he scowled, this had all started with him. *How had he known about Isaac?*

Ahead lay miles of stunted shrubs, bent trees and crooked grasses, cruel and uninviting. No Tribeling lived here for a reason. In every direction he saw nothing of interest to aim for. He groaned outwardly. Then, water began to fall from the sky. At first only in drops. But slowly it gathered momentum until it fell in thread-like ribbons. Was this a sign from the Gods? He could no longer control his Power Element? This *water falling from the sky thing* never happened within Caradoc. He held out his hands and collected some. Rubbing it between his fingers, and whispering a spell – nothing! It had none of the substance he was used to. It was useless, only soaking his clothes and making him feel cold. *What was the point in that?*

Just stay alive, he said the words over and over again, before slamming his foot into a pile of rubble. The shadows were lengthening. That could mean only one thing - *Light Exchange* was fading. With all that had happened, he hadn't been paying attention to how many *Shadows* were left. He needed to find shelter before *Dark Exchange*.

But first, an idea came to him. If there was ever going to be a chance of getting back home, he had to mark where he'd left. Then he could hold on to the hope that he might one *Turn* be able to find the entrance, even if it no longer revealed itself.

He took out his Power Element. Slowly and carefully, he drew out a line of droplets and said Elfland words he'd known since he was young. A silvery circle formed, and spanned furiously. He waited patiently for the blue glow to appear inside. Once it was a deep enough, he released it onto the grass and let it fade. He then tested the spot. Stepping into the circle, the whole area shone blue. It was game he'd play with his brothers. He thanked the Water Lord that something had worked and hoped it would last for however long needed.

Adjusting his bag of arrows, he spied a narrow track that lead over the nearest rise. Perhaps there was shelter on the other side? He headed off, trying to protect himself against the falling water. The darkening sky felt like someone was shutting a door on him. Shadows began to appear. Lurking to ambush. He had heard that the most dangerous Moorland creatures hunted during *Dark Exchange*. He wondered if they were like the images he'd seen in his father's books? Perhaps night creatures weren't his worst problem; perhaps it was other Tribelings, on patrol, protecting their homeland border. *A lone Elf…. easy prey.*

A raucous caw sounded above him. He fell like a stone to the ground and grabbed his bow. It slipped through his damp hands. Another ripple of squawks, liked an animal being strangled. Daniel locked an arrow. A bead of sweat dripped from his forehead as he studied the skyline, waiting. The damp, wet grass soaked his trousers. Out from the clouds swooped a flock of flying creatures. They were long in body, with brown feathers, like dreadlocks of unwashed hair. Their green beaks open wide, filling the air with deafening screeches. They were here to kill him - Eastling Elves in disguise, come to seek revenge. Frozen to the ground he wished a hole would open up and swallow him. Below each winged beast mirrored a dark replica, travelling at speed, rippling across the Moorland and heading towards him. Even the wind, was holding its breath… *waiting.*

Daniel fired an arrow. It was a direct hit, but went straight through the grey images. He grappled for another, but was too late, they were nearly on him. He ducked, wrapped his arms over his head. He held his breath. Nothing, he felt nothing. No pain, just a monotonous note that rang in his ears. Daniel tentatively uncurled his head, peering through his fingers. Their tail ends and dark followers had moved down the hillside. He clambered to his feet, trying to ease his rapid breathing. Where there actually creatures that flew here! He was sure no Elf had even mentioned that before.

He looked about to see where the arrows had gone. He couldn't afford to lose any. Skirting across the path to the ridge, he peered over, only to be greeted by a sea of prickly bushes and shrubs. The arrow couldn't have gone far, so he waded in. The going was trickier than expected. Daniel battled against a mass of brambles, using his knife to cut off long arms of thorns. Rounding a thick hedge, he reeled at the smell of a festering carcass. It was a hare, or at least it had been. The bones laid bare. He edged his way around, dodging the flies and began to wish he'd remained on the path. His arrows jutted out from a thick shrub, mottled in ivy. He grabbed them quickly and looked about. Perhaps he'd also found his shelter for the night? It was not open like the rest of The Moors, and gave him a chance to hide. He jumped down a sharp ledge, into a deep sided hollow. A waft of damp soil reminded him of home. His stomach grumbled. He took out a few bits of the bread his mother had put in his pockets and found a cloth of wrapped meats. He gobbled them down quickly. As he finished chewing, he recognised a familiar tumbling gurgle. His eyes were playing tricks in the failing light, but he thought he could just make out a silver thread, weaving around tree roots meandering down the hillside.

He ran the last few paces and collapsed by the stream's edge, plunging his hands into the cold water. Relief washed over him as he gulped down his fill and stared at his broken reflection. How was he here? How had this happened? If only he could bring Thaen back to life and start this *Turn* again. He knelt there for a long while.

Using his Power Element, he lit a circle of small blue flames. He then set about searching the surrounding area for fallen branches and ferns. As he'd done hundreds of times with his brothers, he began to build a makeshift shelter against a protruding tree trunk and its roots. By the time he was finished, his energy was gone. None left to hunt for food, but at least he'd had something. He crouched with his back pressed against the bark. He hoped this would protect him, at least from behind, and the blue flames would last long enough if he did fall asleep. His mind wandered to his father; despite his tenderness to him in the hall once the Council had left, he still couldn't understand how he'd allowed this to happen to his eldest Elfling? The one he said he treasured so much - *clearly not enough*. So much for Trevarak love. He closed his eyes and covered his ears, trying to block out the animal cries that wailed louder and louder, telling him, *Light Exchange* had ended for eight whole *Shadows*.

12

A STAGINOURISM

Daniel had stayed by the stream, hidden from the bleak Moors, for two *Turns*. He'd hardly slept. Each *Shadow* in *The Dark* had tested him to his limit. He had to keep the blue fire constantly burning, otherwise he could see yellow eyes peering from the gloom. If it faltered, their breathing, growls and padding paws would come closer. He was sick with hunger, only one arrow had rung true and killed a rabbit. Its meat had been lean and guts, putrid.

He left his shelter reluctantly, but knew if he stayed, he'd die there. He'd hoped that when he got back into the open he might see something familiar from one of his forbidden trips. A tree, a pathway that signalled he was near home. He wanted the comfort.

He walked aimlessly. Water fell relentlessly from the sky forming a thick layer of confusing mist. In places it was so thick he couldn't see his own hand if he stretched his arm. Only periodically would it lessen to allow him to see further. His clothes hung next to his skin, as if he'd just gone swimming. The chill and damp fuelled his anger, increased his bitterness, to all that had happened. To the Caradoc Council for taking the Eastling's side, to his father for not being stronger, to Seb for waking only him, to Thaen for starting it all. None of this was fair. None of this was his fault. He hadn't taken

Isaac. He hadn't been the one on the bridge trying to kill him.

He repositioned the sodden rabbit's fur, under the strap of his bow. A meagre prize from his kill. It helped to stop the strap from digging into his shoulder; and trudged on. A cluster of unusually tall trees appeared through the soaked mist. He checked his Element pouches, all three thankfully in place, and headed on. Perhaps the trees would give him shelter? The pathway narrowed and rose. He clambered over boulders hidden amongst gorse. It must have been the mist because Daniel hadn't noticed how close the trees were to the edge of a steep cliff. He was beginning to wish he hadn't bothered. The grasses quickly gave way to rocks and scree, laced in slippery dank moss. He had to use his hands and feet to scramble onwards. The strap of his holdall dug further into his skin. He paused to eat some of his mother's bread. He was so thankful for every mouthful and wished there was more. A bramble hooked itself around his exposed forearm as he pulled the bread out of his bag. It made more red lines to match the already crisscrossed patterns, bitter rewards from his failed hunting skills. On cue, his stomach began to groan. He had never been so hungry. The bread was nowhere near enough. He would have done anything for cooked sardines and some of his mother's pickles.

He urged himself on. His legs getting heavier with each step. He could see the trees more clearly, precariously positioned, unusual looking. A rocky outcrop lay above, the final hurdle. He took a long swig from his water bottle and began to climb, carefully selecting where to put his feet and what to grab hold of. Eventually he reached the final ledge and pulled himself over, but something tore from his clothing. He rolled to the side and felt his trousers. His pocket had ripped. He looked over the edge and saw Isaac's torn cloth tumble down through the fog. Daniel watched it fall. He hung motionlessly, drifting in and out of haunted morbid thoughts. Was this a bad omen? A sign from Ostric that the mighty Water lord, now had his brother? Daniel shuddered and prayed to Istria if she thought anything of him, to make sure his brother was safe.

Roots and bushes jutted freely around him, dangling into the air. He pulled his gaze away and looked up at the wide, straight trunks of thick silvery bark. Each one disappeared into the sky, like the great Elder statues that guarded Algor. In awe he followed the network of branches twisting into the clouds. Each muted branch and hanging leaf drooped with the weight of water. Wearily he clambered through the dense ferns and shrubs, until he reached what he thought must have been the middle. He stood alone, looked through the branches. At least less of the water reached him there.

"Why?" he shouted. "If only you hadn't taken by brother." The wind replied fiercely. He stamped his numb, cold feet, and wiped droplets from his face. Exhausted, Daniel leant against the peeling bark of a trunk and wrapped his arms across his chest. Even The Moorland animals had gone into their shelters, they weren't so stupid, as to be out in this! His mind unfairly wandered to his father's warm arms and calm voice, locked together after the verdict. Bitterness and confusion muddling in equal measure as he tried to work out what his father had told him to do. Find a Sprite called, Mary, Martha, Rowena? Or was it a Pixie? Which Elements were good allies? He kicked the head off a gigantic mushroom, only for his bow to slip off his shoulder.

As he stooped to pick it up. A clear hoof print just visible by his foot, lay in the soil. Daniel knelt closer and ran his hand over the outline. It was larger than any he'd seen before. He looked around, another identical print lay ahead of it and the undergrowth around was only just resetting itself.

Guardedly Daniel rose to his feet, if the print was that big, then the creature that it belonged to was also big. The mist unfairly transformed each bush and sapling into contorted ghosts. A sharp snort resonated behind him. Daniel's heart crashed across his chest, as he fumbled inside his tunic. Twisting a droplet into his shaking hand, he cast the first spell that formualted. A surge of water sprang from his hand. Daniel stared through the broad flowing film and turned his hand around. It followed his movements and protected the front of his grip. *An Elf's shield*, he whispered in astonishment.

Another snort. Now on guard, the fog parted, like a blanket slipping off a bed. On the edge of the copse, he glimpsed a creature. Two horns crowned its head, matching the outline of the trees. Strong hind legs rippled with muscles, completely encased in thick stubby, brown hair. Suddenly, its front legs rose into the air, like a warning, he was lord of this copse. Hooves slammed into the sodden ground. Daniel shivered. The creature then swung it head, bellowing and sending clouds of steam and looked straight at him. It knew he was there! The eyes, black as the deep lake waters of Caradoc. Daniel's shield cast rays of silvery lights across the woodland floor. He took a few steps closer. Its two ears flapped, and front legs scrapped against the ground, as if warning him to stay back. Then, something jogged in Daniel's memory. Hadn't a few of The Council members described a beast like this when they returned from fighting in the *Great Fire of Vearmoor?*

Daniel lowered his shield to get a clearer look. He remembered the Elves boasting how they had seen these magnificent beasts but had never got near. Daniel stepped closer. He could feel the heat radiating from its body drifting on the wind. Every one of his nerves alive. Its nose was a soft brown, flared and breathing rapidly. He crept even closer. His hand was nearly able to touch it. He stretched out his arm.

"I know what they called you," Daniel whispered. "A Staginourisum." It lowered its head towards Daniel's outstretched fingers. Daniel balanced on one foot. *I'll call you Stagin, its easier.* The Stagin gave a clipped bark, and bared grey, dagger teeth. Daniel lost his footing and fell to the ground. The Stagin reared its front legs into the air. Daniel rolled onto his side, scrambling and wriggling to get out of the way as the hooves crashed down, just missing his back. Hot steamy breath showered down on him. Daniel waited for the teeth to land. The mud squelched and wheezed, as the hooves slipped away, with a roaring bay, the creature bolted through the undergrowth.

"Wait..." Daniel yelled, scrambling to his feet, caked in mud. His shield, now a puddle beside him, rippling. Daniel stood and watched it disappear into the mist. How could it just go like that? He ran back to where he'd first seen the print. Maybe there were others? He remembered the Elf saying they travelled in groups. He frantically examined the woodland floor. But after scouring the copse he couldn't find any more signs.

He returned to the original print, to look at it more closely. What he couldn't understand is why he hadn't recognised the animal originally. The Elves had described every aspect. But this one had something different - a crescent shape indented in the centre. *That had never been mentioned.* He paused, running his hand around the outline. Then he took out the stone his mother had thrust into his inner pocket just before he'd left Caradoc. He'd spent several moments rolling it around in his hand, while he thought. He placed it into the print. It fitted exactly. He lay the stone in his palm, and for the first time examined it properly. It was jet black and such a perfect shape, just like the moon of *Dark Exchange*. Might the stone and the beast be linked? Folding his fingers over the stone, Daniel vowed, if he survived the next few *Shadows*, he would find that Stagin again.

13

THE VALLEY ON THE MOOR

"Which way?" Eleanor moaned. "It can't be much further, can it? We've been walking for *Shadows!*" Her sister was standing by an enormous blackberry bush, eating as much as she could. Three paths lay ahead; Eleanor had no idea which one to take. "Well you wanted to walk..." Elerday retorted, "if we transformed it would have taken half the time. You said yourself you were feeling much better, so I don't understand why we didn't." She continued eating. "Anyway, it doesn't matter now, we're getting close." Pointing at the grassy track in the middle, "when we've got to the end of that one. The border is just beyond those trees."

"But there isn't a path beyond those trees."

"Exactly, that's the point."

"Is this some sort of trap?" Eleanor protected her face from the strong rays that caught her off guard, as the branches parted. She felt disappointed there were no magnificent golden gates or enormous statues. She'd never been near Vearmoor's border, but had dreamed of its magnificence.

"No wah, of course not. Come on, you wanted to do this," Elerday ran passed. Eleanor raced after her. Together they tussled, pushing and shoving each other, until they reached the end.

The trees and bushes were much thicker than Eleanor realised. "This can't be right," she huffed, as she pushed aside straggled branches.

"Don't you trust me?" Elerday gave her a sharp look. "Yes... of course," Eleanor replied, "but there's nothing here. Where are the guards, or the fanfare?"

"What world do you live in? Wait and see. Do you want to go first?" Eleanor didn't need to be asked twice. She waded into the thicket, battling against the army of prickly twigs. Her hair kept snagging so she had to stop to unravel strands and if it wasn't her hair, brambles caught her clothes. She could hear Elerday grumbling close by. Eleanor quietly promised that as soon as she was able, she would buy Elerday her favourite cocoa nuts as thanks.

"No wonder," Eleanor said, "Sprites don't leave Vearmoor unless they have to." She yanked another bramble from her skirt. "I didn't know the border was so overgrown. It's a tangled wall. Couldn't we have thought up a better way out?"

Elerday let out a loud sigh. "This isn't the gates, E. There are three; on the western, eastern and the northern side of Vearmoor, and Sprites guard them all. Surely you knew that?"

Eleanor felt stupid. "Huh, sure... I, I just haven't seen, or ever really asked about them." She knocked a clump of lichen aside. "So, aren't we meant to leave Vearmoor this way?"

"No wah!" Elerday replied exasperatedly. "To go through Vearmoor's border you must ask The Sprite Council and get written permission." Eleanor said a silent prayer to The Wind Lord, thanking him for Elerday knowledge. So why would Morwena want her to do something against Council permission?

"Look, we're nearly through," Elerday said. "I can see it."

Eleanor caught a glimpse of something shimmering. "Is that really it?" she gasped.

"You are cute." Eleanor swallowed her annoyance and looked at the spreading silvery web of light. Her spine tingled. Quickening her pace, she pushed on through.

Her hand fell through to the otherside - no twigs, no more trees! There was an arm's length between the edge of the firs and a wall of gloopy liquid. It reflected a multitude of greens and silvers, and stretched into the distance.

"You ok?" Elerday said, as she burst out into the open and started to pull out stuck twigs. "It's beautiful..." Eleanor gazed at the wobbling film. She leant forwards, "But how can this be strong?"

"You can only get through with a spell," Elerday replied. "It protects us from other Tribes and *Dark Exchange* animals." Eleanor could see The Moors stretching tantalisingly within her reach, but it was reassuring to be on their side of the film.

"Maybe we shouldn't do this?" Eleanor looked at her sister.

"Yeah you're probably right," Elerday replied quickly. "Come on then, lets head home." Elerday turned and pulled aside some fir branches.

"Uh, really," Eleanor said urgently, "you're going back?"

Elerday turned around, with a flounce. "We've made up all those lies to Mother. Come all this way. Caught my hair on numerous damn twigs and now you wanna go home?"

"Ok, ok, ok," Eleanor replied.

"And," Elerday went on, "I forgot to mention... I've postponed seeing Jake for this."

"Really...? Wow, sorry... so see him next *Turn, yeah?*" Elerday grimaced.

"So how do we get through?"

"Watch this..." Elerday picked up a handful of soil and began to grind it between her hands. She held her palm flat and said a curious spell Eleanor hadn't heard. The powdery earth span into a spiral and rose into the air. She directed it towards the border.

"Wooowa?" Eleanor whispered.

"Shh..." Elerday's eyes never left the moving dust. It hit the film and soaked in to leave a hole. Elerday then circled her hand, expanding in an increasing circle. The hole grew. "Come on," she whispered, "it won't hold for long." Eleanor quickly glanced back - she was actually leaving Vearmoor! With a deep breath; she ducked her head. The watery hole sparkled like an emerald. It bent and wobbled. Eleanor felt as if she'd been sucked into The Moorland world. Once they were both on the other side, the gap snapped shut like it was ashamed of letting them through without The Council's approval. "I hope no one detected that breech." Elerday looked worried.

"Could they?" Eleanor asked.

"It's too late to worry about that... anyway we won't be long. Hopefully no one will notice." Eleanor tied her hair into a bun, as the wind was stronger without the border's protection.

"That was incredible, Elerday," Eleanor gave her sister's arm a squeeze. "You're full of surprises. Where did you learn that?"

"Mother," Elerday replied. Eleanor knew Elerday was their mother's favourite daughter, even though she tried to keep it hidden. She'd always show Elerday things first.

Outside of Vearmoor's tree canopy the light was different. Brighter, stronger, not the usual dull greens and browns; but rich blues and greys. There were no branches or leaves to stop the rays from reaching her. Even though the warm, orange sun was already halfway across the sky, Eleanor relished the comfort it gave through her thick clothes.

"It's taken us longer than I thought to get through Vearmoor," Elerday said. "We only have a few *Light Shadows* left to find this place." Eleanor reached into her satchel and pulled out a rope in preparation. The rope began to glow as she tied it around her waist.

"Is that another thing we need to talk about?" Elerday said wearily.

Eleanor chewed the side of her lip. "Yeah I suppose so. I'll tell you on the way." She grabbed Elerday's shaking hand. "Let's get this over with."

*

"This is useless," Eleanor moaned. "I can only just see Vearmoor trees', and I've no idea if we're going in the right direction - the sun keeps moving! And... this Moorland is boring, nothing stands out. Maybe we should head back." Elerday lay in a mossy bank collapsed between a mass of tiny white flowers and tufty green ferns.

"Did Morwena say anything else to you," Elerday replied, "that might help?" Eleanor looked up to see her sister lying on her back with her face basked in sunshine. She looked as if she was enjoying being away from Vearmoor.

"A yellow bush... but really! I must have lost my mind, what are we doing?" Eleanor moaned. "The only thing I remember was it stood alone in the valley we're meant to find." Eleanor flopped onto her back. "But seriously this is a joke. Look how many bushes there are around here and they all come in packs and there is no valley in sight." Eleanor gazed at the clouds as they floated by. Different creatures appeared and disappeared. She loved deciding what shape each cloud could be. Shapes of animals from home, a finch, a butterfly, a tree, a...

"Bees!" Eleanor exclaimed. "That's it, Elerday, bees. Morwena mentioned that this particular bush thingy would be covered in bees."

"And?" shrugged Elerday.

"Listen, I know what to do." Eleanor got to her feet and cupped her hands around her mouth. A high-pitched whooshing sound came out.

"What are you doing?" Elerday exclaimed, "You're buzzing!"

"I think I'm meant to ask the bees to take me there." Eleanor knew that sounded ridiculous, but she just had to give it a try. She called again – hoping the bizarre noise would mean something to them. She buzzed even louder, trying to ignore Elerday who was now standing with her hands on her hips.

"There, there," she called. Two bees flew forwards and hovered at her eye level. Eleanor held out her hand. They landed neatly on her outstretched palm. All she could hear was the beating of their wings and pounding hearts. Hesitantly she spoke, in their strange tones, using clicks and whistles. Beady black eyes stared like angry teachers. Nodded and chatting very quickly. When they finally stopped, they flew up and down, hissing noisily. Eleanor took it as her cue: *follow us*. She looked hesitantly at Elerday, who stood with her eyes wide and head tilted. The scowl across her face was similar to mother's, just before she was going to give a real telling off.

"Come on," Eleanor said, "we've got to follow." She quickly transformed, ignoring the pain. The Moorland flew by. It was almost impossible to keep up. Eleanor kept checking behind to see if Elerday was following, but it was hard to keep an eye on the bees and her.

They flew on up the undulating rise. Eleanor knew if she went down the other side she wouldn't be able to see her home anymore. She looked back to Vearmoor's border, as the tips of the firs disappeared. Refocusing ahead, the bees were nowhere to be seen. Eleanor slid to halt, misjudging her speed. Tumbled out of dust travel and clumsily fell to the ground, rolling ungainly over and over, until she caught hold of a thick clump of grass. One leg swung over a ledge. She pulled sharply on the grass and swung herself to safety. There below, lay a deep-sided valley. Filled with a rich, wild mixture of grasses and flowers. A single gorse, dominated the valley base. The two bees appeared and buzzed around her head. It was almost as though they were laughing. Eleanor missed what they said, before they flew off towards the meadow. She yelled a *thank you*....

"What were you thinking?" Elerday collapsed on the grass behind her stammering for breath. "If it wasn't for the bees I'd never have seen where you'd gone!"

"Oh." Eleanor felt bad. "I'd forgotten about that."

"Yes, you disappear, remember!"

"But they were in a hurry. Something to do with the *Shadows* and needing food I think... they only agreed to take me, after I pleaded. And they talk so quickly, I... er..."

"So," Elerday exclaimed. "You did talk to them? I thought you said you hadn't remembered how to do that."

"Well, I didn't... or maybe I do, anyway, we've found what we were looking for, haven't we?" Eleanor pointed into the valley. "Come on," she said, "let's just get this over with." She leapt over the earthy ledge, onto a narrow path. "Are you coming?" she called as she tumbled down the track.

"Wait," Elerday cried, "I need to check..."

14

THE BIG BUBBLE

Eleanor raced over tree roots and rocks, tumbling into the valley. Her hand floating gently across the tops of the barley heads, taking care not to knock the blue cornflowers. Maybe, Eleanor thought, Morwena just liked it here, she could understand why.

The pathway narrowed channelling damp earth and sweet scented Scabias, reminding Eleanor of her Grandsprite, who'd often had a vase on her windowsill. The solitary gorse stood proud yet alone in the middle of the sea of tufty pampas. A shiver crossed her body; the area around the gorse was similar to the clearings of Obakeech at home. They were the only places within Vearmoor you could stand and see the sky clearly. Eleanor slowed her pace; she had been to Obakeech their *sacred place of reflection* once before, and that was for her Grandsprite's burial.

So where was Morwena? Eleanor walked on through the flowers, picking her way carefully. The bees clearly loved them and ignored her as she passed. There still wasn't any sign of the old Sprite.

"Morwena?" she called. But only the sound of the Larka bird replied. Surely, Morwena would be here somewhere. This was definitely the right place, and the old Sprite had made such a fuss to get her to come.

As Eleanor got nearer something about the bush wasn't quite right. The yellow flowers were too bright, too perfect and it wasn't moving with the breeze like the rest of the valley's flora. Long shadows distracted her, crawling across the valley and into the meadow, warning her *Dark Exchange* wasn't that far off. Eleanor's nerve faltered. She stopped, check she hadn't missed anything, twisting her hair through her hands; a habit she couldn't break since being a Spriteling. She suddenly wanted the safety of Vearmoor. Her parents would go wild if they knew she was here. The air clung heavily to her skin. *Elerday!* Where was she? Eleanor span around to search.

"Are you coming down?" she tentatively called. "Elerday where are you?" Her words answered by her own echo. The Insect hum seemed to quieten at the same time. Then a movement caught her eye. Eleanor started to jog back through the flowers.

"Elerday, are you coming?" she broke into a run, trampling on the flowers she'd previously been so careful to avoid. A thunderous crack burst from nowhere and rippled through the valley floor. The hairs stood up across her arms. Muffled notes replied. Eleanor froze. It came from where they had been on the ridge.

"Morwena, I've come as you asked....Stop this," Eleanor shouted. "Show yourself, no need for games?" The air pressed coldly onto her skin. Her feet sank into the grass, as she broke into a run. She was almost at the meadow's edge, when her body unforgivingly hit into something hard, cold and firm. She folded like a pack of cards.

Eleanor didn't know how long she'd laid on the ground. But when she woke, the valley was alive and filled with a tormented wind. It moved more strongly than she had ever felt before, tugging at her clothes and carrying clouds of dust, leaves and sticks. Eleanor ignored the pain in her shoulder as she scrambled up and lifted her hand to touch the clear and watery film she hadn't seen before. It was gooey, like runny slime and flexed, bending with her hand as she pushed. It reminded her of Vearmoor's border. It hadn't been there when she'd come into the meadow, so how was it there now? Her heart skipped a beat. *Was she trapped?*

The wind grew stronger, making her shield her face as it hit from all directions, as if angry she had dared to be there.

"Elerday," Eleanor called, trying to be heard over the crescendo of roars. A faint sound responded. It was her! Eleanor reached for her rope. Her hands circled the fibres emanating a welcoming glow. Instinctively, she threw one end through the wobbly barrier, holding firmly to the other. The rope went through. *If it had got through, Eleanor thought, so can I.* She began to drag herself along, fighting to stand up. The faint voice of Elerday became urgent and louder. The wind battered against her bent head with ever inch. Each grip was harder to secure, and at any moment Eleanor felt as if she could lose her grip and fly across the valley. She vowed never to trust Morwena again.

Then a second crack broke as suddenly as the first. Eleanor lurched and lost her grip. Debris collapsed all around her. The wind instantly stopped and the barrier of watery liquid evaporated.

"What are you doing, Blaydoc?" came a clear and strong voice. Eleanor dived for cover behind a cluster of rocks. Her heart hammering.

"That question should be directed at you," came his reply. "You've been acting most curiously since my abrupt summons to your tent on Festival Day." Eleanor glimpsed Blaydoc, at the valley's summit not far from where she hid.

"You still haven't answered my question. Why are you here?" Eleanor nearly choked; the old Sprite, Morwena, was standing right behind where she'd been.

"Disappearing and reappearing," Blaydoc continued, "all over Vearmoor as if on important business. Forgetting our Council meeting, acting as if you've something to hide. And what was that crazy wind? Why create such a smoke screen, are you trying to hide something from me?" Eleanor choked.

"Perhaps it is this mysterious young Sprite," Blaydoc boosted, "you're trying to hide?" He bent to the ground and pulled something up. Eleanor's throat dried. He had Elerday!

"I have a notion she's one of the Paraquinn daughters," Morwena retorted. "But she is of no importance to me." Eleanor crawled to the other side of the rock. *If she could double back through the adjoining trees, run up the valley slope, she could attack Blaydoc from behind.*

"Will you stop fighting me?" Blaydoc commanded. Eleanor peered out to see Elerday was no longer free but encased in a big bubble. It glistened against the sunlight, trapping her inside. *She had to do something and quick.*

"Don't lie to me this time, I will not tolerate it," boomed Blaydoc. He moved the watery bubble to the edge of the valley. Eleanor could see Elerday's hands and legs were splayed within a star position, as she slowly span within.

A loud thwack rippled. Eleanor span round to see Morwena's hood fly back, as she kicked something into the air. Eleanor ducked as it whizzed past the rocks, just missing her and shot up the valley. Blaydoc was knocked like a fallen tree to the ground, and the hold on the dust bubble broke. The bubble and Elerday, plummeted.

"No," Eleanor shouted, scrambling out from behind the rock, "that's my sis..." but the words stuck in her throat. Followed by her arm locking, then her shoulder and the rest of her body. Eleanor screamed, but nothing came out! She was left like an imprint on the rock.

"You've gone too far, Morwena," Eleanor heard Blaydoc shout through her locked spell, but she could no longer see him, as she was pushed securely behind the rock. "You must believe this Sprite is important, possibly even the one who had made that rope. Otherwise you would have never challenged me like that."

"She is not, Blaydoc," Morwena replied. Eleanor could just see her out of the corner of her eye. "Don't take your anger out on her." Morwena shouted. "I am here because the bees called me regarding the unrest within Caradoc and the lone Elf that walks The Moors. He has been befriended by The Staginourisum..." Morwena paused, "and if she was the *Wind Whisperer* wouldn't she be wearing a rope and free herself?"

"Well if you're not bothered with who this is," Blaydoc replied, "I will take her back to Vearmoor and return her to her parents, as any good Council member would, and I'll explain to them where she was. I am sure they will have plenty to say about that." Eleanor shivered, struggling wildly against her spell. She managed to get her hands to her rope. The spell weakened as she caught hold. She stained to lift her head over the rock, just in time to see Blaydoc wrapped his cloak tightly around his waist slowly fastening each clasp. Then he flicked his hand and a sprinkling of dust floated down the valley side. It linked a lasso around Elerday's bubble. The middle of the bubble flexed inwards as it tightened.

"I suggest this time, Morwena du Gwent, you don't try and stop me, otherwise our alliance will cease to exist." The words floated through the air and bounced down the slope as Eleanor watched her sister punching the sides of her prison. Like a dog on a lead, moving to its owner's command, the bubble bounced over the valley's summit and out of sight.

15

YELLOW TEETH

The final rays of light disappeared from the copse like the release of a lover's hand. Daniel felt every part of him pulsate with energy, as his eyes darted haphazardly. He wasn't prepared. He hadn't had time because of The Stagin, to build the right type of shelter. *Dark Exchange* had, as it seemed to do, arrived in an instant. The trees loomed over him like haunting curtain drapes, thick and unforgiving. The woodland floor darkened, festering with a rotten compost, unwelcoming and cold, a stark contrast to the scented ferns of *Light Exchange*.

He couldn't decide if he was better to stay under cover or go out onto The Moor. He looked around. The mist was still patchy but had lifted, yet not enough to be certain he didn't misjudge the pathway? He might end up where Isaac's cloth had gone. And how was he going to sleep. He slid his back down the tree trunk and sat on his haunches, carefully placing his bow to one side, so that it was still in easy access. His pouch to the other, ready. How was he going to protect himself. His blue fire was getting weaker, because he was, and he'd no time to build a shelter. His thoughts turned to his father and his relentless lessons on water spells. He'd always been rubbish at listening, preferring to practise with his bow. The one who'd listened, was Isaac - he was good at performing spells. Daniel rolled a water droplet around his palm, thinking of the memory of his little brother. Flicking it into a shield and out again. Each time it became easier. The words came naturally and distracted him from the murky shadows. An owl screeched, from somewhere in the trees. He jumped and lost his hold. Scanning around to check nothing had changed, he tried again. But his eyes felt heavy as he watched the water swirling. He fought to keep them open, as his head nodded against his chest.

He awoke, not sure how long afterwards. To his relief he was still crouching, so it couldn't have been long. He checked his bow and pouch, they were both still in place. Rubbing his eyes, an idea came to him, he set about thinking of the correct order of words. *If only he could remember.* His first shield grew to quite a width, almost oval in shape and big enough to cover half his body, but it went no further. It shimmering silvery glow, sent several scurrying mice into the thicket. He traced the journey of one, to something that caught his eye. Further away, masked by an enormous privet. Daniel lowered his spell. A rustling came from the ferns to his side. Daniel turned to look. Something was there too. He grabbed his bow, securing it over his shoulders. A ground mist played around the base of the shrubs. He swung to look at the privet. Was that a paw? His senses locking onto its size. A steady panting filled the air. He edged his way to standing, formed a shield and held it as if it was the only thing left in the world. Pinned against the bark, he waited. A low, deep growl rumbled in response. If he ran now, he would be chased and couldn't use his shield or fire his spells. He pulled out several droplets of his *Power Element* and swirled them furiously in his hand.

A jowl almost dog-like, brushed the leaves aside and appeared into the open. Its eyes the matching silver of his shield, with ears pointed and flat back against its head. Long, shaggy black fur drooped to the ground. In a flash the creature snarled bright yellow teeth. Daniel flinched. As it stepped further out of the bush, a fat scaly tail appeared dragging behind, half dog and half snake. He threw a barge of water droplets directly into its path, casting a spell he was forbidden to use. The droplets exploded, fizzing in all directions. The creature's howls filled the trees. Instantly more appeared, growling and snarling at him.

Lunging away he threw more droplets, he didn't care if he used up his entire *Element*. But his spell wasn't as powerful as the first. It halted them only for a moment. A loud, sharp snort came from behind. Daniel span around armed. His arm froze in mid-air as he saw The Stagin, pawing the ground, kicking up its front legs. Daniel shuddered, had it returned to watch him die? He loaded an arrow and fired at the closest. Sinking the arrow directly into its chest. It wailed and halted in its tracks. Another lunged forward in response, his paws flaying into the air. Daniel fired again, followed by a bombardment of droplets. He didn't wait to see where they went. He hurtled towards The Stagin praying it wouldn't run away.

With trembling hands, Daniel slammed into its nuzzle, feeling the prickly bristles. Keeping his eyes cast down, Daniel hurriedly slid his hand across its neck, feeling the wild heart beat and seeing the whites of its eyes follow his every move. Daniel's shoulder was level with its neck flank. His mind raced... he jumped. The Stagin threw its head in the air. Daniel wrapped his long arms around the beast's neck and clung on. It gave a wild bray, desperate and urgent, then bolted sideways. Leaping the ferns and swerving between the trunks as if they were miniature play skittles. Wildly they flew, out of the copse into the open Moors. Daniel's eyes watered, as the wind slid by and the raw stench of a wild animal filled his senses. He turned back to see his attackers had reached the copse edge, dots of glistening yellow, marking his tracks. He promised - he'd never return into trees like that again.

Flashes of grass flickered between the foggy patches - the first signs of *Light Exchange*. Daniel sank low, savouring the thrill of the speed, as they had covered some distance. The warmth from its body soothed his aching limbs. They crossed a rise and slowed to a walk. The Stagin panting as it went into a valley. A wide stream, bubbling through the bottom, almost cutting it in two.

Daniel pushed himself up and wiped his eyes. The sun was just poking its head over the horizon sending rays into the deepest corners. Water had stopped falling from the sky. He had only just noticed. Sunlight revealed more animals, not frightening hunting *Dark Exchange* beasts, but something similar to the mighty Stagin, he rode. Instead of the towering tree branches on their heads, they had bizarre long ears, or was it hair? Whatever it was, they fell like a dress about their head and in pools around them as they munched on the grass.

Several stopped eating, and watched them approach with interest, but showed no sign of fear. Some of their hair was different colours, mottled shades of black, grey and even some blue.

A squawky series of calls rained around him. In the sky were several flying creatures. Totally different to the ones he'd seen on his first *Turn*. Beautiful yellowy brown feathers and unusual wild head plumage. Daniel closed his eyes and rubbed them several times to check he wasn't dreaming. In this moment he could see more animals than he'd seen in several *Turns*. His Stagin kept walking on, seemly oblivious to Daniel on his back.

He was soon in their midst. The flying creatures above and hairy Stagins beside, surrounded by their calls and chatter. Daniel cowered into the tangled mane. The Stagin, abruptly slid his heels into the ground, sending Daniel down his neck and unkindly to the ground. The herd nestled closer; drawing towards their leader and curious. Their breath felt warm on his skin and each pitched grunts, barks and snorts, a language he didn't understand. Some were bold enough to come close enough for him to touch their noses, before jumping back, almost giggling.

Then, through their calls he heard something familiar. Daniel flinched - *it couldn't be*? He merged into the grass. The herd became alert and twitchy. They scattered giving him space. He scrambled across to a tall clump of reeds for cover. Closer than he'd expected were two Tribelings. The Stagin in that split moment, leapt into the air, and galloped away. The rest of the unusual herd followed, screeching and calling after their master. They ran down to the water's edge and followed its path through the valley. Daniel lay dazed, and as if he was in the wrong place at a spectator's game, he flicked back and forth between the curious herd and the Tribelings. Eventually the herd settled by the water.

He cast a viewing spell, forming a clear watery film. The two Tribelings, hadn't seemed to have noticed all the commotion from the herd. They stood at the brow of the hill, framed by a thick, tall barrier of firs, which stretched from east to west across the horizon.

"You cannot just leave like this," came a deep voice translated and clear through his spell. The other Tribeling threw her arms in the air in protest. "You have to get Council permission," he continued. Tall, well built, with a metal chest plate on both sides of his body. The golden colour reflected the sun. "I have told you," he said. "I will let you out as soon as you are safely returned to your family. You've broken several rules by breaking out like this. Whatever made you do it? The Moorlands are not to be trifled with." Daniel had only seen other Tribes when they came into Caradoc on official business. Leading Elders met them, always dressed in the finery. He could tell they weren't Imp, but wasn't sure if these were Sprite or Pixie.

A long blonde plait fell down the guard's back, and he kept stamping a wooden staff into the ground after he spoke. Daniel couldn't hear what the other one was saying. She looked a similar age to him. Her skin pale, with piercing clear green eyes. Her tunic was different to anything his mother would wear, brownish in the places that weren't covered in various patches of mismatch fabric. She was clearly desperate to get out of the bubble thing. He felt sorry for her. What had she done to be put in there?' Then suddenly, in a haze of green dust, another Tribeling appeared. He spoke sharply to the guard, something Daniel didn't catch. The bubble instantly burst sending her tumbling to the ground. The new arrival quickly picked her up, wrapping his arms around her shoulders. She looked like she was sobbing into his chest. The green haze formed again, this time when it had dispersed there were all gone. Daniel slumped into the grass. *Could this Turn get any stranger?*

16

THE COMBINODIUM SPELL

leanor wiped tears from her sleeve. "That was my sister," she cried, as the spell released its hold. Morwena was rubbing her side, staring at the top of the valley, with an annoyed frown. "Why did Blaydoc take her?" Eleanor shook as she stood up. "Morwena," Eleanor paused, feeling the valley press in and her head spin. "My sister?' Morwena flexed her shoulders and arched her back, as if she was stretching after exercise. Her steely set glare turned on Eleanor. Then a sort of smirk crossed her face and a high-pitched gurgle came from her mouth.

"Are you laughing?"

"Yes," Morwena replied, "because you should see yourself, such a mess; the image of a startled finch and covered in twigs!" Eleanor began brushing her clothes and straightening her hair.

"Your trick of bringing along your sister has cost me dearly." Morwena tone changed, "it will shorten our time together."

"So why did you ask me to come all the way out here? Why not just stay at home. It would have been easier."

"Home... puh! No privacy, peering eyes and snooping noses. You wanted answers," Morwena replied. "And, I need to work out how good you are. No... no...no... we couldn't practise anywhere in

Vearmoor."

"But I can't stay out here. I thought you meant have a quick chat. It's getting late and... I'll have a lot of explaining to do, when I get home." Eleanor grabbed her satchel and pulled out her fur shrug, fastening it hurriedly over her shoulders. "We'll have to do this another time." She picked up her rope; thankful it wasn't lost in the windstorm.

"Blaydoc is a powerful and unpredictable," Morwena said, as if she hadn't listened to anything Eleanor said. "Despite our alliance he wouldn't hesitate to kill me, you or your sister," Morwena paused, "if he finds out why you're here."

"Great..." Eleanor snapped, "and my sister's with him! You gave the impression she'd be fine."

"I don't believe Blaydoc will hurt her at the moment," Morwena replied. "He will take her safely back home, of that I'm sure." Her tone was curious, almost eery. "But, your parents and The Sprite Council will know shortly that you are here... with me. The boundaries of Vearmoor will be put on alert and in a *Turn* from now, they will send a guard team to find you," Morwena finished her sentence slowly.

Eleanor interrupted," well it won't come to that, as I'm leaving."

"Blaydoc will say I'm holding you prisoner. His final blow will be to issue my death warrant." Morwena finished with an extravagant swish of her cloak and mock bow.

"He will never manage that," Eleanor said. "It'll not get that far. Elerday will explain, she knows I came because I wanted to.... And, and I'll be there! So NONE of that matters."

"Oh, you'd be surprised," Morwena shook her finger. "Blaydoc can be very persuasive."

Eleanor could believe it, but didn't care, the old Sprite was crazy. She had to find a way to get away, and quickly. "So," Eleanor edged cautiously, "you're trapped in this valley, because of me?"

"Yes, but that isn't important. I brought you here for a reason and we must focus on that. It is essential to begin your teachings while we're alone." Eleanor nodded, pretending to agree, taking small steps towards the path.

"Now," Morwena turned her back and started to pick up stones and pull petals off flower heads, as if she was a frantic treasure hunter. "You have a great deal to learn." She threw rejects stones over her shoulder. "You certainly don't know as much as I hoped. Not even able to get out of a Lock Spell." Eleanor missed some of what Morwena was saying, only catching a few words, as she continued edging away. *I... if... time... Wind Whisperer.... paramount importance...* Eleanor had reached a ledge.

"You're not listening!" Morwena turned around. "You're not even where I left you!"

Eleanor froze and saw a rich blue light jump into life from Morwena's hand. "You're actually trying to run away!" Eleanor shielded her eyes feeling like she was on a large stage. "I thought you wanted to learn?"

"Please, Morwena... I just need to go home," Eleanor said urgently. "I have to sort this mess out. My parents will be having a nightmare and I'll be in serious trouble."

"I don't think you truly understand, Sprite." Eleanor didn't like her tone. "This is no longer about you... me... or your sister... it's about Vearmoor. You can't just go back home." Eleanor felt the words knock her over. "You NOW have a different path to follow. I must try and make you understand. If you are *important* you'll no longer be in charge of your own destiny."

"Look," Eleanor stammered, "I'm not that Wind Wispy thing you keep mentioning, or important. You've got the wrong Sprite. My sisters are far more talented than I am, and... and... didn't you get it wrong with my Grandsprite? Look, I should never have come... it was a mistake." But Morwena was chanting a steady flow of words. Suddenly the call of a Larna bird rang across the valley. A bird, distinctive to her home district and nowhere else. It was a sign. Her parents would have sent it out to tell her to come back. It was all the encouragement she needed. Eleanor took one last look at the old Sprite and the entrancing valley.

Morwena had a swirling ball of dust between her hands. Eleanor felt her gaze lock, she frantically tried to look away but couldn't. Entranced by its movement and energy. She forgot where she wanted to go, why it was so important. The valley faded into the background as the ball expanded and fought against its boundaries. Flashes of fire leapt about inside, drops of water rained through it, and lumps of what only looked like mud formed and exploded. It was beautiful. Eleanor was full of hope. Her dreams and potential - possible.

"What is it?" Eleanor whispered walking towards it. Morwena didn't reply. The ball grew and soon dwarfed its creator. Suddenly it began to quiver and left Morwena's hands to hover. Morwena was visibly shaking. It was growing darker in colour, getting bigger, no longer enchanting, more nightmare. Eleanor clasped her hands over her ears as something crackled loudly and began to howl. Then the old Sprite collapsed, lying uncomfortably on the floor. Eleanor stood alone. Had the spell gone wrong? What was she playing at? Eleanor suddenly felt her head hurt, thumping a warning. Fire suddenly shot wildly from the ball, lighting the valley floor, then burning everything it touched. Arches of mud spewed out ferociously. She awoke from her trance and ran for cover, just before a gust of wind burst past her. Eleanor peered from behind the safety of a large rock. The fading sun light in the valley sucked into the ball. The only sound was her panting. Still it grew pulsating and angry. Spitting fire and sending out bolts of wind. The ground around Morwena turned black. The water from the spell was gathering together into pools. Eleanor's mind was on slow time. She couldn't just let Morwena drown, the water was going to cover her. She leapt up and run, with no more of a plan than dragging Morwena to higher ground. But the murky water rose like a thick wall of watery fog, as dense and black as rotten moss. It started to slither forwards. The chill in the air turned to a wave of prickly heat. It moved with incredible speed.

A bee buzzed around Eleanor's head. "Help me please," Eleanor cried. "I need to destroy this thing, it's killing everything!" In seconds, a swarm of glowing bees of all shapes and sizes appeared. They began to chatter noisily. She took hold of her rope and repeated the words they were telling her to say. Words she'd never said before. The rope twitched and grew. She kept repeating the spell. The rope grew so big she was struggling to hold it. Then, with speed and skill, they took it from her. It was now so long that Eleanor couldn't see the ends. The bees flew towards the encroaching wall of fog. Eleanor didn't dare stop the chanting which mixed in perfect harmony with the drum of their beating wings. As soon as the rope touched the darkness a bright flash filled the valley floor. Eleanor shielded her eyes and fell.

*

Opening them again, Morwena was peering over her.

"You're strong, young one, you're strong." Morwena held out her hand. "Maybe I'm right this time, just maybe?" Eleanor got up without taking her hand. "You're clearly a bee master..." Morwena looked into Eleanor's face "...and that's good. The bees are your allies. They choose few." Morwena handed Eleanor her rope back.

"Did... did you just perform The Combinodium Spell?" Eleanor said in disbelief.

"Come, you must be tired... and, I think you're now ready to listen."

"But we could have died, that spell is forbidden! You've just conjured up *The Darkness!*"

"Those bees have just given their life to save you, so don't waste it," Morwena retorted. Eleanor felt her body sway. "Come, it's time to tell you about The Book of Spells."

17

THE EARTH GUARDIANS

Daniel lazily chewed a piece of grass, and stared. He had explored the line of trees for a whole Turn, trying several times to push through the wall of twigs and branches in multiple places, but became so tangled and trapped, all he could do was retreat. Something powerful propelled him away. He had walked along its edge for as far as he dared. But nothing… no entrance, no gates, no gaps. He groaned as he turned onto his back, lying between the white heathers, watching the bulbous clouds float by.

Surely another Tribeling would appear? If they did, he'd made up his mind, he was going to approach them, whatever their response. Halgelan, the name he'd given The Stagin, had remained close, with both the herds. Living amongst them during *Dark Exchange* had given comfort – no weird dog, snake like creature had dared to come near. *Thank the Water Lord.* He yawned and searched the horizon. It was getting late. He had to prepare for another *Dark*, and was accustomed to how long that took. He went to fetch water from the river, using an empty pouch, and headed back to his camp. Even he was impressed with how well it was hidden amongst the rocks. A group of Halgelan's herd were grazing close by and took little notice of his approach. Daniel squatted in front of his shelter fire's and eased the burning embers into life. He tried to keep it going all the way through *The Light,* so it won't fail him in *The Dark.* He noted each landmark of importance, checking that nothing had changed. Then, settled to cook a thin rodent he'd pulled from its burrow earlier. The crackling flesh and warmth from the fire made his eyes droop.

Vivid images of his homeland danced amongst the flames. He could see himself walking familiar paths. His two brothers played in the streams. He wanted to join them, get their attention. He called their names, but to no avail, unable to get close enough. He tried several ways to reach them but each time a barrier stopped him. He woke with a jolt, surprised he'd actually fallen asleep, and saw the charred remains incarcerated in the fire. *Great,* he grumbled *charcoal for supper.*

"That wasn't enough to eat anyway." A voice, rich and clear made Daniel jump. His senses prickled. He traced the pale rays of moonlight, along the ground to four stout Tribelings standing like death lords in front of their kill. The hairs on the back of his neck rose. He grabbed his bow and loaded an arrow and aimed it directly at the nearest. A distant animal screamed as if caught in its captor's jaws. Daniel aimed the point at each Tribeling in turn. Sweat slithered down his back - *what were they waiting for?*

"We are not here to harm you, Elf," one of them spoke, his accent strange and coarse. Daniel recognised the language of Naraling. Thankful his mother had taught him. She had always said; it was important to learn the common tongue between the Tribes.

"What do you want?" Daniel replied not trusting them one bit. He glanced for Halgelan, who stood silhouetted, caught in the moonlight, close by.

"To learn why you are alone on The Moors," came the accented reply. "We sense trouble. We want to understand what is happening within your homeland."

"How would I know?"

"One of our Caradoc spies have been killed," he continued and looked at his comrades, in a way that made Daniel even more nervous. Daniel threw his bow to the ground, wildly grabbing for water droplets. *He was going to stop them before they tried anything.* He chanted the first thing that came into his head. Rushing water burst into life; and to his surprise swirled around his body. He swore to himself, as it grew to form a tunnel. He was unable to see a thing - not the clear shield he needed. Why could he never get a spell right! Suddenly the ground flexed and bowed, making him stumble and fall to his knees. His spell broke, the water collapsed, and soaked him to the skin.

"Like I said," the Tribeling was grinning, "we mean you no harm, Elfling." His smile, Daniel thought, still had a threatening edge. "Do you need help?" he asked with an outstretched hand. The moonlight danced across his body. His clothes seemed to blend into the surroundings, making it difficult to see him clearly. Daniel couldn't work out if he was wearing material or the grasses of The Moors.

"No..." Daniel leapt to his feet. "Stay back," he said, shaking the water from him.

"What Tribe are you?"

"Pixie," the Tribeling replied, with a slight smirk on his face. "I'm Tristan Corrinium." He gestured towards his companions. "This is Christian de Verren, Vagen Ornsvik and Edward Glamis, we are the four Earth Guardians of Poldaric, and..." he paused. "we give our word we've come in peace. "

"We would like to keep it that way. " Edward said, "Unless, you throw another water spell." Daniel's feet sunk further into the muddy ground. His breath twirled into the cold dark air. Suddenly The Stagin rose majestically into view, his silent hooves sliding in the wet ground towards them.

"Ahh, my old friend." Tristan spoke warmly and raised his hand to stoke Halgelan's head, as if he'd done this several times before. "It's been a good while since I was last on The Moors. Have you been looking after this Elf?" Daniel thought he saw The Stagin nod in reply.

"Do you... kn... n...ow, this animal?" Daniel stammered.

"Yes... we're old friends. I like to think this fine Staginourisum is a good judge of character, so that makes you, Elf, important. He doesn't appear to all Tribelings who wander The Moorland." *Earth and Water are friends...* some of last words his father had said to him. Perhaps this is what he had meant, the Pixie's power element was *Earth.* Cautiously, Daniel gestured to his shelter, The water had soaked the rocks and moss seeped through the cracks.

"I think we should make another one," Tristan's companions all began to talk to each other in a language Daniel's didn't understand.

"I will form a wall for protection," Vagen spoke in Naraling. "Keep those creatures out." He winked at Daniel or so he thought, before holding up his palm, and placing it across his heart.

"It's a sign of peace," Tristan explained. Edward and Christian did the same. Daniel replied with the Elf's oath, by crossing his arms over his chest and bowing his head. Daniel watched in awe as Vagen picked up a handful of earth and held it close to his mouths, as if talking to it. Suddenly the earth around Daniel's feet began to shudder and emanate a strange groan, cracking and heaving. Then it cracked and moved upwards. In only a matter of moments, a steep earth wall grew into a hoof-shaped curve.

"I think we should be safe enough within there. We also have the herd protecting us. We will know if anything approaches." Tristan gestured for Daniel to enter first and asked, "Have they been with you for long?"

Daniel was still entranced by the earth spell. "Uh, no, not long. Halgelan found me only two *Turns* ago."

"What did you call him?"

"Hal-gel-an. It means *hope* within old Elfland." It was the first time Daniel had said the word aloud.

"I like it," Tristan replied. "Let's pray he is." The other Pixies gathered into the earthen structure. Daniel settled close to the exit.

"Can you make a fire?" Edward asked. "I've heard Elves can with their *Power Element*." His voice was different to Tristan's, deeper, gruffer. He had a strong dark gaze, giving the impression he was testing everything you said. "I have wanted to see the blue flames burn," he continued.

"Yes," Daniel replied more nervously than he wanted to sound. He gathered a few rocks to form a circle and using a water droplet to make the fire. It immediately began to burn brightly. Edward clapped his hands. "There is surprising warmth from it," he grinned. "It's remarkable. They say you can see images in it with practise. Is this true?"

"Yes, if you practice," Daniel said, shuffling uncomfortably, remembering the last painful images of his bothers playing in the rivers at home and his inability to reach them.

For the first time, he could see their rich, muddy coloured skin. Encased by clothes of an intricate network of leather straps, leaves and silk-like material, the colour of deep brown and green tuffs, blending with the wall behind them. Only their leather belts were clear. Each displaying a number of metal emblems, of various shapes and colours crisscrossing their chests. A thick wooden baton poked out of a pocket. They were slightly shorter than he was, stronger looking, thicker shoulders and chests, with dark brown long hair. Tristan's face was etched with concern; as if he held a great responsibility on his shoulders. Daniel's father had the same look sometimes. Vagen was the joker, his face smiled easily, showing his emotions openly. Edward tested everything, was interested in all aspects of being Elf, wanted to learn more, as they discussed trivia. He couldn't work out Christen yet, but he was the oldest of them all. As they began to talk, Daniel's unease lessened. Despite being outnumbered, he hadn't felt so upbeat since his banishment.

18

TREVARAK'S FALL

"Have you had any contact with home, while on The Moors?" Tristan removed a small wooden box from his belt.

"No, nothing." Daniel gratefully accepted the offering of salted fish. The smell of cooked flatbread made Daniel's stomach groan.

"Before I tell you about Caradoc, we must understand why you're here. There hasn't been a lone Elf on The Moorlands for a long time, and this is no place for any Tribeling, let alone one of your age." Daniel cringed; he wasn't that young. And, he didn't want to explain about his banishment. What would they think? He studied the flames.

"You're unable to return?" Tristan's voice was almost a whisper. "Why else would you be out here alone?" Tristan shot a worried look at his companions. "What family are you from?"

"I am Daniel Elf Trevarak. Eldest Elfling of the Grand Master." Daniel concentrated on his blue flames. "I did something wrong, very wrong." Feeling his shame hang in the air like poison, "And this is my punishment... Caradoc is lost to me."

"What did you do?" Edward's words sounded like a snarl.

"I killed an Elf - Thaen Tremaine Eastling. Struck by my arrow and knocked into our sacred waters. His burns haunt my dreams."

"But how did you see his burns? Only Council Members of the Elvin Tribe can enter your waters," Christian said. "You couldn't have seen the body, as it would have been left as a gift for Istria and her Glows."

"It wasn't left – I pulled it from the lake."

"But that's impossible, Daniel," Tristan sought agreement from his companions.

"Don't lie to us, Elf," Edward growled, "we don't have time." Tristan placed a hand on Edward's shoulder.

"I'm not," Daniel looked at Edward directly. "Only my mother knew."

"Anta Trevarak?"

"Yes," Daniel looked at Christian with surprise, "do you know her?"

"My mother does and so does Tristan's." Before Daniel could ask how, Tristan interrupted, "But why kill an Elf?" his tone harsh.

"Thaen and five other Eastling Elves were torturing my youngest brother in full view on our Unity Bridge, dripping water onto his skin. He would not have survived for much longer; his burns were already extensive. My shot was meant to be a warning."

"Where was your father?"

"It was early *Shadow*; my best friend woke me, and no one else was up."

"Didn't that seem strange to you?" Edward looked at him as if he was a fool. Daniel turned his gaze. The Pixies began to talk furiously amongst themselves. Daniel hadn't thought about the lead up to firing his arrow for a while. He hadn't had time to mull over the details. Why wasn't anyone else around? How come his father and mother hadn't woken? Questions now that seemed obvious. He bit his lip and ground his teeth in silence... waiting.

"Did your brother live?" Tristan asked.

"I don't know," Daniel shuddered. "The Council tried me for my crimes quickly and the Eastling Elves made sure I was banished before the *Late Shadow*, I only just saw my mother before I went."

"Did your father tell you anything before you left?"

"Yes," Daniel said, "he told me to find a powerful Sprite, but I can't remember her name; and that Earth and Water are old allies."

The *Early Shadow* Larka bird began to sing its first song. The Pixies resumed talking amongst themselves. He stared with an intense concentration into the blue flames. Beautiful images of his mother standing by their open fire, danced in hues of blue. It didn't make sense that she was known by a Pixie. *She'd never left Caradoc?* Daniel heard Halgelan bark, followed by the flying herd's eerie screeches. The images disappeared, his heart felt heavy, as the *Light Exchange* animals were trying to reclaim The Moors from the *Dark*.

"You should know," Edward spoke, "we have also found a lone female Imp, hiding in one of our tree gates, over two *Turns* ago." Daniel looked at him quizzically. "She is a powerful Fire-Maker. But young, like you. She is recovering within our homeland – Poldaric." Christian broke in.

"We have performed the Combinodium Spell, which is more important for you to know." Christian shot a look at Edward. Daniel shifted uncomfortably.

"It would seem," Christian continued, "that events in your homeland are tipping *The Balance*."

"Did you see black in my Element?" Daniel, keen and intent, his throat suddenly drying.

"Yes... it grew quickly."

Daniel clenched his fists, "What events?"

"Our Elf allies have told us, that your father has been overthrown and his Council dispersed. A few of those still loyal to him remain strong, but some have paid with their lives. The Eastling Elves have gained power and kill anyone that disagrees."

Daniel looked incredulously at Tristan. "But how do you know this?" he asked. "My father would never let that happen. He's always been a believer in retaining *The Balance* against all cost. He would rather die than see Ostric rise within his homeland or let Tonurang take over from him."

"Then he might get his wish," Edward answered abruptly.

"But the rest of my family - my mother?"

"There is hope – Halgelan has appeared to you on The Moors. He fights for *The Light*, so we must believe there is something you can do." Tristan looked intently at Daniel. "You have survived for a while," Tristan looked thoughtful for a moment, "and... it must be significant... few can last this long."

Christian offered him some bread and meat. Daniel almost inhaled it at once. "You must head south," Christian said. "Follow the trees of Vearmoor and the setting sun."

"Vearmoor?" Daniel questioned.

"Yes. Those trees you've been staring at Elf," Christian replied "are the border of The Sprites..." Daniel could sense the Pixie's irritation.

"Keep yourself out of sight," Tristan said. "There are those amongst the Sprites who would see a lone Elf as easy target. The Stagin will take you. Move quickly, Vagen and Christian know that a powerful Sprite is in Obakeech, their sacred valley. Her powers surpass many, she might be the one your fathers speaks of, but be careful." Daniel nodded. "Don't challenge her or be fooled by her age, she won't take kindly to it."

"We will try and find you again," Tristan said. "And... don't be so hrd on yourself," he smiled. Daniel couldn't bring his eyes level to reply.

"We must leave you." Tristan stood up. "We can't be away from Poldaric for long with an Imp in our midst." Daniel didn't watch them get up. As they ducked under the lint of the horseshoe shelter, Daniel heard the Chatter Rat cry; *Light Exchange* had arrived. Only Tristan remained.

"You should be able to rest safely within our shelter. I will leave it as it is." Tristan bowed to Daniel. "Good Luck, Elf, I am sure our paths will cross soon enough."

19

THE BOOK OF SPELLS

Eleanor felt the pit of her stomach turn cold. She'd sent the bees to their death. They'd told her what to do - *hadn't they*? A stillness filled the valley. It was cool, quiet, unsettling. What would dare to move first? *The Dark Exchange* had arrived. The moon's silvery path cast across the meadow, accentuating the valley's sacred ora.

"I'll make a shelter," Morwena said plainly. With a shudder, Eleanor realised she would have to spend a whole *Dark Exchange*, with this crazy Sprite. Resigned, she muttered, "I'll help." Eleanor trudged after her. Being with Morwena was better than alone amongst the valley secrets.

"No... no, don't. I'll do it much quicker this way. Just watch," Morwena replied. "I'm far too old to be doing anything by hand." And she began to wave her arms about in a random motion, muttering angrily at anything that got in her way. Eleanor stepped back, wary. Sticks, branches and leaves flew in all directions by Morwena's command. Her bizarre angry grunts seemed to tell each piece what to do. If one twig went the wrong way, Morwena would bark noisily and it redirected itself. Eleanor almost laughed. Why didn't her parents know how to do this?

"Uh, should I do anything?" she asked over the din.

"No... no," Morwena said briskly, "this won't take much longer." At the sound of a loud breaking branch, Morwena shouted, "There... move back," and drew a dramatic circle in the air. "Now, where do you think would be a good place to make our camp?" *What is she talking about, Eleanor inwardly groaned.* Then, just to say something, "there under that willow tree."

"Perfect," Morwena muttered, "go and stand in the middle." Eleanor hesitated. "Hurry," she demanded. Eleanor ambled over and stood awkwardly. Within seconds a dome-shaped structure appeared. It fell over her, she sank to the floor, cowering. When Eleanor dared to look up again, she found herself nestled under a canopy of interwoven branches, lined with a thick under blanket of moss. Broad arching trunks formed a curved roof, with a small opening in the middle that allowed smoke to escape from an already lit fire. The fire was brightly burning within a ring of stones.

"There," Morwena announced, "better than expected, as I haven't done that for ages." She appeared at the arched door, "and these should keep you warm." Eleanor followed the crooked finger to a haphazard pile of bracken, covered with furs. It looked almost as cosy as her own bed.

"Don't look so... what's the word?" Morwena said abruptly, "shocked, that's it. It looks so stupid in young Sprites."

"I... I just haven't seen someone do that - well nothing like it even."

"Oh, it's nothing and if we'd had more time on the fun stuff, I might have shown you... but we don't. Now go and make yourself comfortable, I am sure you're hungry and tired. All young Sprites are." If only Eleanor hadn't been in a valley far away from home, she might have liked being in such a place – there were even fireflies lighting the canopy. Instead, she quietly settled herself and pulled a fur closer.

"So... uh," said Eleanor. "Er... what happens next?"

"Well at least you're talking to me. That's a start." Morwena bent forward and pulled something from behind the fire. "Now eat, while I talk." Eleanor couldn't believe it – cooked rabbit and her favourite selection of berries and nuts, handed to her on a leaf plate.

"Morwena, no Sprite can do this!"

"Have you heard of *The Balance of NaraRose?*" Morwena ignored her, but Eleanor could see her eyes were sparkling. She liked the praise.

"Huh... a bit..." Eleanor struggled to swallow her mouthful. "My father believes in *The Balance*, I think, but they don't speak about it much."

"*The Balance of Nararose,* you understand, is kept by the unity of our four Tribes, Imps, Elves, Pixies and Sprites and their four power elements, *Fire, Water, Earth* and *Wind.*"

"Uh huh... that's common knowledge," Eleanor said.

"True, so you also know, that if a war breaks out within a Tribe or between Tribes it upsets *The Balance?*"

"Sort of, but my mother doesn't believe that fighting is the only cause that tips it." Eleanor gulped down a chunk of meat, amazed at how delicious it was.

"And she'd be right," Morwena replied. "If history has taught us anything it is that *The Balance* is unpredictable." The crackle of the fire was eclipsed by a fox's call, urgent and near. Eleanor suddenly felt very aware of where she was. She hoped *Darkness* creatures didn't come into the valley.

"Is there a protection spell around our shelter?"

"Yes of course, and the whole valley." Morwena replied irritated. "I believe it'll keep most of the problems out. So may I continue?" Morwena flicked her hand at the fire and the flames jumped higher. Eleanor shuffled uneasily.

"We've been existing in a time of tribal peace."

"But what about the Great Fires of Vearmoor?"

"Yes, it's unusual that *The Balance* didn't tip afterwards."

"So what happens when it does?" Eleanor put her empty leaf onto the ground.

"Ostric or Istria rise." Eleanor felt a chill run through her body and wondered if she'd just imagined the flames shudder.

"But neither came that time." Eleanor's eye's clouded with the terrible memories of the uncontrollable flames.

"We don't know why," Morwena replied, "some of us believe that Ostric not Istria is waiting for something. It is feared that when he next comes, it will be the start of *The Darkness* supremacy. That he is quietly becoming strong, and plotting to become supreme God."

"But surely that's not going to happen, Istria and the others will never allow it, for starters." Eleanor twisted her hair through her hands. Morwena fell silent. Only the fireflies still dared to hum. "She is weakened for some reason, that no-one understands. And remember Eleanor - neither God or Goddess domination is a good thing. She can be just as ruthless as he.

"So… How is Ostric destroyed?"

"No one knows for sure, each time he appears we have to try different ways. Different Elements work at different times." Morwena looked up, "if we knew the correct pattern, it would potentially help us to stop Ostric once and for all."

"So how did he start… I mean at the beginning?"

"That's sketchy too. We only know it's aligned to our *Elements*. When we were given the powers to manipulate *Wind, Earth, Fire* and *Water*, Ostric appeared on Nararose. As the legend goes, Istria appeared at the same time and gave Turgred, the first Pixian Elder, two power gifts: an Amulet and Ridge Goblet. No other tribe was given anything from her. Penda, our first Elder, made our Book of Spells. It wasn't a gift from the Gods. It was formed to hold all our knowledge of the Sprite way of life. Since its creation it has been handed down to worthy Sprites, who only possess it for as long as they stay true to the Sprite Way. It has become, as legend states, a place where every encounter with *The Darkness* and *The Light* has been recorded - for good and bad."

"But no one knows where The Book is," Eleanor muttered, only repeating what her mother often said. Morwena grunted something that Eleanor didn't catch.

"What do the Imps and Elves have?" Morwena's eyes shone in the firelight. "A Torc and The Elves a Stone, but The Stone isn't in their possession." Eleanor was about to ask, how, when Morwena continued. "Did you notice I started that spell with the four Elements? It's an incredibly tricky spell to master – The

Combinodium Spell, but if it works, it can predict *The Balance* within the Tribes." Eleanor remembered seeing the flickering fire and water droplets. "The results weren't expected," Morwena continued. "*The Darkness* caught me unawares and without you I would have struggled to stop its advance."

"Surely not... that's madness ... you're so powerful," Eleanor stammered.

Morwena continued, "My concern is not only... at the creation of the Darkness, but that it started so quickly and grew so wildly within the *Water* Element. Something troubling is happening within Caradoc and Ostric isn't far from appearing there."

"Then I must go home." Eleanor went to stand up, "warn my family."

"You cannot wander The Moorlands alone in *The Dark Exchange*," Morwena thrust her hands near the flames warming both sides. "Haven't we been through this already?" she snarled. Eleanor hesitated, her head bent at an angle touching the ceiling branches. "Now sit down..." Eleanor obeyed.

"I'm afraid," Morwena continued, "I've brought you into something that is greater than I first thought. You can't go back to your family in Vearmoor for now. I'm certain we're heading towards an imminent rise of *The Darkness* and you are a part of it somehow."

20

LUXYLAN

Eleanor paused, flopped amongst a drift of long grass, staring at the solitary yellow bush. Her rope lay in a coil by her side. Morwena pranced into view; her eyes were gleaming as she flapped her arms like a mating Prima Bird. Eleanor sighed, as she had done several times during the last *Turn*. She heaved her aching limbs to standing; Morwena was acting like a Sprite half her age.

Two full *Turns* had passed since she'd left home. Morwena hadn't stopped teaching. Recounting spells, demonstrating dust control, *apparently she hadn't been doing it properly before,* and flying the entire circuit of the valley, many times to practise dust travel. She'd hardly had time to feel home sick. Morwena was fascinating, she didn't give her a moment to linger or dwell. One amazing result was transformation no longer hurt.

"What are you doing resting?" Morwena bounded closer.

Eleanor rubbed her ankle. "We haven't stopped for ages."

"Pathetic. If another Tribeling comes over the edge of the valley, what are you going to do? Tell them - sorry, you can't fight at the moment, your ankle hurts?" Morwena scoffed as she leapt into the air. Eleanor glared at the ground, gritted her teeth and snatched up her rope. Warmth rose through her arm. *Right, she'd show that old Sprite.* She began to spin it skilfully into a lasso. It looped and grew, creating a vast circle in the air. Once it was big enough, she chanted the spell Morwena had made her learn to heart. A rich yellow glow filled the circle.

"Now," Eleanor shouted.

"Hold it," Morwena hollered. The light grew stronger. Eleanor fought to control her shaking arms. Gradually the colour crept towards the ground, creating a golden dome.

"I've done it," Eleanor shouted.

"There," Morwena replied, "you're not so weak after all." Between rope rotations, she marvelled at the shimmering encasement. Eventually her arms, could continue no more. Eleanor let go of her rope and watched the light sink to the ground. "Wow," she said, "an actual Sprite's protection dome – how cool?" Morwena clapped her hands and it disappeared completely.

"Ooww!" Eleanor protested.

"Never a good quality Eleanor, I don't like Sprites that gloat." Eleanor sank heavily into the long grass and stared at the sky. If only she could show her father, he'd have loved it.

Eleanor noticed a thin dusky film had settled across the sky, the approach of *Dark Exchange* was so much more real out here than at home nestled within the trees. She checked to see where Morwena was, and couldn't see her for a moment. Thankfully some rest, Eleanor dared to close her eyes. Her thoughts turned to home. Her parents pacing their tree house, her sisters arguing with The Sprite Council to be allowed on The Moorlands. Sprite guards... golden gates... thick impassable hedges...

"Wake up." Eleanor blinked. Morwena was bending over her.

"It's late and you've been sleeping," Morwena sounded techie. Eleanor sluggishly raised her head; shocked to think she'd actually fallen asleep.

"Are you alright?" Eleanor asked Morwena groggily, noticing the youthfulness of the last couple of *Shadows* seemed to have left the Sprite's appearance.

"No... I'm not alright," she replied, "we've a change of plan."

"What?"

"I've been checking my protection spell around the valley and it has been breached," Morwena looked affronted. "Yes, can you believe it?' Eleanor tried to hide a smile.

"They've caught up with us." Morwena threw a sprinkling of dust over a clump of grass. It shrivelled, turned black and disintegrated into ashes.

"I have also performed another Combinodium Spell."

"No... wah!" Eleanor stared at the patch of dead grass.

"Oh, only a small one this time, don't look so worried." Eleanor couldn't believe it. "More importantly we have had a visitor."

"Who?" Eleanor couldn't take it all in. Nobody had been anywhere near them for the whole time she'd been in the valley.

"Not who... well I suppose sort of... more like a what."

"Go on." Eleanor sat up.

"Luxylan, over there, my Tan-taller Bird, isn't he beautiful," Morwena said boastfully. "He..." Eleanor looked at her incredulously, "it's a he! He's your pet?"

"Oh, no... he's a wild Moorland creature. He and I have a mutual understand."

"A what!"

"Oh, shhh. Look he'll come over when he's ready. Meet you." Eleanor wasn't so sure.

"And who's breached our border?"

"That I don't know, but it can't be good. It wasn't Sprite.

"But you said, they caught up with us."

"Did I? You must have miss heard." Eleanor looked about her, *Morwena was lying to her.* "Anyway..." Morwena continued. "Luxylan has told me something importance. A Tribeling on The Moors, with red hair. That can mean only one thing. An Imp is out of Arramond and we must find out why." Eleanor shook her head. "I'm not chasing Imps. If I'm going anywhere it's home, that was our deal. A few *Turns* teaching and then back to Vearmoor." The valley reverberated with a loud caw that rippled into cackles.

"He's coming over," Morwena beamed, and let out an almost

exact replica of calls. Eleanor flinched. An enormous yellow shaggy-haired bird swooped towards them, flying gracefully across the tops of the long grasses. He had the longest feathers Eleanor had ever seen. Each one drooped around his head, narrow body and outstretched wings. The bird landed with a thud and shook its elegant head to reveal bright, shiny green eyes, rimmed with gold. Its emerald green beak bent into a broad hook, and each of his feet were nearly the size of Eleanor's hand. His tail feather spilled out behind him like the head dress of an elaborate veil. Morwena was right, this bird was beautiful and Eleanor instantly fell in love.

"This is Luxylan..." Morwena announced, "you are honoured to meet him."

Eleanor wasn't too sure how to greet it, so just held up her hand and gave a little wave. "Uh, hi," she muttered. Morwena sighed and went up to the bird, wrapping her arms around its neck. They both began to exchange short sharp squeaks and chirps. Eleanor suddenly an intruder on a private conversation. Then, he took off, opening his wings to full stretch. Circling around them before swooping up the valley slope and disappearing.

"It's not good," Morwena came up to her. "He says that he can feel *Darkness* and we shouldn't stay here. He's warning me, the darling." *The darling, wow, Morwena did have feelings!* Eleanor pushed that thought aside.

"Here?"

"No, not in here. Somewhere on The Moors."

"That can't be true?" Eleanor flinched, "you said it would form in Caradoc?"

"He's sure, and I saw it in my Combinodium Spell too. But he doesn't know when or what form it'll take. So he's moving his herd, travelling south towards the land of the Imps."

"Why south?"

"Because only Fire can destroy a *Darkness* creature that flies. Our Power Element can stall, but not kill it." Eleanor clutched her rope; she must hurry and make it back across The Moors to Vearmoor.

21

RED HAIR

The herd were unsettled; each of their calls, trill and echoed uneasily between the valley walls. It was mid *Shadow,* Daniel had slept only for a few hours. Something, had disturbed them. He stared. All that the Pixies had spoken of, whirled like a sand storm in his head. He stared at the lines of dirt etched into his skin, and the thick dark stains around his fingernails. Every time, the lines merged and became a snakelike *Darkness* creature that chased his family. Perhaps his father had been right, maybe he was better out of the way? But, live a life of solitude? Wait for them all to die. Was that his destiny?

Should he head south as Tristan had said, perhaps this Sprite was the one his father had told him to find. After all it was the only lead he had. Or stay put? Live amongst the safety of the herd. He decided to talk to Halgelan. He knew the Stagin couldn't say anything, but it might help.

Daniel set about covering the traces of the last few *Turns.* Scattering the remains of his damp shelter, stubbing out the fire and brushing over his footprints. It was tiring work and took longer than he wanted. Finally done, he gathered his few possessions and checked his Element pouches, only one and a half left, his stomach lurched. How had he been so careless?

He searched for Halgelan and set off up the valley.

Halgelan was in a fierily mood. Every time Daniel got close, he bolted. Daniel called, coaxed and even begged, but nothing got him near. He then decided to wait patiently for the Stagin to come of his own free will. He waited and waited. The sun turned in the sky and began its descent. *Light Exchange* was on its way out.

"That's it," Daniel shouted. "If you won't help me, I'm going alone." He set off, slamming his feet into the tufty grasses. As if The Moor was working against him, the wind began to pick up and blew more strongly than it had for a while. The sky was greyer, with large bulky clouds. That was all he needed. Daniel hoped it wouldn't start throwing water at him again, he'd enjoyed the time while it had been dry. Keeping the line of trees in sight, he walked on. They were an easy guide in an otherwise barren landscape.

"This is your last chance," Daniel called, as he reached the top of the rise, but Halgelan didn't flinch. "So much for my hope," Daniel mumbled. The Moors and firs stretched into the horizon with no end. Maybe, he thought, Halgelan was trying to tell him something by not helping. Maybe he shouldn't trust what the Pixies had said and that he shouldn't search for this Sprite?

Unsure and wary, Daniel walked on. *Shadow* after *Shadow* passed, until his legs ached and his ankles rubbed inside his worn boots. He took a break and sank heavily onto dried earth, grateful to remove each encasement, to examine his feet. Two perfectly formed, red blisters had burst and oozed a gloopy mush. With bare feet he wearily went in search of dock leaves. Without warning a yellow flying creature swooped overhead. Its giant wings covered the weak rays of sunlight. He tripped dodging its low dive and tumbled down the slope, tumbling and rolling until he came to a halt at the bottom. Dazed and shaken, Daniel rubbed his head and looked around. A startling red-haired Tribeling, as obvious as a female Stagin amongst a pack of wolves, stood tall.

He shouted, having seen him. Daniel froze. The Tribeling roared again, in a language Daniel didn't understand. Daniel stayed where he was. His stomach twisted, there was nowhere to hide. His long limbs were as pale as the white sand of the Algor Lake.

"Help... understand?" he roared in heavily accented Naraling. The words rocketed through his head. Daniel searched the surroundings, the tall grasses, the patches of dark shimmering water. He knelt down and touched the ground in front of him. It was spongy and damp. He looked around, no longer able to see the Vearmoor's trees over the rise. Had he strayed that far eastwards, and made it back to The Great Bog?

"I can't pull... free..." Daniel could see the desperation across his face. His mouth set in a wide tight snarl. His arms fully taught, pulling at another arm. Someone else was there - stuck.

"Hurry..." the voice etched with pain, sweat glistening off the Imps skin. But every bit of Daniel didn't want to move, as if paralysed, none of his own muscles responding. Was it possible to turn and run back up the hill?

Against all his better judgement, Daniel slowly got up. He spotted the large yellow flying creature was sitting halfway up the slope, watching him as if he was toying with the idea of pecking his eyes out. He began to criss-cross the treacherous ground, carefully placing his footing, using only the drier tufts of grasses. He was used to this environment, he knew only too well, that one wrong move and he was in. A persistent wailing, which made his skin crawl.

"Do know spells?" the Imp called, "A water trick, stop this?" Daniel thought of how little Power Element he had left, but he couldn't just watch them sink. He knelt down to dig out his pouch, hoping he could think of something. He had barely begun when the ground began to shake. The grass blades quivered and trembled from the base upwards. He looked up, and both Imps had quietened. They had noticed it too.

"What you do... Elf?" One of them shouted. "Don't trick an Impling of Vanik...."

Daniel felt his throat restrict. "It's not me." The bog began to wobble, shaking like the ripple across a lake's surface. Both Imps began to shout. Every word interspersed by a terrible gurgling and choking. Daniel's hands shone with the effort of gripping twisted reeds. The spongy ground sloshed and rocked. Daniel swiped aside bull rushes and flattened them under his foot. He leapt backwards onto a drier patch and held on, watching. Something was appearing from the bog, dripping in gloopy mud, thin and long with flashes of blue. Through a spiralling mass of water, like a wild tornado.

"I've always hated getting out of Caradoc this way," came a voice through the sloshing droplet. Daniel felt his blood run cold, as if he had just jumped once more into the cold waters of the Great Lake. He formed a protection shield, keeping low and hidden. The words were Elfland. The swirling water fell to the ground, it was like the slow and embarrassing unveiling of a pointless plaque. Daniel scanned the horizon for the Imps but couldn't see either of them. He watched in frozen horror as the Elf began to clean the bog from his clothes. The process was laborious, like he had all the time in the world, caring only that he looked good. The silver hair reflected against the sun light, shining more and more brightly until, eventually any last trace of dirt was banished with a flick of his hand. The commanding figure carefully checked every aspect of his cloak, and made sure the royal blue shone. Daniel's head span, his father had a cloak like that. If it hadn't been for the silver hair.... but who else does he know with hair that colour? The commanding figure turned, so his face was facing him, but the sun's glare blocked him from view. Daniel saw the Imp rise to his feet in response. Two contrasting Tribelings as different as the two Gods they worshipped.

"So there wasn't just one of you!" the Elf said exasperatedly. Daniel trembled at the voice. A pain shot into his head. He knew that tone, it sent memories of his trial flooding back. He flattened himself into the mud, breathing heavily. Guilty... guilty... guilty... replayed over and over and that Elf had started it all for him.

22

SILVER WEB

Eleanor slowly drew the cold air in through her nose and steadily from her mouth, with the name *Ostric* reeling in her mind. She remembered how Amber, her eldest sister would pretend to be one of his forms – a Gulabird. She would stretch out her arms, jut her chin, bare teeth and chase her, screeching. Eleanor never thought one could actually exist.

"Morwena," Eleanor said quietly, watching her gaze lovingly after Luxylan who had long disappeared from sight. "I'm going back to my family," she paused, "I don't care, I'm not following you to the south." Morwena turned to face her, "I'm grateful," Eleanor continued, "for everything... your answers, lessons... really I am... but I'm done." Eleanor rammed her hands into her deep fur pockets so that Morwena wouldn't see them shaking.

"I shan't stop you," Morwena replied briskly. "But... I'd hoped you'd understand," she glanced over Eleanor's head, "that, this," gesturing around her at the wider valley, "is more important than just one family. But you're not my prisoner and I won't keep you against your will." Eleanor didn't expect those words. Relief washed over her, she ran to get her satchel from the shelter. The quickened drum of her heartbeat sounded impatient even to her, she knew she couldn't falter now. She returned to Morwena, who had made a chair of branches and sat on it, as if it was a throne, waiting.

"I will explain everything," Eleanor said hesitantly as she drew closer, securing her rucksack over her shoulders, "to my parents, The Council, even Blaydoc if I have to, that you weren't holding me captive." Eleanor fastened both buckles tightly across her chest. "If there's a death warrant, I will tell whoever I need to, it's stupid." Eleanor looked back at the little arched doorway, and for a moment felt herself falter. "Won't you come with me?" she said quietly.

"No, there's too much at risk." She toyed with a handful of leaves, running them through her fingers. "I must find either the Elf or perhaps the Imp, they might help to explain a few things." Eleanor bit the top of her fur tunic; listening to the wind dancing through the meadow grasses.

"You should hurry," Morwena said, "*Dark Exchange* isn't far away."

"Where will you go?"

"Southwest - between Arramond and Caradoc, my movements might encourage *The Darkness* away from Vearmoor."

"And mine?" Eleanor suddenly went cold, colder than she had been for a while.

"I doubt neither you or I will make that great a difference." Eleanor wasn't sure she was telling the truth.

"I'll go," she said and took one more look around the valley that had been her home for the last few *Turns*.

"Then take this." Morwena held a delicate silvery web in the palm of her hand.

"But, it's yours.... and er... I couldn't."

"I will make another," Morwena said.

"You can make them?" Eleanor almost sputtered out her words. Morwena chuckled, her body shook in a way, that made her look almost likeable.

"There wasn't time for your parents to give you one, before you left. This should protect against the unexpected."

Eleanor took the web and held it gently. "How does it work?" she said inspecting the intricacies of the pattern and feeling its silky texture.

"Hold it as if you want it and say the connection spell I taught you." In excitement, Eleanor muttered the spell. It began to sparkle, then it shot off her hand and whizzed around her waist, to her back. Eleanor wriggled and bent her head to watch it slide up her spine and expand across her shoulders. She felt the slightest of tingles as it took hold. The fact there was a ruck sack in the way didn't seem to matter. The slivery glow faded and she could hardly tell she had it on.

"Wow... that's... uh... thanks." Eleanor held onto her rope, "and it's been surreal."

"Huh," the old Sprite shook her head. "Now go... before I change my mind." Eleanor studied the grey outline along the ridge. She could feel Morwena's gaze intense and critical, as she set off and suddenly wanted to run, she knew what Morwena's change of heart was like.

"Ask the bees for help," Morwena called, after Eleanor had gone a little way, "they will come."

Eleanor didn't look back; she didn't want to be persuaded to stay, it was too late for that. She felt already wildly nervous about crossing The Moors alone. She would never have had the strength to do that before. She continued on, scrambling over the boulders and up the muddy path. She reached the second ridge slower than she hoped and pulling herself over. Resting to catch her breath. She looked around the valley for one last time. Morwena wasn't anywhere to be seen. The valley lay still, desolate as if they'd never been there. Their shelter and traces of the fire pit were no longer visible. Eleanor blinked and rubbed her eyes, that was ridiculous, she can't possibly have done all that in the time she had only got this far. But the black patch of meadow was replaced by a sea of delicate white flowers. It was beautiful... as if the spirit of Istria had been there herself. She could see the lone gorse bush, once more shrouded in the brightest of yellow flowers. The meadow had grown back, billowing stems of willowy grasses floated gently, as if they were pleased to be there. Eleanor shook her head, Morwena was remarkable.

Eleanor looked out onto the bleak moor, it wasn't making her decision any easier. The full realisation of what she was about to do hit her, like a warning from her father. *Look what you're leaving behind. We will be fine, just stay, be safe.* Her blood pumped faster. Then the thought came to her; why had Morwena let her go without any fuss?

Searching the adjoining hills she tried to calm her mind and see if there were any landmarks she recognised. But nothing looked familiar. She had no idea which way to go, and Morwena hadn't told her either. Which wasn't right, as Morwena loved telling her how to do things in precise detail. Perhaps the old Sprite had decided she was no longer of importance? That she really wasn't *The Wind Whisperer* and it didn't matter if she lived. Eleanor chewed a clump of hair and reached around to touch the web. Something her father said, *be careful Morwena is only interested in you for as long as you are useful to her.*

A yellowy flash of light glistened across her eye, a reflection. It was followed by several more. Not the friendly type, welcome images of friends comings to see you, but hopeful eyes staring at her, waiting. Eleanor wasted no time and transformed. She'd be safer hidden from view, no one could possibly sense she was there, could they? She darted away from the reflection, hoping it was in the right direction of her home.

23

THE WORD OF AN IMP

The yellow beast glided above Daniel, leaving the safety of the slope. Its head swivelled as if on a piece of string, looking at him with green glass eyes, amidst a mop of spiky, yellow head feathers. Daniel wanted to fire an arrow at it, *it was going to give away his position*. It glided on, as Tonurang began to speak.

"You Imps are all so stupid, I live for the day when I actually meet an intelligent one. Hasn't anybody told you how to get into Caradoc the easier way?" Daniel peered through the tall reeds. How was it possible for him to be standing out here in full view? Tonurang splashed his staff into the water, as if announcing his arrival. But Daniel knew what he was doing. Moments later the bog heaved and spluttered as if about to be sick. Then the disfigured body of the dead Imp rose from its depths. Awkwardly and reluctant, the bog gave up its victim. His head tilting, and once bright red hair was dulled with gloppy mud, which clung so thickly, like wet clay being stretched to its limited.

"Oh, it really is pathetic," Tonurang mocked. "At least now the body won't fall into Caradoc and surprise anyone!" He waved his hand in a circle and the body twitched haphazardly into the air. "Take him back to Arramond." The remaining Imp leapt forward to catch his friend. "He is of no use to me." Daniel looked at the scowling face of the rugged giant that cradled the white limbs as if they were the holiest of gifts. A multitude of bulging red veins travelled up his neck and shone proudly through his pale skin.

"Now..." Tonurang said, shaking his cloak. "You're obviously here for a reason." Carefully he flicked a clod of mud from his staff. "Well Doric Vanik, don't you speak? Why are you here and who sent you?" Doric, laid his friend reverently by his feet and stood to his full height. He was a commanding figure, nearly twice as tall as Tonurang. Daniel couldn't understand why he didn't just batter him.

"I've come to see the leader of Eastling Elves, bring him message." Each word he said, spat into the air, like bullets.

"It's your lucky day," Tonurang replied, "that Elf is I... and I've been waiting for you." The Imp raised his arm to silence Tonurang. "My message is... been a change of ruling family - The Garnaforts no longer. My family, the Vaniks, now Arramond's rulers, my brother seeks your support."

"And what do I get in return?" Tonurang demanded.

"The Stone of Innvericum," Doric replied. Daniel's arm slipped and his foot fell into a sludgy pool, disturbing a cluster of dragonflies.

"Did you hear that?" Tonurang snapped. Daniel pulled his foot quietly out of the bog, his mind reeling... *The Stone of Innvericum - their power gift, was he making a joke?*

"There... many strange sounds here," Doric replied.

"No... not those, something else. Yes, that's it... I can sense it – there's an Elf!" he roared, brandishing his staff aloft. Daniel reached for his pouch, his breath tight and short.

"Yes... you didn't know..." Doric jeered.

"What?" Tonurang shouted. Daniel shook and shuddered; he didn't want Tonurang to drag him out by a spell and knew he'd get a better aim, if he faced his enemy. He slowly got to his feet, seeing how little bog there was between them.

"Ahh... the Elfling who won't die," Tonurang snarled and with a swirl of his arm, several water discs skimmed, hopping and jumping at great speed towards him. Ducking, Daniel raised his protection shield. He stood firm, shaking with the effort to dispel each hit.

Several fizzed into the cold bog around his feet, releasing jets of steam.

"So, you've learnt something useful, while you've been here," Tonurang bellowed. "But it won't help Elfling, you're no match for me and neither is your father. He's been destroyed within Caradoc." Tonurang leapt with the agility of a jumping hare. "His allies run to me like flies," he said, "I have taken control of the Trevarak Council."

"That isn't true," Daniel shouted back, deliberately speaking in Naraling. "My father would never let you win. You've no right to rule Caradoc." Tonurang jumped to another clump of grass, as if he was playing a game of chess.

"Are you challenging me, Elfling?"

"No... just telling you the truth," Daniel took his bow and locked an arrow. "What you're doing..." he said, his line on sight on Tonurang's heart, "all this... killing... it's tipping *The Balance*. Soon it won't matter who's in command... we'll all be gone." Daniel felt his actions slow, as the bog began to move and blur around him. He pulled the string tightly.

"Take that thing out of my view." Daniel's bow flew out of his hand and went spinning across the bog. "What you're saying is ridiculous," Tonurang said. "I have spoken to *The Glows* and you're wrong, there's no *Darkness* coming, because I am the rightful leader of Caradoc." A reflection glinted across Daniel's shield; Halgelan. The beast stood proudly with his tree branches stretching into the sky. His whole herd, both flying and walking, covered the hillside.

"You're wrong and you're too stupid to see it." Daniel threw several water droplets at him. Tonurang laughed, which made Daniel even more angry, "And what have you done with our Power Gift?" Daniel bellowed. The Imp drew a thick wooden baton from behind his back. He shouted a series of words that Daniel didn't understand, but it got Tonurang's attention. He then spoke in Naraling; each word resonated across the water.

"He," Doric pointed at Tonurang, "traded your Power Gift for life of Elfling during Fires of Vearmoor." Daniel buckled. *How could the whole of Caradoc's Council and his father be so deceived with a false stone?*

"Enough, Imp, hold your tongue." He turned to Daniel. "See,

your father's a fool! The Trevarak's can't even tell," he paused, "and they're weaker without the real one and that suits me well." Suddenly, hundreds of water droplets appeared, changing Tonurang into a mirage, and it began to rain around him, shooting into the sky and flying overhead. Daniel slid under his shield, urging it to change shape, into something that would protect him. The droplets changed colour as they flew through the air, a multitude of yellows, reds and oranges that jarred against the dull Moorland palate. The herd began to scatter, thundering hooves drummed chaotically. The air filled with wild calls, as if they were urging each other to run faster. One small liquid bubble fell by Daniel's foot, a vivid yellow and spilled across the mud, as if it was a hot poison, fizzing wildly, before, eating the soil and disappear through a hole. Daniel watched, this throat dried and palms clammy; *what Darkness magic was this*? He searched for Halgelan, trying to spot him through the curtain of colour, but couldn't. He caught Doric thundering grunts, "The Seventh Shadow at Rock of Vespic." Daniel's mind whirled, had they just agreed to meet? The grasses swished in response as he realised Doric was running away. With the speed of the Darter Fish, the bog was squelching and sloshing, beaten by the Imp's speed.

"So Trevarak Elfling," Daniel shuddered. "It's just you and I." Tonurang looked strangely taller, with Doric gone. Daniel stood up, the bombardment had stopped and edged onto a drier patch of earth, its boundaries flanked by tall reeds. Halgelan gave a distinct rich, urgent cry that told Daniel he hadn't left him. He wished he could run to The Stagin but, he was no Imp, and the bog was too difficult to cover with any speed. So, he held up his shield ready; his only defence.

"It looks like I don't have to do anything," Tonurang boasted. "I think that *Darkness* Staginourisum will have you for a snack." Daniel reeled around to see what Tonurang was talking about. There wasn't anything Dark about Halgelan and his herd? "And this should stop you from getting away from him." Daniel felt himself suddenly lift off the ground. His back bent into a curve and his head jerked sideward. His arms splayed violently either side, as he began to rotate slowly in a circle. The bog's puddles glinted like silver coins. Tonurang had a mean grin that made him look tormented.

"I wish I had time to watch," he grinned. "Unfortunately, I have a lot to prepare before my meeting with the Imps," he continued, "and to think I accused you of liaising with them and your father's Council believed me." He adjusted his lavish cloak, as water began to swirl around his feet.

"Goodbye, Trevarak Elfling. If only you could follow me home." Daniel struggled against his invisible hold. But it only made him spin more quickly, as if he had become an offering to the sky. The bog, gurgling and squelching, telling him Tonurang was leaving, but he was facing the other way and couldn't see. The noise of the moving water seemed to go on forever. Then came a silence, the moment of awkward indecision. He felt as if The Moors itself was deciding what to do with him. Only the gentle moans from the herd interrupted. Daniel shouted, but no words came out. He tried to see what was wrong with the herd, but nothing would stop his body from spinning. Then suddenly and cruelly he dropped like a stone. He wasn't prepared. Ungainly he plummeted. His body hit something hard and unforgiving. His legs swung awkwardly, missing the ground and sank into cold water. He yowled in pain. He tried to grab hold of the grass, but it came away in his hands. He dug his fingers into the mud, as his feet sank, followed by this leg. His fingers slipping.

"Halgelan," he wheezed, as his body started to follow, below, his waist in water. The cold stung like angry wasps, his feet numb, no longer his own. The muddy embankment and water boundaries blurred as he flayed around for something, anything, to hold on to. Stealthily and unkindly, he felt a pouch slip, edging its way from his tunic pocket. He wriggled to shield its fall. He last felt it touch his knee, on its journey to the depths of the bog. He laid his head onto his shoulder, he should stop trying to resist. He felt cold, tired. *Perhaps The Moors had won, what use was he now?* He thought he heard shouting, he looked up but couldn't see anything except blades and reeds. *Would the Eastlings finally have their wish — ridding Caradoc of both father and Elfling for the end of Trevarak rule? Isaac was already dead, only Karn would be in his way. He failed.* Something sharp knocked his head. He couldn't move. He felt another knock; but as he tried to look up his vision blurred mixing reality with images of home. *Why hadn't his father come out of The Moors to find him, if Tonurang could manage it?* Another knock and a muted void consumed him.

24

SILVERBARK FOREST

Nausea rose in his throat, his head lulled from side to side. But Daniel was soothed by a gentle beat, like the satisfying rhythm played by a contended musician. Was he alive? Or had he passed through to the murky underworld of Caradoc's Terra Algor? Short constant beats, thrum thrum thud... thrum thrum thud... an irregular machine, matched his body's back and forth sway; one side warm, the other cold. He wriggled his fingers, his arms dangled, and damp strands of hair flapped against his exposed skin. The familiar stench of raw animal filled his nostrils as he lifted his head tenderly. The short stubby bristles brushed against his cheek. He rubbed his hand down the mass of brown fur and hoisted himself up. How had Halgelan saved him? He wanted to wrap his arms tightly around the animal, full of gratitude and disbelief. Instead he gingerly swung his legs into position and pushed to sit up. His head ached, his clothes were covered in bog. He looked around; *Dark Exchange* was near. He checked for his bow then remembered how Tonurang had knocked it away. He reached for his belt. A pouch had gone, but it wan't the full one. He still had one left.

Both herds surrounded them; filling the air with flamboyant calls, as they travelled in irregular patterns, intermingling across each other's paths. Daniel checked around. The usual group of beautiful female stagins he'd grown used to seeing, flanked Halgelan, as if they were his guards. But where were the beasts that Tonurang had taunted him with, the ones he had left him to die by? He shuddered - had Halgelan fought them off? He looked at The Stagin's body... he saw the marks of Tonurang's colour magic, patches of raw skin, exposed and weeping. Daniel looked at the nearest female. She too had wounds, but none of them showed any signs of anything more severe. The wind rushed about him in playful gusts. Halgelan made easy work of the steep valley, they were all climbing. But there was a warmth in the air that he hadn't felt before.

Daniel slumped low to Halgelan's neck, completely at the herd's mercy and felt his eyes grow heavy. Several, had already reached the summit and were beginning to sink over the brow. The flying creatures were the first to disappear, as if in a hurry. Halgelan halted, and gave several loud snorts. Daniel sat patiently waiting, as the whole herd trudged by. When every beast had finally passed him, like some elaborate circus, their grunts, snorting and braying its music, Halgelan followed.

The slope steepened quickly. Filled with crooked glistening trees, the silver bark shimmered in the dimming light. Dancing silver and copper leaves; interspersed by narrow twisting paths. Daniel had never seen anything so enchanting. How could The Moors hide such a place? Halgelan slowed to a stilted walk, making Daniel rocked from side-to-side. The rest of the herd had dispersed, disappearing in and out of his view, grazing and resting. While the flying creatures had settled in the branches, their wings folded and heads bowed. Halgelan dug his front legs into the ground and lowered his head. Daniel slid ungracefully to the ground.

"Found a nice patch of grass?" Daniel pulled himself up, rubbing his sore shoulder. "Next time, just a little warning, old friend." He patted Halgelan's neck and held on for a moment. *How could he ever repay him?* Halgelan gave a sharp, angry snort.

"You're just cranky and tired," Daniel said soothingly, "like I am. Everyone's safely here, you've done your job well. Lets eat. I'm gonna, and rest, this is the perfect shelter..." Daniel looked about him. The trees although short gave good coverage and there was something about the silvery colour that felt like a protective layer. The tree branches, arched and bent intermingling into each other. A clump of cob nuts filled the bushes beside him. He set about picking and eating as much as he could.

"Hey, what's up?" he said as he looked up. Halgelan's head swung from side to side, as if he was trying to look directly above him. Daniel shivered, "Come on... there's nothing here. Your herd's content. You can relax." Daniel reached out his hand. "it's okay." Halgelan sidestepped.

"H...?" Daniel's voice lowered to a whisper and watched Halgelan's shiny black eyes darted like a warning. Daniel reached for his remaining pouch, but a blast of air came thundering from nowhere knocking him. He thumped into a trunk, just managing to stay on his feet. Another wind bolt sent debris slamming into his face, in a continuous jet.

"Don't move," a voice came through the wind.

"I can't!" Daniel replied half choking and battling with breathing. Halgelan let out a whimper and angry snort. "And no tricks... do you understand," came the voice in a funny accent, smooth and soft.

"Stop whatever you're doing, I can't see a thing and the herd will leave."

"They're with you?"

"Yes," Daniel spluttered, "turn it off." The wind slowed and he lunged for his pouch, chanting a protection spell. A thin film exploded in front of his outstretched hand and formed a tall strip of water that covered his body. The rest exploded burst everywhere, which wasn't planned.

"Oowha," came an angry voice. Halgelan yelped. Then someone began to splutter and a figure gradually materialised, splayed across the ground, flickering in and out of view, as if it was a mirage. Lying over a thick root, was long black hair clung around a face; coughing mouthfuls of water onto the grass. Followed by a green dress, dull and worn with patches, bound by a thick old rope, which looked just like ones from his boat, used to anchor it to the quay. She rolled onto her side and quickly got to her feet. Daniel noticed something silvery shimmer across her back.

"What did you do that for?" she said between coughs.

"Uh... you blasted me with a *wind*... something or other, and I got a face full of leaves," he replied.

"Well what else could I do? Suddenly all these animals appeared from nowhere." Her eyes shone a bright green, It made him jolt, they were identical to the flying creature he had seen above the bog.

"The water... it didn't hurt you," Daniel took a step closer.

"And?" she backed away, "Were you trying to?"

"Uh, well... no, but usually it does," Daniel said. There was an awkward silence, as she wrung out her skirt, and removed a shoulder bag.

"I'm armed, and I won't hesitate to use it." Shaking the rope at him. "Stand back, I need to dry off." Daniel suppressed a laugh, but did as he was told. She waved her hands around her body and he felt a gentle warm breeze. Her hair was very dark and not the golden colour he'd seen on the Sprite near Vearmoor, but she was no Imp or Pixie. Daniel adjusted his protection shield so that he could defend anything else she was preparing for him.

"Are you alone, Elf," she spied him warily, her clothes and hair now dried. She was busy tying it into a plait.

"Er," Daniel replied.

"Well," she said, "are you alone or not?" Her eyes widened as she finished her hair quickly tying it with a twine from her rope. It glowed a bright golden colour when in her hands.

"Well... technically no. I'm travelling with him," Daniel pointed to the brown horns protruding through the silver branches.

"Are you kidding me?" She smiled.

"He's hiding since you appeared."

"Wow... he's amazing. Is he really with you?"

Daniel nodded. "So he doesn't look like a beast to you?"

"No... he's a Lightness Staginourisum, isn't he? Will he come back out?" she asked, "So I can see him properly."

"Maybe," Daniel shrugged, "but he does what he likes, I just tag along."

"You look... uh... terrible..." She said staring at him in a funny sort of way. Daniel looked down at himself. Suddenly embarrassed by all the mud and torn clothes. A swarm of shadowy insects appeared, flying in army formation and congregated noisily around her head. He could see their black and yellow bodies, their tails glowed similar to her rope. Surprised, she seemed pleased to see them, making no effort to beat them off. Then out of her mouth came a series of clicks and buzzes. Daniel watched in amazement clutching his shield tightly. In moments they flew away, a line of glowing yellow into the distance.

"Did you just talk to them?"

"Uh... yeah," she said challengingly. "So." She adjusted her fur and fastened the front buttons.

"So apart from being friends with those things,"

"They're bees."

"What are you doing here?"

"Going home. And I'm not alone... so don't try anything." A long-eared female stagin came slowly up to Daniel. He couldn't help but smile as he reached out his hand and she nuzzled it. He had spent a whole *Turn* back in the valley by Vearmoor trying to get her to do that.

"There's another Sprite," she interrupted, "and very close. She's really powerful. I wouldn't even pick a fight with her."

Daniel's stomach lurched. "Who?" he asked.

She hesitated, "You wouldn't know her."

"Tell me," Daniel felt his anger rise.

She took a step back. "Morwena du Gwent," she said, "one of the most powerful Tribelings of NaraRose, she'll be here any moment, so don't get angry." Daniel spied her defiance stance, and knew she was lying. "So why are you here?" Images of his trial, the watery, blue wood of the shields, the bright yellow Glows across the ceiling. His father's warm arms... the words Morwena...

"Elf... Elf?"

Daniel blinked. "This Sprite of yours. Is she really coming."

Her expression changed and she hesitated, one of those long moments of decision, before she said quietly, "When I left," her rope coiled around her hand, "Morwena performed a complicated spell, containing the four Power Elements of NaraRose.

"I know it," Daniel replied, "The Combinodium Spell."

"Yeah, that's the one. Well, when she'd finished, your Element was cast out full of *The Darkness*." Daniel ground his fingernails into the palm of his hand. "You're the second Tribeling to tell me this in less than two *Turns*."

"Morwena had learnt of you alone on The Moors," Eleanor continued. "She was trying to find you or a lone Imp, but has headed off in the opposite direction, she could be anywhere by now."

25

FOURTEEN TURNS AND SEVEN
SHADOWS

The trees looked like a tangled web of ghostly silhouettes. Nothing warm or friendly about them, like her home. And the Elf, Eleanor thought, had suffered. Her initial fears quickly dissipating at his wet and battered appearance.

"How does she know I'm out here?" he asked, his blue eyes darted like a wild, lost animal.

"Not sure," Eleanor replied. "She seems to know lots of things that doesn't make sense to me." The leaves rustled and branches swayed, playing a whooshing shrill note, that got louder, then quieter. She mumbled something but he ignored her, locked in his own thoughts. "I'm a Sprite, like Morwena," Eleanor decided it was best to keep talking. He looked up at her, as if she was crazy. "It's the hair isn't it?" she blundered, wishing she would just be quiet.

"Guess so... I saw a few Sprites close to Vearmoor and one of them had golden hair." He looked at her closely. " you look different to them, but you're no Imp, so that doesn't leave much."

"You saw another Sprite?" Eleanor felt her blood run cold.

"Yeah, by your border. An old grey-bearded one and one about my age trapped in some sort of bubble thing - weird."

"Was she ok?" Eleanor caught her breath.

"Yeah, looked it," he replied. "Why?"

"It was my sister..." Eleanor replied. *So Elerday had made it home.*

'She just vanished." The Elf continued. She was shouting, then disappeared in green smoke." There was an awkward silence. *This Elf knew which way Vearmoor was.* An animal let out a wild howl.

"I need shelter," he said, suddenly turning his back. It was as if the howl had awoken him from a dream.

"But," she replied, "you're just going to go?"

"Just point me in the direction Morwena went," he replied, his words sounded more like a challenge than a request. Eleanor looked around searching the forest in an almost impossible twilight. Every shadow played tricks and offered no escape. Her nerve was beginning to fail. She couldn't really tell which way she'd come.

"I can't tell you where Morwena's gone, I left before she did," Eleanor said her stomach tightening. The Staginourisum suddenly rose behind Daniel like a towering shadow. She watched the Elf stroke his nose, as if he was his only friend in the world.

"Then we're both lost," he said and leapt with incredible agility onto its back.

"Where are you going Elf?" She felt her heartbeat rising.

"Shelter... like I said, and it's Daniel, not Elf." he replied. "Halgelan will show me, I don't want to wait here for a *Dark Exchange* creature to come." The Stagin pawed his front foot. "And ," he continued, "he's ready to go." Eleanor looked about her; she didn't have any time to think.

"Wait," she said, as he was already disappearing into the mist.

"What?" He face set, taunt and serious.

"I... I," Eleanor cursed herself for sounding weak. "I'm coming with you."

"But. you're going home. It's that way, and I don't need you."

"But we can hardly see a thing, and will be better surviving together?"

"How do I know, that you won't just kill me in my sleep?" He said as he managed to stop the Stagin from prancing.

"My word." Eleanor shuddered. He sighed and looked irritated, then nodded. "If you can keep up."

*

"Here?" she said, trying not to sound too anxious.

"Yes, we stay where Halgelan decides. It'll be safest." He looked at her with annoyance. "I will make a protection dome." He didn't ask for help or tell her what to do. Eleanor stared at the gnarly short moss-covered trunk of a tree. Its branch dripped on her as she touched it. A stream gurgled past, tumbling around thick roots and bubbling over angular rocks. She wished it would stop, it was making her feel colder. She shivered and thought longingly of Morwena's amazing shelter, her warm fire and endless supply of food. She perched uncomfortably on a damp lichen-covered stone, watching his sweeping arm glide through the air, controlling a blue film of silvery water. She needed to do something. So set about drying the surrounding rocks to sit on. His dome complete, he stook like a ghostly thin silhouette rubbing his shoulder.

"How long have you been on The Moors?"

"Fourteen *Turns*," he turned to look at her, "and seven *Shadows*." His stare blank.

"That's long." His clothes hung from his frame and part of his, once smart tunic, lay torn, with only the strap of his bow holding it all together. Exposed scars flickered red across his bare forearms.

"Have you met other Tribelings?"

"Do Sprites have protection spells?" He ignored her and stood with his hand outstretched dancing water droplets from one side to the other as if they were toys.

"Yes."

"Can you perform one?"

"Uh..." She'd only just learnt it and hadn't done one alone, but there was no way she was going to tell him that. "Then, I'd add it to this. I don't know if mine will work for Sprites." He set off to start in a different area.

"Did you know how to do one before being out on The Moors?" Eleanor asked as she hesitantly got up.

"No wah," he said as if she'd told him his trousers had fallen down.

"So have you seen a *Darkness* creature?" His stare went cold. "You talk a lot." She shivered. "In a copse…" he said, "I was attacked. Halgelan came… I learnt quickly after that."

"And he stops them from getting close… And other Tribes, have you seen any?"

"Stop talking," he barked.

Eleanor's hand shock as she raised it to start. She was relieved it was so dark. Beads of sweat formed across her forehead. *If it worked, she was about to lock herself in somewhere with a miserable angry foreign Tribeling.* She chanted her spell quietly and held her rope in the water. It turned dull and droplets ran down its spirals. She tried over and over, but each time the light wouldn't expel into the film. She kept looking behind her to see if he was watching, but he wasn't. He had managed to make a strange blue flamed fire amongst stones and somehow, without her seeing, was cooking a mangled animal over it. He sat hunched and sullen. She quietly swore to herself. This was going to be a long difficult *Dark Exchange*. She wrenched the rope violently and flicked it at the film. Through an angry snarl, she spat out the words of her spell. Within seconds, her rope glowed brightly; a golden film shot from the end and filled the water. It travelled quickly around the circle and over the ceiling of the dome.

"Wow," she jumped back and wiped her hand across her forehead. Casually she went over to sit by his strange fire.

"Pixie?" he said, without even looking up at her. It took Eleanor a moment to work out why he'd said that. "Were they friendly?"

"Yeah…" He pulled a small bit of meat from the cooked flank and crammed it into his mouth. Eleanor's stomach groaned. *Surely he would offer her some?*

"Are you going to find Morwena when *Light Exchange* comes?"

"No."

"Oh…"

"The Rock of Vespic."

"Why?"

"Because Caradoc's fate will be decided there," his replied was flat.

"Your home?" Eleanor quizzed. Daniel nodded and finally offered her some meat. "There's a meeting, between Elves and Imps.'

"So why is that so important to you?"

"The Elves are Eastlings, and I'm a Trevarak." Eleanor looked into the blue flame. *Why was that so bad?*

'So doesn't that sort of thing happen all the time?" Eleanor was trying to work out her Elf history. Who's, who, but little was coming to her.

Daniel handed her another carcass leg. There wasn't much meat on it, but neither was his share. "The Eastlings want to overthrow the Trevaraks and use the Imps to help them." Eleanor wasn't sure she'd heard him correctly. A gentle wind teased its way around her shoulders and whispered within her ears. She looked at the Elf's face and saw his once neatly cut hair that now lay in irregular lengths.

"But that could upset *The Balance*," she whispered.

"I know. And it has, you've seen it." Eleanor looked into the flames "So why are you out here and not in there fighting with your family?"

"My father banished me onto The Moorlands?" Her chest tightened.

"You're own father?"

"Yeah, well and his Council."

"Why?"

"Because I killed an Elf," his sharp blue eyes glared, as if challenging her next move. Eleanor shook her head, she was trapped within a protection dome with a killer... she bit her tongue and chewed the side of her mouth. None of it made sense. Killing someone... in Vearmoor he would have been fed to the Gods.

"Why did you kill him?" She tried to calm her voice.

"He was trying to kill my brother." Eleanor ground her foot into the mud. She watched the goo ooze around her boot.

"Have you any idea where this Rock place is?"

"No," he said, "but I'm hoping Halgelan will take me."

"Does Morwena know you've killed an Elf?"

"No…"

"My father told me to try and find her, she would help. I'm willing to risk her anger.

"So your father did try and help you too?"

"It's complicated." He threw the bones of the carcass over his shoulder. "Look - she might be the only one who could break the spell that prevents me from going home. If she is, and I know the plans between the Imps and Eastling Elves, I could warn my family." The Elf stabbed his dagger into the ground. The sound rippled through Eleanor. "Perhaps… then I could stop the fighting before it starts, so Ostric doesn't come." His shoulders sagged. Eleanor could feel the hopelessness fill the air. He would never succeed.

"I might be able to help…" The words flew out of her mouth before she was ready to say them and immediately she wanted to retract each one as Daniel's face changed, softened. She had offered him something she wasn't sure she was able to give and wasn't sure she wanted to do. "I…," she stammered, "could ask the bees where The Rock is," she said quietly.

"Why would you help me?" Eleanor looked away. There was something about that slanted grin, the only real sign of hope she'd seen, since she'd meet him.

26

THE ROCK OF VESPIC

With his shoulders level, Daniel slammed his body against the rock, hoping that this time it would shift. But again it didn't. He and the Sprite had agreed that this was the best spot to try, but she wasn't helping! She'd done one of her disappearing tricks and had gone missing.

"Hurry," Eleanor reappeared like the arrival of his mother, unexpected and annoyingly. She made him jump. A set frown fixed across her face. "It's the sixth *Shadow*, I'm sure of it," Eleanor said with urgency, "so we've only got one left, before you said they'd be here." He bit his lip, trying to remember that he was really grateful for her help in finding The Rock. If it hadn't been for those bees he would have never got there at all, let alone on time.

"I know," Daniel said, between rasped breaths. A squawk pierced the air, sending a shiver through him. The yellow flying thing he'd seen over the bog swooped along the rock face. Once more it looked as if it was looking for something. He was beginning to think that it was following him. "Can you get rid of it," Daniel shouted.

"No," she replied, sounding indignant. "It's not gonna hurt you." Daniel wasn't so sure, as it landed gracefully, and started to preen its back feathers. She walked towards it muttering and holding out her hand. The creature extended its talons and bowed its head. Its long head feathers dropped either side of his beak. Daniel edged against the rock, the talons looked like they could rip his eyes out.

"I'm sure," Eleanor said crouching down with her hand stretched out, palm flat, "this is the same one that's friends with Morwena. There can't be many other hairy yellow birds like this on The Moors. Or are there?"

"I've seen one before, last *Turn*, but I couldn't tell if this is a different one. And... what did you call it?"

"A bird..." she looked at him as if he was really stupid. "Its name apparently is Luxylan."

Daniel grimaced, "Nothing flies in Caradoc."

Eleanor fixed him with a look, that he really couldn't understand, then said, "Maybe Morwena's near, if only I knew how to speak to it, I could ask where she is."

"Try," Daniel brushed grit from his face. "But quick, if either the Elves or Imps spot him, it'll make them suspicious."

Daniel turned back to the rock he was trying to break and quickly became lost in the task of its destruction. He threw a water droplet aiming at its weakest point, but it didn't do much, only made a few cracks.

"Daniel, look," Eleanor said, breaking his concentration. He turned to see she had given up with the bird and had climbed to a vantage point. She was pointing northwards. He grabbed his pouch to cast a viewing spell and ran around the rock line.

"No," he agonised, "not yet."

"Do you know who they are?"

"Yes, we've the time it takes for them to reach the southern edge of the bog, before they'll sense me." He ran back. When they first got to The Rock of Vespic, they had tried to work out where the Elves and Imps might meet. So had decided to hide inside the rock at the closest vantage point. He had no idea what he was going to do if they couldn't break the rock.

"They'll kill us if they find us out here," he yelled, "isn't there anything you can do?"

"I thought you were the survivalist," Eleanor appeared by his side brandishing her rope. "Stand back," she said as she swung it into the air, circling several times so it got longer and longer It glowed and grew, like a living thing. Daniel flinched, he still couldn't get used to it.

"They won't see that, will they?" He craned to see how far the beams were projecting.

"Shh," Eleanor hissed, "you're distracting me." She flung the rope at the rock. Instantly it shattered, sending a cascade of shards tumbling. The loud whack sent Luxylan screeching into the air. Eleanor heaved the rope back along the ground, until it shrank in size and she was able to retie it around her waist. Daniel rushed in.

"Not bad," he grimaced, "and I think that also got rid of the bird thing. Where did you learn that?" Daniel said as he pulled the last few stones away.

"I didn't," she replied, "but you weren't getting anywhere..."

Daniel let Eleanor climb in first - she'd earned it. He followed her in, covering their traces, making sure the gap was properly sealed. It took some time, but with every rock that went into place, it made him feel safer. He hoped, being inside the rock would mean the Elves wouldn't sense his presence.

"Can't see a thing.," Daniel whispered as he put the final stone into place.

"Yes, we can," Eleanor touched her rope; the glow was just enough. The walls dripped with a sticky liquid, reeking of dank earth. It reminded Daniel of the tunnel he'd climbed through to get out of Caradoc. But, this was narrower, hemming him in, so he had to twist sideways. All he had to hope now was, he'd chosen the right place and they could see and hear what was going on.

"I think there's gaps in the rock above."

"Can you reach them?"

"I'll try." Eleanor led the way and made it look easy. She climbed quickly, clearly used to it. "It's better up here." Daniel used his arm and legs as levers but kept slipping. It took him longer.

"Look," Eleanor hissed peering through a thin crack. Daniel found a hole lower down and pulled away the fern leaves. Cooler air flooded in. To his relief he could see The Moors stretched out below. On the skyline loomed the distinctive outline of Imps.

"I never wanted to see them again," Eleanor muttered. Daniel shuffled uncomfortably, he had heard about The Great Fires of Vearmoor and what cost the Sprites had paid at the hands of the Imps.

"The Elves are nearly here..." he said looking northwards, spotting Tonurang at once. The distinctive Elf was out in front, striding purposefully, a team of six trailing in his wake. Daniel recognised Thansim, a Trevarak Council member, she'd been at his trial. Clearly now a traitor. Stones clattered down the fissure passed him.

"What's up?" he called up to Eleanor.

"We can't risk being sensed," she spluttered. "You said so yourself and I'm thinking this rock won't do much." She began to utter a spell Daniel didn't understand and a film of thin dust came weaving towards him through the murky light. Her eyes shone a vivid green making her look witch- like. Daniel edged away as the dust came towards him.

"Don't move. Let the film cover you."

"But I can use a water shield."

"You can't, remember what you said, it'll be detected. If I use the Sprite's protection spell – hopefully it'll work over you, and there'll be less chance they'll sense a thing."

"But yours comes from your rope..."

"I've just thought of this, I think it'll work..." Daniel stayed as still as he could, watching the ghostly dust blanket float towards him. Silently he prayed to Caradoc's Water Lord. It felt soft, oddly warm, but stifling and for a moment he thought he wasn't going to be able to breathe. It hit the ground around his feet and hovered as if it didn't want to touch something cold and wet. He took several short breaths as it settled. Trapped inside the dust he peered back though. Everything was now covered in a grainy haze. He closed his eyes and shuddered. Imp and traitor Elf would soon decide the fate of his family.

27

RATS WITH RED EYES

The Elves stood like stone pillars. They were not as Eleanor imagined, but taller, majestic looking. With an air of superiority, that suggested to her, they thought they should rule NaraRose above everyone else. They looked nothing like Daniel. Maybe it was their longer face and noses, compared to his angular yet soft expressions; or it was their perfectly straight, neat, hair, to his wavy mess. Even their clothes suggested sophistication, the blue embroidered cloaks, smart and austere to Daniel's battered old jacket. Whatever it was, Eleanor found it hard to believe they were from the same Tribe.

"Do you know them?" she whispered.

"Some," he replied. "That one, there, was one of the Trevarak Council, SHE banished me." Eleanor examined her in close detail. Her black hair wasn't too dissimilar to hers, but she wore it in a plaited style, she'd never seen before. Standing slightly to one side of her male companions, she carried a long grey stick with a metal emblem at the top in the shape of a fish. A thin silver sword protruded from the folds of her long woollen skirt. Her face was curved in sharp points and her eyes darted in murky pools. A hazy mist lingered around her legs, spreading around them all and extending to parts of the Rock. It had appeared when they arrived.

Eleanor wondered if it was their protection spell, blazon for all to see, a warning they trusted no one.

Reluctantly and slowly she turned her gaze across the narrow patch of Moorland. Her Grandsprite had died because of this Tribe's brutality. She had watched Anna that *Turn*, trying to defend their neighbourhood. Her courage and strength had made them all proud, but it was not enough against their speed. She fell at the hands of an Imp twice her size. Breaking her like a fragile dry twig, with not a flicker of remorse. The war had ended soon afterwards, leaving her family forever wishing, if only Anna had hung on a little longer.

Red hair, highlighted their roguish features, every strand stood up on end. Their alabaster skin was so much whiter than she remembered, now illuminated against the dull Moorland sky, exuding a ghostly appearance. An Imp stepped forwards. A shiver ran down her spine, as he held aloft a short dagger with an unusual emblem carved into the handle and down the blade. He shouted a series of words Eleanor didn't understand. She followed the thin wiry tail down the wood, as it materialised into the image of a rat with startling red gems for eyes. In response, the female Elf banged her stick twice and a flag unfurled. A simple white shield, with a blue cross and a picture in one corner Eleanor couldn't quite see. Daniel grumbled under his breath.

No one said a word. Even the relentless Moorland breeze calmed, to a weary meander through the rocks. Eleanor held her breath and felt the thick blanket of silence press heavily over their hideout. The game of stares and intentions was plain to see, and she had no idea who would break it.

Eventually, the Imp who she decided must be their leader bowed, allowing his elaborate headdress room to show off. Its black and red feathers looked a bit like the rat on his dagger. It covered most of his hair and neck. "It's been a while, Tonurang," he said, "leader of the Eastling Elves... or should I now say leader of Caradoc?" Daniel's clenched fist thumped a rock.

"Indeed, Orran of the Vanik family, it's been too long," Tonurang replied. "I'm pleased to see you've kept your word. It's of course a great pleasure to see you again, Doric," Tonurang said, as he pushed his way out of the protective line to stand alone. "I trust there are no hard feelings from events of last *Turn*?" Eleanor tried to see whom Tonurang had address that to. It was a tall, strong looking Imp to his side. The Imp didn't reply. Tonurang continued, "I believe... you and I, Orran Vanik, are in need of each other's help?"

"Indeed, Tonurang Elf Eastling. And... your rise to power is to be congratulated?"

"Yes, The Trevaraks are falling over themselves to die or become loyal to my cause."

Daniel hit something again; this time the sound resonated around their hideout.

"Shh," she whispered and prayed he wouldn't do anything stupid to risk both of their lives.

"After so many unfortunate happenings within Caradoc, it's no wonder," Tonurang gloated. "I don't know why I've waited for so long," and turned to laugh with his companions. "I believe your battle within Arramond happened by chance? I hear you have overthrown the Garnafort family because their young Fire Maker decided to escape?"

"That is correct Tonurang," Orran replied. "You always surprise me by how much you know. Your sources are loyal."

"Yet you haven't won over all the Elders," Tonurang said, "or their families, including that one in the South what are they called?"

"Crewantal,"the Imp Tonurang had spoke to earlier spat. "I would be happy to take you to them."

"Doric," Orran smiled and laid a hand on his shoulder. The giant Imp silenced. "But my dear Tonurang," Orran went on, "I hear the same is true within Caradoc... or else you wouldn't be here?"

"Indeed, as always Orran - the wise. Your words speak the truth. We need your speed and strength in our final battle against The Council. I need to crush their leader, Noah Trevarak, and his remaining loyal Elders."

Eleanor felt a shiver run through her back and lodge in her stomach. She swivelled to look at Daniel. It suddenly dawned on her, who he actually was. Of course, it was so obvious. How hadn't she seen it before? He wasn't just one of the families of Trevarak he was the Elfling of the Trevarak ruler. His father would be the only one powerful enough to stop him from being killed. No wonder they were here and Daniel was so keen to know what was happening.

"Are you alright?" she whispered into the dark. His pale blue eyes shone with anger as he looked back at her. "You can't do anything, Daniel," she said, "there are too many of them." He didn't reply as he turned back to keep watching.

"And what do I get in return?" Orran asked. "Call it a gesture of good will, before I come and fight in Caradoc."

"I will help you in the matter of a Fire-Maker whom I believe is of interest to you," Tonurang replied.

"I've had two search parties looking for her," Orran replied angrily, "and they haven't found a thing. She must be dead by now. So what could you possibly know?"

"Indeed not, she's very much alive. And I can tell you where she is, as soon as you enter Caradoc. And when Caradoc is mine, we'll support the Vanik Tribe as rulers of Arramond, to crush the opposition."

"Deal done, Elf. We have an agreement."

"Daniel," Eleanor whispered, "where are you?" The space on his ledge was empty and her blood ran cold. She touched her rope pushing the glowing light lower into the fissure. Daniel's face loomed up at her and flashed with pain. "What's wrong?" she said urgently.

"My leg, it's stuck, the ledge... gave way." She adjusted her position and shuffled around, the rock began to shake. She glanced through the gap, an Elf's face stared straight at her, their eyes locked. Beyond the Elf, loomed a large, dark figure. Something reminded her of the time in the valley when Morwena had conjured the terrible spell. She pulled her head back slowly moving into the shadows and let go of her rope. Surely the Elf hadn't seen her? Surely, he hadn't heard Daniel fall - *he hadn't*.

"Daniel, we've got to get out of here." Eleanor whispered.

"Why? They've not gone yet and my foot's stuck." She could hear the Imps laughing as she climbed from her ledge. *Why were they laughing?* It made her feel sick.

"I think I've just been seen me."

"That's impossible - surely your protection spell would..."

"I think he did, because I think he was using a Darkness spell." Eleanor shocked as she scrambled down towards Daniel.

"You're not making sense," he hissed. She frantically pulled at bits of rock around his trapped foot.

28

A FLICKERING CANDLE

Daniel's forehead dripped with perspiration. His ankle throbbed as he tried to keep up with Eleanor, who'd already reached the breakout point.

"Wait," he grabbed her shoulder, "you're going to have to tell me why we're risking everything."

"They've seen us, well more like me... I'm sure of it. And I can feel something else."

"But it's not worth going out there," Daniel said. "Even if they saw you, we're safer in here." Daniel shook his head, "The Imps will get us and..." Eleanor pulled at the stones. "Like I said, I think they'll be busy. Daniel yanked her shoulder, "don't Sprite." Wishing he'd never let her join him. But she was too quick for him.

He could see The Moors beyond her silhouette and knew that, in only a matter of moments he would be discovered by Tonurang and ripped to pieces by Imps. He lunged again, but she transformed in an instant, disappearing through the gap. Daniel thumped the rock in frustration. *That was how she could go, without worrying about it - he was never going to trust her again.* Daniel scrambled after her; at least out there he'd have room to fight. Every part of him alive with warnings. The cool breeze seeped into his whirling mind. He raised his protection shield and clung to the rock trying to become as small as a pebble.

"What?" Daniel could hear Tonurang bellowing.

"Sire, did you hear that whistling?" Daniel wondered if it was Eleanor. "And, I can sense Elf!"

"That's impossible," Tonurang roared. "What's going on?"

An Imp shouted, "Why are you preparing yourselves, Elves?"

Daniel drew his shield in tighter and pressed even harder into the cold slab. The wind gusty and playful, flicked and buffeted him. Eleanor was right, there was an odd feeling in the air. It had strength to it, a purpose. He began to move away from the voices, edging out of sight.

"There," an Imp shouted, pointing directly at him. Daniel threw rapid-fire droplets in response, but the Imp was too fast and leapt agilely onto the rocks above him.

"We're being watched," Orran bellowed, "by more Elves. Tonurang is this your idea of a joke?" A flash of golden light, lashed through the air. The Imp howled in pain as it wiped across his back and sent him tumbling down the rock side, landing in front of Daniel, unconscious and still. Daniel swore if he survived, he might take it back about her. His gaze rose to see Tonurang's face dark and cold as stone, bubbling with suppressed anger. His comrades looking as if they had seen their first *Darkness* Creature.

"You're meant to be dead! This must be a trick!" he roared. "Kill him." Daniel weaved his shield into a curved dome and sidestepped the Imp to gain ground.

"So tell me Tonurang," a croaky voice rang over the rocks, loud and deadly. Everyone froze. "Leader of the Eastling Elves - what business do you have with the likes of Orran Vanik of the Imp Tribe?"

"Show yourself, or I speak no more," Tonurang replied. A gaggle of laughter peeled and echoed. Daniel eyes bolted about like loose springs, *surely that wasn't Eleanor?* Then a single figure appeared, hovering between the Tribes, suspended in mid-air, like a puppet without any strings. Firstly, a black cloak, then a flash of yellow. The hood flung aside to reveal a mass of wild hair, and a wrinkled, weathered face. Daniel shuddered.

Tonurang extravagantly lifted his arms. "Aa hah!" he said. "We have Sprite royalty in our midst, Morwena au Leona du Gwent of the Sprite Elite. For what do we owe this pleasure?" He gave a deep bow. Daniel, in a trance, moved his water shield aside to look at the Sprite his father had told him to find.

Her face showing little emotion as she replied, "Flattery, Tonurang, that is worrying."

Two Imps leapt from their positions, as if in response to her voice and bounded across the ground and into the air.

"No... wah!" Daniel shouted. Morwena's head turned like the fixed swivel of an owl, her eyes zooming in on him. The Imps, as if hitting something invisible abruptly veered off course and fell in a muddled heap.

"So you're not alone, Morwena," Tonurang said. "It's to be expected I suppose, but aren't you losing your touch? Two cumbersome Imps and you needed him to help you notice. Well, well, well, maybe you've been out of Vearmoor for too long?"

"Enough, Tonurang. We are not all as violent as you."

"So," Tonurang continued, "I am intrigued, what are you doing with that Elf – a banished one for that matter - of no importance?" Morwena didn't reply. Tonurang continued, "because, Orran, you see he's not with us." Daniel felt everyone turn to look at him, including Morwena; her black steely eyes made him cold.

"I have no care for that Elf," she replied, "I didn't bring him." And she carelessly flicked her hand, as if he was a worthless bit of dirt. Momentarily a haze blocked his view, then something like a pillow hit his chest, lifting him into the air. He catapulted backwards and landed amongst purple heather. Raucous laughter, and a cruel cackle filled his head, as he tumbled across the ground. The last thing Daniel heard was the word *Caradoc*, as he rolled over a lip and dropped down a steep slope. Clawing frantically, he ground his nails into the mud and gasped for breath, slowing to a halt. Using a jutting tree root, he scrambled up and hurriedly climbing back to the top. Cautiously, he peered over.

"You're a fool for taking this so far," Morwena was shouting, her cloak bobbing up and down, like a flaying beast. Something had changed, the Imps were on the attack and Orran was heading for

Morwena. With one long white limb he ruthlessly grabbed her ankle, yanking her to the ground. Tonurang strode over and drew out his pouch. He stood over her and bragged, "Who's the more powerful now?"

Morwena pulled herself to her feet and patted the dust from her clothes. "Keep you hound dog in check, Elf," she replied. Tonurang threw what was in his hand towards the rocks above her. The rest of the Elves followed his lead; so a bombardment of water disks, like a running river flew through the air. There was an enormous crack followed by an avalanche of stones.

"Orran," Tonurang was moving away. "I'll leave you to have the satisfaction of finishing this thing. I think she has disturbed us enough." The Imp stood tall, making Morwena look like a hare trapped by its hunter. "My pleasure," he replied.

"Our deal still stands," Tonurang said, having already reached the far side of the rocks. "Four *Turns* from now at the Eastern entrance to Caradoc." "It's coming to an end, you're weak, Morwena, that's plain for all to see. And as soon as I have control of Caradoc and regain *The Stone of Innvericum*, you, including anyone else will find it impossible to stop me."

"We'll be there," Orran replied. Daniel fleetingly glimpsed what he thought a flickering candle, fading in and out of view as it tumbled amongst the falling rocks.

"Eleanor..." Daniel shouted impulsively and leapt from his hiding place. A reply floated, errily etched and weak. He sent a barrage of water droplets into the backs of the Imps, as he ran on into the blur of reds and white, swirling leaves and batons. The Imps darted in all directions. He charged on blindly. A spell sprung from instinct. An enormous water jet shot into the air. But, through the silvery wave, something sliced into his hand. The spell fizzed out of control as he fell clutching his pulsating and burning hand. Dazed and confused, he choked at the smell of coarse ash filled his lungs. Paces in front, Eleanor's rope flickered a weak yellow glow, on and off, as it floated like a lone feather to the ground.

"Let's finish them," an Imp roared.

29

THE ELFLAND BOW

The tips of muscular long pale fingers dug into Daniel's collarbone. Each sharp nail pressed his skin into a curved divot.

"Well this should be easy," came the course voice. The Imp's breath smelt like stale meat. His captor's body was emblazoned with creamy, white lines weaved in all directions, forming an elaborate network. It might explain, Daniel thought, how there was little evidence of the effects of Tonurang's water disk. Perhaps that was their protection shield. He hadn't been so lucky; his hand still throbbed. A deep cut oozed and glowed a bright red. Daniel looked over his captor's shoulder at Orran, who had spoken, he was nestled between his warriors

"The Sprite is dead," an Imp said sharply, as he broke from Orran's ranks. "Why were you bothering to protect her?" Doric wore a curious expression, as if he was seeing Daniel for the first time.

"She…" Daniel could hardly look at Eleanor lying on the floor. It was all his fault - he should have sent her away, told to her go home. "She… helped me."

"Why are you talking to him, brother?" Orran interrupted and pushed Doric aside.

"Because I have seen him before." Doric replied. Orran spat at Daniel's feet. "Where?" he sneered.

"At the Great Bog, where my servant drowned, he was there." Doric raised his baton and jammed it into Daniel's neck.

"How did you survive that beast?" he said, pushing the baton in deeper. Daniel choked, struggling for breath. "He isn't a beast," Daniel said hoarsely, watching the orangey tinges of Doric's black eyes glow. "He's a Light Stagin," Daniel muttered.

"Why are you interested. brother?" Orran wiped his blade across his outspread hand.

"Because that beast was not a Staginourisum, it was a Natajaw!"

"Does it matter?" Orran knocked his brother's shoulder. "What matters is this Elf has listened to our plans. He could ruin them... And he let Iran die in the bog – you should enjoy his death even more?" Doric lowered his gaze to the ground and withdrew from Daniel.

"Do I make myself clear brother," Orran sneered."

Doric lowered onto one knee. "Yes sire – my apologies," he replied. Out of the corner of his eye, Daniel glanced at Eleanor - *how could she be dead?* He closed his eyes.

"Goodbye, Elf, I shall convey your last moments to your worthless mother when I see her," Orran turned and with the speed of an arrow thumped Daniel in the stomach. He doubled over, folding like a pack of cards. "Just before she dies," his hot breath filled Daniel's ear as he knelt on the floor, his head lulling.

"Now... make it quick, brother. We are going in search of Morwena, she can't have got far. Come and join us once you've finished." Daniel heard their footsteps thud against the hard Moorland floor. Doric remained, his presence looming and real. Daniel coughed up a mixture of blood and phlegm, feeling his injustices mount. His rapid and cruel banishment, his father's part in it all, his stupid and unhelpful, misleading advise - Morwena wasn't going to help him. The mindless cruelty of Tonurang, and worst of all, Eleanor's death alone on a patch of grass, miles from her home, he had never meant for that to happen. She should never have been there. He no longer cared about his home, and what happened to it.

Shimmering lines of black appeared from his hands. He couldn't stop it. He'd become the spell. No longer the master, as it flew in wild circles, growing bigger and bigger. Rushing water ran across the open ground. His arms trembled, releasing his anger on anything that moved.

*

When Daniel woke, The Moor before him was eerily empty. The ground was sodden as if a patchy lake had formed. Daniel spotted Doric, standing alone, on a distance ridge. Distinctive, yet hazy. He thumped his chest as their eyes met and punched the air, just before he ran away.

"Eleanor..." Daniel struggled to his pull himself up, weighed down by the gooey mud. Dark bruises were wrapped thickly around his wrists, as he limped on his hands and knees towards her.

"I wouldn't lose you to an Elf," a voice said above him. Morwena floated to the ground and dropped by Eleanor's side. She changed Eleanor's position, so that she lay on her back with her arms folded neatly against her body.

"She's not dead, is she?" Daniel shuddered.

"No," Morwena said, "but I have to be quick, she's fading."

"What can I do?" Daniel heaved a massive shudder.

"Nothing," Morwena said, "you're good for nothing... shh, I have to work." Daniel fell away as Morwena took a handful of soil and crushed it carefully in her palm. Then, scurrying about like a mouse, collecting moss and heather, sniffing each bit, discarding some, before she was satisfied with her mixture. Grinding it together, she placed it on top of the soil, like a tenderly cradled baby. Then, scooping it up, she sprinkled it in a line, slowly from Eleanor's chin, to her stomach and finally in a cross, which passed over her heart. Morwena began to chant a spell, with her hands held together. A soft whitish glow emerged from the line of soil, floating like a silk blanket and engulfed Eleanor.

"Come closer, Elf," Morwena was barely a whisper, but its command clear. "You need this too." Daniel dragged himself as near as he could get. A gentle drying air twisted around him, soothing his aching body and warming his cold skin. He felt his eyelids become heavy and he wondered if he was dreaming as he thought he saw Eleanor rise off the ground, just before his eyes closed. He dreamed of his home, playing Cross-link and running across the sand with Seb.

*

"So, Elf," he woke with a jolt. "You too have quite a grasp of spells, don't you?" Daniel blinked and looked around. Rubbing his head, as he tried to sit up.

"I dunno," he mumbled, "It just happened."

"Lucky for us," Morwena smiled at him, "it worked." Daniel looked at his hand; it wasn't so red and didn't hurt so much. The bruises around his wrist were lighter.

"But you blasted me away," he said.

"That was for your own safety," she replied, "the Imps were baying for your blood." Daniel rubbed his wrists. He caught Morwena staring at them.

"That was your first time, wasn't it?"

"Uh?"

"That spell you cast, it had *Darkness* magic in it. You need to learn to control it... did you ask for *The Dark* to help you?" She looked at him with her head tilted on one side. Daniel remembered... "No... no never. I won't...."

"Huh," Morwena grunted. "At least that's something."

"Eleanor..." Daniel suddenly realised she wasn't on the ground where he'd last seen her.

"She's alright," Morwena replied.

"Where is she?"

"Collecting sticks." Daniel stared at the old Sprite as she shuffled over and handed him a pile grassy mush. "Here... eat this," she said. "It should help a little more." Daniel looked quizzically at the mixture before gulping it down grateful for anything to eat. He felt it travel all the way to his stomach.

"I think we should move closer to the rock and shelter for the night. We've wasted enough time as it is." Morwena pointed to the base of The Vespic. "And Eleanor cannot travel far," Morwena continued, "so we must set up camp?"

Daniel staggered to his feet. "Have the Imps gone?"

"Yes, for now."

"Hey," Eleanor called, "I've found some." Appearing around the corner. Daniel could hardly look at her, consumed with guilt for what had happened.

"Are you ok?" she asked, as she got closer to him.

"Yeah... you?"

"Yeah... fine," she gave a sort of smile, but Daniel could see her pale face was etched with concern. "Not sure what happened though." she said, "and Morwena won't tell me," Eleanor handed him the sticks. "Least the Imps have gone," she said, "was there a fight?"

Daniel shrugged, "Yeah sort of."

Eleanor looked at him quizzically before Morwena interrupted, "Show me where you hid. It might be a good place to camp near." Eleanor nodded and they began talking in their own language.

Daniel followed quietly. When they reached the spot, he automatically set about building up stones into a wall to start off a shelter. The menial task helped to ease his increasing worry of what had just happened, and what he was going to do next. He could hardly believe he had summoned *Darkness* Magic - only Elders did that. The *Shadows* had moved on; the sky pressed heavily, like thick piles of grey paper layering one on top of the other, as he worked. He knew there wasn't much *Light* left and he needed to sleep. An orange light caught his eye as he worked, and he saw Morwena had created a fire with Eleanor's sticks. The bright flame released more warmth than his blue spell. Daniel paused with a stone in his hand and wondered how he was going to talk to Morwena. He was finding it hard to believe that his parents had known her, certainly in his lifetime, he'd never seen her enter Caradoc.

"Uff... you are taking too long," Morwena interrupted his thoughts, "here, go and sit by the fire and eat." Daniel gratefully did as he was told.

"What's she doing?" he asked Eleanor who was mixing something in a small vessel.

"Oh, she waves her arms about when she's doing a spell. I'm not sure why as it's not normal Sprite behaviour. It makes her look wild, doesn't it?"

"Look... the stones are moving."

"Yes, watch, it'll be done in a moment... amazing, isn't it?" Eleanor grinned.

"I've never seen anyone do that," Daniel muttered.

"There are lots of things Morwena can do, that others can't," she whispered.

"My bow..." Daniel suddenly exclaimed.

"Yes, I found it while I was out searching for the sticks. It had just been left on the grass, near that ridge." She pointed. "Did you just drop it or something?"

"No." Daniel picked it up and turned it over in his hands. "I lost it in the bog." The bow was clean and the deep chip along its length had been covered with twine, a rudimental repair, but nevertheless a repair.

"I'm glad you've got it back," Morwena interrupted, "because I think, we're going to need more than this wall, our protection spells, and your weapons during this *Darkness Exchange*."

PART II

30

POISON & FLAMES

The *Darkness,* Tristan looked out across the chaotic arena, hoping he'd be strong enough to lead the Pixies against it. He held the wounded messenger slumped across his knees, feeling his breathing fade.

"Go and fetch the Medicine Leader," he said, "and bring my sister Enka... hurry." One of the Ornsvik Pixies nodded and ran off.

"Move back..." Tristan ordered the hoards. "We need space to work." He didn't want anyone to see the black raised veins, only his closest allies. "Vagen...?' His trusted friend stepped forward through the throng.

"Tristan, I've summoned the remaining Earth Guardians," he said.

"Good... and get rid of everyone else."

"Yes, Earth One," Tristan watched Vagen long enough to see he was doing what was asked of him. He felt a weak tug at his tunic.

"Time has run out, Sire." Tristan bent his head lower. "*The Darkness* that attacked me came from the sky. It grew within *Wind.*

I've come from the northern Moorlands near The Great Bog." He coughed, spluttering a thin line of black spit from the corner of his mouth. "My fellow watch didn't make it, tell his family he died with honour..." his head tilted and eyes rolled in their sockets.

"Medicine Leader," Tristan shouted. "I need her now; this messenger must live." A short, thin, Pixian, framed by long silver hair, pushed her way through the remaining small circle of Pixies.

"Get back," she barked, "give me room and allow your Earth Guardians to do their work." She rattled her long wooden staff at them. They quickly melted away.

"Can you save him?" Tristan searched her stern face.

"I will need your sister and Wilhelmina from the Verren family," she replied. "But time is against us." She nudged Tristan aside.

"Now go and calm things," she ordered. Tristan stood tall, irritated by her words; he knew what he had to do and didn't need telling. The arena was full to the limit of Pixies jostling, shouting for loved ones, and younglings crying. He saw her, standing alone, with no one daring to go near. Her pale skin radiated against the muted sand and her dress, rippling ochre, mirrored his family flag. Her red hair shone; too brightly, as if a warning sign, making it impossible for her to hide. He closed his eyes wishing she were only a dream. Then, he bent to gather sand from the floor, rolling it in his palm. Satisfied it was ground into a powder of the correct consistency, he threw it into the air. Controlling the movement with his hands, he weaved the sand into a cone shape. Holding one end to his mouth, he blew a single flat note, that grew louder and louder. His eyes fixed on the Imp as she placed her hands over her ears.

Gradually his fellow Tribelings stopped their urgent tasks. The arena's heat, always the hottest part of Poldaric, rose and rippled in mirrored lines. They stood to look at him. When Tristan was sure he had the attention of as many as he was going to get, he began.

"Fellow Pixies," his voice, clear for all to hear. "Do not let your fear get the better of you," he paused. "It is true... *The Darkness* has formed above us, on The Moorlands of NaraRose." The crowd began to murmur, glancing between each other. "Gulabirds within the Sprite's *Wind Element*. They are not our greatest concern but must be stopped. We are the Tribe, who treasure *The Balance* more than any other." His stomach turned, as he realised that it wasn't since his father's lifetime there'd been such a threat. "A group of our warriors will travel onto The Moors to fight." A resounding cheer started as a rippled and grew into a tidal wave, shaking the ground with force.

"We will fight against any threat to our *Light*," Tristan roared through the applause and stamping. "Now go, all of you, prepare your homes and spread the word. We must be ready for whatever comes."

Vagen approached. "Earth One," he said. "The Guardians are here." Tristan nodded.

"Christian," Tristan called, "bring the Imp to me. She probably doesn't understand what's going on and we need to keep her calm."

He returned swiftly to the injured messenger. "Am I too late?" But the lulling upturned palm told him his answer.

"The bite was too severe," the Medicine woman said. "The poison had already reached his heart. Look." She pulled him over and Tristan reeled, clasping his hand over his mouth.

"*The Darkness* is powerful this time, my Pixling," she said, "you will need all your wits about you if you wish to combat this. I will set to work to consult *The Glows*. I fear, Caradoc's troubles have spread like a disease." She tied her grey hair into a bun and stood up with the help of her staff. Slowly she pointed her thin, bony finger through the crowd.

"She, dare I say it, might be of use... after all." Tristan followed the aim of her point. Scarlet looked so fragile and alone at the far end of the arena, Christian still hadn't reached her. "I think she needs you." Tristan looked at her, squinting his eyes. "That Imp can not control her fire; but do not be beguiled by her ways Tristan. Remember Imps are always poison." The Medicine Leader shock her head and turned away. Tristan laid his hand on her shoulder as she went.

"What's going on?" he called across to Christian, as he jogged towards them.

"I can see flames within her eyes Tristan." Tristan noticed his sister, Toria, running at full speed across the arena.

"Toria, don't," Tristan, shouted, "she's losing control, don't get so close." The surrounding Pixies scattered. Scarlet was edging away, gesturing wildly. But, behind her the stone terraces were acting like a cage. She kept shouting words, Impish phrases, Tristan didn't understand.

"Scarlet..." Toria shouted, "it's okay, nothing's happened you are safe."

"It's taking me over." Scarlet yelled in Naraling. "Help me!"

"Try Scarlet... you can suppress it," Tristan shouted, as he slid to a halt paces away. The three Pixies encircled her.

"Please...get back" she shouted. "I don't want you to burn..." her words faltered, as her head fell unnaturally, jutting her chin into the air. Her hands jumped with flames that travelled in criss-crossed lines up and down her arms. Her dress caught alight, rising like a phoenix, consuming her body. Tristan could just see her outline as she erupted into a ball of fire. Her hair floated amongst the flames. Tristan edged back, the heat intense.

"Scarlet, listen to me - reach out - hold my hand, I can help you stop this." Toria said. Tristan quickly thought. He had to contain this. Poldaric had seen enough events for one *Turn*.

"Toria... get back," Tristan called. "You're not strong enough to heal."

"I am... and she's my friend."

"I won't allow it, help me to encase us all, stem the flames and starve the fire and you can work on your spell once inside." But Tristan could see, she had her own ideas.

"Hurry, Tristan," Christian said. The flames are already consuming the wooden seats half way up the arena walls. Tristan performed his spell with skill moving the surrounding sand into a circular wall. It grew effortlessly into a dome. The encroaching walls cast grey shadows over them, intensifying the heat as it rose higher, fighting to stay alive, funnelled into a tube. The flames ate at Tristan's skin and burned the hairs from his arm.

"Scarlet, listen to me," Toria said. "You can't hurt anyone now. But you have to call your fire back, take control; you're its master. Tristan's eyes flickered between the blackness and the roaring orangey flames. Toria was too close.

"Scarlet," Toria continued. "Can you hear me?" Tristan caught a glimpse of her within the flames. "Stop this., Scarlet," Toria said. "Remember, it doesn't control you."

A scream replied. It filled the dome, itching and scratching at the walls. The flames evaporated. Instantly sucked back into their source. Tristan felt a tug on his clothes as the force pulled him in. Leaving a vacuum of total silence, as if all the sounds in the world had been shut inside a box. Tristan closed the hole to the dome. Everything went black. A crude raw stench filled Tristan's nostrils. Fumbling around, he found the dome wall, and punched through, allowing the air to flood in. Whispering a reverse spell, he commanded the sand to return to where it had come from. He ran to Christian who was coughing and spluttering, crumbled under a pile of sand. Tristan pulled him free, "Give me warning, next time you reverse a spell," he grinned. Tristan helped him to his feet. His skin was singed in places and parts of his tunic had burnt away, but he had used his protection spell well. He found Scarlet lying in a foetal position, her hands tucked under her head, and pale skin exposed. He took off his jacket and flung it over her body. Gently he touched her forehead, it was cold and clammy. There were no signs of any burns, and her breathing was steady. Looking at her now, he could hardly believe she was capable of such power. He heard a groan to Scarlet's side.

"Toria," he pushed a pile of sand away. "Toria... noowh!" He pulled her into his arms. She groaned. He could see black patchy skin between the rips in her clothes and clumps of her beautiful brown curls missing.

"Why Toria?" he whispered as he pulled her into his arms and lifted her up. "Is the Imp really worth it?" He staggered forwards, cradling her as carefully as he could calling once more for the Medicine leader and her team.

31

EARTH GUARDIANS

"Earth One," Edward said, "you must address the leaders." Tristan noticed that Edward already wore his family shield.

"You're right," Tristan replied, wishing he didn't have to leave Toria. He watched her being taken off by four Verren sisters, one of her burnt arms lolled awkwardly between their pale dresses. He wrenched his gaze away hoping they would be able to save her beauty, if they couldn't, he would never forgive himself.

"Where is the Imp?" Tristan said.

"She's with Christian," Edward pointed towards the crowd, not far from where they stood. "He's guarding her, and she's been dressed again."

"Is Christian alright?"

"Yes... nothing a good wash didn't solve." Edward smiled, but Tristan knew he was angry that this had happened, angry at Poldaric's situation and at Tristan for bringing the Imp into their scared home.

"How are the other leaders taking to what just happened?" He asked as they began to walk.

"They're not happy, Tristan, you need to prepare yourself." Tristan grimaced. He knew they held him personally responsible for bringing her into Poldaric and after that trick; they will be saying he should have kept her under better control.

"Tristan," Edward said hesitantly, "I have never seen such wild fire," he paused, "do you really think she'll ever control it? Is it why, perhaps, her mother never taught her? Do those Imps know something about her we don't?"

Before Tristan could reply, Scarlet appeared from the crowd, dressed in Pixian trousers and shirt, her hair pulled back behind her head. Her wild look replaced by a docile façade wanting to please; momentarily she could have been mistaken for a Pixian servant. Tristan suppressed his anger at her healthy glow, as the full realisation was plain to see - she thrived off her fire.

"Will she be alright?" Scarlet spoke in her stilted accent, eyes etched with worry.

"I hope so," Tristan replied, "but the burns on Toria's arms might never repair."

"I'm so sorry," Scarlet enthused. "I really didn't mean for it to happen." She reached forwards to touch his hand, but he pulled it back. "You asked me," Scarlet continued, "never to start my fire within Poldaric and I would never have broken that promise willingly. I just didn't know what was going on... all the shouting, the screaming... I was scared. Then my fire started and I couldn't..." she let out a sob.

"I'll show you." He beckoned for her to follow.

"What... what are you going to show me? But Toria..." Scarlet spluttered. "Surely I should go to her? To help?"

"No..." Tristan voice rose, "the Pixies won't let you near."

"Sire," Edward interrupted, speaking in Pixian. "Is it wise, that she sees?"

"Yes... she needs to," Tristan replied, "It's time she learnt what is really happening and that she needs to put her powers to more constructive uses." As they drew near Tristan issued a series of commands and the unsettled crowd parted to let him through. He was pleased to see The Medicine Leader was where he'd left her and the messenger's body was prepared for burial. He inspected the work; checking that the shroud of leaves was properly secured and his family crest, clear for all to see. He liked her touch of the jewelled golden dagger, clasped under his hands.

"Can you see?" Tristan addressed Scarlet. "Come closer." He watched the Imp's face as her eyes turned to black coals and her red lips opened.

"But his skin... it's yellow," she said her voice quivering. "His veins... they're black." She looked up at him. "Who did this?"

"Not who, but what. A Gulabird. Ostric at his most playful."

Scarlet shook her head. "Like our Natajaws."

"There are so many forms. Some, to be feared more than others."

"So, it's true, *Darkness* has formed. It is one of the few things my parents allowed me to know about."

"Yes," Tristan was surprised by her composure.

"Which Tribe?" she asked.

"The Sprites."

"Then why is your Pixie dead?" The Medicine Leader scoffed, and without provocation she spat at Scarlet's feet. Tristan spoke harshly to her.

"Who is she?" Scarlet looked startled.

"My mother," Tristan looked up. "She doesn't like Imps and is angry with me for breaking the ancient rule of bringing another Tribeling into our homeland. She is especially angry it's you." Tristan watched the look of panic cross Scarlet's face and couldn't find it in himself to ease her worry.

"Now come," he addressed said, "the Elders are here. We have to agree on what to do. You can stay and listen; I will ask everyone to speak in Naraling. But if you feel your fire rising again, warn me, is that clear? Otherwise I cannot guarantee your safety."

Tristan turned his attention away from the Imp wanting to prepare, and show he was still in control. He began casting a Moulding spell. Edward and Christian quickly joined in, to his slight irritation, but he knew they too were keen to get things moving. Although they each said the same spell, the chairs that formed, had their own distinctive shape and pattern, rising from the sand like ornamental waves.

He gestured for Christian, Vagen and Edward to sit. Then the eight other leaders quickly followed. The circle established became a focus to the arena, integral and powerful. As they took their places, each chair changed and moulded to represent who sat on them, emblazoned in colour and displaying images. Usually, the leading families, united to celebrate, laugh and drink into *Dark Exchange*; but this felt different, restless even, anxious. He hoped they would be able to make a decision and quickly, for each *Shadow* that passed, *The Darkness* was getting stronger.

Tristan beckoned Scarlet to stand behind him. He wanted to show everyone she was part of this. She looked to him, like a frightened mouse. It wouldn't have surprised him if she fled. But then, he probably would have been the same, if he were alone amongst a gathering of Imps. He ran his fingers down the handle of his precious dagger for good luck; before laying it on the ground in front of his chair – a signal to show the meeting was to begin. He looked at the ancient weapon; still gleaming as if it were just a few *Turns* old. To think Turgred, himself, had once touched and owned it gave Tristan hope. Helena, his mother and their Medicine leader and so much more, paced the outer ring of the chairs, hitting her staff against the ground, with the impatience of a Pixling. He had never been as close to her as he had his father. She had a wild side that even he, at times, found disturbing. He tried to ignore her purposeful disruption, as he raised his hands for silence.

"Why have the Gulabirds appeared?" Vagen spoke first, his long grey beard wrapped between three of his fingers.

"We consulted *The Elements*," Helena said in her high clear tone, "and it was in *Water* that *The Darkness* was predicted to appear." Several of the leaders nodded their head in agreement.

"A few of us," Tristan said, "have just returned from The Moorlands. We went to seek out the lone Elf. We have learnt, he is the eldest Elfling of Noah Trevarak. Events lead to Noah being key in deciding to banish him from his homeland." He paused to let them all digest the information. "A drastic decision indeed for a father, no matter what his Elfling's crimes were, Noah must have been sure something even worse was happening within Caradoc, to do such a thing."

"And since this Elfling has been on The Moors," Vagen interrupted, "we've learnt that the Trevarak Council has been overthrown and The Eastling Elves have captured or killed a great number of important families. This in its entirety is enough to upset *The Balance* and create a swing towards Ostric."

"So it is a mystery that this has happened within *Wind*," the Clamis leader said, his hands clenched on the arms of his chair.

"Then, as I asked before," Vagen said, "why indeed did the Gulabirds come?"

Tristan could feel Scarlet's gaze burrowing into the back of his head.

"We do know there are also Sprites on The Moors, how many we are unsure" Christian said, "but one is a Sprite Elite." Several leaders mumbled between themselves. Tristan glanced at the settlements walls, now a dull amber, reflecting the waning heat of *Light Exchange*.

"Tristan, I've stood by you through difficult times and never doubted your leadership," the Clamis Elder said. "Yet the pressing question on all our minds and something we need to discuss before we agree our plan, is why you've brought an Imp into our midst, at a time like this? You know I, and many others, are not happy."

"Yes... we're all concerned, Tristan," Tomas an apprentice Earth Guardian said. "These are unusual times and we should close our borders, not open them."

Tristan felt Scarlet's fists clenched tightly on the back of his chair as he searched the stone terraces that whispered emptiness. Only *Shadows* before, they had been happily filled with Pixies enjoying the Mud & Bridge game. His mother tapped him on the shoulder.

"Helena," he said, unable to use the word mother. "You must work with the Bablen and Ornsvik families to find out more about the situation within Vearmoor, we need to understand why the Gulabirds have been sent."

Tomas growled, "Tristan answer the question - you've put all of our lives in danger by bringing her here." A small pale hand fell on his shoulder.

"You do not have to speak for me," she said slowly. Despite her fragile position, she showed little fear. Tristan readied himself to counteract anything she did.

"I mean you no harm," she continued. "He..." she pointed at Tristan, "offered me help, when I had lost much." She paused and took a deep breath. "His family have treated me with nothing but kindness and friendship. I will not forget that. If I return home I will either be killed or enslaved, so I am at your mercy." Her gaze held strong, as she looked at them all.

"You may not mean to harm us now," his mother replied harshly, "but you might not be able to stop yourself in the future." She waved her staff towards her.

Arguments erupted.

Tristan looked at the family leaders and fellow Earth Guardians he'd known all his life. He could see the anger and fear starting to weave its web of discord. He could listen no more.

Quietly Tristan rose from his chair. "Stop!" he glanced at Scarlet and smiled at her for the first time since their meal together.

"Have none of you remembered?" he said as he turned to face his comrades. "The most important issue is the Gulabirds. If we continue to argue they will grow." He waited for them all to quieten. "And which Power Element can actually kill a *Wind Darkness* creature?"

All eyes turned on Scarlet.

32

UNION AND HOPE

"Elves, make blue flamed fires, don't they?" Daniel inwardly groaned; he'd heard that before, what was their fascination with it? Morwena had finished creating her wall and was sitting so close to glowing embers of their fire.

"Yeah," he replied, still deep in thought, trying to work out how to bring up the subject of his banishment.

"Can you cook on it?"

Daniel looked up and gave Eleanor a quizzical look, but she just shrugged in reply. "Sure..." he replied before resuming his task of removing grass from his boots. "But you'd know that right? "

"Good." Morwena threw two dead hares at him. "Then you'll be practised at skinning and cooking these, my fire's not hot enough," she retorted. Daniel caught them just before they thudded into his lap.

"Where did you catch these?" Morwena raised her hand to silence him.

"I'll help him," Eleanor picked up a carcass.

"No," Morwena snapped, "you won't. We've work to done on the protection spell."

"But you've just finished one," Eleanor said, the firelight made her green eyes wary.

"Always answers... always questions," Morwena grumbled. "Maybe it would've been better if you'd made it to Vearmoor - not found this Elf."

"Perhaps so," Eleanor retorted, "but I'm here, so tell us what you think is coming?" Daniel looked up and pushed his hair from his face.

"Protection spell first," Morwena knocked her foot against her hessian sack that had mysteriously appeared from under her cloak. It rattled as she stomped off to the perimeter.

"What's worrying you, Eleanor?" Daniel said under his breath.

"Nothing..." she gave him a scowl, before she too flounced after Morwena. Daniel slumped forwards and grabbed the hares, wondering how he'd managed to end up with two moody Sprites. He picked up Eleanor's knife, cut into the fur, and began roughly tugging it up over the neck. To his relief there was a fair amount of meat on the animal. He occasionally looked up at their work. A thick film of grey dust was being added to the protection shield. It made him feel he was back underground. With both hares finally skinned, he spiked a thin stick into the jaw of one and pushed it through the middle of its belly. Sitting crossed legged, he held it into the flames and watched the flesh begin to turn.

"Come on... ask me, Elfling." He hadn't noticed Morwena return to the fire, sitting quietly to one side, cooking the other hare. "Your silence will eat it before it's even cooked." Eleanor was also there pouring a liquid into three vessels.

"Will you help me?" Daniel blundered.

"Do what?" Morwena's gaze searched his face. Daniel felt he was being tested, an exam he was sure to fail.

"He needs to get back into Caradoc," Eleanor answered for him.

"Can't he speak for himself?" Morwena snapped curtly. Eleanor scowled and thrust the drinks at them both.

"Why can't you get back home?" Morwena had a clipped way of speaking.

"I can no longer see the stones of Caradoc's entrances." Daniel felt a wave of sickness at the thought.

"Were you a thief?"

"Something worse," Daniel looked into the flames of the fire unable to return Morwena's stare.

"But what could you possibly have done that warranted such a punishment?"

Daniel hesitated and looked up at Eleanor for support, but she seemed solely focused on grinding nettles into a pulp.

"Look at me, Elfling..." Morwena said.

Daniel raised his eyes.

"Ah, it's beginning to make sense. I thought I recognised something about you. I know those eyes - your father, that's who I can see. You're a young Trevarak? You have the same intensity," she crackled, "but are you as wise as he?" Suddenly his chin was grabbed and jutted upwards. "Clearly not or you wouldn't be out here alone!" She dropped his chin, as if it was a heavy stone. Daniel withdrew from the yellow tinged nails.

"You're right, I'm not as clever as he is," Daniel glared at her, "But he told me to find a powerful Sprite."

"So, I might not be the right one?" Morwena said.

"Morwena," Eleanor interjected. "It's got to be you, you said you knew his father."

Morwena didn't reply. Her gaze shifted to the fire, letting a silence weave its net.

"I was at their joining union," Morwena's tone had changed, "many *Turns* ago," she sighed. "That was a happy occasion and the last time I was in Caradoc."

"You were in Caradoc?"

"Yes," Morwena half smiled, "such an interesting land." Her tone became almost joyful. "Other Tribelings were there too. Some of us, Daniel Elf Trevarak, don't respect the separation clause, that is bound into our laws." Daniel had never heard of that clause. "But what," Morwena snapped, "did you do to make your wise father banish you?"

Daniel felt for the stone his mother had given him, before beginning to retell his story. He wasn't allowed to leave anything out. Morwena relentlessly probed, until every detail lay bare. At times Daniel felt as if he was back in the lake or standing within the Great Hall. Only at the very end, when all was still and being digested, did he notice Eleanor quietly looking at him, her eyes glistening. Daniel looked away, ashamed. He ate the cold remains of his hare silently, knowing Morwena was deciding, and, once her mind was set he was powerless to change it. His food had become a chewy mush as he waited. Eleanor was also locked in her own internal mire. Blindingly staring into the flames. Perhaps now, he thought, she too would despise everything about him and wish she hadn't helped.

"I will honour your parents," Morwena said bluntly. Daniel was unsure he'd heard correctly. "But I can't see what your father thought I could do?"

"Uh?" Daniel spluttered.

"I believe the banishment spell, performed by The Council to keep you on The Moorlands, is binding. Only a powerful Elf would be able to reverse such a spell. I could help a Sprite get back into Vearmoor, but my powers won't work on another homeland."

"So, why would my father tell me to find you? Send me on a false errand?" Daniel could hardly breathe.

"A Tribeling cannot enter another's land without specific invitation. It has been the way of Nararose for several generations. I've given it thought and will continue to, but I'm afraid, Elfling, there is little I can do."

"Daniel," Eleanor's voice sounded distant, "didn't your father say anything else to you that might help?" Daniel struggled to his feet. He felt like someone had just ripped the hope he'd been holding onto so dearly and shown it to be the most worthless piece of emotion possible. How could his father tell him to find someone that couldn't do anything? Shadows merged across the floor, as he stumbled towards the wall.

"Daniel... where are you going?" He brushed Eleanor's hand from his shoulder. Would he ever see Caradoc again? His brothers? His mother? He couldn't be here for the rest of his life. He had to return. He spun around, feeling trapped in a cage. He had to get away, away from the eyes that judged him. He felt tears well, and he didn't want Eleanor or that Sprite, to see them. He pulled at the stones that were almost impossible to move.

"I wouldn't go outside of the protection spell." Daniel no longer cared; it didn't work for him anyway. He had his own *Power Element*.

"Daniel... don't be stupid." He kicked with all his might, finally a stone came away and the spell wobbled. Daniel kicked again. The stones gave way and he pushed his way through. The air blew strongly, its ferocity surprising. He walked haphazardly, allowing his torment to take control. Images of Imps rampaged through Caradoc, while he wandered alone, with no point in being alive. How had all this started? Why had Isaac been taken?

*

A bead of sweat dripped from his forehead. He moved his hands over the back of his neck - it felt damp. He adjusted his clothes and rolled up his sleeves. It was dark, darker than any *Exchange* before. But he was used to this. He'd survived alone for several before. The air was stagnant and rich in musky dampness. A heavy silence made his head giddy. He stumbled. A dark shadow ran across the grass, leaving a sticky haze. The grass darkened and shrivelled before his eyes. He stared at it motionless. His skin prickled. *That had never happened before.* A shiver ran up his back. Something was watching him. Through a crack in the surrounding mire, an irregular ring of light appeared. Daniel looked up. A billowing cloud hung in the sky. It's shape changing. Daniel stared mesmerised. A hare, a small Stagin, a flying fish. It was a rich black colour, and even sparkled alluringly, as it reformed and hovered. It was hot, overwhelmingly warm. His eyes grew heavy. He should lie on the grass, and watch the shapes form. *What else did he have to do?* He leant heavily on this bow, and placed his head on his hands to rest.

33

THE ARMORAKS

"A small group of us, including the Imp, if she will join us, will journey again onto The Moors, to tackle the Gulabirds." Tristan could tell everyone was still digesting the bitter idea that they needed the Imp's help.

"Can I rely on you, Scarlet Garnafort?' he spoke loudly to cover his nerves. The credibility of his leadership was resting on the decision of an unknown young Impling. His mother understood, she paraded like a peacock to show her displeasure, ranting and shaking as if she had a mystical twin.

"I have little choice," Scarlet replied solemnly, "I will," her voice rose, "only if, you promise, that when we encounter Imps, you will swear to protect me whatever happens," she gave Tristan a look through black discs.

"So..." Tristan looked around his close-knit circle, observing each reaction.

"If the Imp will use her fire against The Gulabirds, I vow to protect her," Christian broke the silence that hung like a suffocating fog.

Vagen, grinned at Tristan, as if he thought this all a game. "Count me in, I wouldn't miss this for all the sand in Poldaric."

"But someone needs to stay home. " Edward scowled, "Tomas, is still learning, and we must protect our homeland."

"Agreed, that will be you Edward. " Tristan was surprised he felt relief that Edward on this occasion wasn't coming.

"Settled" Vagen got to his feet and bowed. "All your Earth Guardian's agree," Vagen smiled, "Tristan, your plan's accepted. *She*," he gestured at Scarlet, "is a lucky Imp!" Tristan raised an outstretched palm. Christian, Vagen and Edward all placed their hands one on top of the other.

"We vow to protect Scarlet Garnafort of the Northern Arramond Imps and honour our promise to the Elf, Daniel Trevarak, and," Tristan spoke to everyone, "in the presence of each family leader here, this remains in place, only for as long as *The Darkness* threat exists. Once this is done, our vow is over."

"Agreed," they all chorused.

"You can question my leadership," Tristan continued, "if I fail to bring the Earth Guardians home," Tristan looked to Edward. "Summons the Armoraks, we have a journey ahead. Go spread our plan to your families. We reconvene in a *Shadow's* time by the bridge on the eastern edge of our settlement." Tristan closed the meeting by retrieving his dagger from the sandy floor. Each leader rose to leave, their bright cloaks, stark and bold, against the stone of the terraces. The chairs quietly dissolved into the arena floor.

"Scarlet, stay with me," Tristan said, giving her no room to argue.

"Do I really have to leave Poldaric?" Scarlet said as she jogged along beside him. Tristan knew Christian and Vagen were close by and would be listening to every word.

"Why, have you grown to like our home?"

"It would be perfect if everyone wasn't so frightened of me."

Tristan looked at her. "Imps have a bad reputation and exploding in the arena was a funny way to show you meant no harm."

Scarlet grimaced. She padded on behind him like a puppy.

"Did your mother," Tristan stopped and turned to face her, "not teach you anything about fire-making?"

Her face suddenly crumbled making her look younger. "She never gave me any time, I was kept hidden. I'd never used my fire until I escaped from my Compound. It was forbidden... only Aldrena performed fire spells."

"That explains why you can't control it. I will ask Enka to help teach you if we return from The Moors."

"So, you will let me back?"

"If the Earth Oracle permits it, but not for ever, we will decide your future once *The Balance* is retained." Tristan set off again, "we must hurry, my household will be preparing for our departure." Tristan wasted no more time in reaching the far side of the arena.

A line of heads appeared as he approached the ramparts and was surprised to hear cheering as he marched up the granite steps. The settlement walkways were lined with long tail-like flags. Pixlings held on shoulders waved as he passed. Pots and kettles banged and laughter echoed. So many had gathered. It gave him hope, that they did not blame him.

"See," he called back to Scarlet, "they are not so scared of you," he said.

"They are not interested in me, only cheering for you," Scarlet ducked as if expecting something to be thrown at her. Tristan waved and smiled to as many as he could, shook hands and hugged old allies. The intricately carved stone bridge appeared. He wished he'd been alive to see water flow underneath, when Poldaric, according to legend had been so beautiful - *during Turgred's lifetime*. But now, a trough of coarse sand, where vegetation dried to nothing. Only thorny cacti and sanguro thrived, which he had little care for. He passed the tall stone tree sculptures that guarded the bridge's entrance and paused to inspect the detailed craftsmanship, feeling it smooth marble bark.

"There," he spotted them through the branches, "they will take us onto The Moors - our Armoraks." He turned to see Scarlet had frozen in her tracks, like a white willowing lily amongst the array of colours.

"They are harmless," he assured, "and quite amazing - incredibly powerful and fast. Enka will ride with you."

"I am not getting on one of those," she had a stubborn look on her face, that Tristan could see had come from years of getting her own way. "And they're ugly."

"It's much better than walking — trust me." She proceeded to slowly cross the bridge in silence. The jostling crowd followed at a respectable distance, all vying for a prominent position.

"They're enormous," Scarlet said, as Tristan went to pat an Armorak under its pointy rabbit-like ears. "Will those short legs get us there?"

Tristan laughed. "Wait and see." His Armorak kicked the ground and sent up a great cloud of dust.

"They are amazing at covering our difficult terrain," Enka appeared, "and just as good on The Moors. But you have to be kind to them, as they can get easily frightened. And when they are scared they will refuse to move and go into their shell — then you're in trouble." Tristan smiled at his sister, relieved she had agreed to join them. "Ours is over here, Scarlet," she said, "we're on Daventour. She's strong and calm."

"I don't think I can," Scarlet stuttered. "I had no idea this was part of the deal."

"You are needed - we can't do this without you." Enka lay a hand on Scarlet's shoulder. "You'll be fine, look how much you've done since leaving home." Tristan watched Scarlet's eyes flicker with fear. Enka then linked arms with Scarlet and lead her away." Tristan felt humbled at his sister's forgiveness. Toria their eldest lay injured in her bed, because of that Imp and there Enka was showing pure kindness.

"Enka," he called after her, "remember your armour and a set for Scarlet."

"Yes, brother, don't fuss," she smiled at him. "We've got it covered."

"You will need this. sire," Barron appeared, his oldest servant. "I've brought your armour, headgear and sword," he paused, "and each Armoraks has a sack of *Power Element*, enough for six *Turns* - you shouldn't run out."

"Thank you, old friend, what would I do without you?" Tristan clasped his shoulder. "Toria - how is she?"

"The Verren daughters are caring to her every need. I am sure within time she will recover, but the burns are unusual in their severity. I fear her face may be scared." Barron's eyes clouded and he looked to the floor. Tristan knew how much he loved Toria, caring for her when she was young as if she was his own daughter. "There is food in your saddle bags," Barron said quickly as a reluctant Armorak came into view being dragged by several Pixies.

"Yoken, sire," Barron announced. "Your trusted Armorak. I hope he brings you luck on this journey," Barron said, "and with the grace of our dear Earth Oracle, you will return to us safely." Tristan took the harness, thrust his foot into the stirrup and jumped into the broad saddle. Yoken quivered and shook his head cumbersomely, bellowing out gooey sand.

"I hope Yoken's mood will improve, Barron, otherwise we are all doomed."

Vagen and Christian were already mounted, each surrounded by fusing family. He spotted Enka. It looked like Daventour was reluctant to go near the Imp. Enka was whispering into her ear and smoothing her shell.

"Try food Enka?" Tristan shouted. "Give some to Scarlet." Tristan smiled as Scarlet gingerly held out an orange, precariously balanced on one foot, her head tilted as far away as it would go. Daventour sniffed and edged towards the fruit, then, in an instant, gobbled it up. Scarlet nearly fell into the sand if it hadn't been for Enka who in one quick move, gave her a leg up, and practically thrown her onto the beast's back.

Tristan walked Yoken over. "See they're not so bad," Scarlet gave him a wild look, like a pale fierce ghost on a fat oversized nut; he never thought he would have lived to see this. Enka showed Scarlet how to hold onto the pommel, securing the straps around her waist.

"Surely I don't need straps," Scarlet protested, "they're too fat to go that fast. And I'm use to the speed of Imps."

Enka smiled. "Just in case then! But don't wriggle out, you'll regret it." Once Tristan was satisfied that Scarlet was in place, he moved Yoken on. A boisterous chorus of blubbering and snorting broke out. The wind seemed to match their impatience and blew across the arena in angry whistles.

"Ready?" Tristan called. Vagen and Christian saluted in return.

He turned to the crowd that swarmed across the bridge and the multitude that lined the walled settlements.

"Edward," he called. "Poldaric is now in your hands until we safely return, hold her in peace and serve each Pixie, like they were your own family."

"I will, sire, and may the luck of past generations go with you," Edward replied.

"Poldaric," Tristan called. "Do not let fear get the better of you. We will destroy this *Darkness* and it will never enter our land as long as I am alive."

The crowd erupted in cheers as Tristan nudged the thickset neck of Yoken and pressed his heels into her side. He knew she would take a while to react, but when the command registered, she would know what to do. He led the way, with Enka and Scarlet behind, followed by Christian and Vagen. The pads of their feet ground into the sand, mirroring their grunts and moans, as they gathered momentum. The thuds became quicker and over took the shouts from the crowds. The terrain turned into finer sand and rose up into majestic dunes, making the Armoraks work harder. With the settlement out of sight, and the open desert plains before them, Tristan heard a lone shout. He spotted her standing on the top of a disused building. She framed the skyline, her grey hair almost alive as it flew. He could just make out her chants, about something he would never understand. Calling to their Gods asking for their help to ease his path. A shiver ran down his spine, *never the mother, always the priestess.*

The sand gave way to earth. Yoken knew exactly where he needed to go. Suddenly all went black, the calm yellow light, replaced by the dull grip of a tunnel and the air thickened, laced with a dampness that Poldaric had long ago lost. Slowing, Yoken let out a high-pitched call, the others copied. Tristan took a handful of *Element* and cast his spell. The tunnel rumbled. Clouds of falling earth covered him as he lowered to the saddle and closed his eyes. Yoken leapt towards the light, into a wall of cold.

"May the united *Elements* of *Earth* and *Fire* succeed," Tristan cried.

34

THE BOOK OF SPELLS

"Daniel," she cried. Eleanor understood why he'd stormed off, but hated him for it. He was putting them at risk. If only she'd didn't care enough to be able to leave him to the mercy of whatever was coming. Her actions slowed and throat dried as she tried again; Morwena had given her only a quarter of a *Shadow* to bring him back, otherwise, she was sealing the encasement spell with or without them.

"Grab hold," she hollered. Daniel was staring at the sky - *oblivious*. "What is wrong with you... Daniel can't you hear me?" She could just make out his silhouette, and leapt across the ditch, following the glow of her rope. It was so dark, that every step was difficult. He didn't move. "You can't stay here all *Dark Exchange*." She pushed him sharply in the back. For a skinny Elf he wasn't easy to shift.

"Eleanor..." his voice sounded miles away and his head awkwardly swung forwards, so they both lost balance.

"Elf?" Eleanor's panic rose in her voice. "Look I know the news you heard was rubbish. But we in this together, well er...., we are at the moment, so don't be an idiot and lets get back to the shelter." Eleanor paused. Something itched at her skin. She could feel it, a presence. She swivelled her head and stared upwards. Quickly she pulled her gaze away and screamed, "don't look at it." Eleanor punched Daniel hard in the shoulder. "Move." Eleanor could tell he was trying but, like a drunken Sprite, who'd been on the berry gin, he stumbled awkwardly and kept stopping. Then he stopped.

"I've got to stay," he'd moan, pushing her aside. The heat was unbearable, clawing at her skin, sweat dripped down her back. The Moors were closing in on all sides.

"Morwena..." Eleanor called into the dark, praying she'd hear. "Help."

"About time, I had just started the closure spell," Morwena crackled as she appeared by Eleanor's side, and without another word, Eleanor was propelled forwards in a burst of wind. She landed heavily on the ground, just outside the stone wall. Waisting no time, Eleanor scrambled into the protection dome.

Daniel tumbled in just behind her. He was shaking his head and rubbing his shoulder. Eleanor felt momentarily guilty for hitting him so hard.

"What... was that?" He spluttered between coughs and groans holding his head.

"Phwah!" Morwena huffed, her arms folded across her chest. "It's the nest," Morwena replied.

"Huh?" Daniel sat up.

"*The Darkness* nest, you were entranced by it."

"That thing... in the sky?"

"Yes, surely you were told by your parents never to look at one?" Daniel didn't reply.

"So... are you saying," Eleanor interrupted, "we're alone on The Moors with *Darkness* creatures forming above us?"

"Yes," Morwena said, "not ideal."

"Are you mad?" Daniel asked, "that can't be happening! *The Darkness* was supposed to be forming within my homeland – not here."

"Oh, for goodness sake - keep up Elf." Morwena went to sit by the fire. "You're strop, nearly cost you your life and potentially, that of a Sprite. So at least you could do is listen. I can't abide bad listeners."

"This isn't right," Eleanor groaned. "Is this because we're out of Vearmoor and shouldn't be? What are you not telling me, Morwena? Have all those spells you've performed caused this?"

"No," she barked, "they have not. So before you go accusing me of something or other, remember we're here alone I'm your best chance. Argue and you'll suffer the consequences." Morwena removed her hood, revealing tinged cheeks. "But... I'm not, at the moment, strong enough to keep any of us safe for long."

"Great, just great. So, now what the *Wind lord* are we going to do?" Eleanor was shouting, "for the sake of our sanity Morwena, what nightmare have you got me into?"

"Enough," Daniel groaned. "Do all Sprite's argue like this, my head hurts." Morwena trust him more of the green mush, he'd had before, "Eat this."

"We need a plan," Morwena said in a way that was final, "and we all are part of it."

"Great, I think we should..." Morwena cut her short.

"ENOUGH. This was never something I foresaw. If it was I would not have brought us out on The Moors." Eleanor wanted to throw something at her. There was a long pause with only the sound of Daniel chewing. Eleanor wanted to hit him too. AGAIN but this time even harder.

"I'm going to act as a diversion for you to go." Morwena mutered.

"What...." Daniel demanded.

"To where? Why? " He looked as if he'd regained his wits, bow in his hand.

"You Daniel," Morwena looked sharp, "must get the real *Stone of Innvericum* before anyone else does. Eleanor saw a spark reignite in his face.

"I think it's your only chance to return to Caradoc and have any chance of your family fighting Ostric. The Trevaraks need that *Stone*."

"But, how do you know about *The Stone*?" Daniel said, "even my father didn't!"

"I'm a Balance Warrior," Morwena replied, "it's my duty to. But I also overheard Tonurang. Remember I was there. " Eleanor and Daniel exchanged looks.

"So... where is it?" Daniel's face had turned stony. "Do you know that?"

"Yes - Arramond but I don't know anything else," Morwena replied.

"Where the Imps live?" Daniel threw his arms into the air.

"She will go with you," Eleanor stared at the boned finger that pointed at her chest.

"Did I just hear you correctly?" Eleanor gasped. Morwena turned to face her. "Morwena you're joking right?"

"Together you'll have a chance," she replied. "You can't go northwards to Vearmoor with Gulabirds in your way.

"Gulabirds...!" Eleanor nearly choked. "You're saying that thing is making Gulabirds?" Morwena gave her a withering look. "By travelling south you will be heading away from them. If you get into Arramond the birds won't be able to follow."

"But we won't make it!" Eleanor shrieked. "You've said so yourself, no Tribeling gets into another land, unless they're invited." Eleanor edged towards Daniel. Morwena had clearly lost it; this plan was a death mission.

"Morwena, it's a crazy idea," Daniel said, "firstly we'll never outrun The Gulabirds and secondly we won't be able to kill them without fire. At least that I know." But Morwena was facing Eleanor, with one of her possessed looks. Daniel kept talking; while Morwena moved like a mating bird with a mission.

"Morwena.... what's wrong?" Eleanor tried to push her away. "Why are you so close?" Morwena plunged forwards and grabbed her shoulders, pulling her roughly, so that their noses almost touched. Eleanor's skin, consuming Morwena's stale scent of hare and sickly nettles.

"Stop it," Eleanor shouted. Daniel yanked at Morwena's arm.

"Get off, Morwena you're scaring me!" Eleanor said, but her voice became distant, echoey, and her resistance weakened, as Eleanor felt the dome move enclosing her inside.

"Please..." her last word slid through the pores of the newly formed tunnel. Morwena's steely eyes remained still and clear, holding her on the journey. Rolling and plummeting as if in a tormented wind storm. Then suddenly the spinning stopped and she hit a hard floor. Her surroundings came into view. She'd been there before. During a better time... it was the same place she'd met Morwena at the Sprite Festival. A fire still burned with the same rocking chair beside it. The enormous book sat on the jewelled bench. Eleanor's heart jumped, was this, her chance to start over? Decide not to go onto The Moors, with the Elf, to The Rock, all the decisions she'd got wrong. Survive the Gulabirds. She could run, leave the tent and be home before another *Shadow* had passed.

She bolted, but something invisible stopped her from getting very far. She tried a different way, but the same thing happened. Her hands sunk into clear impenetrable walls and no matter how hard she pushed, she couldn't get through. The only way she could move was towards the book. Reluctantly she touched the spine, a cold shiver consumed her body. It was old, well thumbed; the pages were a greenish cream with brown edges. Her fingers tingled. Brightly coloured images of Tribelings, trees, and animals lit up the tent, dancing in the air. The Book knew what to do, the pages turned without her assistance. Finally it came to rest three-quarters of the way through. An image of a giant Imp with flying red hair soared out. Eleanor ducked as the Imp ran around her head. A strange black creature rose and began to scuttle after the Imp. It had enormous pincers, a body of a spider and several thin long legs. The two images faded as the page turned, replaced by a dark cavern with a shining blue lake. More spider-like creatures ran around inside the cave. Suddenly they turned away and headed out, growing in size, their large pincers reached out like an arm. Eleanor screamed. Words in old Sprent filled the air. The book slammed shut and disappeared. She screamed again, before her throat seized. Blaydoc stood before her.

"Now my dear, how did you get in here, or rather, you're not really here are you?"

Eleanor reached for her rope. "Use it and I'll take it from you," he said. "Now..." Blaydoc leaned forwards gazing into her face. "I know you're there Morwena. Why are you using this Spriteling so? Give her to me, she could easily go home - away from all this trouble." Eleanor kicked and punched against the hold.

"I know you can hear me, Morwena," he repeated. "You'll have to come back to Vearmoor soon; you can't live on The Moorland of NaraRose forever - we both know that. And, we have all felt the presence of *Darkness* creatures there. Was it you? Did you summons them to do your bidding? There is a bounty for your capture... you must give me *The Book of Spells*... I need it to stop all this nonsense." Eleanor could smell burnt ash and smoked rose wood across his beard. His teeth were tinged yellow and his eyes filled with blood vessels that bulged.

"And you... yes you... youngest daughter of Francis Paraquinn, have caused great trouble. Your family are in tatters because of your disappearance. Your father and a sister are at this very moment, on The Moorlands trying to find you. Probably going to be Ostric's first victims." Eleanor felt the air expel from her chest as a vacuum of swirling dust sucked her backwards, with Blaydoc's outstretched hand closing its grip.

35

LADYBIRDS

Earth slid by like a river. Scarlet had never felt so alive. If she'd ever been allowed out of her Compound, her brothers would put her in a wooden carrier. It took four of them to lift her cage, and her only view was through two slatted windows.

"You ok?" Enka called.

"Definitely," Scarlet beamed. Adjusting her position, she lent nearer to Daventour's ridged shell, remembering her previous time on The Moors. Huddled in that tree hollow begging to sleep. If Tristan hadn't found her, she'd have died of hunger.

Daventour's rhythm slowed, allowing the undulating hills to appear out of the blur. Panting and gulping lung-fulls of air, she made a big show of slowing down. Scarlet could see Tristan had already stopped just ahead.

"Is everyone alright?" he called over the commotion, checking the horizon.

"We're late," Christian, said, "I can sense *The Darkness's nest* has formed." His Armorak came next to Scarlet's. "The Imp needs to stay close to me." Tristan nodded in agreement.

"There," Enka shouted, she pointed northwards. "It's there, look at the way it's moving." Scarlet followed the line of Enka's arm, to something small, darker than the other clouds. It had a benevolence, unnatural purpose, like nothing she'd ever seen before. It moved, in pulsating patterns and fought against its confinement. Her thoughts relaxed as she traced the movement.

"Scarlet, don't," Enka was pulling at her sleeve. "We are far enough away at the moment, but when we get closer it has a strange power, if you look at it for long, it draws you in and changes you." Scarlet blinked.

"We'll have to hurry," Tristan said, "It's near to one of our gates and we can't let it get any closer. The trees will give us protection while we work out what to do."

"Until they take flight and turn our gate into ash," Christian muttered. Scarlet wondered if he'd said that just to scare her.

"Ready?" Enka said. Scarlet grasped the straps tightly trying to control her shaking arms. Daventour suddenly leapt from her standing position and surged into a full paced run. Scarlet bowed backwards and touched the Armorak's hind.

"Grab hold," Enka twisted around. Scarlet took her arm, "I didn't expect that," she gasped. "Thank the strap," Enka grinned.

Gathering speed, the mismatch hills swam by. Scarlet looked south wondering how far away her homeland was. Might she be close enough to be spotted by one of Orran's scouts? Or were the Vaniks still occupied chasing down her brothers and trying to overthrow their Compound? She hoped her mother would have enough strength to fight them. She thought of Tam and wanted to tell him she was sorry; hear his strong voice saying it would be all right and together they would work it out, but she knew that *Turn* would never happen. He would never forgive her.

Daventour's hooves cut cleanly through the coarse grasses. A stillness rested heavily, lurking over every branch and leaf. Her fur, now stifling, as the temperature rose. *How could the Pixies think she could kill it?* The trees got closer and closer, and the immanency of what she had to do, clawed at her heart. If it hadn't been Tristan who'd asked, she would have said no, run away. The knot, rose and tighted into an internal tormented mixture of self-doubt and fear. A sharp pain shot across her eyes and a trickle of blood seeped onto her cheek. Hurriedly, she wiped it away, grinding her nails into her palms to feel some other distracting pain.

Pounding up a wide gritted path, the trees reminded her of Garnafort sentries - tall, motionless and dominating always guarding her Compound. But, they or her precious stonewalls protected her now.

"Hide," Tristan bellowed, as he slid off his beast and began running by its side. Scarlet panicked. "Get your Armoraks under cover," he called, before disappearing into tall ferns and giant laurel. Vagen quickly followed, while Christian waited impatiently to usher them under cover. Daventour all the while was letting out soft shrill whistles that put Scarlet's nerves more on edge. She was making heavy work of the brambles and half-grown hazel.

"Tristan is calling us," Enka dropped from her back and began to pull Daventour the last few paces.

"I'll go ahead." Christian didn't wait for a reply, and disappeared between the trees.

"What's going on?" Scarlet landed next to her.

"Tristan senses something other than the nest." Enka quickly covered Daventour with a blanket of leaves.

"She'll be difficult to find now." Scarlet watched mesmerised as Daventour disappeared, the only part of her still visible was her long nose as it rummaged in the undergrowth. "Enka," Scarlet said, but turned to realise she too was gone. "Enka," she hissed, wading clumsily into the undergrowth, her cloak snaring on brambles. Her senses heightened; there was no air amongst the trees. *I thought they were meant to protect me?* It was darker, claustrophobic and unnervingly still, even the insects and birds had muffled their songs as if in compliance to a master conductor.

Where had everyone gone?

Shadows flickered, suggesting Enka or Tristan everywhere, but Scarlet remained quiet her senses alive. She cautiously pushed aside a thick dogwood, peering ahead. A startling clearing broke through to the darkening heavy sky. A grey light filled the void. Her throat dried. Someone was lying on the leafy floor. By the flecks of golden hair, they weren't Pixie. Scarlet leaned in closer. Two Tribelings. One looked the same age as her. With a long plait, olive skin, and something shiny on her back that lead to a green pattern around the side of her neck. Scarlet edged around the silvery trunk. Something slipped into her hand and she nearly screamed.

"Shh, we're still here." Two brown eyes blinked at her.

"Why d'ya go?" Scarlet whispered.

"We wanted to check first." Enka slowly reappeared, peeling her cloak aside. "Stay here – watch," she said and squeezed Scarlet's hand, before walking confidently into the clearing.

"Enka don't," Scarlet whispered, but Enka had started to speak in Naraling. The Tribeling looked up and began to mutter a spell.

"I'm not here to hurt you," Enka raised her hands and formed a barrier of earth. The spell evaporated. A rapid exchange of conversation rippled like ping pong, but Scarlet couldn't catch it.

Enka moved with stelf, as her voices soothed the shadows. Slowly she knelt by the injured Tribeling and began to examine him. *Pixies, were by far the best Tribe.* Every one of the brothers, Scarlet knew would have just killed them.

"Come out Scarlet, it's ok," Enka looked straight at her. Scarlet muscles wouldn't obey.

"I need your help" Enka called again. Scarlet's foot caught on bindweed. She fell pathetically into the clearing.

"Don't be alarmed," Enka said hurriedly as the Tribeling leapt to her feet. "She won't hurt you, she's with me." The Tribeling fixed Scarlet with a distrustful gaze. Scarlet glanced at the Tribeling on the floor. It was enough to see the same raised black veins.

"What's his name?" Enka asked in Naraling.

"Francis, my father, we were on The Moorlands trying to get to Obakeech."

"The bite is serious, but you know that," Enka paused. "If we combine *Elements*, there is a chance we can save him."

"So there is something you can do?" she replied. Scarlet flinched at her desperation.

"Yes, but *The Balance* will have to be maintained in the future. Is that a price you're willing to pay?" A tear welled in the lower lip of her eye, she turned her face as she knelt back down and pulled the male's head onto her lap.

"Surely it's not that late?" she said. The trees groaned and creaked in response, as if they too knew the answer. Suddenly Tristan, Christian and Vagen appeared, panting.

"How many of you are there?" she said, panic skimmed her face.

"That's it," Enka replied, "I promise."

"We have skirted around the far perimeter of the gate," Tristan said urgently. "The nest is on the eastern side, hovering over the next valley."

Scarlet watched Tristan take in the situation before him.

"Has he been bitten?" he looked at Enka. She nodded.

"How is this happening?" His voice laced with anger. "The nest hasn't released anything yet."

"It was definitely a Gulabird who attacked us," the Tribeling replied, "there were two of them and I didn't kill either. It all happened so quickly."

"Which way did they go?" Scarlet felt Tristan's gaze fall on her.

"I don't know... I can't remember," she shook her head, with swollen red eyes.

"Did you say you were trying to get to Obakeech?"

"My sister," she sniffed. "She's there with Morwena du Gwent, one of our Sprite Elite."

"Why didn't you bring more help?" Christian asked.

"We had to leave Vearmoor in secret. There's a Council freeze on any movements outside of our homeland."

"Huh," Christian scowled, "it's beginning to make sense."

"Can you save my father?" she looked at Enka.

"I'll try, but we'll need the help of the Imp." Scarlet felt the Sprite look at her as if she was a piece of dirt on her clothes. "Does she have to come to close?' she said.

"Do you want *The Darkness* to spread?" Enka simply replied.

"No..."

"Then yes, she does." Scarlet did as she was told; something about the way Enka spoke told her not to argue.

"This spell takes a little time. Scarlet, you'll need to join in when I say." Scarlet shuddered.

"But. I've never done a spell," Scarlet muttered.

"Great, that's because you just kill," the Sprite spat.

"Easy," Enka said. "It's either this or the Under Terra." Enka waited for a moment before expanding her hands over his body. A shower of earth spray across his clothes.

"I need you..."

"Elderday," she said.

"Elderday, to blow the earth gently up and down his body." She quickly did as she was asked. Making easy work of the dried earth, keeping it in control.

"Both of you repeat these words with me," Enka spoke softly.

"Ladybirds, ladybirds, come to me, eat and destroy, to set us free." Scarlet looked back at Tristan, who gave her an encouraging look. They began to say the phrase, repeating several times as the wind moved, but nothing else seemed to be happening. Time merged into a swaying trance of words, where little matter. Then Scarlet noticed a line of ladybirds – faint at first; then focused, like mini Armoraks unique and brave, with a line of armoured shells, their red dots contrasting against the earthy tones, they grew. All her eyes could see.

Drawn to the pool of black blood oozing from the wounded Sprite's arm. He groaned and mouthed something that Scarlet couldn't understand. The ladybirds swarmed into the blood making her stomach retch. She wanted to stop saying the spell but couldn't - locked on repeat. They drank and drank, growing in size, bloating like male bullfrogs, until only a fleshy red open scar was left.

"You must burn them." Enka opened her eyes and the words stopped coming from Scarlet's mouth.

"No..." she said shocked. "They'll die and I'll burn everyone?" The insects rolled off the body and collapsed on the ground, with fat legs pointing skywards. Everyone was looking at her.

"Now Scarlet, do it quickly, we'll keep you in check."

"Why can't any of you powerful lot do this?" she snapped, "I can't. I'm not a killer."

"Huh – a Fire-Maker, who won't use fire," Elerday sneered.

"What did you say?" Scarlet looked at her, "We've just helped your father."

"Yes, and if you don't kill them," she pointed at the ladybirds, "we'll all be dead."

How dare she? Scarlet flicked her hand – amazed at how quickly the fire bubbled within her stomach. She flashed her eyes and pointed at the ground where the insects lay, suddenly repulsed by their fat, unnaturally ballooned bodies full of black poison. A direct jet of flames ripped through the air. Intent on their destruction, Scarlet enjoyed the rise of power that filled her veins.

36

A DROP OF BLOOD

"Well you clearly haven't been taught fire skills," Elerday spat. The undergrowth smouldered. It has taken Pixie and Sprite powers combined to prevent the trees and gate to Poldaric from disappearing. Tristan could see her point. And what the Sprite didn't know; it was the second time in just a *Turn*, that Scarlet'd lost control. Tristan watched Elerday return to her father and tenderly help him. Her hands working efficently. Francis arched and shock himself, drawing his feet in tentatively, then gingerly stood. Despite Enka's incredible healing skills it was still a speedy recovery for anyone from the clutches of Ostric. He followed Francis' gaze. It took him back to Scarlet, as if every way he looked led to her. *Was The Earth Oracle trying to tell him something?* Alone, again back to her angels are my equal look, she hung back, head lowered. He shook his head, trying to clear the mire of thoughts. *Was he slightly scared of her?* Her unpredictability, the complete lack of control. *Where did her fury come from?* As if Creoda herself was standing before him; the temptress of old, whose beauty and power were a cruel mixture that slathered her foes in drifts.

"That won't help things," Enka voice dragged him out of his thoughts. She said, while casting a spell that extinguished the last pocket of fire. It smouldered angrily before dieing under a pile of earth. "At least Scarlet has killed them all," Enka said defensively.

"Yes," Elerday snapped, "but we all nearly went up in flames." The air was thick with floating ash.

"Thank you, Pixie," Francis interrupted, his voice shaky. "Your sister is remarkable,"

Tristan smiled. "I don't understand all she can do."

"But, it worries me," he said, "what price did my daughter agree?"

"We didn't ask for anything if that's what troubles you," he said, "but Istria in time will, that is something I can't change." Francis looked away, his eyes shadowing. Tristan waited for a moment before asking, "What would Morwena want with one of your Spritelings?"

"I'd like to know that myself," Francis replied. Tristan could see that he was still struggling for breath, as he leant on Elerday's arm. "Eleanor, my youngest Spriteling, left Vearmoor, to find answers that she thought Morwena could give. For her own safety she needs to come home."

"Morwena is up to something," Christian touched Tristan's shoulder.

"Do you know her?" Francis looked up.

"We go back a long way," Christian paused, "but what answers was your Spriteling looking for?"

"She has... well, special gifts... which Morwena must have somehow spotted." The torment across his face was raw.

Tristan decided he'd asked enough. "Your Wind Lord," he said, "must be your ally. You're still alive and I'm sure your Spriteling will be found safe and well, have faith." He looked up at the canopy, catching glimpses of the monochrome darkened sky and felt sorry for Francis. He was a gentle Tribeling, who didn't deserve to be caught up in these troubles.

"We're time wasting," Christian broke in, speaking in Pixian. "We're all dead if we don't destroy that cloud, and soon."

"He's right, Tristan," Enka agreed. "I can feel the heat rising, even in here."

"I just don't understand how the Gulabirds that attacked them were made? Or where they've gone" Tristan replied. "We'll be fighting on two sides and I don't want to risk more than we have to."

"It's too late to decide a battle plan now or worry about what isn't here," Enka pointed through the thickets and out onto The Moors. Tristan pushed his way through the overgrown field maple and angry brambles, a barrier of vegetation protecting him from The Moors beyond. He allowed the dry, hot air from the nest to wrap itself around him, as he stood in the border of the trees. The safety of his gate with all of Poldaric's protections around him. Vagen came to his side.

"Thank our Earth Guardian's we're prepared," Vagen's voice sounded shaky. Tristan turned to face him, "but the Imps never seen Ostric before and I don't know if I can control her."

"You will find a way," he replied, his stare firm. Tristan looked into the wrinkled face.

"Have you ever seen Ostric's nest so large?"

"Yes, and you have too, we can beat this. He is playing with us, tempting us away from our homeland where we are weakest. We will show him that it makes no difference." Tristan smiled. "I'll attack from this side; you, Enka and Christian from there." His arm outstretched to the west.

"Easy…" Vagen smiled, "it'll be just like a game of mud and bridge."

"Huh, thankfully Edward's not here, he doesn't play by therules."

"Stay safe," Vagen called, as he ran westward. Tristan turned pondering how Vagen continues his relentless fight, despite being three-hundred-and-fifty.

"Where is the Imp?" he called when he reached the Sprites. Elerday pointed across the clearing.

"Stay here and don't follow. Your father is not strong enough to fight and if we fail you'll be the only Tribeling left to save him." Tristan disappeared into the undergrowth giving them no time to reply, and furious that Scarlet had moved. He could feel the long tentacles of heat hotter from this side. *Had Ostric called her?* He stilled by a thick silver trunk. Arms outstretched, he quietly whistled the familiar tune. Leaves upon leave left their place on the copse floor Fragile twigs wove intregral knots. The network combined and covered his chest, neck, head and most of body. He clenched his fists. The network turned a rich grey, like silver interelocking armour.

He spotted her red hair.

"Scarlet," he called. She didn't turn around. Hacking through the vegetation he catch up with her easily. He twisted her to face him, her head tilted to the side, as she side stepped drunkingly.

"Leave muh," Scarlet mumbled, "ler mee go."

"It's the cloud. You're too close."

She giggled.

"Listen to me," he shook her, "snap out of it."

"I'm tired," she yawned and closed her eyes. Tristan saw blood on her cheek and a red line of blood around her eye. He wiped it with his finger and looked at a perfectly formed tear, rich red against his bronzed skin. This meant only one thing - she wasn't ready. Her powers were destroying her. He hesitated. If Scarlet didn't use her fire, Ostric would kill his gate. He muttered another protection spell. It would only go some way. He waited impatiently for its effects to work, while searching the trees for signs of Ostric's artisty. He couldn't see any yet. But a ripe, musty smell filled his lungs, as if he'd step into a sealed cellar. It fell over him in waves, moving as peaks and troughs.

"Scarlet," he gently shook her shoulder.

"Where am I?" her teeth chattered.

"The Moors..."

She looked around, as if she was seeing everywhere for the first time, "I remember... the ladybirds.... they're dead!" A matching screech responded, an echo from The Moors.

"What was that?"

"Ostric" Tristan silently prayed.

"I can't do this, I'm not strong enough."

"You can... just use your *Element*, like you did before. I will do the rest."

"But how?"

"Trust me." Tristan felt the hairs on the back of his neck flicker. "Just aim at the cloud. Ok? Look... its time... we can't delay."

Crouching side by side, Tristan stared at a lone butterfly folding her delicate wings feeding from a thistle. He willed it to take flight, as pockets of adjacent brambles started to turn to ash. He knew they had to work quickly. He had to protect his gate, his priority was to his Tribe, and nothing else.

"Whatever happens keep me in sight," he ordered. Scarlet eyes had darkened, her hair shone. He squeezed her shoulder as she returned a nervous smile.

"I wish my brother was with me now, " she muttered. Tristan turned and focused. He needed more than The Earth Oracle on his side now. With both hands flat and firmly on the ground, he began to chant. The poison mustn't get to the roots. His arms quivered as the ground begrudgingly did his bidding. Creaks and groans filled the air, as the earth began to move. Between the familiar sounds, a rhythmic beat... beat... beat... filled his head.

"No... wah!" Scarlet screamed. "I can see one..." Her words jarred, severing his concentration. Her small body pushing against his side. He could feel her heat even through his armour. His spell collapsed. He had to get onto The Moor. The ground was too old. He leapt over the useless small rise and twisted in mid-air. Landing outside the copse. He could see them now. Giant flying creatures. Black as Scarlet's eyes. Enormous wing spans that dripped deadly ash. He counted six, assassins who scanned systematically for anything that moved, their heads swayed like a pendulum. His chest heaved and heart throbbed. Intoxicating mixtures of choking ash filled the air. The clear views of the Moors obliterated by a mottled grey haze. His head swivelled on his shoulders as he took in the sceen. Then bits of bright orange caught his eye. A fierce arch of flames shot like a deadly arrow to his side.

"Move out," he yelled, her hair dancing within the flames. "Scarlet, no." But her *Element* was once more, the master, she the servant. With all his might he mixed spells upon spells to move and channel her power. He, the mighty Earth Gaurdian, matched by a lone young Imp.

37

HUNTING SCOUTS

"That was awful?" Eleanor gasped for breath. Her hands shook and head twisted in pain.

"She's crazy." Daniel replied. "I couldn't get her off you… her hands, locked like clamps."

"It happened so fast," Eleanor slowed to a jog. "Did you see her face? She was so angry. Was it at…. you, me or that weird dream thing."

"You went mad too." Daniel looked away. Eleanor shuddered, her thoughts stuck together like sap.

"Do you think any of it was real? Could Blaydoc really have been there, and could my family really be out on The Moors?"

"I doubt it, I mean you didn't move from Morwena's clutches. So how could it be true?" Daniel replied, "I think Morwena made it up, she was the one to speak, not you. She's truly crazy. When she's angry, she's angry." Eleanor thought about that for a moment. Daniel continued, "they'd be mad to be out here, right? So I reckon it was all a trick to pretend she knew where *The Stone* was. Make us go. Make us believe it's the only option. Remember the bit about the Imps and those spider things, that's just convienent."

Eleanor collapsed into deep heather and groaned. "Yes but, we haven't got a better plan, and that's all we've got to go on. And she **HAS** got her own way. We are doing what she wanted! Eleanor covers her face with her arms. "Do you even know if we're going in the right direction? Are we actually heading south?"

"Yes... I'm sure." Daniel collapsed beside her. "Look, the grass, its... its changed..." He pulls up a clump and waves it about, "there's more sand, its warmer, but not in that weird way, and that nest things gone."

"This is all rubbish." Eleanor, heaved to her feet. "I need water." Daniel pointed down the hill. "*Bramble*...Do you have some sort of sixth sense where water is or something? You seem to be able to locate it anywhere. I mean it's weird, as it's so different to your *Element*." Eleanor didn't wait for his reply as she stomped off. It really troubled her, how crazy Morwena had gone and all those things she was saying. Her *family, Imps, caves* and *stuff*. None of it made sense. What had she been trying to tell them? The old Sprite had waved her arms and gabbled even more crazily that usual. If she knew one thing about Morwena, it was that she wasn't cruel. *So why do this?*

"We'll rest here," Daniel muttered. Eleanor hadn't noticed he had come down to join her.

"Do you think we've travelled far enough away?"

"Yeah, I mean that flying spell took a while, I thought I was never going to stop floating."

"Yeah another one of Morwena's talents! "

"What are we going to do when we get to the border?' Eleanor's heart lurched. "Are we really going to try and get in?"

"I'm not sure we have much choice." he was looking straight ahead.

"So you reckon we can find it? Dodge Imps?" She grimaced. "Nope, but we're gonna try." Daniel replied, "I can't go home without it, and if we don't Ostric will not only destroy Caradoc, he'll head for Vearmoor next."

"Yes, but it really all can't just come down to one Stone... surely. The Elf Elders will fight Ostric and We do have another choice Daniel." Daniel stared at her. "We could skirt eastwards, reach the edge of southern Vearmoor. I'll get us back home. We could ask my family to help. Speak to the Sprite Council, they would surely do something."

Daniel shrugged. "Yeah... and by then, it might be too late."

He resumed his incessant searching. Glistening water flowed in front of his face. He was always vigilant. His shoulders touched the ends of his straggly hair. Tense and alert.

"Give it up will you..." Eleanor ground moss between her palms and wiped away a dried patch of mud, that stuck to her arm. "I'm gonna try and get some sleep."

"I don't think we'll have to worry about reaching Arramond... "

"What? "

"You need to see this." She got to her feet. The viewing spell felt odd in her hand. An *Element* that held its shape didn't make sense to her. She looked through it and nearly dropped it. A yellow hurtling dot, was flying wildly, wings somersaulting around in circles rising and diving.

"He's trying to get away from something," Eleanor whispered.

"Look behind him." Her eyes travelled across the horizon. "It was hazy but unmistakable.

"Morwena didn't send us far enough."

"I think that bird of yours is leading them straight to us!" Daniel grabbed his bow. "We need to run." Eleanor's blood froze; she had felt like this once before, within Obakeech. She closed her eyes to control her fear... *don't think about it... don't think about at it.* Luxylan's screams suddenly reached her ears and rippled through her body, distant, but urgent.

"Don't run. We won't get far." Daniel's angular jawline was set in a gaunt expression. "I'm going to make a shield, we'll have a better chance if we hide and prepare. "

"But how will we fight? Do you know any *Darkness* spells?" She stared at him in horror. "This is madness, we'll never succeed alone."

"Have you got a better idea? " Two thick, black shapes appeared on the horizon. The viewing spell was no longer needed. Amber's taunting alive and armed. Each wingspan, like Mountains of

ObaMoor, that trailed wispy lines of deadly ash. She remembered how, in Obakeech, the valley had shrivelled to a grey desert at its hands. She looked at her companion, an Elf, who didn't even know her surname. She fell to the ground next to him.

"Hurry up," her throat tightened. "Do what ever you need. Get that dome up." Daniel was fumbling with his pouch and losing several droplets. "Quiet," he hissed, his hand shaking.

"I can see only two," he said loudly, as a giant shield of water sprang from his hands and engulfed them both, arching into a dome. Eleanor entranced, felt instantly safer inside.

"Put some of your light in it.… You know your power thing."

"I can't, I need my rope and space."

"Then, I'm going to move the dome, so there's a gap at the back."

"For what."

"Your stupid rope."

"Why? D'ya mean I'm to throw it at them?"

"It's light? Maybe it can help." He suddenly looked younger, vulnerable. "Doesn't it grow or something?"

"There is a spell," Eleanor said hurriedly. "Morwena showed me in the valley, we created a light dome with it, but she helped me." Luxylan came swooping overhead. A streak of rich yellow like a watery mirage floated across the top of the dome.

"Can you do it again?"

"No idea." Daniel waved his hand over a patch in front of her, and the moving water stilled.

"They've reached the top of the rise." Mesmerised, her eyes fixed on the beasts. They had hit the valley's air current to follow the line of the stream. Green eyes shone like drops of poison. Heads covered in black matted long hair parting over a narrow claw-like jaw. The jaw protruded into a shiny hook. Scaly legs stretched to the ground, ending in wide bent talons ready to pick up their prey. Each talon shone green like the eyes. Nothing at home was anywhere near to it in size.

"They're splitting up?" Daniel twisted around in the dome.

Eleanor could see his arm was shaking with the effort of keeping his spell.

"Here hold the spell," he said suddenly. "I'm going to try something."

"No.. wah," Eleanor bellowed... but it was too late. Daniel thrust the water funnel into her hand. "Focus," he yelled.

Eleanor's hand shook. Their only protection would disintegrate in moments. He disappeared through. She couldn't see him. Twang... Twang..... filled the air. His bow at full stretch. Sweat dripped from her forehead. The dome was getting thinner, slower, it wasn't responding to anything she was doing.

"Daniel," she yelled. He collapsed back into the dome. "Ash..." He was visibly shaking. The air that came in with him, was thick and hot. It filled the dome.

"Take it." Eleanor released the spell with a wave of relief. "Hang on," Daniel spluttered. Eleanor's hand slipped.

"The funnel," he shouted. Eleanor watched in horror as the swirling water slowed. Each droplet froze in mid-air, holding for a single breath, before collapsing to the ground. Daniel's eyes stood out like a circle around the sun.

"Watch out," she screamed as over his head appeared the point of a jaw, covered in spiky hair glistening with wet sticky goo. Eleanor lashed her rope. The light shone brightly and the talon veered away. Ash fell. Eleanor's skin burned. She howled out in pain.

"Your spell... I'll distract it." Daniel ran. She screamed words that faded into the heat. He would die because of his recklessness. Eleanor tried to remember the order of Morwena words. The screeches were as loud as a bell tower.

"Eleanor," Daniel's voice evaporated. With trembling hands, she began to chant. This beast had come for her. Daniel couldn't help her now. This Gulabird was after a Sprite and she didn't want to die. The soft light of her rope brighten and danced, making patterns on the mud around her feet. But its glow was weakened as a strong patch of light licked its long tongue. She glanced up to see an incredible column of swirling orange colours stretching into the sky, burning like a beacon. Eleanor followed the column upwards. There in the horizon was the darkest cloud she'd ever seen. It overshadowed everything. The beast saw it too. Its angry jaw opened to let out an almighty roar. Its green eyes momentarily clouded and turned black. In those fleeting seconds, Eleanor saw her father and Elerday waving, like misty ghosts. Standing on The Moors shrouded in a white mist floating in and out of sight. Her skin itched and something hit her stomach so hard her spine vibrated. She blinked and their images evaporated.

The beast swooped in that instant, cutting the air as it narrowed to dive. Jaw open, revealing mountainous pointy peaks of teeth, lined in ever decreasing rows. Its thick black tongue dripping in anticipation. Eleanor lashed her rope, her revulsion strong and raw. She pivoted as if balancing on a narrow ledge. A bright light filled the air mixed with seeping patches of ash and exploded into a million pieces. Eleanor disappeared into a wind bolt dancing with fear.

38

ORRAN DU VANIK

Orran marched passed the guards, as they saluted. He felt pleased to be back within the confines of tunnels and passageways that made up his family Compound.

He had dismissed his accompanying Imps and issued his brother Doric, another task. He had to keep his younger brother busy, so he wouldn't cause any trouble. He was mildly concerned about Doric. Despite his servant's death, who he knew he was close to, there was something else. Orran decided he would need to prize it out of him when he'd got a moment.

His meeting at The Rock of Vespic had been satisfactory, except for the interruption. How had that Sprite, Morwena, found out about their plans? If he had a leak in his family, the culprit would pay dearly. If it was an Elf traitor, he would enjoy his revenge. But on reflection, he knew that just one old Sprite couldn't do anything to stop their plan now.

He drew closer to his parents' quarters. His first task, much to his annoyance, was, a courtesy visit to his father. This made him irritated. But first he had to check his own chambers - make sure everything was working how it should. He strode on thinking of ways he would run the family instead of his father. He did everything anyway, even his brothers answered to him. All except Seth, the eldest, who he felt, lived in a completely different world to any normal Imp. And... of course the general running of the household was a female's role anyway. So what else did his father do?

Arriving at his private chambers, he stopped at his door and felt its solid oak planks, warm and smooth, before entering. He liked the familiarity of knowing everything that went on. He barked orders to the few servants he saw, feeling slightly uneasy by their lack of a warm welcome. He wondered if they realised what he'd just done. He was securing the Vaniks as the head family of Arramond. Therefore, their future would be more assured. Yet they darted away from him in all directions. No matter... it wasn't important. He quickly set about washing and putting on a fresh set of clothes.

Once he was completely satisfied that everyone was doing what he wanted, he beckoned two servants to accompany him and headed towards his parents' quarters. Their arched wooden doors, were framed by granite guards holding long spears. It wasn't the warmest of entrances. Without knocking, he collapsed his full weight against the wood, and heaved forwards. He ordered his servants to stay by the door. It was important to be cautious even here.

Orran looked around the outer chamber, a large impressive room. A great fire danced in the hearth; he guessed his mother was close. The stone floor was covered in ruby red embroidered rugs and the walls draped in hangings, rich in golds - Mother liked her comforts.

His father entered the chamber from a side door and seemed surprised to see him. "I did not hear you knock, Orran?"

Orran gave a curt bow. "But we have nothing to hide, Father."

His father snorted, "So, what news do you bring?" Orran moved towards the engraved throne chair at the head of a long table, taking time to make himself comfortable. He ushered his father to join him, who declined, with a look on his face. Orran decided to ignore it.

"My meeting with the Eastling Elves went well. I am to help them to gain complete control of Caradoc and by the sounds of things that isn't far from happening. Most of The Council of Caradoc have changed their allegiances to Tonurang." Orran paused wondering if his father was listening, "In return he has promised to rid Arramond of the Garnaforts once and for all."

His father walked over to the fire and threw a letter into the flames. "How do you know he can be trusted?"

Orran slammed his hand down onto the wood. "Oh come, Father, surely you know he can't." He took a deep slow breath. "But he'll do anything I ask of him until he gets the real *Stone of Innvericum*." His father looked up from the flames. "Which, of course," Orran continued, "I have no intention of ever giving him." Was that annoyance across his father's face? Orran felt his irritation rise.

"Who rules Caradoc is of no concern to me, as you well know. All I'm interested in, is that for the time being, those irritating Elves will help me to secure my future... I mean our future. His father walked around the table, "But Orran, if you cross Tonurang, at the end of all of this, you'll make him into a very powerful enemy and that will have repercussions on us all." The fire crackled, as Orran wondered where his mother was. She was much more pleasing to talk to.

"But it won't be our fault," Orran continued.

"How?"

"York has secretly been tracking the remaining Garnafort family. A group is left alive, including Tam the eldest and a few other brothers. As you know I killed Solomon and Aldrena the elders." For a fleeting moment the image of Solomon's weak neck lying in his hands dipped into his conscience. "While Scarlet, their Fire-Maker, is nowhere to be found, lost on The Moorlands and probably dead in a ditch." Orran thought he saw a look of distain shadow his father's face but continued. "York has been successfully tracking them southwards; Tam would be the only other Imp alive, outside of our family, to know of *The Stone*'s whereabouts. They will be under the illusion it will help them regain power, grasping onto any chances without a Fire-Maker."

"You mean, who know about *The Stone*'s whereabouts, alive within the *North* of Arramond?" his father interjected.

"Yes, yes what of it? Orran threw his father a look of venom. "May I continue?" His father gave a mock bow. "I will enable *The Stone*'s release to Tam, making it relatively difficult, so he doesn't expect anything. When the time comes for Tonurang to help us to rule, he will learn of the Garnafort's possession. During the ensuing battle, York will make sure *The Stone* goes missing. Tonurang will only have himself or the Garnaforts to blame."

His father shook his head. "It sounds good, Orran, but I'm still unsure how you're going to manage to fight in Caradoc and ensure York's eventual success. Remember The Garnaforts have been Arramond's rulers for several generations for a reason."

"Yes but at least I have the guts to do something about that." Orran rose from his chair and pushed it aside.

39

OSTRIC'S TRICK

An orchestra of deafening cries tore through Tristan's head, jarring his teeth. But the cries meant the *fire* was working. With a surge of effort, he released his spell. Leaves, mud and clumps of grass amalgamated into a hairy uneven, floating wall. He guided it precariously. His arms trembling. He wanted to try and funnel the flames to the centre. But the heat, like waves of a sand storm, was making it almost impossible to see. Deathly spirals of dark ash filled the gaps, like dancing angry monkeys. He'd lost sight of Scarlet. She had merged into the twists of orange and white. All his knowledge of Imps and their powers had shattered like glass, she surely was a direct decentant of Creoda.

The wall had formed, to shoulder height, linked into a circle. He could see a few Gulabirds had escaped. Oversized, they filled the skyline like floating grey blankets. The trees were a barrier behind him, so each one had flown straight towards Vagen, Christian and Enka, their hunting instincts too strong to be fooled by luring Moorlands. The cloud was at its most vulnerable and cruel. It had halved in size, twisting and turning, as it writhed in agony. Ostric never died without a trick, Tristan just had to work out what it was.

He crept forwards edging onto The Moors. Her claws of prickly heat were subsiding. Tristan steadied his spell. Was she tiring? Had she done enough? He halted his spell. The wall would have to do. He leapt through the ash, surrounding himself within an earth shield. The image of her body flickered. Every last drop of the fire was spilling into herself. Tristan shuddered - Ostric's plan revealed. She was too young to know. Tristan ran faster, stretching every muscle to its limit. Exploding ash turned plants to ghostly remains. He stumbled, as his foot twisted, collapsing onto the ground and rolling on his back. He swore aloud, ignoring the coursing pain. He launched a covering spell. Not a drop of the Darkness must fall onto her. His arms at full stretch, but he wasn't at the right angle. He had to break his wall. He sprang across the last patch of burnt scrub before his spell descended. Charred earth scratched at his throat. The pounding of his heart pulsated in his ear drums.

He parted the earth just enough, for Scarlet to swung into view. Like flowing lava his spell released into the tunnel dome, stopping her *Element*, like collapsing pieces of string. He rolled underneath, panting. He knew Scarlet was in there somewhere, as the sides of the walls descended around them. He lay cocooned by the dark, heaving and blinking. His senses trying to detect where she was. He hoped they had done enough to destroy the nest. The lurid smell washed over him, a mixture of lemon and blood. His stomach clenched. Had he asked too much of her? He knew if *The Darkness* was destroyed his reputation would be restored, and his reasons for befriending her forgiven. But had he just used her, like so many others in his quest against Ostric?

He carefully parted one side of their encasement. Ash floated like snow outside. He saw her for the first time, laying in a foetal position only an arm's distance from him. He called to the surrounding leaves from the copse, asking for their help. They came in hundreds, swirling between the ashes, and entered the dome. With a spell Toria had taught him, he knitted them into a blanket. Although his efforts were poor. He had laughed at Toria, when she was teaching him so earnestly. Scarlet didn't stir as the leaves wound around her. He gingerly went to her side. Her arm was cold and face almost translucent, with red protruding veins. He carefully scooped her into his arms. Fresh blood dripped from both eyes. He must find Enka. He should never have asked her to do this. Was his quest all he thought about? Quickly he ran back into the trees, ignoring the damage done. Finding the pathway with ease back to the clearing.

Enka, Vagen and Christian, were already there.

"You did it." Vagen looked genuinely relieved. Tristan didn't reply. Enka rushed over.

"What happened," she said, "why are you carrying her?" Tristan spoke for Enka to hear only, "I did very little, her fire was so fierce, she killed the nest with only a guiding spell from me." Enka stood back and looked at Tristan quizzically.

"But that's impossible, only an experienced Fire-Maker could do that?"

"I know," he said quietly, "we must help her now, it has taken its toll, look there's blood."

"Give her to me," Enka insisted, "I will need to hurry - lay her down and fetch more clothes from my Armorak, your leaf cloak is terrible, brother."

Tristan gave a weak smile, "I feel I have..." he said.

"Go," Enka ordered, "before Vagen asks questions. Look they are already coming over."

Tristan hesitated. "The Armorak, brother - hurry you must find them." Tristan was grateful to Enka. He would never be able to lead without his sisters.

"Now - go." He turned and ran down the southern pathway. He was glad to get away and hadn't given the beasts a thought during the last *Shadow*. He hoped they'd survived. And thanks to Enka's quick thinking, it would give him time to clear his head before he faced Vagen and Christian. He reached the other side of the copse, and called out to Daventour. He was relieved to see there were only a few scarred branches, and no lasting signs of *The Darkness*. He searched and called. For such enormous animals, they weren't easy to find. He ran his hand through his hair, as he whistled. He tried to ignore the aching pain that ran through his ankle.

"What's wrong with her?" A sharp tongue ripped through the hazel. Tristan turned. "It's been a long time, Tristan Corrinium."

"How did you get here?" Understanding now why his Armoraks weren't appearing.

"I've been fighting with your companions."

"I didn't see..." Tristan replied.

"I know; you were having troubles of your own."

"Were the Gulabirds after you?" He looked carefully into the green sharp eyes.

"You tell me!" she crackled, "Earth One - isn't that your skill or has a certain young Imp clouded your judgement?" Tristan looked at the old face carefully, she wasn't smiling as she said that and her skin was speckled with hints of yellow. She had clearly been on The Moors for a while.

"The Imp," Morwena said, "you carried her."

"She's killed the nest... but the effort was too much."

"Do you care for her?"

"She's under my protection," he felt himself getting annoyed.

"Huh," Morwena said, "interesting. Anyway - four escaped, heading south towards Arramond."

"But how, why? I thought they were all killed?"

"Well we didn't..."

Tristan couldn't read her reaction. "Then who are they after, if you are here?"

"A young Sprite and Elf. I believe you've met him - Daniel Elf Trevarak." Tristan shuddered - *his oath*.

"They will never defeat them alone," he said. The Armorak, Yoken appeared and protruded his long nose forwards. Tristan ran his hand across the shell that protected the soft skin. "Two of my messengers were killed, a few *Turns* ago," he said. "They were guarding our northern outpost. One made it home only to die in our arena. So tell me, what is going on within Vearmoor, Morwena?"

"That I must find out," she paused. "It is time to go home whatever the risks. I will take the Sprites in the clearing with me. Will he live?"

"For a while."

"Will you thank Enka for me, I am in her debt?"

"I will," Tristan was unsettled. He had never heard of thanks from a Sprite Elite. "You must promise me one thing, Pixie," Morwena said, taking in a deep breath. "On your oath you must kill those remaining Gulabirds and ensure those two young Tribelings get to Arramond's border alive."

"Arramond? What are you scheming?"

"He has to find the real *Stone of Innvericum*."

"Is he worthy?" Tristan pulled the leather bag off Yoken's back.

"I don't know. But his father is wise - one of us - so hopefully he banished his own Elfling for a reason."

"You are playing with *The Balance*, Morwena, Ostric is clearly mad with you and if you're not careful many of us will pay for it. And Daniel could die, if he isn't."

"But if Ostric does rise in Caradoc, the Elves will need their Power Gift or else the land will be overrun."

"Another pawn in our game against the great Lord Ostric." Tristan roughly pulled the saddle bag off Yoken's back. "I must hurry, Tristan continued.

"Yes - back to your Imp." Morwena reached out to touch Yoken's shell. Tristan looked at the yellow old skin, troughs and rivets like the undulation of a farmer's field. "It would be a good idea," she said slowly, "if you sent your Imp home, it will only cause more trouble the longer you keep her."

"Whatever happens," he sharply replied, "she is the least of our problems. I must tackle those loose Gulabirds which now have a massive head start on us. And..." He paused.

"Tristan, you must do what is right for your Tribe."

Tristan pulled the saddle bag over his shoulder. "Sort our Vearmoor first Morwena, then you can start telling me what to do." He turned back into the clearing.

40

POWER OF THREE

At meal times, Daniel remembered his father liked nothing better than describing how other Tribes lived, what powers they had, and how their lands looked. The Imp border was one of his favourite topics.

"We need to rest." Eleanor had her back slightly turned. Daniel glimpsed the scare she was tending. It was a deep greyish purple, trickles of blood ran down her forearm. She was squishing something green over it. He wondered if her spell had backfired. When she turned to look at him, thick grey rings circled her eye. Patched of skin looked dark and sore. The ash had done its work well.

"We can't afford to," she replied, while chewing on something and glaring at him. "Killing those birds hasn't changed a thing." Daniel knew she was right; the mugginess still wrapped itself over them - Ostric was still alive somewhere. If The Moors had taught him anything, he knew he could never rest.

"I saw something," Elenor muttered. "when that things was above me."

"You mean, just before you killed it," Daniel paused.

"Yeah, well. It was a column of fire."

"Where?"

"Into the nest."

"Are you sure?" Daniel stopped talking abruptly as bits of earth had started to fall on his clothes.

"Eleanor, what are you up to?" he rolled onto his front and pushed his arms into the ground.

"What's that?" Eleanor was looking in the opposite direction over his shoulder and protecting her eyes. Daniel thought he could hear a whooshing sound.

"Give me your viewing things, quick," she said. Time slowed, Daniel lay paralysed watching a flying clump of earth, with bits of tree and roots sticking out of it whizzed through the air towards them. He had neither the time or energy to move. Wobbling from side to side. It flew at a crazy pace down the valley, before collapsing into the hillside, exploding noisily, and spewing bits everywhere.

Eleanor let out a panicky scream. Her reactions jaded and slow. Mud and earth rained down around them, like a violent hail storm. Several thuds hit the ground. Daniel raised a water shield, just as one large cloud of clay bounced above his face. Blinking and protecting his face, he gazed through the dusty haze. Something red came rolling into view. *A warning party?* Images merged between the flaky dirt and red twisting strands. He threw a handful of droplets chanting a spell.

"Don't attack," came a voice. Daniel froze, holding his breath. He slowly lowered his shield. Something made him stop.

"Daniel." A Tribeling shaped tree was poking out of a massive pile of earth.

"Vagen," Daniel said tentatively.

"Yes," he sputtered, his cloak appearing. "Give us a hand." Half his body was sunk in deep. Daniel scrabbled over. "How... did...? I mean... what was that?" Daniel grabbed his hand and pulled. "A form of travel I hate," he replied bitterly. "But we had to get to you."

Tristan appeared, "That didn't go to plan," he grunted, no displaying his usually composure. Daniel smiled - he was covered head to foot in branches, twings and leaves and furiously shaking mud from his hair. "Our Armoraks were too frightened to come any further. Christian returned to Poldaric with them. It was either earth travel... that," he pointed to the remains of earth, or run.

Vagen smirked. "Which I think I would've preferred. Tristan, that was your worst yet." Vagen thumped his chest. "Good to see you're alive, Elf."

Daniel smiled.

"Tristan, I'm making it next time." Daniel looked at the female Pixie who'd spoken, her olive skin was deathly pale and she was holding her stomach.

Eleanor appeared from her transformation spell, "was it you who created the fire?"

"No," Tristan replied, seemingly unfazed by her arrival. "It was her," he pointed to the Imp. Daniel's gaze fell on the pale Tribeling – she was so small, compared to the males he'd previously seen. Her striking hair looked wrong against the mutted colours of The Moors, as if her creator had never meant her to hide.

"She did?" Daniel said quickly. No one replied for a moment until she muttered. "My Element's - *Fire*," her accent was rich.

"I'm pleased to see you," Tristan broke the unease. Daniel quickly turned from the Imp's intense gaze. "You look awful," Tristan grinned. Daniel made a peace sign, "And you too."

"So who is your Sprite companion?" Tristan asked. Daniel noticed part of his beautiful leaf cloak was burnt exposing most of his shoulder.

"Eleanor, Eleanor..." Daniel mumbled.

"Eleanor Paraquinn." She cast Daniel a look. Tristan introduced each of the Pixies in turn.

"We've encountered Morwena du Gwent," Tristan said, "and two others."

"Sprites?" Eleanor asked rapidly.

"Yes, Francis and one of his daughters Elerday. Do you know them?" Daniel watched Eleanor stumbled, her hands sprang to cover her face.

"They are both well, honestly." Daniel noticed Tristan give Enka a look. His stomach notted, Tristan wasn't telling the truth. "Morwena is indestructible, only tired." Tristan continued, "she is going to take them home to Vearmoor. They will be out of harms way very soon. We are here to kill the remaining Gulabirds and help you too...."

A sudden gust of wind roared and sang over the rocks. The heat doubled in an instant. Eleanor instantly disappeared. Daniel swore to himself. "So soon?" he yelled.

"They're quick," Enka shouted, "they've caught up with us."

"Unite Pixies," Tristan shouted, "form a barrier wall." The atmosphere thickened, and the skyline darkened almost instantly.

"Run... get to the border, Elf." Tristan called, "Morwena is right, you must try and get *The Stone*." Tristan's gaze left no room to argue.

"Eleanor?" Daniel shouted. A renewed surge of energy pulsed through him, united with other Tribelings. A Gulabird appeared and dropped from the sky, skilfully twisting into a dart. Daniel knew this time it didn't want to make a mistake. Whistling as it cut through the air, raining black ash and crying its battle sream.

"Get down," Daniel bellowed. He threw several droplets. He covered his last arrow with a water spell and shot at the beast's head, but it continued its decent. With the speed of a hare, a series of fire bolts rained over his head. The Gulabird stopped in mid-air, hovered with its wings fully stretched. It glowed red. The red turned into an orangey haze and spread over the whole bird, its eyes shining a warning green, before exploding into grey ash, and scattering across the ground. A thin wall of earth appeared above them and spread like an opened umbrella.

"Keep running," Tristan shouted, "go." Daniel leapt up. "Come on," he yanked Eleanor by the arm, who had appeared like a mirage by his side. With the Imp, they ran. Sweat slipped down his back. The Imp was sending wild fire bolts in all directions. But wasn't as fast at running.

"Keep up," he called.

"I can't," she puffed. Then to his horror she abruptly stopped in her tracks, gasping for breath.

"What are you doing?" Eleanor, yelled, "we're too exposed," she shouted, her voice sounded like notes played on a flute.

"Get behind me," the Imp replied. Daniel flinched at her tone. Fire shot from her tiny hands. It hit the grass in front of them and patches burst into flames. "I'll create a wall," she shouted, "can you do anything?"

"I'll help." Eleanor sent a torrent of wind bolts into the flames. Daniel rooted to spot, *useless*. His *Element* would only hinder. He moved slowly behind the growing wall of fire. He prepared for attack from above. The scene quietened. Feeling as if every heart beat took a full *Turn* to complete. His vision blurred, as the sky murged into hazy blotches of white, with an almost spring like feel. Lavender replaced the ash and filled his senses. He closed his eyes and breathed deeply. Looking up, instead of the fire wall, darkness and confusion, he saw his mother, her face as clear as the last time he'd seen her. *She has said she'd come.*

"Is it you? Are you really here?" he whispered, and reached out to touch the outstretched hand, her rough skin, warm, familiar. A sudden longing washed over him. Her face broke into a veiled smile, parting thick clear, tears. She pulled him close. Her felt her hand slide into his tunic pocket and pull out his remaining pouch - he let her without question. She said something that he didn't understand and the pouch shone a rich blue. She gently replaced it and stroked her hand across his face as her image began to fade. She mouthed something to him, that Daniel couldn't understand. Daniel reached out his hand, "where are you going... No wah!" he bellowed.

"What is wrong with you.... fire something." Eleanor screamed in his face. He shuddered as the smoke fumes, black ash and swirling dust appeared.

Eleanor shouted again. "Move!" As she swung her rope and a rain of fire bolts missed their target. A Gulabirds, hauntingly hung in the air, still very much alive. Its enormous wing span dwarfing all other parts of the sky.

"This isn't working," he yelled. Eleanor looked back at him, with a mixture of anger and fear.

"We can see that," she snapped, "and she keeps missing for some reason. But you're just standing there."

"We need to throw our *Elements* together."

"Are you crazy?" Eleanor shouted, "firstly we'll never manage it, and secondly yours works against hers."

"Trust me, this'll work," he ran in front of them, with the heat burning his face.

41

BETRAYAL

"Do you think there'll be any more?" Eleanor sat in bracken. No matter how she tried, she couldn't get comfortable, every part of her ached. She placed the handful of redcurrants into her mouth, wishing she had some of her mother's honey loaf to go with them, she was starving.

"No, they're definitely gone," Tristan sat apart, on a high rock, basking in the first rays of light exchange. "Your united attack was brutal," he shielded his face as he turned to her.

"Impressive team you three." Vagen patted Daniel on the back as he strode by. "Who'd have thought an Elf, Sprite and Imp would work together?" Eleanor was busy studying the jumble of battle scars that scorched the earth, like pathways of death across the landscape. She had to keep checking just in case one more appeared, even though she knew they were gone. Eventually she looked up at Tristan as he spoke to his fellow Pixies. She studied his clothing, reflecting the greys and blues of the sky and the mottled grassy greens.

"How was my father?" she interrupted still in shock that Morwena's crazy rantings had been true and that Blaydoc had actually talked through her.

"Okay" he replied too quickly. Eleanor's throat tightened. "How okay?"

"After we... helped him." He stopped. Enka came up to her and placed her hand gently on her shoulder.

"Your father was hurt," she said. "But is better now. I will explain when we are in a safer place."

"But I need to know now..."

Daniel interrupted.

"I've just seen my mother," His stare blank, as if he'd been dreaming.

"Crazy Elf," Vagen chuckled, "that's impossible. You're just going mad from being out here for so long."

"No, really," Daniel stood up, "I know it sounds stupid but I'm sure it was her..." he paused. "But I can't have - right?" he stared at them all, "I must have dreamt it?"

Vagen smiled. "So, while we were fighting Elf, you were just having a chat with your mum!"

Daniel stared blankly. "Actually, it might not be... crazy." Everyone looked at Enka. "Did your mother, uh... do anything?" Eleanor could see furrowed lines wrinkled around her eyes and the smooth curve of brown lips.

"She was crying, which she never does." Daniel shook his head. "And she took my pouch... only for a moment."

Tristan looked up, "What did you say?"

"Took my pouch. Well it happened so quickly," he said. "And those things were above our heads. Uh... her hand was almost translucent." Tristan and Enka exchanged looks.

"Daniel!" Tristan jumped to his feet, "and you didn't stop her?"

"It was my mother," Daniel shouted.

"Tristan," Enka said firmly. "Daniel, can I see your *Element?*" Daniel fumbled inside his tunic. Eleanor could see his hands were shaking.

"It's darkened," Eleanor said aghast as the leathery material spilled over his hand. She had grown used to seeing it. Vagen reached for his sword.

"It's alright," Enka said, holding her arms out, as if to stop them all from moving. "It's not Ostric, I would know..." she said. "But someone or something did come to you, Daniel. Given you something, maybe a fleck of Istria's *Light*; look at the rich blue - it's remarkable. Did you call on Istria?"

"No wah," Daniel looked startled. "How would I?" Enka spoke quickly in Pixian to Tristan and Vagen. Their words like a song, rhyming, with high and low tones.

"What are you saying?" Scarlet interrupted. Eleanor turned quickly, she had almost forgotten the Imp, who'd been sitting quietly, apart, like a hunter, hidden, waiting to pounce. Clearly she'd just been listening, plotting. Eleanor didn't like or trust her.

"We need to understand what Daniel's been given." Tristan replied. "Would your mother know how to call on the Goddess?" He shock his head, "of course she would... its Anta isn't it."

Daniel eyebrows crinkled into a frown. "Yes," Tristan rubbed his hand across his chin. "Enka thinks you thought of her, to give you strength, and somehow that created a link. Did your mother give you anything when you left."

"This." Daniel pulled out the moon shaped stone.

"Can you make a lump of earth hover for me?" Eleanor realised Tristan's odd question was directed at her.

"Sure," she replied, "why?"

"If the earth is moving around in a continuous circle we can cast our viewing spell. We need the stone to be dropped into the moving spell when I ask. Can you do that Daniel?"

"But how is that going to help Daniel?"

"You'll see," Tristan replied. Scarlet edged forwards, Eleanor could feel her presence. It made her heart beat quicker.

"But how will it show us anything?" Eleanor asked.

"Patience," he said quietly. Tristan knelt and scooped a handful of earth into his hands; then positioned himself closer to Daniel and stood with his feet square, concentrating. He nodded to Eleanor. She closed her eyes and tried to block Scarlet's red hair from her mind. She hadn't wanted to let on that no one had taught her how to move an object using her *Element*. It had been the lesson Morwena had promised before she left the valley. Quelling the rising tide of potential failure. Eleanor thought of every spell, she knew, words swirled inside her head, mixing. She said the only vague spell relevant she could think of crasping a bits of Morwena's teachings. She opened her eyes to see the earth pivoting in a circle. She surpressed a smile.

"Now Daniel," Enka said, "drop the stone and think of your home."

"I can see Caradoc," Daniel suddenly shouted. Eleanor jolted and the spell collapsed. A flicker of exasperation crossed Tristan's face. "Let's try again," he said through a strained smile, shaking the dust off his clothes. "Daniel – you will see your homeland as it is now, maybe even your parents, so are you ready? Whatever state they're in?"

"Yes," Daniel replied, his slanted smile unusually strained.

"Eleanor... you?" Tristan said. She gritted her teeth. She felt as if the whole Moorland had quietened around them.

"I can see The Great Hall," Daniel said quietly. Eleanor dared not look; she focused solely on the flying earth. "I'm actually walking inside," Daniel's words carried around them. "Someone's lying on the floor, in a black pool of something. I can't see who... look! My father," Daniel exclaimed, "by the great altar." Eleanor held her breath. "He's firing water droplets... no... wait. He's sending out a droplet message."

"It that normal?" Enka asked quietly.

"Yes... to call Elves together."

"Tell us, everything you can see," Enka urged. "We can't hold this for much longer."

"He's watching the ceiling, like he did at my trial. Shadows and glowing lights are darting everywhere." Daneil's voice rose, "There... there's my mother. She'd hiding... Behind a pillar. That's how I saw her, she's crying, she's holding something – she's sending it into the ceiling. But my father isn't seeing her do it..." The circle shock and hesitated. Then disintegrated.

"What... wait," Daniel said angrily. "Where's it gone? Tristan, I want to know why she's doing that. Get it back." Tristan's face was set into a frown. "Don't challenge me Elf..." he growled.

"I'm not..." Daniel grew taller, "but I want to know if she was helping him?" Eleanor laid a hand on his shoulder, "Daniel calm down." He angrily brushed it aside.

"Your father was trying to predict the future of Caradoc." Tristan turned his back. "Maybe she was trying to make the outcome more positive."

"But that's wrong," Daniel shouted. "And doesn't make sense. She would never do that. Anyway we know what's going to happen," Daniel hadn't lowered his tone, "I was there at the meeting between Orran and Tonurang. It is set from now, in two *Turns*, there will be war! And if that happens we all know Ostric will return stronger than ever."

"Why do you use his name so freely?"

"What?" Daniel looked as if he'd been smacked in the mouth.

"You're not an Earth Guardian or an Elder, and have not won the right?" Eleanor moved away from them both.

"She's playing with all our lives..." Tristan yelled, "whatever the spell she was doing, it disturbs *The Balance*." Eleanor saw fear etch into Daniel's expressions.

"But that's impossible. It's just my mother, and she'd never go behind his back or challenge the Gods." Daniel slipped his hand to his bow. Eleanor felt her protective web come alive.

"You must get the real *Stone* and quickly," Enka moved to stand between Daniel and Tristan. "Try and get back into Caradoc before the Imps do. Daniel can you hear me." Not an insect buzzed or bird sang as she spoke. Its life seeping away like the ebbing of a tide.

"I will go with you."

"What?" Daniel span on his feet. Her voice calm yet strong. "I won't be returning to Poldaric. I would never belong there. I can get you into Arramond, otherwise you'll never cross the border."

"That makes sense." Vagen answered. Tristan held his baton, his knuckles tightly looped around the wood.

"Yes, you should go." Pain flickered across the Imps face at Tristan's words. "Remember Elf," Tristan continued, "only those who are truly worth can pick up *The Stone*. Do not ask Istria for help. This won't work in your favour."

"Daniel...." Eleanor stepped in.

"My family would never harm the Balance," Daniel retorted.

"That's as it maybe Elf, but only time will tell if you're right."

"And you?" Daniel said aggressively, his gaunt and desperate expression etched in thick lines as he stared at Eleanor. Eleanor wanted the ground to swallow her whole. She felt as if a thin veil had suddenly appeared and wrapped itself around them both, blocking out the others. Daniel's blue eyes bore into her as a strand of his hair fell across his face. All she wanted to do was brush it aside, rather than decide if Arramond was her fate.

42

IMP BORDER

Mangled thin branches like a spider's web stuck around Scarlet's hand. She needed to get a better view of the border patrol. They had covered the final part of their journey in silence, which suited her well, she had a lot on her mind. The Moorland was awkward to manoeuvre as sand over took the grasses. Her feet sank deeply. Rocks were buried under the sand and kept tripping her over. She was so much slower than the other two, which really annoyed her. She hated looking weak.

Squinting, she could just make out the guards. It was strange seeing her own tribe again. Her thoughts turned to Poldaric. He hadn't wanted her to return. Even though he had promised her she could. It was obvious. She didn't belong. She had been a problem. Imps and Pixies don't mix. Despite their outward kindness, really she knew, she had only been used. An Imp who had no control. She was useless in their minds. Her thoughts lingered on Toria. Her only true friend whom she'd harmed.

Eleanor sighed a long withering groan.

"You ok?" Daniel mumbled, breaking the silence.

"What do you think?" she replied gruffly. Scarlet kept quiet. Scarlet knew that neither of them wanted to go into her homeland; and who'd blame them, Imps weren't exactly liked. She had no idea if they could find the *Stone* thing, but perhaps the journey would lead her closer to finding out what had happened to her family. Or what Orran was up to. She did have to at some stage face her past. Memories of being chained in her carrier, Orran's prison, his hands on her skin and his breath. How his Vanik henchmen had fought her brothers. Her eyes clouded in shame.

"I can see three on patrol," Daniel whispered. He was looking through something.

Scarlet twisted around. "What's that?" He came forwards and held the film in front of her face. She screwed up her nose. "That's useful, Elf," she said. "And another three to the north," she followed his line.

"We'll aim for there," he replied pointing to the middle.

"What about that way?" Eleanor nodded in the opposite direction. "There's no one over there!"

"Because, that's the cliff edge," Scarlet replied, "and there's nowhere to go except the sea."

Eleanor threw her arms in the air. "Great," she huffed. "Imp warriors or plummeting to our death."

"We must travel as quickly as we can, once we're through," Daniel paused. "Will you know which way to go?" His voice hoarse.

"Yes," Scarlet replied simply. She bit her lip, not wanting him to suspect she hadn't a clue. "The word will get out though, Elf," she continued to compound her lie, "that the border was breached; so we'll be hunted."

"It's Daniel, yeah, not Elf?" he said.

"Ok..." Scarlet replied, suddenly realising she sounded like her high and mighty mother.

"Brilliant," Eleanor sighed. Scarlet pushed her way out from the shrubs.

"What are you doing?" Daniel blurted, "they'll see you and we haven't made a plan." She looked at the distance between where they were and where they had to go. She pushed back in.

"Can you get to the border unseen?" She looked at Eleanor.

"Yeah... sure ?" she grunted.

"So you can get close without them seeing you?" Scarlet said.

"Yesss," she hissed.

"Good..." Eleanor eyes widened. Then with a look of pure hatred, the Sprite muttered something and disappeared. Scarlet wondered what the Imps had done, to make her so angry. "I will get Daniel through the border and come back for you." She called into the air. Scarlet felt a surge of energy, finally in charge and not the one being bossed. This is what she had dreamed of while trapped within her bedroom.

"So we're just going to walk right up?" Daniel had his arms folded.

"Yes," Scarlet replied. "Got a better idea? Anyway if I take your bow and arrow, you'll look like my prisoner." Scarlet could tell he was thinking this over.

"Are you sure you're not just going to use it on me?" Daniel looked a little worried.

"Remember I don't need arrows to kill you, but the guards don't need to know that." Daniel handed over his bow and she slung it over her shoulder, it was heavier than expected. She wanted to look like she knew what she was doing, so tried to lock an arrow. Daniel had made it look so easy, but it was tricky. He pushed his way out of the shrubs.

"This had better work," he growled as he walked ahead. "And hold your arm up straight with the bow, you look pathetic."

"Well... try and act like my prisoner, that might help," she hissed. He shoulders sunk in character, while she adjusted the bow. Scarlet looked up. They'd definitely got the guard's attention. With a drop of sweat from her brow, she locked the arrow and pointed it into Daniel's back, praying her fire and the arrow would stay under control.

As they got closer, two giant hulks glared through the glistening border, hunters, as fierce as caged lions. Her fire began to bubble inside. She breathed deeply. They haphazardly climbed at the gravel path. The guards taunts and whistles got louder. Scarlet had forgotten how rough and wild they were compared to the Pixies, and suddenly missed Tristan's kind expression.

"A prisoner?" one shouted. "How come you're out alone?" He spoke in Impish and his red eyes glared at her in warning. Scarlet felt her fire react. "Orders from Orran Vanik and yes... he's my prisoner," she tried to make her voice sound strong. "Orran, could only trust me to do such an important job." Daniel jerked around, he clearly didn't understand. She roughly pushed him in response. He wasn't easy to manoeuvre.

"We haven't been told. You're lying. Orran always tells his guards." The Imp's tongue fell awkwardly out of his mouth when he spoke, followed by drool.

"Don't be insolent, guard. What's your name? I'll report you." They exchanged looks, as Scarlet drew nearer. Her fingers tingled with nerves.

"So, who are you really?" he snarled through his teeth. His face was jutted forwards into the filmy border. His nose touching, slightly on a slant. Scarlet could see thick black hairs poking out.

"That," she said, feeling sick, "is none of your business. I will only address Orran when I see him. I believe he is waiting for me." The guards stepped back and rapidly talked between each other. Scarlet was close enough to almost touch the watery film. It's multicolours glistening. If she reached out her hand now, she could melt through.

"Well, what are you waiting for Imp, let me through? Isn't that what Gentle-Imps do?" She untied her hair and shook it out. She knew they were watching her with interest.

"I reckon I know who you are."

"Of course you would, I live in Orran's compound... I'm his Imp." Scarlet pushed Daniel to one side and held a ball of fire in her hand. "Now let me through." Suddenly a golden flash of light flew through the air from behind her. It whistled through the boarder and whipped the back of the Imp who'd been speaking. He howled and collapsed. The border fizzed and wobbled, as if something had been sucked through. Daniel swore loudly. Scarlet melted through the border. Her fire had spread up her arm and was covering her body. She yanked Daniel through. The Imps ran for her. "Stay back," she yelled.

"Why are you doing this?" the guard faced her, stretching to his full height. "You're an Imp. The new rulers – the Vaniks – will have you killed for threatening his guards."

"I care nothing for the Vaniks," Scarlet retorted, her fire wiping up over her head and covered her completely.

"I know who you are... you're the missing Fire-Maker... you're Scarlet Garnafort." Scarlet saw him shake in fear, which made her feel strangely powerful. She clapped her hands above her head and savoured the power that coursed through her veins.

"But they're all dead!" he spluttered. "Garnaforts destroyed. We were told you were dead!"

Scarlet's hands trembled and the flame faltered - her family, her beloved Tam and Shanakee, gone! "Stop talking..." she screamed. She felt her heart break, *it can't be true*. Her arms swung down beside her and she felt a great release of agony. Her mind clouded and she felt herself falling, as the flames grew.

*

"Scarlet... Scarlet... wake up...." Daniel's voice, coarse and angry, came whispering through her foggy mind. She suddenly shivered. With a jolt she realised she was soaking. Her clothes were wet, her hair lay in damp tangles.

"Oh no," Scarlet shuddered. She raised her head and held it tenderly. Her sight blinded by early *Exchange*. "What is that?" she groaned.

"The remains of the guard, who challenged you." Daniel's face was deathly pale, his hair soaked.

"No..." Scarlet's hollered, "I can't have?"

"Yes, and you would have killed the other two," Daniel said angrily, "if I hadn't been here, but they are in there."

Scarlet looked at the weird water tower beyond the pile of bones, ash and tattered clothes. "But I didn't let my fire loose for long?"

"Long enough..." Daniel retorted, "we've no time left, your fire will have been seen for miles. More guards will be coming this way."

"But," Scarlet muttered, "I have to do something, help him.... anything."

"Scarlet," Daniel shouted, "he's dead... and look at my arm."

Scarlet felt her head spin, Daniel's red blistered forearm glared at her through his torn shirt.

"Face it," he snarled. Scarlet quickly did as she was told, hating the way the Sprite looked at her, *never again... never again would she let that happen*. Eleanor and Daniel stood silently, staring at the dead remains.

"Did I do anything else?" she looked at them both.

"No, luckily my *Element* works against yours. At least something does," he said. "Now let's go." Daniel glared at her. "Which way?"

Scarlet knelt to the ground, she shakily reached her hand out to touch the charred skull peeling away a piece of his remaining hair. Sick rose to her throat, hot and putrid.

"I don't know," she said quietly. Scarlet's eyes began to ache as blood fell down her cheeks; this time, she did nothing to wipe them away - she deserved the pain.

"What?" Daniel almost spat out his word.

"Look... I don't know." Scarlet turned around. Daniel and Eleanor took a step back. Eleanor had a bizarre look on her face, almost like pity. "I've been a prisoner most of my life," Scarlet shouted, "and I really don't know."

Eleanor walked over, and in a quick movement wiped some of her blood from her check. "Then would one of them know?' she pointed to the swirling water.

Scarlet shrugged. "Imps hate water and will do anything to get out."

43

ARRAMOND

"Are you sure you won't lose it again?" Daniel pressed his hand over his throbbing burn, wondering if it had been a good thing that the Imp had come along.

"Yes," she replied sharply, as she moved to the water tower. Thick black bruises in criss-cross lines covered her skin. He hadn't seen that before. Eleanor stood close by, her glowing rope ready in her hands. He collapsed the spell. It swamped his feet and ran away in thick rivulets. Both Imps, released like birds from their cage, began to shout in growling song.

Scarlet raised her hand, alight with flames. "Silence," she said etched with nerves he'd seen before. The time in their cage had only fuelled a rampant anger. Without warning one of them leapt into the air, twisting in mid-flight, like a hare released from the jaws of a hungry boar. Daniel raised his bow, but he was slow. The Imp like a ray of light stretching into the distance, and was gone.

"He'll warn everyone," Daniel seethed, "hold the other one, Scarlet!" She snarled at the remaining Imp releasing a jet of fire directly at his feet. He halted and turned to face her. They began to talk in words that made no sense.

"What are you saying?" Daniel edged closer. The Imp turned,

looking at him as if he was an irritating fly to swat.

"What choice... I have?" he said louder, "I dead either way. I run like him and Orran kill me. I stay... take what comes."

"Your name?" Scarlet said using Naraling.

"Reuben..."

"What family?"

"Inaat..." Daniel thought he saw Scarlet flinch.

"There isn't much time," Eleanor echoed Daniels' thoughts, "we should get out of here. Scarlet does he know?" Scarlet began again to talk to Reuben quickly in Impish. She held a flame close to his face. Daniel could smell singed hair. The Imp's shoulder hunched and occasionally he launched his arms to the sky. Eleanor paced up and down stamping in the remains of his spell.

"I can," Reuben suddenly said in Naraling, making Eleanor spin around to look at him. The sides of his mouth curled into a warning it was sent to each of them. "But can you keep up?" his red eyes flashed against the lowering sun. Daniel wondered why he was asking him specifically - did he look slow? It would be Scarlet who'd struggle. He gave the Imp a curt nod. Reuben smiled, which made Daniel feel sick, it showed too many bright teeth. The Imp ran over to Scarlet and scooped her into his arms. "We go..." he called. Eleanor threw her hands in the air and sighed, but transformed easily. Daniel momentarily taken aback by Scarlet's complete acceptance of being carried, stood alone. He looked briefly at the transparent border. He, a Trevarak Elf, was in Arramond. He hoped that if he didn't make it back to see that border again; his family would get to hear of what he had tried to do and perhaps his father respect him.

It was hard to keep up. Unused to the terrain, Daniel found the pathways and rocks difficult and had to use various spells to keep himself going. Throwing water droplets to slide over, when the rocks became too irregular. They travelled on for most of a *Shadow* in silence, places he knew he would never be able to identify again. Too many grey bits of granite, rising above his shoulders and blocking out everything of interest. Only the sound of their footsteps told him he was moving. The sky, if he craned his neck upwards, had dulled, no longer the heat of mid *Light Exchange*. There was something alluring about the stillness to the air. For the first time Daniel noticed the relentless wind that blew around him on The Moors didn't reach here, instead if felt like a cotton sheet covering him. In places sand squashed around his feet, reminding him of the lake's shorelines. At least he took comfort that in this network of passageways they were less easily seen.

"We rest here." The Imp had jumped onto a higher boulder. Daniel halted, panting deeply and holding his knees. The Imp pranced to the edge and dropped Scarlet unkindly to the ground. Daniel noticed he'd hardly broken into a sweat. Eleanor clumsily transformed beside him. Her clothes reappeared in a mess, she stumbled into him and he helped her to stand up. She roughly pushed him away. Scarlet was muttering something under her breath as she pulled herself up.

"Why here?" Daniel asked, when he regained his breath.

"There - my dwelling, you eat... rest," Reuben pointed, "you'll never make it if you don't." His face crumbled with distain.

"Have we been followed?" Eleanor gasped.

"No, I sure." Reuben's clipped tone would have made Daniel laugh if they'd been anywhere else. The Imp jumped down from his advantage place and pointed to a large gaping hole between a cluster of rocks. The only tree Daniel had seen on the journey was growing beside it. Short and stunted. Prickly thrones adorned its branches, spreading into a flat wide network of thin leaves. It was the start of several more that grew between the rocks ahead.

"Do you live there?" Scarlet's eyes were wide open.

"Yes," the Imp challenged. Daniel knew he'd slept in some pretty rough places recently but this wasn't inviting. "No one will look, you here," Reuben continued, "or me."

Scarlet gave him a look of suspicion, "What's that?" she pointed to a rusty black cauldron.

He grunted with disgust. "What I use, cook." Daniel wondered why Scarlet didn't know what it was for, as he had a similar one at home, albeit it was used outside.

"You'll find places inside... sleep," Reuben ushered them towards the entrance.

"No..." Scarlet said, "you lead the way." Forming a fireball in her hands. Daniel ushered Eleanor to go with him, he was worried about her, she wasn't herself.

"Don't you live underground like this?" Daniel asked Scarlet, as they entered the cave's dark mouth.

"Yes..." she hesitated, "but not like this." They all filed in, like a line of chained prisoners. The room suddenly opened up, as if a balloon had been blown up to its full capacity. A dome-shaped cavern with several alcoves. Some used for storage and others wide ledges with thick seats in stone. Daniel smiled, he hadn't expected this.

"Then what's your place like?" Eleanor said.

"Bigger..." Scarlet picked up a blanket between two fingers like it was a piece of dirt. Daniel dodged several wooden utensils that hung from the ceiling.

"Sleep," Reuben pointed to the alcoves. "I'll keep eye out."

"I'll watch him," Daniel whispered to Eleanor.

"No. You're half dead," Scarlet said, "I'll do it." Daniel didn't argue, he could hardly see her without his vision blurring over. He went to the nearest ledge and clumsily scrambled on. He pulled a skin from a hook and yanked it over his shoulders. Momentarily he registered it was from an animal he'd didn't recognise, before awkwardly leaning on his side and closing his eyes.

*

He woke in complete darkness, unsure how long he'd slept, unable to hear any of *The Dark Exchange* sounds he was used to. He swung his legs off the ledge, noticing Eleanor was still on close by. Her back was turned, as she lay on her side, but he knew she wasn't sleeping. He looked down to check his hand and burn. It had been covered with a thick fleshy leaf. He carefully lifted it to see a green gooey liquid that smelt of aloe. He stifled a yawn.

"You ok?" he whispered into the dark.

Eleanor shuffled but didn't turn around. "No," she mumbled.

"You looked like you were struggling when you reformed," he said, hoping she wouldn't get mad.

"Go away."

"Eleanor..." he laid a hand on her shoulder. She swung around, her skin reflected her angry green stare.

"My transformation spell isn't working properly, it hurts." Daniel didn't say any more, as Morwena's words came back to him. *That she would have to go home, unable to stay out on The Moors for much longer.* He stared at the cold grey stone above her.

"It's just because you hate being here. It'll pass." He moved on, pushing aside an over hanging pan. "We should go and find them."

"I'll be there in a moment."

He walked in a daze towards the moonlight flickering across the entrance. Blinking, at the brightness of the sky littered with white stars. For a moment he thought of home. Scarlet and Reuben came into view, sitting silently around a small camp fire.

"It's the Ninth Shadow," Scarlet looked up, her eyes swollen as if she'd been crying.

"Eat quickly," Reuben said, "then we leave."

Scarlet handed him a plate of food. "Reuben's explained there is a curfew during *The Dark Exchange* for all Imps, only Vanik Guards are allowed to be out." Scarlet said. "That's why it's so quiet."

"So, it's a good time to travel."

"Yes, as long as we are silent," she replied.

"Does he know which way?" Daniel looked at Scarlet.

"I know," Reuben replied for Scarlet. "She explained... but you mad, you... never come out alive." Daniel followed the long muscular arm to where he pointed. He hadn't seen it earlier. The rocks ended and a wall of grasses sat on the horizon, like an impassable barrier. "It's that way," he grunted.

44

VANIK GUARDS

They set off after Eleanor had eaten. *Darkness Exchange* wrapped around them. Daniel was uneasy; he had always sheltered during these *Shadows* because of *the creatures*. He thought he remembered his father saying that Arramond didn't have any, like elsewhere, but couldn't suppress the increased feeling of unease. Reuben led the way; this time Scarlet wasn't carried. Daniel didn't ask why. She ran at the back. He noticed Reuben's pace had altered, he was slower and constantly looking back to check where she was. *Imps with a caring side*, Daniel found that hard to swallow. Eleanor – flew above somewhere. She had managed to transform after a few tries.

They hit the wall of grasses, like waves of tall willow, unforgiving and at times brutal. Tall, course stalk sprang up and hit his face. If he deviated slightly from the Imp's giant footsteps, a truncated stem spiked tender skin through his leather boot. They stopped, in a flattened area, where the stalks had been squashed to form a perfect circle. Reuben rasied his hand, commanding and threatening in a simple move.

"Where are we?" Daniel looked at Scarlet, whose head was swivelling like an owl's.

"The Balithaque Grasslands," she whispered.

"Don't talk," Reuben hissed. Daniel stood as still as he could, to listen, but heard nothing other than a host of insects. Scarlet edged nearer.

"Imps in grasses, I sense..." Reuben whipsered, "that way, they are," he pointed to the north-west. "We got go faster, you too slow."

"Guards?" Scarlet's eyes were dancing with red flames.

"Yes," Reuben bit back.

"Eleanor," Daniel looked into the air, "can you go and see how far they are from us?"

"No," she reformed and landed by them, "I can't fly anymore." Her face was pale with a slight tinge of green.

"How far is it until the grasses end?" Daniel looked urgently at Reuben.

"Half *Shadow*."

"I won't make it." Eleanor looked ill. Daniel moved to her side.

"I think Reuben's right!" Scarlet knelt down and laid her ear to the ground. "Footsteps from the north, they're running fast," she said. Daniel saw genuine fear across her face. "We have to go..."

"Are they hunting us?" Eleanor said.

"I don't know, maybe, maybe it's just coincidence, but we should go."

"Then run," Daniel grabbed Eleanor's arm. "Come on." Daniel focused on his feet pounding against the hard sand, trying to keep his eyes firmly on the Imp's back, as it flickered between the grasses. He said a silent prayer to The Water Lord. Scarlet gasped for breath. Reuben seemed to be getting faster. He became harder to see, only by the bends in the tall stems, until he'd disappeared. Daniel slowed, confusion at the confronted blank wall. The trail unsure.

"He's left us." Eleanor spat.

"He can't have," Scarlet wheezed between breaths. "Shhh," she hissed. Daniel paused - *maybe this sensing thing was some Imp skill.* "I don't want to be captured by them again."

"E, how much further can you go?" She shook her head. She was visibily shaking. "Damn Reuben..." Daniel muttered. "And if you Scarlet use your powers here, the whole place could burn, with us inside."

"Then we'll have to hide," Eleanor said. "Daniel your shield thing - we used it with the birds." Daniel didn't wait to think, he hurriedly ushered them into the nearest, thickest grasses. Huddling low to the ground, he started to perform his spell.

"The water...?" Scarlet spluttered. Daniel couldn't look at her, he didn't care.

"Shut up," Eleanor snapped, "Daniel, what happens if they walk into it?"

"Then it's over," Daniel banged his hand on the ground to make the spell hurry up, as a barrage of shouts and calls floating over the swishing grasses.

"What about Reuben?" Scarlet muttered.

"He's left us. He's going to have to defend himself?"

"But then we wouldn't know where to go." Eleanor was chewing her hair.

"Shhh," he hissed, "don't move."

"They're definitely searching," Scarlet murmured.

"What's that sound?" Eleanor whispered. "They're cutting the grasses." Scarlet murmured. "What with?" Eleanor looked like she was going to be sick.

"Long blade knives - every Imp warrior carries one."

"Will this dome withstand a knife strike?"

"I don't know.... now just shut up." As if time slowed, each slash of the grass was matched with a groan from Scarlet as she crouched like a curled cat. Daniel's arm trembled, his hand white. Each deep voice grew clearly and louder. Their footsteps no longer running, but walking, searching. Every step a thud into Daniel's conscious. Then, like an vile smell he thought, if the Imps passed by, they would be in front of them; exactly in the direction they were heading. His mind raced with possibilities. An almighty howl and scream seemed to answer. It dislodged his dome, slipping it sideways revealing a gaping hole.

"No," Scarlet trilled. A large white hand reached over her mouth and slid her backwards.

"Get up," came Eleanor's frantic voice. A blast of wind erupted. Scarlet's body disappeared out of the shield.

"Fight Elf," came a snarl. Daniel threw a handful of water droplet into the air, shouting a spell. They burst and rained down for as far as his strength could throw. Several red blotches, like bobbing shark fins, jumped above the grass line.

Eleanor screamed. Daniel turned and fled, heart hammering, throwing *Element* after *Element* behind him. The grass lashed at his face, blinding his route. He pushed, shoved and dodged. He could feel the strength of Eleanor's spells coursing through the grass. The force of each wind blast pushing.

Daniel felt like he was going in circles, *did the grasses ever end?* He ran on and on, twisting his head spadmodically to check. Their pants, breath stretching across his skin. A body of long white limps rose, like a marble statue. An arm fully stretched towards his bow. He shook his shoulders, weaving away from the outstretched fingers. Daniel jumped and somersaulted leaping free into clear air. Sand and grasses mixing into a jigsaw. Extending full length he landed shoulders first and rolled. Recovering awkwardly, he scrambled to his feet. He ran on, with speed he never knew he had, his feet sinking into ankle-deep sand.

Eleanor's voice came from above him. "They've stopped, Daniel... Daniel they aren't coming through..."

Daniel slowed, gasping and panting. "What, are you mad? There are hundreds of Imps chasing us... don't stop."

"No, Daniel," she pulled at his arm. "Look... look." Daniel could barely focus on anything as he stumbled around.

"Why, why," he gasped.

"They're not crossing over." Daniel could hardly believe it, interspersed between the tall bamboo-like canes, he could just make out in the murky *Darkness Shadows* pale figures, standing, watching their every move - fierce, silent, and knowing. Daniel shivered.

"Why aren't they following?" he hissed.

"I don't know or care. Lets head for those hills get away from here" Eleanor panted.

*

"Where's Scarlet?"

Eleanor shrugged, "disappeared, just like I thought she would."

Daniel looked at the looming hills ahead. "I think she was taken... someone grabbed her." Eleanor flashed him a look that made Daniel smile. They jogged on. Daniel kept checking over his shoulder to make sure they really weren't being followed.

"It'll be *Light Exchange* soon." The deeper sand underfoot started to thin as they climbed upwards. "This place looks lifeless," Eleanor wrapped her arms around her. Through the pale glimmers of light reflecting from the rocks, little vegetation, except small spiky plants with wide thick stems, seemed to survive.

"Where is she?" Daniel frowned, "Eleanor this isn't right. Its because of me she's here. She did offer to help, remember. And... why wouldn't those Imps follow? Don't you think its odd, that every Imp has just disappeared?"

Eleanor face shadowed.

"We should wait, go no further." Daniel began to feel like he was walking in a trap. The stillness fell in thick stifling layers.

"This is Crewantal Territory, the land of the Southern Imps," Daniel jumped and looked up. Satnding on the rocks above him, stood a pale figure. "Northern Imps can only cross with permission. Between the two lands, are these hills. They are sacred and few will enter unless they want to angry the Gods." A small ball of fire appeared behind a large cluster of sandy covered rocks.

"Scarlet..." Daniel said, "you're ok." Relief washed over him. "You were grabbed...."

"It was Reuben..." Daniel gazed at the giant shaped Imp that appeared ungainly behind her.

"You not safe yet..." Reuben grunted. "I sense more Imps ahead."

"What?" Scarlet glared at him. "You didn't say... and I CAN'T."

Reuben tutted in disgust, "I don't know... you call yourself Imp.

First you help Elves, and now you, *no sense.*"

"Do we have to go through these hills?" Daniel asked.

"Yes," Reuben answered, "on other side... Crewantal territory. No other route, and that's where... you need."

"Then are these other Imps - Crewantal?" Eleanor asked.

"We rest briefly, then you go find out." He glared at Eleanor

"If I go in transformation, I still won't know if they're Crew... whatever they were called, Imps, or not," she replied curtly.

"Look..." Daniel said, "if we get close enough we'll see them with my viewing spell and track around. It'll be *Light* soon and we need to know what we're dealing with." Reuben grunted, and set off, without another word, launching off the rock into a narrow pathway flanked by tall walls of rock.

Scarlet pulled at Daniel's arm as he turned to follow. "Wait," she hissed. Eleanor pushed passed and walked on. "There is something about Reuben," Scarlet said urgently, "that I don't trust. He's hiding something."

"But he's been true to his word so far, and he rescued you in the grasses."

"I know, but there's something."

"Maybe thats an Imp thing. Look we can't get left behind...." Daniel shouldered his bow. "None of us," he turned back to her, "are sure about him. Or... each other for that matter. Just don't let him give us away." The moon cast a silvery beam between them. Scarlet shook her head, as she turned to follow.

45

GRASS RATS

"I can sense fear," Scarlet whispered. Daniel pushed aside a large myrtle shrub to see what was going on. A sly hairy spider sat on his shoulder, one leg pointing at his ear. Daniel swiped it off. He wasn't too happy about the small crawlies in Arramond. A deep longing surged through him for his lakes, at least there he knew what he was up against.

"They're ahead," Reuben coarse voice sounded too loud. He lay sprawled like an albino snake, peering over a ledge.

"Scarlet, look through this," Daniel handed her his spell, "tell me what you think." She held it with a trembling hand, like an explosive parcel.

"I don't know how you think I'll know who they are, I've hardly ever meet anyone."

"You've a better chance than Eleanor or I." Begrudgingly, she wriggled into position. Daniel checked the sand floor for more approaching spiders. Scarlet became tense and alert, like a solid tree trunk, unmoving, yet fizzing with energy.

"What is it?"

"Uh," she stammered, "it can't be..." she pulled away from the spell and shook it out of her hand.

"Scarlet – what's the matter?"

"It's, it..."

Reuben was suddenly be her side. He grabbed Scarlet by the shoulders and pushed her roughly, his face touching hers.

"What are you doing?" Daniel yanked at his arm.

"It's her brothers," he growled.

"I was told," Scarlet, spluttered out a sob, "that they were dead, my family destroyed. All dead... All because of," she hesitated..., "Orran and his filthy Vaniks killed them all." She physically spat her words out.

"What's going on?" Eleanor said.

"She saw her brothers," Daniel words were clipped.

"How many are there?" Eleanor looked horrified. Daniel shrugged. Scarlet let out another sob, that sounded more like a moan, "They're alive... you lied."

"But how I know any different. I'm just guard – remember."

"So what are they doing here?" She looked directly at Reuben.

"What do you think?" he replied fiercely. Daniel automatically raised his hand covering Scarlet.

"It's alright," Scarlet voice was almost a whisper. "Why do you hate me so?" she directed her question at Reuben. "I know there's something. Something you're hiding. Why you helped us so readily. Why you carried me. Was it to show me this. To torture me?"

"Maybe, as I glad" he spat. Don't remember?" Scarlet shook her head. "You young, you no understand. But you family took my sister..." He dug his finger into her shoulder.

"Your sister? Who?" Her words echoed off the hillside. Daniel shuddered - *they were being too noisy.*

"Searka, or Shanakee, your servant." Daniel caught Eleanor's look. Scarlet raised her hand to her mouth. "Is she dead?"

"How I know? I'm nothing..."

"You knew who I was from the beginning." Reuben didn't reply.

"But why would your brothers be here?' Daniel interrupted.

"They after *Stone* like you," Reuben snarled.

"But why?"

"They need it, advantage over Vaniks, without Fire-Maker," and he gestured at Scarlet, "they nothing..." Daniel looked at Scarlet. A cold, slow realisation dawned on him. If she helped him to get *The Stone* it would go against her family, if she helped them, he was going to fail. He slowly backed away. His head clouding. Suddenly the chill of air, was no longer refreshing.

Eleanor interrupted. "We can't just stand around here, someone will discover us." Daniel looked at her, and slowly saw the shadows creep over her expression. She realised too.

"You're her brother..." Scarlet turned back to Reuben. They switched into Impish and Daniel no longer understood.

"What are we going to do?" he spoke softly to Eleanor, whose arm almost touched his, they had both slid slightly apart from the Imps. "I never thought we'd have this sort of competition for *The Stone*."

"Well I guess we're going to find out pretty soon which side she's on."

"How can you be so calm?" Daniel wanted to shake her.

"Because I'm tired, cold, angry... hungry." Eleanor turned away from him. Daniel ran his hands through his hair, staring at the ground.

*

"We go - observe." Daniel stared blankly at Reuben. He had no choice but to let them go. Time had slipped through their fingers for too long, while waiting for an answer. Without giving Daniel a chance to respond, the Imps disappeared out of sight. Daniel paced the ground, running scenarios through his mind. *They weren't coming back... or they were coming back but with Scarlet's brothers... they would lead them into a trap...they would leave them to rot alone in Arramond.* Eleanor had her eyes closed soaking up the first rays of *Light Exchange*.

"Grass Rats." he pivoted around to see Reuben's leg muscles flexing as he jogged towards him. "Scarlet saw..." he pointed. "My sister there, alive." His long arm pointed over the sandy dune. Scarlet came slowly into view. Eleanor pushed passed Reuben.

"What did you see?" she demanded as Scarlet drew close.

"It's her - she's alive. Only Four of my brothers - but they are using her."

"So who's side are you on? You need to decide?"

"E," Daniel rested his hand on her arm. She shrugged it away. Green and red flashed together in a warning that froze Daniels blood. He flexed his bow and paced back.

"Stop, both of you, this isn't going to help. "

"Shanakee is important to me. My only true friend," Scarlet relaxed.

"My brothers are using her in their usual controlling way. They are seeing if she's a Fire-Maker - she has no choice." Daniel looked at her quizzically.

"They are preparing her... going to put her into a fenced pen with hundreds of Grass Rats. She'll die, if we don't do something." Daniel was unnerved by her plea. She was genuinely asking.

"You must help... Elf." Reuben interrupted. He looked like a rabbit that had just been caught. His usual strength evaporated. "I help you."

"But what do they need those creatures for?" Daniel looked at Scarlet.

"Distraction," Reuben answered for her. "Over there - Crewantal settlement. Those rats let loose, cause havoc, give time to search." The first rays of *Early Shadow* creep along the ground and spread across Daniel's boots. "So does that mean Imps you are still helping an Elf to retains The Stone?" The wind teased the edge of the rocks with a growing heat.

"Scarlet..." Eleanor snapped as she shook her long black hair free of the dust and began to plait it to one side. "I'm here, in a land I hate, with two Imps, that over six *Turns* ago, I would have laughed if someone had said I'd be near, but, I know we have to get that *Stone*. You were with us Scarlet, you saw what that nest produced... its growing within Caradoc and getting stronger. But that," she pointed, "over there is your family."

Scarlet turned away from Eleanor and pace the sand making small footprints. Daniel bit his lip.

"I can't go back..." Scarlet said quietly, "not yet," her reply directed at Daniel.

"What?" Reuben looked as if he was going to throttle her.

"But we must help Shanakee first, make sure she's alright." Scarlet laid a hand on Reuben's arm, almost, Daniel thought, tenderly. "I promise she will live."

"My quest stays with you Elf." Scarlet declared.

"But Scarlet, that mean if we succeed in getting *The Stone*, your family will suffer," Daniel's blue eyes flashed.

"But it was yours to begin with." Her eyes dulled as she folded like paper, holding her stomach.

"Scarlet...?" Eleanor approached.

"I can feel it," she winced, "Shanakee, she's hurting." Reuben jumped into the air turning with the speed of a hare, as if released from a cage. "Don't," Scarlet managed to say, through gasps, "you'll ruin everything, if you go charging in." Reuben didn't stop. Scarlet reached out, her arm shaking, and shot a neat fire ball. The pain was clear to see. Reuben slammed his hand over his back, where it hit. He growled something and skidded to a stop.

"Scarlet, can you move?" Daniel held her shoulder. "Take us to where she is - we'll think of something." Scarlet pulled herself up. Daniel helped her walk.

*

Daniel was surprised by their organisation. Twelve Imps surrounded a makeshift wooden pen filled with bizarre looking creatures. The most Imps he'd ever seen.

"Who are they all?" Eleanor gasped. They crouched hidden behind a cluster of rocks and thorny shrubs.

"From her compound, brothers and servants," Rueben grunted.

"Were you the only female?" Scarlet smiled.

Each Imp looked like they knew exactly what they were doing - calling to each other in codes. Moving in unison. Not a single animal was escaping. Daniel thought there must be at least fifty creatures. Each about knee height, fat-bellied, with four short stout legs and rat-like faces. Stubby round ears and sandy colour hair, with a long, furry tail.

"Oh no," Scarlet murmured. "look they're going to put her in!"

"No – wait… I can hear them speaking - that's my old cook, she's telling *Shanakee, to feel the fire from within her.*"

"But impossible - you, can't hear her?" Reuben looked annoyed.

"Can't you?" Scarlet almost spat, "You said I couldn't possibly be a real Imp and now, you can't hear what I can…" Daniel smirked.

"Daniel can you get me closer?"

"Yes, we'll use a shield. They won't see anything other than the desert as usual."

"Eleanor can you transform – I know its hurting?" Scarlet said, "gently blow the rats away from her or something - it'll keep them occupied." Eleanor sighed, then nodded. "Reuben don't follow… don't do anything," Scarlet demanded. "Do you promise or your sister is left to be eaten?" The giant Imp nodded compliantly.

Daniel and Scarlet edged as closely as they could. Daniel covering Scarlet in a shield bubble.

"How will your fire work through the water?" he hissed.

"It won't, you know that. But if I can feel and hear Shanakee, doesn't that mean, she might actually be like me – a Fire-Maker?"

Daniel looked at Scarlet in surprise. "So you can help her - guide her?"

"Maybe," Scarlet shrugged.

"This is as far as I dare to go." Daniel halted just behind a dried out thorn bush. The ghostly figures were clearly visible through his shield, like hoovering ghostly mirages. "I'll part one side," Daniel pulled his gaze away. "But you'll be partially exposed, so be careful." Scarlet shuffled into place. Her breathing steadied, and body stilled.

Shanakee stood like a single marble column amongst a mayhem of scurrying bodies. The snapping of the Grass Rat's jaws, were like the chopping of wood. She had accepted her fate calmly as she walked defiantly into the middle. Eleanor was doing something. The rats scurried this way and that, but none got close to Shanakee. Scarlet's brothers were shouting praise, as if this was a sign, it was all her doing. The scene went on for a while until, suddenly a thin long line of fire, spread from Shanakee's hands, like a hovering blanket of orange, it spread across the heads of the rats, high enough not to burn. Daniel watched transfixed as they quietened, their biting and scratching stilled. The flames flowed over the whole of the pen, covering every animal. Once it had reached the corners of the pen, it evaporated. Its work done. A raucous cheer went up. Daniel quickly pulled Scarlet under the shield and filled in the gap with his spell.

"Did you see how they calmed?" he muttered. "Was that you?"

"I don't know."

"Let's get out of here." Daniel nudged her. "You've done all you can, come on. She'll stay alive for a little longer."

"But did you see my eldest brother Tam?" Scarlet pulled his face around to look at her. "How he ran to Shanakee, wrapped his arms around her. He thinks she will save the family." Daniel didn't reply, but he could see the pain across her face. They scrambled back to the others in silence.

46

THE PRESENT

Eleanor stared at Daniel, it was the first time she'd seen him relax. His face looked even jovial, as the curved lines of his mouth creased. She knew exactly what he was thinking. He'd said the words before she had a chance. "The ruling family of Arramond! You could have said..." Eleanor studied Scarlet's skin and hands, for the first time she saw how smooth they looked, how little work they'd done.

"So that makes two of you," Eleanor said jokingly. Daniel threw a handful of leaves at her. She blew them easily away before they landed.

"That's not fair," he laughed.

"Well I'm not," Eleanor said, "my father's a simple wood carver, nothing more." Scarlet smiled from her curled position, on a wide sandy ledge.

"And you had servants!" Daniel almost choked out the words. "My father may have lead the Trevarak Elves - but we never had anyone to do anything for us." He made a face as if they'd clearly done something wrong.

"Would you have treated me any differently?" Scarlet looked suddenly serious.

"Yes, made you run more," Daniel replied. He continued his taunting, as Eleanor looked across the adjourning valley from their vantage position. She was enjoying the rest, coupled with the welcome shade of a large olive tree. Grateful that Scarlet's brothers were now a safe distance behind them. The Crewantal settlement sprawled across the flat-bottomed valley below. Reuben had gone. Decided to go to his sister, Shanakee. He had promised not to breath a word of their existence or that Scarlet was alive. Scarlet's threat had been real and frightening. Eleanor felt better without him. Somehow that Imp had divided them. Daniel rose to his feet. "Have you eaten enough, princess?"

"We wouldn't have eaten at all if I hadn't started that fire..."

"Huh... I had it covered." Eleanor raised her arm to protect her eyes from the sun's rays - the simple carpenter. Her father was so much more than that. The relentless click, click of insects matched his rhythmic beat of his hammer. He had been on The Moors to find her, his youngest. *How could she have made him do that?*

"So, should we go over this plan once more?" Eleanor said trying to distract her thoughts.

"Eleanor, it'll be fine," Daniel nudged her shoulder, "we have an Imp – with crazy uncontrollable fire, you, who no one can see, and me, and no idea where *The Stone* might be. Except its in that village in front of us. What could possibly go wrong? Oh yes – a crazy dream of where it might be from a mad Sprite, and her brothers are after it too."

"I wish Tristan and the Pixies were here," Scarlet muttered, "Enka would know more."

"But they're not," Daniel said more agitated than Eleanor expected, "so that's how it is. "Anyway - we've only got until the end of next *Turn* and Caradoc is at war. So no pressure either."

"Reuben said to rest until mid-*Dark Exchange*. He believed my brothers would attacked at first *Light*."

"Seriously Daniel - the plan. We've agreed to split. Scarlet to divert attention by creating pockets of fire, but keeping out of sight. You and I to search. Follow Scarlet's brothers, who might know where it is - right?"

Daniel finished his mouthful of meat. "Yeah, something like that."

Eleanor took a long drink of the minty water and stared at the line of ants that marched up a rock.

"Can you sense other Imps approaching?" Eleanor asked, "Like Reuben could?"

"No, not all of them, it would seem only those with Fire."

"Then... that narrows it down - right? There aren't many of you?"

"Uh, there should be twelve, I think," Scarlet replied. "Seven in the north, one in the grasslands, and three in the south."

"But that makes eleven?" Eleanor looked at her red hair. It needed a wash.

"Not sure about the twelfth. Apparently that one comes from Ostric or Istria as a direct descendant every seven hundred years. But we haven't known one to descend directly from the Gods for many generations, or if one ever has. I reckon that's another lie my mother told me, just to scare. But at the moment I know of only four other Fire-Makers alive." Eleanor dreaded the thought. Four more, like Scarlet, who could burst into flames and destroy anything without thinking twice.

"So how do you," Scarlet stared at her, "feel when on fire?"

"To begin with amazing, then when I can't control it, and feel cold, lost small hurting."

"Huh yeah... that's what transformation does to me." Eleanor thought of her spells and *Element. A curse or a gift* – sometime she wondered? She looked at Scarlet, who was busy running sand through her hands. Eleanor could see she belonged to this land, it resonated from her. He skin shone brighter and she looked somehow stronger than she had on The Moors. Eleanor wondered if she look better in Vearmoor? Something inside her worried that she didn't.

Eleanor lay on her back tucked under the overhanging ridge. It was still dark, but the yellowy lights amongst the sand dwellings were soothing, helping her forget where she was. She closed her eyes, content in hearing her companions breathing.

*

"Wake up," Daniel flicked water droplets into her face.

"Don't do that," Eleanor winched. "Or I'll blast you off this ridge into the settlement."

"Berries." he held out a handful.

"Thats better." she sat up and yawn. The long arms of *Light Exchange* were creeping into the valley. Her stomach clenched. She wanted *Dark Exchange* to stay.

"We need to get into position, before my brother's release the Grass Rats." Scarlet was already up. Her hair tied away. A baton she taken from Reuben secured by her side. The trousers she wore, were too big, and looked odd.

They crept down the valley side in silence. Scarlet let the way. Eleanor wasn't ready to transform yet. She needed to prepare for the pain. The base of the slope was sandy, deep rivulets shaped with each stride. Tall eucalyptus bushes provided cover.

"Lets head to that shed, we'll split from there." Daniel pointed. "Scarlet, you need to reach that far thatched building. It near that cluster of huts." She nodded, her face set with concentration.

"Eleanor, we'll head there." Eleanor shuddered. A track of lone huts and outbuildings dotted a dangerous path into the centre of the village.

"So where are the rats?" she whispered.

"They'll come down there, I'm sure of it," Scarlet replied. "Its the only way from the scared hills. We should be out of their way if we stay this side. I'll go." Scarlet eyes were large.

"Good luck." Daniel replied. Eleanor couldn't bring herself to say anything, as she watched Scarlet disappear. They waited for her signal. Two short low whistles, mimicking the Larna bird. Eleanor could just spot her red hair as she leant out from behind the tumble-down stone building. The goats inside bleated in response. Eleanor hoped Scarlet would be able to do what she said she could. Her part of the plan was essential. There had been no mention of what would happen if one of her brothers discovered them.

A fireball appeared in the dark, it was Scarlet's signal to indicate her family had begun their attack. Eleanor grabbed Daniel's sleeve. He gave her a funny look, and she quickly released her hand.

"Don't you want to transform?" he whispered. "You'll be out of sight and above the rats." His nerves were raw and intense. His fingers repeatedly tapped his bow as the water shield flowed madly around them, she had never seen it spin so crazily. She suddenly caught glimpse of a bubbling red sun appear on the horizon behind them, with small shadowy lines.

"Daniel, there," she whispered.

"Oh no, they're coming from our side," he replied. Eleanor froze as the shimmering images of Imps appeared, lead by Scarlet's brothers. Reuben the traitor - she wanted to scream, but it was too late for that. The Rats, their tall elaborate tails stood up like swords, marched like a line of needles. Moving in a trance spread out across the hillside. Seemingly controlled by Shanakee herself, with Reuben, tall, important, close by. The liar Imp didn't look like he'd kept his words about not helping Scarlet's brothers. Suddenly a red pulse of flames rippled over their heads; Eleanor spun around to check on Scarlet.

"What's she doing?" Eleanor nudged Daniel.

"No wah... she's gonna blow it for us," he cried. "Quick, we've got to get her back under cover." He spun his water shield around between them and grabbed Eleanor's hand. Eleanor felt a pulse run up her arm as they bolted into the open.

"Scarlet, get back," he hissed as they got closer, but she remained standing like a frozen statue. Like the speed of a Stagin, Daniel flew over the jumbled stones and dived at Scarlet. In one quick move, he bundled her behind the wall. Eleanor scrambled in behind them panting.

"What is wrong with you?" Daniel gasped. Eleanor saw her flames dancing in her eyes.

"Why did you do that?" she fumed. "I could have burnt you!"

"You were in full view, someone would have noticed. And what would've happened if you'd gone out of control."

"I had to... I wouldn't have..." Scarlet looked indignant. "Shanakee couldn't have done it alone."

"Are you sure - or do you just not want her to?"

"Daniel!" Eleanor said, "what's wrong with you. Scarlet was trying to help. It's all ok, no one has seen us - I'm sure." Eleanor peered over a pile of rubble, her heart pounding. The calls were a wild mixture of mouse squeaks and wolf howls. The Grass Rats had been released - whoever's fire it was, had worked. Desperate to get away from their captor, they fled at random. Disorientated and unsure where home was, they flew down the hill, letting the world know they were free.

The surrounding settlement burst into life. Lights brightened the darkest corners. Voices shouted in panic. Babies began to cry and for the first time, Eleanor knew that even Imps were once young and fragile.

"We need to get off the ground." Daniel eyes shone. "Eleanor - transform." The command was short and angry. "Scarlet - climb those hay bales, we might be able to escape the jaws and let some of them pass." They all fled, like hares before the hounds. Scrambling with desperation. Pulling at the hay in great handfuls to get higher. "There - some rafters. Get onto those." With one foot nestled in his cupped hands, he practically threw Scarlet onto a beam.

"Eleanor - I don't understand." He scrambled up and pulled her behind him. "Why, for the sake of my Water Lord - can I still see you?" He had his arms firmly clamped on each of her shoulders and Eleanor could feel herself begin to shake uncontrollably.

"I can't - I can't," she almost sobbed t.

"What?" Scarlet looked at her, as if she had gone crazy. "But you did when we were travelling in the hills?"

"That was just it - I was getting more and more sick each time, but now it's different. Now the spell doesn't work."

"It's gonna be fine... it'll be..." Daniel squeezed her shoulder.

But Eleanor lost his last words as the first rats ran into their building. Squeaking like tiny high-sounding bells mixed with scratching metal.

"We've gotta get out of here," Scarlet said in panic. "I can't use my powers or the whole building with go up and you can't either..." An Imp burst in, shouting and flailing. "Don't move," she whispered. Eleanor wrapped her fingers over the aged oak, gripping tight. The jaws of a rat were clenched firmly onto the Imps leg. He jumped about madly, desperately trying to shake it off. Eleanor held her breath. Another rat appeared from the other side of the wall and leapt at the Imp, sinking into his arm.

"We can't just watch," Scarlet whispered.

"We can't risk being caught up here," Daniel glared. Eleanor thought for a moment. Silently she whispered a spell she'd known since birth. She blew it out of her hand towards the dying Imp, relieved that something still worked.

"What are you doing?" Scarlet span around, wobbling on her beam.

"Watch." Eleanor saw her spell landed where she wanted it to. It began to work immediately, picking up small stones, leaves and sticks, making them dance. The closest rat saw it first and dropped his prey. Like a playful dog, it went to try and catch the moving debris.

"That's brilliant," Daniel whispered. "So you haven't lost all your powers?" The second rat joined in and released the Imp. He shot from the barn, clutching his arm, leaving blood trails, like a silk carpet. Several rats joined in. "Can you make it bigger?" Daniel asked. "No," Eleanor whispered, "but I can make another one."

When three more spells were working, "now's our chance," Daniel whispered. He silently jumped from his beam. Eleanor followed. Her foot sank deeply into the first bale. With Scarlet just behind.

47

AN IMP'S OATH

"WHere are we going?" Daniel shot a rat with a droplet, flat onto the ground. Its comrades scattered. With the barn behind them, Daniel knelt fixed against a cobbled wall and rooted to the spot. He was grateful there were height, bricks and wood to protect him. He never thought animals could create such pandemonium.

"No idea... where are we going to start looking?" Eleanor's green eyes gazed at him, watery and challenging.

"Can you see your brothers?" he asked Scarlet.

"No, but they're not far away, so we can't just stay here," she replied urgently. Daniel pressed himself into the wall, holding his breath. Slowly he edged around the corner. A wide pathway, lining the base of the valley, leading directly into the village. Like an army of angry wasps, with batons raised, Scarlet's brothers, fierce and ready for battle, walked in military formation. Daniel's skin prickled.

"We could get to that dwelling, it looks derelict." Daniel pointed over his shoulder. "We can hide inside." He raised a water shield, pushing Eleanor and Scarlet in front of him, not givingthem any time to think. The dust underfoot blew into his face, as they pounded across the open track.

"There," Eleanor was first, "through that window." Daniel knew his shield was bouncing all over the place and that parts of them was exposed, but he couldn't do anything about it. The sandy cob wall felt cold to touch as he scrambled over, following Scarlet and Eleanor inside. The gloom of the room was thick and heavy. It took his eyes a moment to adjust. Like a cage, he instantly felt trapped. It was the first time, he realised, in a long while since he'd been inside a dwelling.

"Can you hear anything?" he looked about him.

"There's too much noise outside." Scarlet's breath was erratic and filled the void. A wooden chair lay tipped on its side. An old cupboard, with one door open, swung wide on a single hinge. Tattered shreds of curtains hung limply either side of the window.

"Doesn't feel like anyone's been here for a while," Eleanor whispered. "Look there's another room." She crept across the slabs of broken slate. There was no door to open, as she disappeared through. Scarlet followed. Daniel stayed back, crouching beside the window. He wanted to see where Scarlet's brothers had gone and if they'd been followed. He peered out, as far as he dared. The track outside was deserted. The chaos had moved into the village. He lent out further. They were still only on the outskirts. He could hear shouting and the sound of wood against wood - their batons in action. A few rats were lingering, scurrying aimlessly, as if lost souls. A draft of wind tugged at his clothes from behind. He swirled around to see a thick stream of light lying across the floor. He fled to the opening, where Eleanor had disappeared. Scarlet's head was pressed against a thick set chest, with a blade to her throat. Her eyes dancing with flames. She shook her head, as if warning him not to do anything. Daniel reach for his pouch.

"Don't come any closer, Elf."

"Its you..." he gasped. Eleanor was slumped onto a chair. Reuben held her hair tightly in his fist, her head pushed down towards her knees.

"Why?" Daniel blurted.

"Shut up," Reuben looked like a painted wild animal. He had a thick band of dried blood smeared across his chest and streaked over his face. His hands were covered in thick red lines, that ran in broken patterns up his arms. "An Imp's Oath..." speaking in Nararose, he grunted. "Her brothers heading to hillside ... other side. There - shrine door. You need get there."

"Huh, then get this idiot off me..." Scarlet almost choked out her words.

"Why that?" Daniel noticed the thick blade had moved to Scarlet's eye level.

"That Imp doesn't speak Naraling. He think we kill you. Your brothers saw something, I said I investigate."

"Then how are we going to get out of here."

"You need do something..." Reuben growled at Daniel. The other Imp began to shout, panic rippling across his face. Scarlet joined in. Her voice high, urgent and angry. Daniel wished he still had some arrows. Instead he chose a spell. He hoped Scarlet would see it coming. He threw a water droplet directly at her captor. It hit him squarely, with the force of a brick. His nose cracked, as his head jolted upwards. Scarlet slid away. The blade scattering to the earth tiles. Reuben let go of Eleanor and shoved her towards the door.

"Go," he yelled. Daniel ran. Linking under Eleanor's arm, they fell outside. Scarlet came tumbling behind almost falling on top of them.

"Run," she yelled. "That won't keep him down for long." Daniel could see a red line across her cheek, with blood. They fled into the open, like startled rabbits, spinning around to see which was the best way to go.

"How do we get across to the village?" A shout roared. Reuben and the Imp were at the door.

"That way," Daniel yelled and they tore across the ground, desperate to reach the first house.

"We're not going to make it..." Scarlet screamed. "Reuben is too quick."

"Then burn it, Scarlet, burn anything. We'll lose him in the smoke."

"But what if someone's inside?"

"Just do it, they're all so fast."

Reuben's presence felt overwhelming. Daniel knew the Imp couldn't let them go the second time. They covered the ground, with thundering footsteps. He was nearly there, if they could only reach the alleyways, they had a chance. A loud yowl sounded, as several fire balls shot past, disappearing with great accuracy into the thatch. It took no time before the roof caught alight. He spun around and threw a barrage of droplets into Reuben's path. He watched long enough to see them fall to the ground as he ducked around the corner and into the shadows. The flames had taken hold. Eating hungrily at the roofs. The buildings were made of all the materials that fire love. Combined with the heat from the rising sun, making the perfect combination. The fire jumped above them, moving quickly onto its next victim.

"Daniel - it's not going to stop." Scarlet held her knees panting out loud.

"There's nothing we can do now," he replied, "come on, we need to get out of here." He pointed ahead. That way." They ran on. Daniel felt as if he was bouncing off the walls, half running, half checking behind him. They flew out of the end and straight into the thick of the fighting. It was like a slow action play. The smoke from the fire gave it a dreamy quality, with misty white tones. The Crewantals had clearly recovered from their surprise and were fighting back. They knew how to defend themselves. Individuals locked in combat; their brutality at close range was frightening. Daniel wondered how many of Scarlet's household wouldn't make it.

"We should edge around, try and get out the other side."

"You go..." Scarlet grabbed Daniel's arm. Suddenly a Grass Rat ran straight for them, as if it could see them through his shield. Daniel nudged Eleanor. She flicked her hand and blew it away with a blast of air.

"That was close," he muttered.

"Oh no..." Eleanor gasped. The Grass Rat and several others were sprawled on their backs between a group of fighting Imps. "It was too strong! " The Imps momentarily stopped their fighting and were looking about them. "That's Tam, my eldest brother." Scarlet almost shrieked. Daniel could see he was hurt, one of his eyes was blackened and blood dripped down his leg. "Can they see through this, Daniel?" Scarlet muttered.

"That Imp is looking straight at us!" Daniel felt her edge closer to him.

"Don't move," he said, "they should just be seeing a reflection."

"What's he doing?" Eleanor took a step back. Tam leapt into the air. Flying over his opponents. He yelled something Daniel didn't understand. One of the larger Imps took off after him, like the leaping Stagins on The Moors, they bounded across the square with incredible speed.

"Go..." Scarlet said again. "I must stay... they will never survive, if I don't."

"But Scarlet," Eleanor blurted. "We can't leave you."

"I'll meet you, on our ledge, at the end of this *Light Exchange*. If I'm not there by the time *Darkness* falls, go on without me." Daniel could see she wasn't going to change her mind and he had no right to ask her.

"If that's what you want," he said quietly. "I'll wait until you've got back to the safety of the alleyway, before we go." To Daniel's surprise, Eleanor smiled at Scarlet.

"Stay safe," she whispered. Daniel decided he'd never understand females, as he waited long enough to see Scarlet was hidden. He then secured his dome, making sure every bit was in place.

"Let's get out of here," he whispered. He and Eleanor skirted the perimeter of the square. Remaining in the shadows and fending off angry Grass Rats. Fireballs began to fly in all directions. He hoped Scarlet wouldn't lose control.

"Where did her eldest brother go?" Eleanor's pale face looked haunting next to the spinning water. "He's disappeared down that alleyway." A putrid smell of burning animal dung filled his lungs. They left the square and headed after Tam.

"Where have all the other Crewantal Imps?" Eleanor said quietly. "There were a lot in that square." "Yes, but not enough to fill a whole village. Where are the babies we heard crying or the young ones?" she said.

"Look ...it's Tam - there ahead." He was fighting. Another one of Scarlet's brothers was there, who Daniel recognised from the Sacred Hills. There were five Crewantals surrounding them.

"We need them to survive," Daniel said. "If they don't we

wouldn't be able to follow them to this place in the hills Reuben was talking about."

"That's stupid," Eleanor replied. "If they don't survive, we just have to find it ourselves and it'll be easier."

"And what do we tell Scarlet, if she does make it - we let her brothers die?"

"Well what do you suggest? We can't do much through this shield." Daniel reversed his spell; the shield fell instantly to the ground. "Wind Lord," Eleanor cried and bolted into a darkened doorway, pressing herself into the shadows.

"They'll never notice," Daniel murmured, as he ran down the narrow passageway, as quietly as he could. With the light touching his boots, he threw a barrage of water droplet over the attackers' heads. The droplets fell like a shower of rain, which to him would have felt gentle and soft, but Daniel knew to the Imps it was like falling sharp needles. Faces turned upwards, followed by screams of bewilderment.

Eleanor ran to his side. "Are you crazy?" she gasped and sent a blast a wind into them. Several Crewantal Imps were knocked sideways, stumbling and tripping over themselves like younglings learning to walk. *Run Tam, run...* Daniel prayed, as the giant Imp hesitated. Then seeing his advantage he took off at speed. "Hurry, E, we can't lose him."

48

THE LAKE WITHIN THE HILL

"Why aren't there any guards? And this vine!" Daniel watched Eleanor's hand float over the long mottled curtain of tangled leaves. The small door lay hidden beneath, barely visible. Thick with knots in aged oak. The wrought iron handle seemed too big for the arched frame. A stone plague lay above with an inscription Daniel couldn't understand.

"We would have never found it, if it hadn't been for them," she muttered. "Do you think they're inside?"

"No idea, I lost them once we ran over the hill. Its taken us ages to find this door. They could be anywhere."

"It's weird how this green stuff covers everything. The only thing that grows in abundance around here."

"I haven't seen it anywhere else on our journey."

"Me neither - but, it reminds me of stuff that grows in Caradoc." Daniel paused checking around for anyone approaching. "We should try and get in, this looks like the place Reuben said." "If there were guards, they're gone."

"Daniel, " you know who'll have to deal with if they're..." Eleanor nodded her head to the door. A shiver ran down Daniel's back. Eleanor's expression etched with concern.

"Perhaps," Daniel said, "lets hope not. Come on, lets get a move on. Time is running out, there only four *Shadows* until we're meant to meet Scarlet again."

"That's if she makes it." Daniel gazed around at the settlement; black spirals of smoke filled the valley. Shouts and screams hadn't dwindled. If Shanakee hadn't managed to make any fire, Scarlet had certainly done her work well. Almost half of the village was charred burnt out remains baking in the late *Shadow* sun.

"Can you open the door?" Eleanor asked. Daniel pushed his shoulder against the wood, nothing happened.

"What if only Imps can open it?"

"Great – that's all we'll need," he sighed. Eleanor slumped to the ground, burying herself behind the overhanging leaves. "And... if you do get in," she said, "are you ready to find what's in there?" Eleanor's tone caught him off guard.

"What do you mean?"

"You might actually get to hold the Elves' Power gift. I mean - imagine that? The one Ostric gave your great, great, whatever, Grand Elf, Ead... something or other." Daniel studied a long-legged flying thing that crawled across the door. "And... don't some Elves die trying to touch it?"

"That's what Tristan said" Daniel shuddered, "my father never mentioned it." A violent explosion erupted in the village below, sending a column of bursting flames spiralling into the sky. Daniel could feel the heat radiating onto this skin.

"Scarlet, maybe she's lost control." Eleanor uttered as she rose to her feet. A group of female Imps with their Implings came running out of the village.

"We've got to get in, they're coming this way." Daniel shoved the door as hard as he could, but it didn't budge. "Let me try." Eleanor brushed off her skirt and aimed. Her spell ricocheted off the wood like an angry snort. The door flung open, crashing back on its rusty hinges. She grabbed his arm and pulled him though. Daniel smiled and quietly shut the door behind them.

*

The air clung heavily and smelt damp, like wet clothes. Daniel shivered, it was a stark contrast to the heat.

"What is this place?" Eleanor whispered, "it's freezing."

"Look," Daniel said, "down there." He was surprised at how wide it was. Well built, with high brick walls and worn footprints indent into the cobbled stoned floor. Neat rows of tall iron baskets framed either side, burning brightly with recently lit fire. Each one cast elongated shadows that darted over the walls.

"They must be here, oherwise, who light those?" Eleanor had moved away from the door. "You don't think a Fire-Maker is with them?" she said quietly. Daniel shrugged.

"Look." He took a few steps, "and there's only one way to go." Stone columns, he hadn't noticed, loomed ahead. *Someone has gone to a lot of trouble to build this inside a hill.* Daniel's mind raced. He was back underground. He pressed his hand over the curved surface of a column. "Look, there are carvings."

"So," Eleanor muttered. "It's not like Imps have any culture." Her foot slipped across a cobble, and she cursed.

The tunnel sloped down into the hill and narrowed, curving around a series of gentle bends.

"This is going on for too long," Eleanor muttered. "Where could they have gone?" A series of water droplets fell from the ceiling and splashed loudly.

"That's odd," he said, "there's more water underfoot. But Imps hate water, so why is it here?" He caught a drop in his hand and tasted it. "Eleanor it tastes of home."

"But that's impossible, it's not your *Power Element* is it?" Daniel muttered a spell with what he had in his hand. It didn't move. He dropped it to the ground.

"It would have been good, if it was. You could do with some more." Daniel instinctively wrapped his hand around the leather, his stomach twisting.

"Look, a blue light, ahead," Eleanor exclaimed. A pale tinged glow crossed her face. Daniel froze in his tracks.

"Why've you stopped?"

"Its the same glow as home." Eleanor looked at him quizzically. "Daniel. You're just home sick."

"I'm not... that light really is like home. Look," Daniel turned to face Eleanor. "I don't think its gonna effect me badly."

"What! *The Stone*?"

"I can touch my *Power Element* without using magic."

"Well I can see that, you throw it all over the place... so."

"But that's not normal, all other Elves use spells to touch it and spend years learning."

"So you just different - whats the big deal" Eleanor turned away. "But..." he stuttered, "its part of the reason I was banished, all of Caradoc found out and they didn't like it - thought I wasn't a real Elf."

"Great, so I'm stuck in Imp territory with a fraud..." Eleanor stomped off towards the blue glow. He stared at the water droplets falling to the floor, feeling the cold stinging water run over this skin as if was from The Great Lake itself.

Daniel paused. He could hear voices ahead. Slowly he edged along, feeling the veins and damp moss in the rock. The air on his face was drying.

"I wish I understood Impish," Eleanor face loomed in the shadows. "They're up ahead talking."

"Did you transform? You moved quickly."

"No I still can't."

"I'll go and look," Daniel said. Eleanor did nothing to stop him. The passageway immediately opened into a large, dome-shaped cave. It wasn't big or grand. A dead end. A simple perfectly carved dome, no status, alcoves or doors, except one wide hole cut into the middle of the floor. Rays of blue light streamed through the gap. He felt Eleanor's presence next to him.

"They must have gone down there," she said. Eleanor edged passed him and walked around the perimeter. "What are you going to do?" She held his gaze with a look of steadfast defiance; and he knew she was not going through the hole. Bending on all fours he slid to the edge, peering as far in as he could.

"There's an enormous cave below. It's like a mini Caradoc!" Daniel looked again; hardly able to believe it was here underneath Arramond. "It has the same blue light as home, with a lake. Eleanor..." he looked up. "You don't think there could be a way into Caradoc from here, do you?"

"Don't be stupid, we're in Arramond. The two lands are nowhere near each other."

Daniel shrugged, in disbelief. "But that looks so like home."

"With Imps in it!" she said exasperatedly. Daniel sat back, "they're at the bottom, near the water."

"Then there's no time, it must be down there." Eleanor said. "And you've got to get it first."

"BUT HOW?" Daniel looked about him. Eleanor gingerly peered into the hole. After a moment she brought her head up.

"By the railings," she said. Daniel looked again. He saw what she was meaning. A series of rusty black handles hung, like small staples, from the ceiling. He would have to lean half his body through to get anywhere near. If he managed to reach the first one, hang on and swing to the next, it would be a miracle. The drop to the ground would be enough to kill him, and how was he going to do it without the Imps noticing?

"Daniel, you said so yourself we're running out of time." Eleanor stood with her arms folded.

"I wish you could transform." Eleanor wasn't budging. Her face locked into a thick stare.

Daniel shuffled over and eyed the first rail. Now he knew why the Imps had hidden it down there. The whole place was designed so that only the most agile would succeed.

49

THE STONE OF INNVERICUM

Daniel edged around the hole, trying to get the right position to start. Eleanor paced around the dome. *If only she could fly down there, grab the damn Stone. They would be quickly out of there, without encountering Scarlet's brothers.* He bit his lip. If he didn't go now, he never would. He slid to the ground and contorted his body, then launched into the air. His legs swung free, with his hand outstretched. He caught the cold iron, his muscles taught and burning. His hold cold and rigid. His body swung like a pendulum. He daren't look down. Releasing one hand, half his body dangled freely. He went for the second rung but missed. Swinging back and forth. He tried again. His knuckle, small and fragile. Sweat broke over his body in prickly waves. He reached the second rung on the next lunge. Bit by bit he edged forwards... his arms trembling, as if they were pieces of cotton blowing in the wind.

In a wild surge, as if Eadric himself had pushed him, Daniel lunged onto something solid. He flicked his body against the wall, balancing precariously on the top step with the ball of his foot. Clasping like a limpet against the slimy rock, twisting his fingers into the cracks. There was just enough room to turn around and look down. The Imps still gazed at the mirrored water. Melting into the side of the cave wall, Daniel started to descend. The steps were slippery. Each footing a tenuous placement, contorting into shapes to fit. He gazed down, he was almost halfway. The cave opened into a vast cavern. It looked like it stretched under the Crewantal Village. Another land, secretly hiding below. Daniel shivered, *what was this place?*

He went on, trying to formulate a plan. How could he get passed the Imps, into the water, without them catching him? And why hadn't they gone in? What were they waiting for? The lake was wide. It dominated most of the cavern's floor. Flat billowing platforms of grey rock lined its shores, like piles of pillows. All it needed were waterfalls and it could be one of the Sky Lakes within his homeland.

Suddenly his foot slipped from under him. His whole body weight followed. His grip slid off the rail. The blue light weakened, mixing images of floating rock and silvery water. He hit the sand with force.

Daniel came to. A sharp pain ripped through his shoulder and down his side. He tried to turn over, but his body wouldn't respond. A foot, twice the size of his own, wrapped in a hard-soled leather casing pushed into his stomach.

"What are you doing here?" sharp, aggressive, but in perfect Naraling, its lilt similar to Scarlet's. Daniel tried to pull himself up, but the foot pushed his shoulder back. The pain made his eyes roll. He lay still, listening to their heated words.

"Who are you?"

"Daniel," he said croakily, "Elf Trevarak."

"Then... Elf," The words were like sticky treacle, "you've come at a good time. A gift from our Gods. Get *The Stone*. Bring it back to me." Daniel glanced at the hole above him but couldn't see Eleanor. The thick muscular arm pointed to a glowing blue light in the centre of the lake. He could see *The Stone* clearly. Hovering on a plinth of majestic black rock.

"There is no way out of here except through that hole," the Imp pointed, "if you get it, we will spare your life." Daniel gazed up at Tam. He knew it was her eldest brother. The similarities were obvious. Tam had the same sharp angular jaw line and wide forehead. His eyes were set deeply into his skull shining with a jet-black sparkle. Scarlet's eyes turned the same colour when she was frightened. They both had an almost regal look, that set them apart from other Imps. It had taken Daniel a while to notice this. He then saw the blood as it dripped freely by his foot. Tam was battered and had been severly injured.

"Get up..." Tam barked, his foot lifting. Daniel gingerly lifted his tunic and felt a thick deep open wound down the side of his chest. The source of his pain. Blood came out on his fingers. His vision blurred. He knew now, he wouldn't be able to make it out of the cave.

"Don't try anything, Elf... you're outnumbered." Daniel felt for his pouch as he took a few steps toward the water. Foot steps sinking into the damp sand. He swayed, as blood seeped into his sinking prints. He pulled out his pouch. A hand grabbed his shoulder, "I said, don't try anything." The pouch slipped to the ground, but Daniel could see it was empty. He had no means to defend himself. He looked ahead, staring through the hulk of white flesh, to the glistening water. It beckoned, urged him on. He hadn't felt water of a lake since the day of his banishment. Images of his trial, his brother Isaac falling from the bridge and the contorted face of Seb merged together in equal cruelty.

The water came as a welcome relief, cold and soothing. The cavern merged. Rock formations became one large slab of grey. He took several steps in. The lake reached his knees. His foot hit something hard. He plunged his hands in and felt a shelf – steps? He stumbled taking the first. Seeing his reflection, he screwed his eyes momentarily shut. Older, haggered. Barely recognisable. Thinner, with ridiculously long hair. He could hear the Imps shouting, demanding his urgency, but he didn't care. Nothing seemed to matter. He climbed over the first ridge and down. The water rose to his waist touching his wound. The shock stopped him in his tracks. It stung like thousands of angry bees. Then he saw it clearly, *The Stone*, small, egg shaped, black in colour and quite insignificant. It could be mistaken for any other stone found lying on a beach. All this trouble for something so small. He didn't care if it killed him or not. His life, worthless, his father obviously thought so. If he died, at least he wouldn't have to face Scarlet's brothers, Eleanor's disappointment or Caradoc's destruction. He walked on, gliding on tiny waves that lapped against his skin. Drawing closer, Daniel noticed the patterns had changed direction. Something ignited through the murky haze of Daniel's mind. Each ripple began to move towards *The Stone*, as if dragging him closer. An overwhelming sense of calm descended. He could hear voices from Caradoc, Elves speaking to him, hundreds of words of old knowledge. Some he recognised but some in old Elfland, that made no sense. He knelt down, so that the water reached up to his neck, and for a moment stared at The Elves' Power Gift. Their most treasured possession – stolen by Imps and here within Arramond. How could his father have fallen for such a trick? *Or was he part of the sham?* All he had to do was lift his hand and take it.

*

Daniel held *The Stone* gently within his palm. It was small, yes, but more beautiful, midnight blue, not black and a perfectly smooth egg shape. A wave of energy pulsed into his hand and up his arm. It travelled hurriedly and quickly filling his chest. A tingling sensation covered his wound. He felt himself warmed, even revived. He savoured the feeling. It grew stronger. He was saved, important even. With this he was powerful. Then it dulled, returning to its inert state. *Don't do that*, Daniel shook it, willing it to glow that beautiful blue again. He looked up as Tam shouted something from the lakeside. Daniel scanned the lake, ignoring the idiots. This was his chance to get away. He wanted to keep it. He had travelled far to get this. The Imps should never have let him get it - he would show them.

To his annoyance a veil of grey smoke masked which way to go. He was sure it hadn't been there before. Which way had he come? He heard an unusual howl, like a war cry. Daniel wanted to laugh; maybe the Imps knew he'd beaten them. He had the Power Gift and had no intention of giving it up.

The sound came again. Were they getting into the water? Fools they'd die. Dizzy with excitement; wouldn't his father be amazed? Anyway, his stupid father, what did he know; he'd fallen for the fake one. And..., he'd sent him out on The Moors alone. Why should Daniel help him? The water was swirling in circles. Quickening, even bubbling and frothing in places. Daniel put *The Stone* into his pocket; next to the one his mother had given him, and zipped it in. Jumping off the plinth, he plunged forwards.

Behind, a jet of water spurted, hot steam flew into the air, trothing where it landed. A voice, as if speaking in his head, was chanting a spell, which made him push on, battling the swirling water. Daniel covered some distance. Without warning, his body slammed into something hard. His arms roughly pushed behind his back and face plunged into the water. Thick fingers clamped around his neck, his fist was prized open.

"Where is it? Give it to me," muffled words came through the water. Daniel violently shook himself from side to side. His head was roughly pulled up. Gasping for breath. "It's too late," Daniel, shouted.

"This is you, you've done this Elf, you deserve to die." His contorted face glared down at him. "Brenn, stop," Tam shouted. "Daniel give me *The Stone*, we had a deal." Tam's bulk loomed over them.

"Never," Daniel roared, "it doesn't belong you!" Suddenly Tam flew aside. Daniel struggled free from Brenn's hold, grappling *The Stone* from his pocket and held it aloft. Brenn circled him like a prowling tiger. "Are you playing tricks Elf?"

"No… you fool."

"Have you started this… with your Elf magic? Brenn was almost screaming. Daniel took in the full cavern. Something caught his eye. Lurking in the far side. His memory jolted. He looked at the water. It was darkening.

"Tam, Imp scum." Daniel shouted.

"How do you know my name?" He lunged, dragging Daniel with enormous force through the shallow water and onto the sand. Drawing him closer. "You said my name, how do you know my name?"

"Because I know your sister," Daniel snarled. Tam dropped Daniel. "That's impossible."

"No it's not… and she's here helping me…" The water was bubbling and swirling now a rich black-like oil.

"But this?" Brenn interrupted. "You Elf, have summoned *The Darkness* – why would you and our sister do that?" Daniel pushed Brenn aside. "This isn't my doing." Daniel looked to where Brenn pointed.

Daniel felt only anger. He raised a viewing spell. It looked like an oversized ant, six bent long legs trying to hold up an overweight oval body. A funny bulbous head with two, sword-like, antennae, framing one red eye. It flicked its head from side to side the same ridiculous movement as The Gulabirds. Several more were behind their leader. Still relatively small and not the terrifying size The Gulabirds had reached. Their red eyes in row formation. Red eyes like the Imps.

The Stone felt warm again in his hand and it began to glow. Daniel spun around. The Imps were already halfway up the steps.

"You called them, you can kill them." Brenn shouted, "we'll be waiting at the exit, when you're done." The leader launched its attack, as if spurred on by Brenn's words. Followed closely by its army, like determined soldiers, they scuttled across the rocks. A regimented line of red making wavy lines through the gloom.

"Die," Daniel shouted, but there was no reply. He scooped handfuls of water from around his feet that hadn't changed black, and blew it at two rapidly approaching beasts. The water flew like bullets, direct and true, with accuracy he'd never achieved before. Their howls and screams echoed and filled the whole cave, before each one exploded into black dust. The kills fuelled his anger. Daniel lunged to reach his empty pouch left lying on the sand, hurriedly he filled it. Then ran towards the steps. Several beasts were scurrying over the side of the cave, able to run on the vertical angle with ease. He glanced at the hole in the ceiling. Tam had already reached it. Brenn was close behind. Daniel fired water after water droplet, to keep Ostric's beasts at bay. The air hung around him in thick folds of heat. The temperature had soared, but it didn't affect him. Taunt nerves and thumping heart, he was enjoying the fight. He reached the first step with speed and pulled effortlessly at the rail. Firing accurately at anything that moved.

50

NATAJAWS

Eleanor shakily pressed against the wall of the tunnel, wandering why she hadn't fled.

Tam rose to his feet. "I know you're near, so show yourself." At his full height Scarlet's brother filled the dome, his head touched the ceiling. "Why would a Sprite be with an Elf, who knows my sister?" Eleanor thought his words were like stabbing daggers. His presence sent a mirage of fear jumbling into a contorted web. Her hand skimmed her rope - instinct. She cursed herself. Its glowing light illuminated her position. Tam's eerie reflection loomed hauntingly. His red eyes catching her. Thick jagged scares marked his skin. Not just battle wounds - *the water had burned.*

"If you stay here, you'll die," Tam said, "those are *Darkness* creatures - our Natajaws, your so called friend has brought them into being, and they won't just kill Imps. Ostric had been summoned, and I think he is to blame." His contorted glare masked a twinge of fear, she had seen before in Scarlet.

"Your sister's near," Eleanor blurted. The Imps exchanged glances.

"That's impossible – she's dead," Brenn snarled.

"She isn't," Eleanor mumbled, "The Elf was telling the truth.

Scarlet's helping us... and here within Arramond."

"You lie, Sprite." Brenn lunged for her. Eleanor flicked her rope and lashed his hand away. He flinched.

"Daniel," Eleanor glimpsed his hand through the hole. Tam twisted swiftly and pulled him roughly through the hole.

"How have you made it?" he snarled into Daniel's drawn face as he held him in the air, Daniel's feet swinging "who are you both?" Tam dropped him heavily.

Daniel shoved Tam; the way he did it, took Eleanor by surprise.

"Why shouldn't I make it?" Daniel, retorted, "Elves are not weak like you think." Defiantly Daniel adjusted his jacket, "and you," his face set in angry glare, "won't stop those creature." Eleanor's heart thumped violently. "The waters filling the cave, bubbling black and hot," he continued calmly, even cruelly. "The beasts are scurrying above it, they'll soon work out the exit." Eleanor hardly blinked before a thick arm wrapped around her, Brenns' coiling like a python, a dagger held to her throat. "Then you'd better stop them, Elf," Brenn said, "or she dies."

Eleanor's screamed. An antenna appeared looping over the threshold. She felt a wave of heat like a red-hot poker. She itched with fear and squirmed against Brenn's slippery hot skin. Daniel stood majestically by the hole, his face locked in dark concentration. *Had he gone mad?* "Daniel, get away," she cried. "Let's just get out of here."

"I will kill her," Brenn repeated. "Do something Elf..." Eleanor fought against the strong arms. Daniel raised his hand. *The Stone,* he had it.... A fountain of water burst forth. She had seen such force before, it was like Scarlet's uncontrollable fire. It engulfed his thin frame, cascading like a water fall. Filling the dome in an instant. Tam disappeared under a cloud of trothing foam, as the water propelled in swirling circles. Gasping for breath, Eleanor tumbled, half submerged - kicking and padding. The silvery dagger floated by. Her feet hit the cobbles, her back scrapped the tunnel wall. A blue light filled the water like a blast of cold sunshine. On a wave she sped around the bend, up the tunnel. Brenn's legs and arms, knocking her as they tumbled over and over. The sound roared and crashed, deafening. With a flick of the waves' tail, it beached her, soaked, a distance from the cavern. Eleanor lay gasping. The tunnel had turned to a milky silver. The roaring ceased. An eerie *drip, drip drip*, filled the void. She looked around for Brenn and Tam. She lifted her head and pushed aside her soaked hair. Daniel lay collapsed in a puddle. His arm lulled across the floor, bent under his weight. His body in a haphazard foetal position. She pulled herself up. He was cold, his face unusually calm. She said a spell. A soothing, warm gentle breeze rose in her hand, and spiralled around them both. While it worked she hunted; opened his hands, checked in his pockets. It wasn't there. She held her rope, and using the yellow light, searched the floor, hurriedly scurrying through the water like an erratic mouse. *It had to be close.* She found it lying in a puddle. It looked so small, so insignificant, but she didn't like it. Something was wrong, it gave her a strange feeling. It had done something to Daniel. She hesitated. Then, because she thought he would go mad, placed it back into his hand.

"Wake up," she shook him, "we've got to get out of here." Daniel began to cough and splutter. He looked at her blankly. She watched him clutch his hand and transfer *The Stone* to an inside pocket.

"What?" he mumbled as he flicked a few drops of water from his hair and got up.

"Get out of here," Eleanor urged.

"Huh…" he stared right through her.

"In the hillside, remember," Eleanor looked about them. "That crazy spell you did. It worked. But I don't think we should stay around to check." He got shakily to his feet.

"Did one get out?" he snapped coldly. Eleanor hesitated.

"Dunno." A shiver ran across her body.

"What, you don't know."

"Uh, hang on…. was water everywhere."

"Great," he grunted.

"You ok?" she tried to sound lighter. He pushed passed her and started walking away.

"Hadn't we better be on guard for the Imps?"

"They won't come near me now," he replied. Eleanor bit her lip and swallowed her anger. They walked on in silence and covered the length of the tunnel quickly. Eleanor wished she was as far away from here and Daniel as possible. Clearly now he'd got *The Stone*, he didn't care much about anything else. She had been a fool to think otherwise. The door loomed. Daniel lunged against the door, pushing it open. The air sucked into the tunnel and pulled them through. The natural light made her blink, and for a moment everything went white.

*

"There they are," shouted a deep voice. Dusty sand blew in tiny swirls, between a long line of wooden spears and white limbs. To Eleanor it seemed the whole of the Crewantal Tribe had gathered, standing in a wide arch, like death warriers. Each held a weapon, whether they were young or old; long spears, shields, axes and swords, glittered in the late *Shadow* sun. Their stares mirrored hers - utter disbelief. She studied the mixture of scars from the recent battle, red raw and not easily forgiven. Behind lay the bitter backdrop of destruction. Smouldering lines of black smoke billowed between tumbled down walls of shattered huts. Adjacent, stood a line of Imp prisoners, watched by guards. Shackled by long chains and pushed onto their knees. Reuben was amongst them and further down the line was his sister Shanakee. His gaze caught hers, and his eyes flashed a bright red. Eleanor quickly spotted Tam and Brenn, held separately from the others. Chains linked around their necks and three swords pointing at their chests.

"*The Stone*," an Imp stepped forwards from the line. His head was adorned with an elaborate crown of orangey feathers, joined together by what Eleanor thought looked like teeth. He had dried blood smeared across his bare chest and part of his face covered in soot. "Or I'll start to kill them one by one." He pointed to the line of prisoners. His Naraling was basic, but his defiant stance said enough to show his intentions. Eleanor looked at Daniel in alarm. She wanted nothing more than to reach out and rip it from his hand.

"Daniel," she whispered, hoping for some sign of the Elf she knew.

"It is not your Power Gift," he bellowed. "It's mine – and responds to me. You have no right to hold it." Eleanor stepped away. "If I hadn't been here, you'd all be overrun by Natajaws." The wind blew strongly down the hillside. Eleanor felt a chill spill down her spine. She glanced to see more Imps appear and position themselves behind them, amongst the green vine.

Daniel held his palm flat for all to see. It glowed a rich blue, rays of pastel light burst across the desert sand. Gasps rang through the younger Imps, but no-one moved. "Wait," Tam shouted, his chain clattering. "Don't use it, Elf," he struggled against his binds. A guard roughly hit him across his face. A young Impling screamed.

"Go, Elf," Tam cried through his pain, "go, get out of here." Eleanor could hardly watch as he was hit again and again. "Tell, my sister... we forgive her, and I will always wait for her return." Eleanor struggled to hold back tears as several guards set on Tam and battered him into silence.

"Scarlet seeks her own destiny," Daniel's tone flat, his stare blank. He swirled *The Stone*, chanting words Eleanor had never heard before. An enormous water dome appeared, engulfing him inside. It roared and crashed, looping around and around. Not a drop moved out of the shape. Eleanor bolted. Her mind raced. How could he? The idiot... he'd left her... as if she didn't exist. Eleanor in a fit of rage muttered her transformation spell. Cries of anger filled her senses. Pain rippled with intensity. She looked down to the ground. Dodging the spears and random arrows, she flew as close as she could to Tam's crumbled body.

Furious at Daniel's deception, the Crewantal's were throwing everything they had at the water dome, but nothing was penetrating its walls. It was an odd sight in a desert. The water wobbled over the sand, like an iron box, grey and impenetrable. The guards had left Tam, joining the others in the attack; chasing the dome.

"I will tell Scarlet your message," she landed beside him. His head rose slightly off the ground. Eleanor could see a tear glisten across his cheek and for a moment, she didn't feel fear or hatred. "She was helping you in the village, before all this. Scarlet was on your side. I think she will always be."

"Please give her my message. We need her home, I need her..." his voice trailed.

"I will..." Eleanor bent and loosened the chain around his neck. She blew at the bolt binding the links together and released the pin. She quickly set to work on the ones around his wrists. Tam groaned at her touch. She could see the bruises forming through his white skin. "Go, you've done more than enough," he muttered, "find my sister....?" A shout made her look up. Imps were approaching. "I will," she whispered and quickly flew away. Drifting over the burnt out dwellings and fleeing cattle. The village, in charcoal lines etched into the earth. The Grass Rats had long gone. She saw some of the Crewantals returning from the hills, lumbering ghostly giants beaten and worn. Eleanor wondered if Scarlet had seen her brothers being captured? Whatever Scarlet had seen, Eleanor didn't care. All she knew was, she had to find her first. At least together they could work out what to do about Daniel.

51

THE BANISHMENT SPELL

The ridge came silently into view. Eleanor landed on the sandy gravel and reformed, every part of her hurt, she could even feel her skin pulsing in pain waves. She bit her lip, *why was it so bad?* She sank under the shade, deperate to feel hidden. She knew she should give the birdcall signal they had agreed on, but could bring herself to. Locusts and crickets, mingling with the distant cries from the village. Everything looked so small and unimportant for up there. She took a long drink from the tiny stream that bubbled down the hillside and splashed water over her face. The quick glimpse of her reflection was enough, she looked a mess. Defeated and conflicted, she settled behind a rock, under the olive tree and lent against its trunk. Her eyelids grew heavy.

*

"Daniel," Eleanor jumped, he seemed to appear from nowhere. "I didn't hear you coming."

"I'm not here for long?" he snapped.

"What did you say..." Eleanor replied furiously.

"You heard."

"What is wrong with you? You left me….. I could have died or worse been captured. You're a senseless idiot... got what you want now, so to *Under Terra* with everything and anyone else. " Eleanor grabbed her rope and felt her pulse racing, his cold stare infuriating her further.

"It's *The Stone*." Eleanor leapt out of her skin. A voice purred. Standing on the ridge, with an elaborate pattern of the sandy hillside dancing across his chest

"Tristan…?" Eleanor cried.

"Don't rattle him. Step back." Tristan face taunt. Enka appeared by Tristan's side. "Daniel, you need to give *The Stone* to me," Enka urged, "we can hold it for you, until you're back within Caradoc."

"Never," he said, the word rang against the ridge.

"Listen to them," Eleanor fumed.

"Daniel," Enka said, "its too strong for you, while you're out here." Enka began to walk towards him, a shield of leaves before her. "Daniel, can you hear me. I won't steal it. It belongs to the Elves, but you must relinquish it. You are already changing." Eleanor could see him fighting something internally, his eyes darted like fish and his hand seemed to be pushing against an invisible force.

"Now," another voice! Eleanor spun on her heels. Her eyes fixed on the pale Imp. Whose clothes were in shreds and hair even wilder than normal. A burning flame danced in her outstretched hand. The side of her face was tinged blue and she limped awkwardly. No one spoke as Scarlet approached. The heat pushed Eleanor away. Daniel looked into the flame, mesmerised and vacant. Scarlet stepped closer.

"Daniel, give it to Enka." Scarlets voice left no room to argue. His hand went forwards and backwards like a flapping curtain.

"Now…." Scarlets flame grew. Slowly Daniel lifted his hand and opened his palm. Scarlet quickly took it and threw it to Enka.

Daniel wobbled on his feet and shook his head. For a moment Eleanor thought he was going to fall. Scarlet's flame disappeared as she steadied him.

"Tristan," Daniel muttered, after a moment. "How… you… Scarlet, that's hot… why are you? Er were you holding a fire bolt at me?"

"You'd lost it," Scarlet walked away and sat heavily on a rock.

"I've been following you out of the village. It wasn't pretty." Daniel looked at her quizzically.

"We must get out of here," Tristan interrupted. "The Armoraks are waiting for us, along with an old friend of yours, Daniel."

"Halgelan?" His eyes sparkled.

Daniel's gaze met Eleanor and he flashed a broad grin. "We did it," he said, "we got *The Stone*." He came over and flopped his arms around her. Eleanor stiffen in his hold. She wasn't sure whether to thump or hug him. "Never again," she replied. "Seriously, never again or I'm going back to Vearmoor. No offence Scarlet, but this place it worse than what I reckon the *Under Terra* is like."

"We have to get away from here." Tristan interrupted. "The Imps won't take long to cover these hills and discover the trail of the dome."

"What dome?" Daniel's eyes back to their usual blue. Scarlet rolled her eyes and threw a fire bolt at some twigs. They burst into flames. "Next bolt is for you, Elf."

"What.... whats the matter with you all? Seriously I can't remember anything since lifting *The Stone* in that lake... I thought I'd die."

"It might have been a better solution." Eleanor snapped, "so watch your back Daniel. The Crewantal's won't forget you for a long time." Daniel looked at Eleanor with a worried frown. "Lets just say," Eleanor continued, "you've got a lot of making up to do."

Tristan's shadow covered the ground between them. Daniel looked up at him. "So, do you believe you're a real Elf?"

"Huh," Daniel stuttered. "And it didn't kill you," Vagen stood behind Tristan. Eleanor hadn't noticed him before. She would never get used to them appearing as they did. "No it didn't kill him, but made him really weird," Eleanor retorted. Although the Pixies laughed, Eleanor wasn't sure it was that funny. She had no idea how Daniel was going to be able to use it again and fight *The Darkness* without going completely evil.

"How are we going to get back through Arramond, without the Vanik guards attacking us? We won't make it," Scarlet asked.

"We're going to use the Poldaric tunnel." Scarlet, Eleanor and Daniel exchanged looks.

"The Armoraks will make quick work of it." Tristan began to cast a spell and the bank at the back of the ridge under the rocky ledge began to move. Eleanor smiled in disbelief.

*

"It's within this area…" Daniel said, trying to stop Halgelan from prancing, "I'm sure of it."

"But it all looks the same," Scarlet's irritation raw, "and this is the third, *I'm sure*, in a short space of time." Daniel ignored her and jumped off Halgelan's back, gently patting the warm neck. It had been a relief to see his old friend again.

"Did you do anything to mark it?" Enka asked, as she walked over.

"Yeah… cast a spell, but I doubt it's lasted."

"So," Scarlet said, "why can't you see your spell? And why do the Elves hide their entrance so much?" She sat proudly on the strangest of beast. "Imps don't. They just guard theirs."

"That's just it," he rebuffed. "…I can't. I'm like the rest of you… I was banished, remember." Daniel felt his frustration rise. "And they hide the entrance, to make it harder for you lot to find."

Eleanor dismounted. "So, how did you mark it?" she said. She was holding tightly onto a beautiful Staginourisum, clearly not willing to let it go. It had made Daniel smile when she'd chosen that over Tristan's beasts.

"A blue circle will glow when I step into it."

"Did you cover a large area…?" Daniel suddenly felt stupid, he remembered the circle being only big enough to surround his feet.

"Huh," he replied shrugging his shoulders.

"Oh," Eleanor gave him a look. "Do you think if I stepped in it, it would glow too?"

"Might do."

Tristan sighed behind them, "then… Daniel, this could take a while," he said, and he jumped down from his mount. And we haven't got much time."

"What did you find out about *The Darkness* within Caradoc, when you were home. Tristan?" Tristan was standing on a cluster of large rocks, majestic surveying The Moors. "*The Darkness,* was already there, lurking, but not formed."

"So my family could be underneath, not knowing they're in real danger."

"They could be. But you're family and several of the Elf Elders are no fools Daniel, they will know something is happening." Daniel felt the air press in on him. The shadows were failing. There was only a few left until *Dark Exchange* and he wanted to be in Caradoc before then.

"Daniel – let me try a spell," Enka called from the middle of overgrown ferns. "Does anywhere look more familiar and I'll start there?" Daniel wanted to scream... he really couldn't tell, so much had passed since then.

"Try anywhere around here..." he picked a spot.

"Are you sure?" she said. He nodded, trying to cover up his doubts. Enka began to work a spell with tumbling words that meant nothing to him. Daniel looked around at his companions, unrelated Tribelings helping him. How had this happened? How close he felt to them. He glanced again at Tristan. His image part sky, part rock, his mass of brown hair neatly tied at the nape of his neck. An Earth Guardian, leader of all Pixies, willing to help him, a banished Elf. Daniel vowed to one *Turn* return the favour, despite their differences.

"That hurt!" Scarlet suddenly shouted. She was blocked from view by Halgelan. "Look... I can't walk across here," she shouted. Daniel pushed through the gorse and jumped over a wild clump of heather. He threw a handful of water droplets to where she was pointing. "Hey," she shouted and dodged to the side, "they could have hit me!"

He grinned. The droplets landed where she pointed, but nothing happened. He punched the air in annoyance.

"Aargh there must be something I'm missing..." he shouted.

"Then try something else..." Scarlet shot him a wild look, "it's getting dark and I don't want to be out here any longer."

"Why not use *The Stone?*" Tristan said as he approached. Daniel felt the waves of doubt ripple through the air, Eleanor had said how he'd left her to face the whole of the Crewantal Tribe alone.

"No, Tristan, you can't ask him," Eleanor interjected, "he just needs to get it back into Caradoc for someone else to use it."

"But, look." Tristan pushed his hand into the same area Scarlet couldn't enter. "I can't either... This is the place, Daniel, you need stronger magic to break that spell." Daniel felt cold. *He remembered the words of Morwena.* That was why he'd started the journey into Arramond. Everyone was staring at him.

"It is why you risked all," Tristan voiced this thoughts aloud.

"All you need is a little help," Enka added.

"Yes..." Tristan looked across at Enka. "You've had help from your mother while on The Moorland before... ask her again, she can protect you." Daniel looked uneasily at *The Stone* that lay in Enka's outstretched hand.

"But none of you were sure she had doing good last time we saw her."

"Its a risk we're going to have to take?" Daniel suddenly felt very aware of sights and sounds of The Moors. The Stone called to him, in a way that unsettled him. It was tempting, powerful, almost too easy. He could rule all he wanted with its power. He shook his head.

"Do it, Elfling!" Tristan suddenly shouted, "you and Caradoc are running out of time." His aggression, Daniel noticed, even made Scarlet flinch. "You," Tristan's tone was hard, "must return, you are the only one who can stop this!" Daniel looked into the brown Earth Guardian's eyes, lost for a moment in a different world of power. "If you falter now, Elves will suffer and so will Nararose. It won't stop with just Caradoc. You have come too far to hesitate."

Daniel thought of his family, his brothers, Karn and Isaac; his father, those feelings still confused. His mother. He closed his eyes. *The Stone* pulsed in his palm. A wave of energy coursed up his arm. He looked at the ground around him and saw it fill with blue light. His aches and pains once more faded, and his eyes brightened, seeing more of The Moors than ever before. His companions, even Halgelan, no longer clear, their outline merging into a blue fog of energy. He wished for the barriers to Caradoc to break. He was bringing their power gift home.

A long pale hand extended slowly through the haze, welcoming and kind, he instinctively took hold. With a jolt, he fell into the mist, losing control of time and where he was going. Holding tightly to the hand for what felt like a full *Turn*, his body somersaulting over and over. Eventually and unforgivingly he hit the ground. The rich blue dissipated into the familiar soft glow he had so missed. He could smell the rich dampness and wanted to jump for joy, he was actually home, in the land where he belonged. Daniel rose to his feet and shook soil from his clothes. He opened his palm to check, but his mind knew the answer, *The Stone* was no longer within his clasp. He felt in his tunic and trouser pockets – but it wasn't there either. He searched the ground around him, scrabbling and scratching at the gritting pathway. But it was nowhere to be found. His elation tainted, as he wondered whose hand it had been.

52

SKY LAKE AND WHITE FALLS

Eleanor crouched against the prickly grass, trying to stop herself from shaking; *this can't be as bad as going into Arramond.* A narrow, dark trench had opened, cutting through the tufty earth, where Daniel had disappeared. She looked back at Scarlet.

"You are coming, aren't you?"

"Yes, I've already promised – twice," Scarlet face was set in a look of utter determination, "now go, before we both change our minds." Eleanor heard Daniel calling her name and breaking the spell that barred her from entering. Eleanor briefly smiled at Tristan and Enka, whose silhouette blended with the skyline. They had said their farewells. Eleanor could tell leaving the Pixies for Scarlet was hard. Eleanor took one more look across the horizon. She wanted to see Morwena, talk to her. Know she had made it back with her father and Elerday.

"Go Eleanor," Tristan said, "keep safe, you can stop Daniel from being consumed by *The Stone*, he'll listen to you both." He gave the Pixie's sign of peace.

"We will see you again," Enka said kindly. "We will help as much as we can from Poldaric." Enka paused to steady the Armorak she sat on. "Remember, Eleanor, whatever has formed will be no harder to kill than the Gulabirds you've already faced - there hasn't been enough time." Eleanor wasn't so sure, as she lowered her feet into the hole. She gave Enka a smile and launched herself into the earth, thinking how, she - the youngest Spriteling of Francis Paraquinn - was friends with a Pixie, been into Arramond and about to enter Caradoc. Would her family ever believe her?

She half fell and half ran through a earthy tunnel. So small and cramped. Praying to her *Wind Master* for a safe landing. It was as if a billowing cushion shrouded and protected her. Magic was certainly stopping her from falling, but it wasn't of her making. Suddenly it gave way and she fell through the air. Daniel pulled her to her feet.

"You ok?"

"It's an odd way to get in," she said as she brushed soil from her clothes. "I thought I was falling but weirdly under control. Its not very welcoming."

"Its not meant to be, remember we don't normally spend time with Sprites or Imps." Eleanor thought he looked nervous as he looked back up the tunnel. "Is Scarlet coming?"

Eleanor nodded. "But you know, she's focused on revenge. I think she saw more in Arramond than we realise." Eleanor paused for a moment. "And do you remember what was said at The Rock of Vespic? It's been worrying me."

"Which bit... so much has been said."

"What Tonurang said to Orran... his first promise. He had information about a Fire-Maker who'd escaped. A powerful one.... that must be Scarlet."

"You're right," Daniel looked worried. "Orran will be just as keen to see her, as she is for revenge. She could be in real danger."

"Should we say something?"

"What good is it going to be now?" Daniel shook his head, "I just hope she's strong enough to keep Orran at bay. Or we're all in trouble." A pile of loose stones and soil came tumbling from the ceiling. "She's coming..." Scarlet fell through the air and landed skilfully. Eleanor felt a stab of jealousy.

"Wow, Scarlet, look at your hair," Eleanor said. Scarlet held a clump in her hand, "It's gone black!" she exclaimed. "Like mine," Eleanor reached out to touch it. "Why would that happen?" Scarlet looked startled.

"Not sure, maybe it's the light here," Daniel said. "But this could be good, it means you won't stand out so much."

"My powers…. have they changed?" Daniel shrugged. "We'll find somewhere less open to try. But don't here."

"And you," Eleanor said, "you look… well… sort of better." Daniel examined his arms, "That's because of *The Stone*," he said, "it healed a huge gash I had down my side in the cave. It's strange. Whenever I hold it, it's as if it transfers powers and makes me feel stronger."

"Its the Power Gift healing?" Scarlet said.

"We should move from here," Daniel said, "there are probably Elves about, and I'm not ready to see anyone yet." Daniel set off up a path. Eleanor fell in step with Scarlet behind her. Together they climbed the rocky incline. The panoramic view slowly unfolded. A huge cavernous underground network of misshapen caves stretched as far as Eleanor could see, dotted with wide glistening lakes. It was so much more impressive than she'd ever imagined and the gentle soft hazy blue light made everything look dreamy. She liked it.

"This is the outer territory," Daniel came to a stop, "the main Trevarak settlement is over there. You can just see its edge."

"It's beautiful," Eleanor said, then wished she hadn't.

"There doesn't seem to be anyone about?" Daniel muttered.

"Yes, a bit like Arramond." Eleanor replied. "The curfew on Imp movements. Do you think Elves have the same, or are they in hiding and watching us now?"

"No," Daniel replied. "No Elves live up here. Only in the settlements. Its safer, away from falling water. Remember don't touch the stuff in the lakes."

"Great," Scarlet sighed and wrapped her arms tightly around her waist.

"Was Tristan all right"? Daniel suddenly asked, as he looked about.

"He's gone, but you knew that, he doesn't seem to come into other territories willingly," Scarlet's tone was annoyed, "but he said to give you this." She took out from under her jacket. It looked like a carved disk. It was no bigger than her hand.

"It's ash," Eleanor said.

"Interesting..." Scarlet smirked. "Definitely a carpenter's Spriteling." Eleanor scowled.

"What is it?" Daniel looked at it curiously.

Scarlet shrugged. "I've seen similar being worn by other Earth Guardians. Look it has writing on the back."

"Do you know what it says?" Daniel asked Eleanor. She lent in to have a closer look.

"What would I know?" she replied, glaring at Scarlet. "Never seen anything like it."

Daniel tucked it into his jacket. "Well there must be some use for it, as Tristan never does anything without a reason."

"Why aren't there any guards here, or at the entrance?" Scarlet said.

"There usually are," Daniel replied. "When I was banished I was sent through those." Eleanor looked at the giant boulders he was pointing to, proudly guarding the end of a flat valley floor. "Most of the Trevarak community was gathered."

"Daniel, you ok?" Eleanor asked quietly.

"Sure..." he shrugged.

"It's so quiet?" Scarlet continued. "Except for the awful running water."

"Come on..." Daniel said. "We're still too close to the exit." Eleanor was mesmerised by the tranquil sloshing against the shoreline, to her it was soothing. She didn't think she would ever tire of it. There were only a few lakes within Vearmoor and her mother had never been interested to take them to see one. So she had, had to satisfy herself with rows and rows of trees.

"Daniel, is the water always so dark?" she asked.

"No," he replied, clearly lost in his thoughts. "I think we'll stay off the main path, head towards Sky Lake via White Falls. Few Elves go there and it'll get us closer to where we want to be."

"Can you transform, Eleanor, it might be better?"

"Sure," she began to mutter the spell. "Remember you left me surrounded by Imps? It came back thankfully....." Eleanor watched Daniel flinch as she repeated her spell. Her body ached with pain.

"You're still here," Scarlet said, her hands on her hips.

"I can't," a wave of nausea swept over her. "Not again!" Eleanor cried.

"But your rope is still working, look, its glowing," Scarlet said reassuringly.

"Can you make fire?" Eleanor asked hurriedly. Scarlet flicked her hand and a small flame leapt to her command.

"Then why can't I?" Her throat tightened, "why is this happening?"

"Forget it," Daniel said, "We'll manage." Eleanor grabbed her rope and twisted it in her clenched fist.

"E, it doesn't matter," Daniel said. "Scarlet and I won't let anything happen to you."

"Yeah, until that damn stone takes control of you again." Daniel's face was etched with concern. "Come on," he gave her arm a squeeze.

"Wait," Scarlet said, "Daniel, talking of The Stone - you're fine. You've not gone weird. So where is it?" He stood on a rocky step shadowed by a torrent of white water, surrounded by thick layers of dropping ivy.

"I've not got it," he said quietly.

"What?" Scarlet screeched. Eleanor looked wildly between them both.

"It's gone... when I came into Caradoc, someone took it."

"But that's impossible," Eleanor spluttered, "no one could do that, there wasn't anyone with you! And... and... what... are we going to do now! You've no Stone, and I can't transform."

"I think I know who has it," Daniel said.

"How...?" Eleanor shook her head.

"Come on, we're time wasting. Trust me. I don't think its bad." Eleanor hesitated, wondering if their plan was on the verge of collapse. Daniel ran on.

The path began to widen. The deafening sound of thundering water filled her body, with a regular drum beat of vibrations. They ran into a tunnel through solid rock, where water seeped through the cracks, dripping relentlessly onto the already soaked ground. Her feet squelched into deep muddy puddles. Scarlet's fire, lit the way, like a bobbing fire fly. The tunnel ended as quickly as it began, and they stood behind a vast wall of foaming white bubbles. Protected by a ceiling of rock and surrounded by a multitude of shining white crystals.

"Is there only water in this place?" Scarlet shivered.

Daniel gave her a smile, "This won't hurt you, but that in the lake, will."

"So that burns?" Eleanor looked startled.

"Yep, and it's worse for other Tribelings."

"That's mad," Scarlet said, "having so much of something around you that actually hurts - you lot are weird." Scarlet dug her arms under her fur.

"We need to go through to the other side," Daniel said, "but no more fire, Scarlet, we're heading towards the main settlement and the Great Lake." Reluctantly Scarlet obeyed.

Running past the waterfall, Eleanor found herself once more enveloped in the heart of the rock and without Scarlet's fire, found it difficult to avoid the stalagmites that dotted the pathway, it was the slowest obstacle course she'd ever done. The darkness felt, as if it had swallowed them whole. Only to spit them out the other side, slightly bruised and panting. Eleanor could hear her first sound of Elves, muffled and difficult to decipher. Daniel ran ahead. Eleanor stood to catch her breath.

"Don't you wish you were home?" Scarlet had found a dry spot to rest.

"Nearly every *Shadow* of every *Turn*, but this, whatever it is, is like a web and I'm trapped until the end," Eleanor replied.

Scarlet sighed. "For so long I wanted to escape and have some freedom. Now I have, I would do anything to go back to the way things were. Even trapped in my chambers." Eleanor was about to ask more, when Daniel reappeared, tense and alert.

"Elves are dead on the path ahead," he said guardedly.

"How were they killed?" Scarlet asked.

"By blue Elf spells," he was visibly shaking.

Scarlet pushed past him. "Are you sure?" she ran on to look. He didn't stop her. "Daniel," Eleanor said slowly, "what does this mean?"

Scarlet interrupted, "I can see Orran," Scarlet called, "I know it's him."

"Wait Scarlet!" Eleanor got up. "Don't do anything stupid. And stop shouting, you'll attract attention."

"He's mine," Scarlet said with such ferocity Eleanor paused. "I have lost my family because of him."

"And you will," Daniel said calmly, "but we have to think this through." He paused thoughtfully. "Can't you feel it?" he said quietly.

"What? Feel what?" Eleanor replied guardedly.

"It's hot... hotter than usual."

"How would I know that? Neither of us have been here before," Eleanor replied angrily."

"We'll divide." Eleanor gasped. "Look," Daniel continued, "I think *The Stone's* been taken by an Elder. The hand that pulled me through, I think I recognise it. They will have gone to Algor, with it."

Eleanor cried out, "So Scarlet flights Orran alone, while you walk off to some place or other?"

"I don't look like an Imp anymore without my red hair and can stay under cover."

"This is crazy..." Eleanor looked at them both. "Can't either of you see that?"

"Once they see Scarlet fighting against Orran the Trevarak Elves will rally to her side," Daniel reassured. "Eleanor you just need to keep her alive long enough."

Eleanor could hardly control her frustration. "So I'm going with her.?"

"You'll be safer together. I'll take you as close as I can, to where the Imps are."

"So how will we find you afterwards... if we make it that is?"

"I'll be in Algor," Daniel replied, "any Trevarak will help you, I know they will."

Eleanor shrugged. "I don't think I know anything anymore. Now you're asking me to chat to Elves to find out directions."

"There's only one way into Algor, from where I leave you... its easy. I know you can make it. The Elves will not kill another Tribeling unless threatened - they aren't Imps." Daniel looked at Scarlet momentarily. Scarlet shrugged. They both continued talking but Eleanor felt the words stick like glue. She really hated the plan. It was going to break them all and she didn't seem to be able to make them see that. They could only suceed if they stayed together.

53

REVENGE

Slumped shoulders and grim set jaw line told Scarlet, Eleanor wasn't happy. But, there was nothing she could do. Fate was set. She had to face Orran, gain some sort of revenge.

They had reached the place where the path divided.

"I really think this is stupid." Eleanor's green eyes were glaring so intently it made Scarlet shudder. "This is your land, Daniel, you will be the strongest here. Scarlet didn't leave us in Arramond and she had plenty of reason to."

"It's too late for that," he replied, but he didn't look at her when he spoke. "Over there, by that lake," he pointed, "if you run along the northern edge through the fern grove, you'll be heading into the Trevarak settlement." A slightly awkward slant crossed his face. "Scarlet," he turned to face her, "this is your chance. There will be several Elves fighting, if The Trevarak's see you're on their side, they'll help you." Scarlet felt her stomach twist. "Avoid the Eastlings."

"How will I tell the difference?"

"We need cloaks," Eleanor blurted out, "every damn Elf except Daniel seems to wear one," and you and I stick out in our clothes."

"That was on The Moors," Daniel said, "they don't wear them much in here."

"But, what about those dead bodies up the pathway?" Scarlet replied. "They did."

"You're kidding," Daniel eyes bulged.

"They won't look at us so much if we have them on." Scarlet darted away without giving anyone a chance to stop her. The bodies were heavy, rig amortise had set in. Her hands trembled. She kept checking over her shoulder just in case someone was coming.

There was an awkward silence when she got back. Panting for breath, Scarlet handed Eleanor a cloak. Eleanor grabbed it without a word and stuffed her arms into the sleeves. It dragged on the ground, but she doubled it over and tied her rope through the fold.

"I need to find out if Orran has brought another Fire-maker with him," Scarlet blurted.

"And what if he has?" Eleanor replied roughly.

"I'll just have to deal with her first." Scarlet focued on her cloak, it smelt of sweat, and weighed her down.

"I'll go..." Daniel said. Scarlet nodded.

"Good luck," he said, "that's both of you..." Scarlet bit her lip, she had begun to think of him as a friend. He nodded and smiled at her, "See you in Algor." He disappeared down the path.

"So you really want to do this?" Eleanor had her arms crossed.

"Yes... my brothers need something." Scarlet launched down the gravelly incline. If Daniel hadn't had the guts to tell her that her brothers were being held captive by the Crewantal Imps, then she doubted Eleanor would.

"Wait," Eleanor called after her, but Scarlet carried on. It was up to her now, she has started all of this for them, and she would never forgive Orran for holding her prisoner.

"Scarlet, look…" Eleanor grabbed her shoulder.

"Its Okay, I saw you try and free Tam, that's enough." Scarlet shook her off and ran on.

They quickly reached the track. One side fell away into the water.

The other, hung thickly with a dark mist, like a shirttail over trousers. Scarlet shuddered at the proximity to thick dark liquid. Over her head hung a criss crossed network of thick interwoven fern. The perfect cover. Scarlet pulled up her hood and headed on.

"…. We're getting close to the end," Eleanor whispered.

Scarlet stopped, transfixed, listening. The thin leaved archways masked the exit. She parted the remaining few branches. It happened so quickly and so unexpectantly that she almost lost her footing. Elves were everywhere, filling the open spaces with blue flashing lights and disks of flying water. Scarlet's skin crawled, as if an army of ants had run over her body. Their shouts and screams bursting into stereo, like walking into a carnival.

"Watch out," screamed Eleanor as water flew into the ferns.

"There are so many," Scarlet said through gritted teeth.

"Did you really think there wouldn't be?"

"Uh… I thought it might be like Arramond, Imps hidden within their Compounds." Scarlet peered out. "If we head over there, we'll see more." The wide expanse of plateau between them lay bare like a skinned animal. Scarlet's throat dried. With a deep breath, she gathered her cloak and ran with a surge of speed. Ducking blue spells and praying a water disk wouldn't hit her. Out of breath and panting, she fell into a doorway. There were more dwellings adjacent, covered in thick roof thatch that touched the ground in places. Eleanor stumbled in behind her.

"Do you think anyone saw us" Eleanor panted,

"Scarlet peered out, trying to catch her breath. "Can't see much, through the blue haze."

"Huh," Eleanor held her nose. "What's that smell?"

Scarlet began to cough. "Erghhh, don't know." She edged forwards and looked down the cobbled path. She could see a younger Elf lurking in a doorway and a mother carrying a baby wrapped in a thick blanket, running between the shadows. The grey street had no lights to ward off the gloom, leaving an eerie grey twilight below the thatch. She leaned out to see where the mother was going. A flash of white streaked across the path, Scarlet blinked. The mother fell brutally against the wall. Scarlet shot her hand to her mouth, as the

Elf slid down the wall and her Elfling fell from her arms. Something ripped into her shoulder. Scarlet stifled a scream as it burned her skin. She crumpled into her cloak.

"Scarlet," Eleanor knelt over her. Scarlet rolled onto her side, and through a clenched droopy gaze saw Elves walking towards them. A tall, male, with something swirling in their hands. Two arrows pointed at Eleanor's head. The air felt heavy and hot.

"I'm ok," Scarlet pulled herself up, holding her throbbing shoulder. The Elves encircled them.

"Imp!"

"I am," she said quietly in Naraling, "but not here to kill Elves." She formed a small ball of fire in her hand.

"Then why are you here?" Suddenly blue flashes rocked over their heads and the Elves returned fire. Eleanor dived sideways, dragging Scarlet with her. Barging through a flimsy side door. They fell into a dark room.

"Are you badly hurt?" Eleanor gasped, looking like a frightened hare. Scarlet took away her hand, to see the raw patch of flesh.

"Daniel's right, this stuff does burn!" She tried to give Eleanor a smile. "Ironic....!"

"You're not getting away that easily," a grey hairy face peered into the room. His nose was longer than Scarlet's whole hand and made her feel queasy. "What is a Sprite and Imp doing here... *and together?*"

"I'm here to take Orran Vanik back home," Scarlet spoke as commandingly as she could. "He doesn't belong here."

The old Elf's face broke into a broad snear. "You... and her, alone? Couldn't the Imps have sent someone better? If we can't get rid of him ourselves and we've been fighting the Imps for over twelve *Shadows*, then how will you?" Scarlet could feel her fire begin to rise.

"She can," Eleanor spoke for her. "Are you....?"

"Trevarak," the Elf replied, "what of it?"

"Do you know Noah Trevarak?"

"Camundra Volwine, one of his few remaining faithfuls. Why do you speak the name of our leader?" His tone was tight and Scarlet noticed a deep scar across his head that sat in a white bald patch.

"Because his Elfling, Daniel is back." Eleanor stood tall. Camundra slammed the door shut behind him. He pulled Eleanor towards him grabbing her roughly.

"His Elfling.... you said, his Elfling!" Camundra demanded. "But that's impossible, a banishment spell was performed." Scarlet placed her hand on his shoulder, she knew it was on fire. He quickly let Eleanor go.

"Surely this news is what you wanted to hear," Eleanor demanded.

"Yes, but how can I trust you?" Camundra replied. "This," he pointed at them both with distain, "is not normal!"

"There's no time, "Scarlet interjected, "Daniel's gone to Algor and I must deal with the Vaniks – will you get me closer to them?" Scarlet knew her pupils were dancing with flames.

"I will," he bowed. "I will ensure your safe passage, for as far as I can. My Elves will rally under my command. But, be warned. It is not a fair *Shadow's* walk out there, and I cannot say that you'll make it."

"Just get me as close as you can," Scarlet held her shoulder hoping it won't let her down.

"Can you find Noah Trevarak," Eleanor said, "and tell him Daniel has returned with the real *Stone of Innvericum*." A shadow fall across Camundra's face, and Scarlet thought, darkened slightly.

"The real *Stone*, but that's in our Great Hall?" Camundra spoke calmly though his teeth.

"It isn't," Eleanor continued. "Well, then," Camundra said, "we should hurry." Camundra gave another curt nod. "We have no time to lose."

54

ALGOR

Muffled cries echoed through the thundering torrents, as cold spray settled on Daniel's face. It had none of the sting of the falling water on The Moors. Daniel knew he'd give eternal thanks to whichever God listened, for returning him home.

The familiar mixture of pebbles and grit crunched beneath his feet. He had often used this track with his mother, and loved the hidden pockets of lakes, their thick green ferns and giant Panicum grasses. There was nothing like it *above*. Familiarity gave him strength, reassurance. But what he didn't understand was why he hadn't seen anyone? No reflection seekers, no Elfling's playing, no fishers in the lakes. It was as if they had all disappeared. As Daniel ran on, his worry intensified. If there was no one here, they would all in Trevarak, with Eleanor and Scarlet. He should never have left them. Eleanor's powers were weakening and Scarlet alone was no match for Orran and his henchmen. *What was he thinking*? But *The Stone*. It called to him, relentless and longing. He needed to touch it one more time.

Daniel jumped across an arching step onto the sandy plateau, the entrance to Algor loomed ominously. Two giant stone carved Elder Elves, peered at him from their seated position, as if they knew exactly what he was up too. He moved to hide, and crouched behind thick set fern bushes, listening. His mind wondered to the last time he had come here with his mother. It had been a whole *Light* season ago. He was shorter then, only tall enough to touch a protruding toe and the sandal strap of the seated stone giant, if he balanced on the ball of his feet and stretched an arm to its limit. Cascading waterfalls fell between each figure. It formed a curtain of white powdery foam making it difficult to distinguish other sounds. Daniel waited for several moments to check that no one was around. He ran out in the open, crossed the short distance quickly, and with bounding strides, jumped through the opening. His hair soaked, he stood in the mouth of Algor - their *reflection sanctuary*. It was the only place within Caradoc that dazzled golden rather than blue. He paused, bowed, and bent to collect a handful of sand. Inhaling its rich aromas, savouring the way it ran through his fingers. The cave exuded a sense of calm, soothed by the harmonious lapping of the silvery water on the sloping beach edge. An intense relief washed over him. *He had survived.*

Daniel set to work, checking the outer perimeter and skirting the lake's circumference. He needed to make sure that he wasn't alone. Zig zagging, to the main lake where the altar stood proudly, he knelt to run his hand over the rippling waves and savoured the thought that he no longer had to hide his ability.

"Well, well, well."

Daniel looked up. His skin tingled and hairs stood on end. Tonurang, surrounded by a multitude of guards, walked boldly across the sand - as if they owned Algor. The guards fanned outwards, protecting their leader on all sides. From the plinth of rocks by the altar, floated two objects, skimming the surface of the lake, like soaked logs. His stomach tightened.

"The prodigal Elf...." Tonurang's familiar sneering tone, jarred every bone in Daniel's body. "So you've seen for yourself how busy I've been." Daniel's eyes darted. "Oh, you don't know yet... do you? Imps in Caradoc, Trevarak's defeated, Eastling in power. And no sign of *The Darkness*. Just Elves under control. And those who aren't, will soon be brought into line." Daniel shuddered. Something else was banging in his head, a warning... a fierce warning. He went towards the water's edge ignoring Tonurang. He stared at the floating objects, *something was familiar.* Daniel waded in. The lake rushed around his ankles. A jolt like an arrow hit his chest.

"Mother!" Daniel screamed. From the corner of his eye several water droplets, came into view. Daniel raised a shield, wide and strong.

"It's too late anyway," Tonurang shouted over the din.

"What have you done?"

"Oh, she's still alive... and her companion – Sorrel - your friend's mother, Seb, I believe, now loyal to me." Tonurang laughed. "They've, " Tonurang pointed to the bodies. "Been very useful." The guards began to circle, like hunters. "You, your father and all the stupid Trevarak's will not win this battle," Tonurang spat. "Anta has foretold of my victory - fancy that! Your own flesh and blood. The Glows have promised me glory. Your reappearance, will make no difference." His words resounded around the cave walls. "Special or not, you can't stop me now." Daniel fought to hold back the wave of searing hot bile that rose in his throat.

"Why?" He yelled. "Can't you feel *The Darkness* rising?"

Tonurang laughed. "You are all the same. You think it is only your family that can control *Light* and *Dark,* maintain *The Balance* – well you're wrong and I will prove it." A ripple of agreement murmured from the other Elves. Daniel could not bear seeing his mother's drifting body any longer. He didn't care about Tonurang. He extended his shield into a dome and waded on. A barrage of water disks came from all directions. He dived cleanly under. The disks fizzed into the water, a dart boart and he the bulls eye. His lungs quickly reached bursting point. Through slicing lines, he dodged and contorted his body as he swam. He lunged for the surface, coming up between the bodies. He dragged Sorrel and his mother into the dome, his nose lying just above the lake's surface waiting, watching. The cold water stung. The disks missed their target and now silent.

"It'll give me great pleasure to see your father's face when I tell him you did actually make it back into Caradoc but died next to Anta, once more a prisoner."

"You will never get near to my father." Daniel roared, treading water.

"Oh, but someone will…"

Daniel recognised Thaen's father, the Elf he'd killed when all this started. He was shouting abuse, that drifted and echoed over the cave walls. Daniel stared in horror… as Tonurang waved his hand and a series of water droplets span into the air and sped across the sand. The entourage began to run. Sprinting towards Algor's mouth, as if they had seen a *Dark Exchange* creature. Daniel legs were tiring his arms shaking with the effort of holding the dome. One by one he saw each guard disappear through the entrance's mouth, consumed by the white foam. Tonurang remained, a mist of blue, hovering. Daniel began to drag and push his mother's lifeless body, towards the edge. When his feet hit the sand, he looked up to see Tonurang had gone. With both hands, he dragged her body onto the shore and wiped her hair and water from her face, checking for breath. The golden glow of Algor warmed her pale skin. Daniel's heart skipped a beat, could she still be alive? He raised his gaze, to the entrance. Instantly he leapt to his feet, and began to run as fast as he'd ever done. Daniel's feet drummed into the sand. *What has he done?* If he could just touch it, he had a chance. Daniel leapt towards the white, his arm fully extended, his body at full stretch. His fingers straining. Like a stone he dropped short, rolling to a halt. A few drops fell on his head. Pain coursed. He scrambled away. The beautiful white curtain, tumbled silently, stopping from the top in splurts, then silence. Stop to reveal the plateau beyond. A deathly roar filled the walls and the white turned grey, bursting into life once more, falling to the ground in violent pulses. With every meter, the water turned darker and darker.

*

Anta's auburn hair lay wet and limp; her soaked clothes exuding a coldness that made Daniel think it was too late. The earlier glimmer fading with every moment. He pulled her onto his knees.

"Mother, I'm home," he said quietly, "I stayed alive, like you said I would. I made it. It's your Elfling." She didn't move and he knew she wouldn't. He didn't even know if she could hear him. If only Eleanor was here, she could use her drying spell, it might do something. Daniel looked up and saw Sorrel's floating body. He couldn't leave her there, so waded in and dragged her out. Lying her body beside Anta. *Had Seb really betrayed his own family?* Daniel yelled loudly into the void. A torrent of words howled from him, echoing into the darkening abyse, leaving him exhausted and spent. He lay his head on his mothers shoulder, watching the tumbling grey curtain of water.

A concertina of bangs, lurched him from his trance, like the applause of a wild audience. He shuddered.... Were the Gods speaking to him? Replying to his ranting? Moments later a rippling wave of sand bubbled towards him, making snake patterns across the cave's floor. It seemed to come from every direction. Daniel froxe to the spot, letting the ripples pass underneath. They travelled on and entered the water. The lake bowed in response and gradually the warm glow began to fade even more. Daniel's heart started to pound. *What had Tonurang started?* Surely he wouldn't risk Algor? He got up quickly and started to drag his mother up the sand. He ran back for Sorrel. Sweat dripping from his forehead. If the water rose, they would be safer where he'd put them.

Daniel rested, and waited. The air hung like a heavy curtain. Daniel was glad his mother was oblivious to what was going on. Rocking the silence again, came another thunderous drumming, louder than the one before. Daniel was ready this time. He saw where it started. The wave came tumbling across the sand, from where Tonurang had first appeared. This time they were bigger and travelled like rolls of moving tubes. He knew he had to get to where they originated. He could feel the heat rising and soon it would be too late. Something was making this happen. If he could get to it, he might be able to stop it. He looked to the lake, watching the ripple end at it edge. It was like ink spilling into the water. Not the black of the Moorland sky, which had scared Daniel enough for the first few *Exchanges*, until eventually he'd become accustomed to see the small flecks of forgiving light. The lake's water had turned the blackest of the coldest stone, with not a glimmer of hope.

55

TEARS OF BLOOD

leanor was pleased they'd met Camundra. It was proving
easier hidden between billowing orange and reds, than
navigating the cobbled pathways alone. None of the other
Elves had questioned their presence after Camundra had spoken;
only Elfland words, but it didn't matter, as they were being protected.
She hadn't been able to get close to Scarlet, who was at the front.
Blue spells and burning clouds of murky haze shrouded them as they
sped along, confusing their every move. The settlement was
deceptively bigger. Brick alleyways closed in on Eleanor, tall and
strong. A stark contrast to the network of trees she navigated at
home. The smooth green lines between the bricks gave direction.

Camundra side stepped. Eleanor was roughly pushed after him.

"We're getting closer," Camundra's breath fell onto her face. She
pressed into the cold granite wall and turned away from the smell.
"Beyond that wall, is the harbour, where most of the Imps are fighting
by The Great Hall. It's the last Trevarak stronghold." Scarlet appeared,
with a wild look on her face.

"What are you telling her?" Scarlet roughly shook off the Elf's
hand, who seemed to be her shadow. Camundra smirked. Eleanor
didn't understand why Scarlet looked so angry. "How many Imps?"
Scarlet demanded.

"I haven't got close enough to count..." the sides of his mouth curled. "Its up to you to find out." He snarled.

"Will Noah be here?" Eleanor asked anxiously. He shrugged, his scowl still set.

"So you'll just let us go?" Scarlet's pupils had changed to flames.

"That is what you wanted, isn't it?" Eleanor noticed her hands were glowing red.

"You'll go to find Noah," Eleanor repeated urgently, "tell him Daniel's back."

"Of course." Camundra pulled his coat around him and replaced his pouch. He turned his back, checked up and down the alleyway. Then darted out without another word, dissolving into the grey. The others Elves followed like silent ghosts.

"I don't like this one bit," Scarlet whipsered, "they gave me the creeps."

"You hate everything Elf," Eleanor replied.

"We should get out of here." Scarlet crept forwards scanning before disappearing in the opposite direction. Eleanor hurriedly followed, constantly checking about her, ever nerve twitched. They ran to the edge of a majestic dwelling where the windows glimmered with flecks of multicolours. The harbour wall was ahead.

"Why did you tell him so much?" Scarlet breathed heavily. Eleanor pressed in against a corner stone.

"Who?" she replied as she tried to see how far the wall went. The water lapped hungrily on the other side. There was a fishy smell and a salt taste that dried when it hit her face.

"I don't trust him," Scarlet seethed.

"You mean Camundra?"

"Yes... why did you tell him about *The Stone*, didn't you see how he changed?"

"No..." Eleanor snapped. Scarlet's tone was scaring her. "He was just confused about *The Stone* – that's all. They all believe they had the real one."

"You're wrong, Eleanor. There was something else. And I think you've made it worse."

Before Eleanor could reply, a loud crash pounded into the back of the harbour wall and the ground shook beneath her feet. Eleanor peered over. Imps fighting, filling the settlement with flashes of white. A long sandy beach following the line of the lake jutting at an obtuse angle, filled with Imps and Elves. She couldn't see where the noise was coming from, but there was, what looked like charred tree trunks, dotted across the sand, bobbing with the ebb and flow. "We're never going to do this, Scarlet. There are so many and *that sound*, its not right. I think we should just forget the Imps and find Daniel." A series of blue spells flew over the wall, missing her by a hand span.

"It's too late," Scarlet's face set.

"Then, how?" Eleanor looked into her translucent skin and for a moment saw the Imp she'd first met and feared.

"Lots of fire. I can't hold it back. "Just make sure no one tries to put the flames out."

"You'll die... and I don't want to?" Eleanor stared at the sandy slab of rock beneath the folds of the heavy cloak she wore, feeling her fragile bond with the Imp breaking.

"For my brothers." Eleanor felt a draft of wind blew across her tunic. Eleanor looked up. Scarlet cloak lay over the wall, tumbling ash filled the air. The necklace, collapsed by her feet and rich heat warmed Eleanor's cold face.

"Wait," she screamed, scooping to pick up the necklace. Scarlet had burst into flames. It coursed from her arms and chest in orange bands. Her hair had changed back to its glowing red and danced in the flames. Eleanor stared in horror at the silent white giants in the mid distance, savouring the scene. Eleanor shed her heavy cloak and whispered Morwena's spell. She needed all the protection her web could give.

*

Orran could see Scarlet had changed; wherever she'd been, had made her stronger. And to just think, if it hadn't been for her stupid escape attempt, he, Orran, would've met her that exact *Turn*, as The Garnaforts' proposed betrothal! Scarlet would have been made to be his partner. But seeing her now, in Caradoc of all places, his mind, set, like a solid wall of his Compound – she was alive and he wanted her. She would be an even better partner now. He didn't need Tonurang Eastling to help him any more. If Scarlet Garnafort were under his control, she could be very useful indeed.

He barked a series of commands to his fellow Imps to encircle her; after all it was only one against them all. He wanted her alive, no matter what the cost. He must start persuading her immediately, show her his family are the powerful force within Arramond and that her Garnaforts were no longer worth her efforts – together they could rule, he could see that now. Orran held his arm up to protect his face; her fire was impressive as it swirled like a scorpion's sting, but she had little control, clearly inexperienced. His mother would be able to show her.

"Lower your flames, Scarlet," he bellowed, "we're all Imps here. There is no need for this."

"You're no Imp - Orran Vanik," she spat, "that I wish to be associated with." Her gusto was marvellous. He dodged a fireball that hurtled towards him.

"Now that's no way to treat your leader," he held up arms to show he was defenceless. "Look, even the Elves are watching you. Everyone has stopped to watch." Orran was drawn to her anger, his words seemed to release more fire that weaved magically from her hands.

His fellow Imps were being rightly cautious, trying to enclose her but unable to get close enough to be effective. Steam rose in isolated pockets where her fire met puddles of dark water. Orran could see The Elves were doing nothing to intervene, their focus had been diverted to something else, something happening in the lake, the unusual sounds that filled this forsaken land. It was of no importance to him. This was all working nicely. She was chanting like a wild Imp. He had to break her.

"Your mother's dead," he spoke loudly, and watched with an element of enjoyment as she stopped in her tracks; her arms and hands still burning. "If you kill me now," Orran stood as close as he dared, "you'll never know what happened to her or what has happened to your father."

"It's lies," she screamed, "she can't be dead." But he had stopped her.

"She is," he replied, "and I know who is to blame." he waited for her to look at him, "and I could help you save your father." That had got her attention, her fire bolts stopped.

Then behind Scarlet, with her flames lowered, he could see something he recognised. He swivelled on his feet, remembering The Rock of Vespic. He sprang into the air. Within moments he sped around Scarlet. He ripped the glowing ropes from her weak hands and flung it to the floor. He had seen that working before. She was as light as a feather. He locked her into his hold, his arm clenched around her neck. Her thick dark hair unusually beautiful against the olive skin, yet her smell, too woody for him, as she choked, struggling and kicking.

"Let her go," Scarlet yelled, holding a ball of flames directly aimed at him. Orran chuckled and wondered how such an impressive Fire-Maker of their leading family could be messed up with a tramp of a Sprite.

"Scarlet, you belittle yourself. What would your brothers say, how could you associate yourself with this?"

"She is worth a thousand of you," Scarlet spat at the ground. Then to Orran's astonishment she lowered her flames completely.

"No, Scarlet don't," the Sprite, shouted.

"Yes, lower your flames," someone said from behind him. Orran spun on his feet twisting the wriggling Sprite, to be confronted by a united line of Elves. They had appeared like spirits, silently and commanding.

"This is not your fight, Imp Orran," one of them said, holding a ball of circling water. "Take, whatever is happening here, home with you, your time within Caradoc is over." There was something about the way the Elf spoke that Orran recognised, but he couldn't place it. Doric stepped forwards and took the struggling Sprite from Orran's arms.

"Brother, look," he said. Orran turned to see Scarlet's flames had been extinguished by several Elf spells. And blood dripped down her face. Tears of red falling across her snowy white cheeks. She looked as if the slightest puff of wind would topple her. Orran knew he must get Scarlet home, otherwise her strength and powers would disappear altogether, and she would be no good to him or anybody. He hoped it wasn't too late.

"You are right, Elf, the game has changed," Orran replied, "this is no longer our fight." He gave a slight bow. He scanned the beach and harbour for Tonurang. But the treacherous Elf wasn't in sight. After their initial side-by-side combat, Tonurang had soon disappeared on some errand. Well, he no longer needed Tonurang to secure his future within Arramond, Scarlet was a much better prize.

"Brother," Doric whispered so no one else could hear, "look at the water." Without the heat from Scarlet's fire, Orran could feel the change in the atmosphere. The air was thick, claustrophobic, unpleasantly. This was perfect, Orran thought; he knew exactly what was happening. He silently smirked. He might not even have to deal with Tonurang ever again.

"I want safe passage for all of my Imps, including that one and this Sprite," Orran shouted. "We will leave via the Southern Exit, without delay."

"Give your word, Orran du Vanik," the Elf replied, "all Imps will leave immediately?"

"Yes, every last one," and he looked at Scarlet who was lying on the ground. She had collapsed like a broken twig.

"But leave the Sprite," the Elf shouted. "She's of no use to you." Orran hesitated. He had wanted a play thing. But wasn't going to argue over a Sprite. He gave Doric, the signal. Doric released his hold. She fled like a frightened hare, bolting across the open granite. How foolish Sprites were. He leapt across to Scarlet. Within moments she was secured in his arms, still and unmoving, her skin the colour of the purest marble and cold to his touch. It was tantalising. Without another look, he led the way, signalling for Doric to stay close. He wasn't about to lose his favourite brother. They sped across the sand and launched into the Vanik battle cry he so loved, his heart elated. His comrades joined in loudly, clearly relieved to be getting out of this wet and miserable land. The harbour wall was long behind him, as he lead the chase across the rocks, feeling the thick blanket of heat peel away and his prize securely in his hold.

56

TEELASORS

Another enormous explosion shook the floor and echoes rippled across the harbour, as Eleanor stood shaking, trying with all her strength not to sob. She shielded her ears.

"Who are you?" The Elf spoke roughly. He had the same slanted smile and earnest look as Daniel. His hands like clamps of iron on her shoulders. His weather-beaten features riddled with furrowed lines, framed by grey tinges. There was a coldness there that she didn't like. Eleanor tried to speak; but felt as if her voice had been taken, ripped away and buried. Her strength was going, she knew it.

"What are you doing here?" He spoke in Naraling and gave her shoulders a slight shake.

"Daniel," a whisper rose in her throat, closing her eyes to rid her memory of Scarlet's drooping arms.

"Who?" he said urgently, his grip lessened.

"Daniel," Eleanor croaked. Elves leant in like bending willows, taking her air. Her interrogator struggling to keep them at bay.

"Trevarak," she said more clearly, "he's here, we... she... I.... together." Her resolve close to crumpling.

"Daniel...?" another Elf shouted. His blues eyes piercing. He was too close. She couldn't think clearly. "Here..." His face loomed in, blurring everything from view. She couldn't see around him. Then everything went black.

She came to, with sand in her ear, her cheek squished and sticky. A blanket swaddled over her curled-up body. It was too small to make her warm, but the gesture gave her hope. Two Elves peering came into focus. Behind them was Daniel's father, she knew it was him. He pushed them aside and knelt down by her. An intense expression of worry rooted into his face.

"Are you strong enough to get up?" he asked quietly.

"Yeah," muttered Eleanor, not sure if she could.

"Good," he said quickly, "you must stay by my side." Eleanor's head was pounding and thoughts murky, as she struggled to stop herself from toppling. Quickly, she realised they were at the edge of the Lake and hadn't gone far from the harbour wall. There was a large gathering of Elves with them in all colours including blue. No longer fighting. Some were on their knees, others, coiled in flowing water. Elfling's of all ages, the youngest being carried. Several with bows locked and ready to fire. Not at each other, but into the water.

Daniel's father walked away. Elves bowed to him, as he passed. He looked like he was going forth to command an army. Eleanor struggled to keep up, and suddenly became very aware of the strange looks she was getting. Noah stopped close to the water's edge. He sank to his knees. Eleanor slowed. Its colour was as black as Morwena's eyes when she performed a spell.

"Try not to look at it," an Elf appeared by her side. "The Grand Master wants you close when we fight; it will be the best place. You've done us a great service by bringing Daniel home – something he will never forget." Eleanor shuddered. The smile across his face was a bitter one, that came with the knowledge - bringing Daniel back had made no difference, he would only die with them.

"It's too late," she said, "isn't it?" The Elf didn't reply; his grim expression confirmed all Eleanor needed to know. She wondered how Daniel was – had he made it to Algor, had he found the...? Another explosion, thunderous and deafening, erupted from the centre of the lake, shaking the very foundations of this strange land she was in. Eleanor clasped her ears in despair, knowing Ostric's Gulabirds had been mere puppets in comparison to what he was creating with that sound. *"The Stone,"* Eleanor cried out, "your Power Gift," over and over she cried the word *Stone.*

"What of it?" Noah reached her quickly taking her hands from her ears.

"Daniel's brought it back with him," she gasped, "that's how he broke the banishment spell - didn't Camundra tell you?" Eleanor gasped.

"No," Noah shook his head, "he's one of Tonurang's henchmen, why?" Eleanor felt her blood drain. "He... he was heading to find you...." Noah eyes flashed a rich blue. "I told him to find you." Eleanor instinctively reached for her rope - but it wasn't there.

"No, he wouldn't." Noah leant in closer. "So where is Daniel?"

"Algor," Eleanor replied, as if it was the hardest of secrets to tell, "Camundra must be heading there too."

"We need to get to Daniel first..." Noah said, "Otherwise Camundra will take it." Eleanor couldn't look into the Elder's face - this was her fault, she had been the one to trust Camundra. Scarlet had known. Why was she so foolish? Noah began issuing a series of instructions and Elves dispersed hurriedly in all directions.

"This won't take long." Noah turned to face her. He studied her carefully as he took out his pouch. "Hold still," he said. Eleanor edged away as a few droplets began to circle her body. "Don't move." Before she could blink the droplets disappeared into her arms, her legs and back like a Tala bird catching its prey. She pulled her sleeve aside to see where it'd gone, but couldn't see anything. "It won't hurt you," Noah said. Eleanor checked her flesh all over. Feeling stabs of pain, but was too tired to resist.

"You must come with me to Algor," Noah, instructed, "the Trevarak's will stay and deal with whatever's coming out of our *Power Element.*"

"Will we make it?" Eleanor could feel the heat of *Darkness* wrapping its claws around her, like it had done on The Moors before an attack. It made every part of her twitch with fear.

"If we're quick."

An Elf appeared from behind Noah. He awkwardly thrust

something at her. Eleanor's heart jumped. It had been cleaned and something woven into the threads. She tied it securely in place, whispering her thanks, but Noah set off, breaking into a run. Three Elves fell in behind. Eleanor followed running as quickly as she could across the deep, dry sand, her feet sinking in places over her ankles. They ran passed rows of Elves, like lines of guards.

"What are they doing?" Eleanor shouted at Noah.

"They're about to begin the spell – you should transform," Noah replied, "it'll be safer." Eleanor felt like laughing, if it'd been funny - she would have. Little did he know, she couldn't. She wished with all her might she could. It would be so much easier. The sound of flowing water filled her ears. Elves, stationed at intervals along the whole length of the beach, had begun creating great water columns. Each spreading out to reach the other. The entire edge would soon be surrounded. The wall stretched as far as Eleanor could see. Her heart soared; perhaps this might work – perhaps nothing will make it through – the perfect barrier, the Elves united against Ostric.

"Transform," Noah shouted again, having already reached the first series of boulders. *Oh for the sake of The Wind Master?* Just to prove to him it was futile she bellowed the spell, so that anyone could hear. She waited for the pain. But none came. She looked around and realised she was actually flying, Daniel's father, a small outline. Lost in the joy, safe in her invisible state, Eleanor flew above the line of water barriers. Four large lakes swung into view. The walls of water tall and strong. She spiralled around and headed for Noah, she couldn't afford to lose him.

"Where are you?" Noah was shouting, stading on the edge of a rock, close to the path where she'd left Daniel. He had already skirted the fern lake. Eleanor flew as fast as she could.

"I'm here."

"You're almost invisible," he said, his gaze intense. "How are the lakes looking... are they all surrounded?"

"The ones close to us are."

"They need to be... what about the sky lakes?" Noah pointed eastwards. "Did you see those?"

"I'll go." Eleanor disappeared. They were smaller and awkwardly placed, between a sheer cliff face and a network of thick palm trees. Elves swarmed over the rocks. Some had already reached the lakesides. Eleanor skimmed the cliff face. Something caught her eye. Bubbles and ripples shimmering across the surface of a small lake. She swerved along the crooked path, and as she did so, a black jaw, long with silvery scales, broke through the surface. Her skin pricked as a wave of heat stopped her in her tracks. Hovering, she could see black droplets falling from the beast's skin and staining the water like oil. Elves were still running towards it. In Eleanor's horror, she realised they were like swarming ants to a meal...

"Stop..." she yelled, but her words were consumed by the cries. The heat was getting too much, like a wall of Scarlet's fire, she couldn't get any closer. Each Elf fought bravely on, surrounded in a watery dome. They were going to try. She didn't want to watch. She spun round and flew off, finding Noah as he appeared from a tunnel within the cliffs.

"One of the lakes has been broken," she gasped landing on the path beside him. Her feet tingling, as if they had pins and needles.

"What did you see...?" his face turning the colour of the surrounding stone.

"A jaw."

"No," Noah clenched his fist and slammed it against the cliff wall. He turned to his fellow Elf and spoke rapidly in Elfland. When he'd finished he turned to Eleanor, "You'll have to go on alone to Algor. I cannot risk any of those creatures getting out of our water," he paused. "So... I must ask you one more thing. I know you have already done so much. But this is important. Find Daniel. Tell him to come to Sky Lake eight with *The Stone* - give it to no one or anything, especially not the water." Eleanor nodded as Noah jumped over the edge of the path, like an owl silently taking flight and disappeared.

57

EADRIC'S STONE

Daniel knelt beside his mother, listening to the shouts from outside of Algor piercing the tumbling water, tormented and powerless, as the word *Teelasor* bore into his conscience. The ancient Elfland name that brought fear into any fireside story. Tales of how the beast's long jaw lolloped from side to side, catching their victim in iron-like teeth. Daniel knew he had to find the *Stone* - now more than ever. Without it, the Teelasors would overcome Caradoc, and maybe Ostric, would be strong enough to appear. He shuddered uncontrollably.

Shakily he kissed his mother's damp forehead; if only she'd wake, she'd know what to do. With a heavy sigh, he rose. He had to look. Scanning the cave. It was here, he knew. He headed off to the far corner. With an agility that came with growing up in the environment, he skirted the back of the cave, lifting loose stones, peering into cracks and checking gaps. He fought to push back the oppressive sinking doubt that threatened to overcome his movements. He examined the edges of each pool, circling them slowly making sure he didn't miss a single bend, before venturing onto the plinth where the sacred altar sat. His hands trembling as he lifted each sacred white crystal. Hoping Istria would forgive him? Surely, he thought, its dull form, would be easy to spot amongst such beauty? The fear of time lost, began to feed off him like a parasite.

"This is hopeless," he shouted to no one in particular. "If you're listening, Istria - why take it away?" Daniel threw a sacred crystal into the water. He watched it float, bobbing on the surface, before laboriously sinking. The water, Daniel realised, was not only black, but was thickening too. It made him feel sick.

Suddenly a shout came from beyond the black curtain of water at Algor's mouth. He froze. The voice came again, in singing tones. It couldn't be? He ran. Crossing the sand like a bolting hare. Skidding his feet, to slow himself, to dodge the stray droplets. His face was as close to the water as he dared. Nerves taut. The radiating heat mixed with a powerful magnetic pull.

"*Daniel... Daniel are you there?*" Eleanor? With all his strength he tried to listen, to be sure. Something was pulling him closer to the water. He pushed against the invisible heavy black mire that drew him in. He struggled and kicked the sand. Then a tumbling fountain of black droplets rained, covering the sand in a black splattering gloopy poison. Daniel dived to the side. He raised a shield. Cowering underneath, hardly daring to breath. A long protracted jaw sliced through the waterfall. It quivered and shook as if enjoying a wash. The black leathery skin glistened. Suddenly thousands of small soothing voices filled his mind.... *Daniel, Daniel join us. Together we could win. Daniel are you there?* Daniel slammed his hands over his ears. He mustn't listen. *Remember the cloud.* His head span. He had to get up, he had to run... *Eleanor?*

Another jaw appeared, smaller, with thick silvery armour that ended in a shock of sharp teeth. It extended further into the cave. Its two wide, thick nostrils sniffed the air. Each sniff, sent a mountain of ash crashing to the ground, blackening the sand and burning deep holes. The jaw was followed by a leathery-clawed foot, which sank deeply into the sand, claiming the new territory beyond. Daniel knew the waterfall wouldn't hold them back.

"Daniel," rocked his conscious. The same voice that had lured him to the entrance.

"Eleanor," he cried. "Ostic?"

"Yessssss..."

"Who....?" His head thumped as droplets fell onto his shoulder, making him recoil in pain. They had pierced his shield! A jaw appeared just above his head. It shot through the curtain with deadly accuracy. Knocking the first Teelasor sideways. It's teeth protruding in an evil smile. Daniel knew he shouldn't have spoken. An eye opened. It lay on the underside of the jaw and looked directly at him. Daniel collapsed under the weight of hot air. His heart pounding, shaking under the strain of keeping *poisoned* water from engulfing him. He backed across the sand, sliding onto his knees and feet until he reached his mother's side. If the beasts got into Algor, he doubted the rocks would protect them for long. But there was no time to move her. He closed his eyes and leant his head onto his mother's chest. *Forgive me, I've failed.* The laboured rise and fall of her breathing was his only comfort. Something knocked his forehead, protruding out from under her tunic. A piece of string around her neck. He wriggled it free from her clothes and tugged it wildly over her head. He placed the small pebble on his damp hand and twisted it over and over.

"Is she dead?"

Daniel span on his feet, nearly dropping the necklace. "Eleanor," he leapt to his feet, looping his arms around her. "How did you get in? How are you alive?" She collapsed into his hold.

"With this," she turned around. He had seen it many times, but never so clearly, it glowed a rich silver and neatly covered her back, neck and most of her head. "It's Morwena's and it has just saved my life," Eleanor frowned. "It stops that stuff from getting anywhere near me." Her smile was weak. Daniel scanned her broken look. He wanted nothing more than to take her away from all of this.

A roar filled the cave. With her hand over her ears Eleanor screamed. "Use it!" A beast filled the cave like a swollen balloon. Daniel ran, skirting the edge of the pool. The Teelasor's was cumbersome and slow. Its jaw swung through the air, like a giant fishing rod. Daniel slid under its belly towards the thick tail and rolled to the other side.

"Eleanor, keep it away from the altar," he bellowed. He could feel the force of her wind bolt as he got to his feet.

With *The Stone* in his hand Daniel chanted. The Teelasor's tail came lashing towards him, cracking the air, like a whip. Daniel leapt aside, careful to keep on his feet, as he followed the line of pointy scale plates rising in spikes across its back. He aimed. The sense of power surge through him. A wild jet of blue water flowed from his hand. Curving like dancing ribbons. The beast let out a deafening howl as it fell onto its knees. Daniel fired again, hitting it in multiple places. This time it fell onto its stomach, and rolled onto its side, until finally its head crashed to the ground. Sending ripples shuddering across the sand.

"Get down," he shouted to Eleanor. The power all consuming. The water jets no longer going where he wanted. They hit the cave's wall and roof. Rocks crashed to the ground, in warning thuds. The Teelasor he'd hit was trying to get up. Daniel felt his feet spin, the force of a jet knocking him sideways as he completely lost control. He lurched forwards, his body tilting. In a slow motion of water haze, he saw one of his jets rip across the entrance's waterfall. Frantically, he tried to cover his hand to close off *The Stone's* power. His arms trembled. A strange rumbling filled the air. With quivering strength, he closed his hands. *The Stone* went cold. He landed flat footed. The Teelasor was stumbling from side to side, shaking its head. The last wave of Algor's water gate tumbled to the ground from just below Daniels stray water jet. It quietly lay in black puddles.

"What have you done?" Eleanor hovered above him. In disbelief he stared at the mouth of Algor, now left wide open. Three more Teelasors stood across the threshold. Like guard dogs, their tongues lulled out of their jaws as they panted.

"If the Teelasors get into the source we're lost," Daniel cried through a chorus of deafening roars, and rattling crystals.

"Daniel, look..." Eleanor shouted. A group of Elves, liked an army of ants, came into view. Firing relentlessly at the beasts. Fighting with all their strength around the stone statues; their silvery domes, reflected Algor's glow.

"It's Camundra," Eleanor said, "don't let him near you, Daniel."

"What?" Daniel looked startled. "Why?"

"Your father, he knows you're back and that Elf is no friend." Eleanor threw a torment of wind bolts, just before she lashed with her rope at a Teelasor's head. Its wide jaw lunging straight for them. Daniel and Eleanor dived to the ground side by side. "If *The Stone*," Eleanor whispered, "doesn't kill them, what will?"

"I have an idea?" Daniel couldn't hear Eleanor's reply, as the Teelasor swung its jaw at them again. He could feel the blue eyes of the Teelasor lock onto his pocket which held *The Stone* inside - it wanted the power. Daniel could feel the beast was coming to receive his prize. Daniel felt himself sinking into its hold; there was nowhere for him to hide, his energy fading. His power to resist folding. The silvery shielded Elves were gaining ground, halfway into the cave, skilfully fighting their way through. Daniel edged away from Eleanor, towards the bubbling angry lake behind. He could hear Eleanor calling his name, but the Teelasor's heartbeat was stronger, not regular like his, but slower, louder, two thumps then nothing, two thumps, then nothing. Locking onto his, like a father holding his offspring. It was a hold that wouldn't let go.

"Daniel... Daniel give it to me." He could hear a cool clear voice ringing in his ear. Camundra, whom he hadn't seen for several *Turns*, now urgent, up close and in his face. "We can use it, kill *The Darkness*. Daniel you have to listen. Everyone will die if you don't." Eleanor was close too. She was defensive, arguing against them, her words playing in a battle ground, urgent and raw. But Daniel now knew his purpose. Why Morwena had told him to find *The Stone*, why Tristan had been such a friend - it had never made sense to him. He was their pawns, another piece in the eternal game of *Light* and *Dark*. They were the Earth Guardians that fought *The Darkness* first and foremost. He was only helped back into Caradoc for one reason. Even his father hadn't come to Algor to find him, leaving him to play out his own destiny. He had remained with his Elves, to fight, a Grand Master to the end. Daniel - just another sacrifice along the way to save Caradoc.

He looked up at Eleanor, just able to make out her outline, "Stay safe," he whispered, "go home." She had grown important to him. More than he had ever told her. Her mouth moving with words that he no longer understood. *The Stone* was now his and his alone. He was its power and its power was his. He would never let the Teelasor have it, or Camundra. Neither were deserving. Ostric roars call him forth, he was going to join the God himself. The Teelasors were still. Standing guards, watching, their jaws no longer searching. Waiting patiently, tasting their victory. Daniel backed towards the water's edge. Utter confusion flickered across Camundra's face. Daniel smiled to himself. For he alone would be the bearer. Take *The Stone* back to the place where Eadric had first put it. Why, after all, had his mother shown him all those *Annuls* ago? Her actions were another notch in his fated path.

58

THE GLOWS

"No wha, Daniel," Eleanor ran towards the water's edge. "You'll never survive," she howled. But it was too late. He had already slipped into the gloopy lake surrounded in a shadowy dream, and slowly disappearing. Eleanor stood momentarily confused. The water was as thick as rich, dark honey. *How would he breathe?*

"He's mad, the source will devour him." Camundra's hot breath stank of stale fish.

"This is your fault," she howled, twisting around to stare into his blue eyes. Eleanor began to mutter a spell through her anger. She willed Morwena's web to protect her. With her glowing rope clutched tightly, she lashed it across the ground, chanting the final words. Camundra swirled water droplets in response. The Teelasors replied with deafening roars, as if Daniel's disappearance had awoken them from their trance. A wind tunnel, small yet perfect, danced across the sand to her command. Eleanor flicked her rope allowing its light to fill the tunnel. Navigating it, with a speed born from patience, it lashed into Camundra before he could throw a single droplet and knocked him into the closest Teelasor. The other Elves scattered. Eleanor commanded the tunnel onwards, lashing her rope, with every ounce of anguish she felt — her lost home, Daniel's sacrifice and Scarlet's humiliation. The beast exploded, sending bits of leathery skin and scales flying. She stood tall within her silvery web. The black poison trying to find its final victim, but none could penetrate Morwena's creation. Eleanor turned her anger onto the next Teelasor, directing the course of her tunnel into its path. The beast's white bulging eyes locked on its approach. Something nestled deep within Eleanor's conscious ignited - there was no need to be scared. For her Element *Wind* was the one to destroy these beasts, like Daniel had silenced the Natajaws and Scarlet killed the Gulabirds. The Teelasor knew this too. Conscious of its last moments, the beasts lashed their jaws, rushing at her with an urgency to survive. Jabbing with sword like swipes, cutting and slicing the air. Defiantly calling to their foes, this wasn't the end. She dodged and ducked to maintain control of her tunnel. Screams filled the cave as more beast arrived and devoured Elves as if they were mere blades of grass to chew. Then something hit her squarely on her side, pain tearing across her arm. Her heart fell still as she glided into the air, through a glowing mixture of swirling mist. She landed with a thud, sending up clouds of sand. A furiously intense blue light filled the cavern, burning her gaze, as her head collapsed onto the sand.

*

Hurt, groggy and confused, Eleanor awoke, seemingly an eternity later. A clear image of her bedroom, the bedside table and her favourite candle burned invitingly, in the haze before her. Had it all been a terrible dream? Could she really have been at home all this time recovering from her Passing? With some effort, she pulled herself up, expecting the familiar pillows and furs. But they were not there; sand filled her hair and stuck to her cheek. She tenderly touched her arm. The sharp pain jabbed as she lifted the flap of her sleeve. A small dark line crossed her pale skin. She bit her shaking lip. She looked up. A natural light filled the cave. In a bitter dawning, she could see the beasts had gone... the deafening roars and screams were silent, replaced by the stillness of an exam hall. Large piles of black ash peppered the cave floor. Camundra, and his one remaining companion, knelt, hands clamped around his head. He groggily rose to his feet, stumbling like a drunkard.

"It's over, it's over...," he repeated to no one in particular, like a drifting ghost with blood seeping down his face, staining his once majestic silk jacket.

"Where is he?" Eleanor shouted her voice raw, "has he resurfaced?' Camundra shook his head, looking through her as if she didn't exist.

"That can't be." Eleanor scrambled to her feet and stumbled towards the water's edge. "He has to..." she cried, "he has to come back."

A harrowing cry, rare and unnatural, echoed from behind her. At first Eleanor thought it was her own words. She turned to see a hunched shuffling figure. Her arms flaying and rich auburn hair dragging into sand. Bent over looping from side to side, she stumbled forwards crawling on all fours, muttering words Eleanor didn't understand. Her clothes, wet and tattered.

"Anta," the name rang out, echoing and bouncing off Algor's walls. Eleanor swirled around to see an army of Elves, with Noah as their leader flooding across the open mouth of Algor.

"Anta," Noah shouted. But the bedraggled Elf had already reached the water and was floundering in. A young Elfling broke from the crowd, weaving a clear path through the survivors and tore across the sand. The Elfling was yelling and shouting. He ran right past Eleanor, as if she wasn't even there. Swathes of red scars glistened across his exposed skin. She choked back tears. She had never felt so empty. She wanted nothing more than her family. Be held in her father's arms again. She didn't belong here and didn't want to. Daniel was no longer alive; they had lost their united quest, even Scarlet had been ruined in the process.

"Are you alright?" Noah's arm lay gentle and kindly on her shoulder.

"He wouldn't stop, I tried to stop him, but he wouldn't. *The Stone*... it has powers over him... he... he wasn't himself." Noah pulled her close and she felt his cloak cover her shoulders.

"You are a remarkable Sprite. I thank our Water Lord Daniel found you."

Eleanor shuddered. "But I failed... I've failed him. We didn't win."

"But we have. The Teelasors are gone. *The Darkness* vanquished."

Eleanor shook her head. "But I have lost them, lost them both ..." She buried her head into Noah's hold. The Elves were all shouting around her, like a swarm of bees drawn to honey. The water sloshed noisily and a steady chanting had begun. Several flat notes repeated rising and falling ina a tone that rocked Eleanor's core. Droning on in repetition, until she could hear nothing else. She pushed Noah aside and started to walk back through the crowds to the mouth of Algor, she had to leave.

*

"Hey...?"

"Uh..." Eleanor turned around, taking in the mass of soaked hair surrounding intense blue eyes. The chanting had silence, and a beautiful golden glow fell across his path.

"You're alive..." she whispered. Every once of him soaked, but he was there standing as tall as ever. Stronger, his slanted grin raw and intense.

"Well?" he smiled and shrugged his shoulders.

"Just this once." Knowing exactly what he wanted. She blew her drying spell into a warm tunnel and gave the spell enough time to completely dry him.

"I've waited for ages for you to do that."

"Huh?"

"Well, you've always dried yourself and left me hanging."

"I thought you liked being wet," she protested, "you're an Elf!" He gave her a gentle nudge as he wrapped his arms around her. Eleanor winced as the pain shot through her arm.

THE END

To be continued in

VEARMOOR STORMS

GLOSSARY

Nararose	The world (see map)
Caradoc	The land of the Elves *underground*
Trevarian Settlement	Where Daniel lived before his banishment.
Algor	The Elves sacred place of reflection.
Arramond	The land of the Imps *above ground*.
Compounds	Underground stone dug out dwellings.
Garnafort Compound	Where Scarlet lived before she escaped - Northern Arramond.
Grasslands of Balithaque	A vast grasslands in the middle of Arramond.
Vearmoor	The lands of the Sprites *above ground*.
Paraquinn Territory	Where Eleanor lives.
Obakeech	The Sprites scared place of reflection.
Poldaric	The land of the Pixies *under ground*.
Corrinium Settlement	The main settlement where Tristan lives.
Coravolt	The Pixie sacred place of reflection.
The Moorlands	Area *above ground* covering Caradoc and Poldaric.
The Rock of Vespic	A granite Tor where the meeting happens between Vanik Imps and Eastling Elves.
Copse	A cluster of tall silver birches. These are the gates of Poldaric.
The Great Bog	Area on The Moorland that lies above Caradoc.

GODS

Ostric	The God of Darkness.
Natajaws	Darkness creatures formed within Arramond.
Teelasors	Darkness creatures formed within Caradoc.

Gulabirds	Darkness creatures formed on The Moorlands.
Istria	The Goddess of Light.
The Glows	Creatures that live in all lands. Messengers of Istria.
Wind Master	God of Wind.
Flame Goddess	Goddess of Fire.
Water Lord	God of Water.
Earth Guardian	God of Earth - they have representatives in Nararose of which Tristan Corrinium is one.
The Balance	Creating an equilibrium between Light and Dark to maintain peace.
Balance Warriors	Those who protect The Balance at all times There are two within each tribe. Morwena du Gwent and Tristan are both one.
Eadric	The first Elf to be given the power gift from Ostric.
Pendra	The first Sprite to be given the power gift from Ostric.
Turgred	The first Pixie to be given power gifts form Istria.
Creoda	The first Imps to be given power gifts form Ostric.

POWER GIFTS

The Stone of Innvericum	Belongs to the Elves. A small round smooth pebble that can easily fit in the palm of your hand. To those who are unworthy it kills. To those who are worthy it can give great powers.
The Book of Spells	Belongs to the Sprites. A large old leather covered book. It contains all Sprite knowledge handed down through generations. Only possessed by Balance Warriors.
The Torc	Belongs to the Imps. A golden colour neck ring made of Titanium with two flame as finials.
The Amulet	Belongs to the Pixies Amulet - decorative

| | necklace. Highly decorative in rich colours of green. |
| **Ridge Cup** | A simple beaker with two handles and ridges up the sides. |

TIME WITHIN NARAROSE

A Shadow	Equivalent to one hour in our time.
A Turn	Equivalent to 16 hours.
An Annul	Equivalent to 1 year.
Light Exchange	Made up of 8 Shadows where there is light.
Dark Exchange	Made up of 8 Shadows where there is dark.

ABOUT THE AUTHOR

Growing up in the rugged clay scared landscape of Cornwall author Kate Rosevear was drawn to the moorland scenery of her homeland and Dartmoor. Holidays on the Isle of Scilly provided the perfect environment for The Moorlands of Nararose to be born. The unity of wind, fire, air and earth mixing in equal measures to provide a beautiful backdrop of underground lands and magical characters. Kate has been writing for over ten years and this is her first novel in the NaraRose Series – Vearmoor Storms is the sequel.

Printed in Great Britain
by Amazon